COLLISION

A Phobos novel

D0228503

904 000 00641626

THE PHOBOS SERIES

Ascension
Distortion
Collision

COLLISION

A Phobos novel

VICTOR DIXEN

Translated by Daniel Hahn

HOT
KEY
BOOKS

First published in French by Éditions Robert Laffont, S.A. Paris, in 2016

First published in Great Britain in 2019 by
HOT KEY BOOKS
80–81 Wimpole St, London W1G 9RE
www.hotkeybooks.com

Text copyright © Victor Dixen, 2016, 2019
Translation copyright © Daniel Hahn, 2019

*This book is supported by the Institut français (Royaume-Uni)
as part of the Burgess programme.*

All rights reserved.
No part of this publication may be reproduced, stored or transmitted in any form
by any means, electronic, mechanical, photocopying or otherwise, without the prior
written permission of the publisher.

The right of Victor Dixen and Daniel Hahn to be identified as Author
and Translator of this work has been asserted by them in accordance
with the Copyright, Designs and Patents Act, 1988

This is a work of fiction. Names, places, events and incidents are either the products
of the author's imagination or used fictitiously. Any resemblance to actual persons,
living or dead, is purely coincidental.

A CIP catalogue record for this book is available from the British Library.

ISBN: 978-1-4714-0723-9
also available as an ebook

1

This book is typeset using Atomik ePublisher
Printed and bound by Clays Ltd, Elcograf S.p.A.

Hot Key Books is an imprint of Bonnier Books UK
www.bonnierbooks.co.uk

For E.

For Francine and Kim

Waltham Forest Libraries	
904 000 00641626	
Askews & Holts	23-Apr-2019
TEE	£7.99
6019663	

I can't change the direction of the wind,
but I can adjust my sails
to always reach my destination.

James Dean (1931–1955)

GENESIS PROGRAM – SEASON 2

CALL FOR CANDIDATES

Six new girls. Six new boys.
Six new love stories. And even more babies!

You too can make History with a capital H!

Are you a fan of the Genesis program? Have you spent the last few months thrilling along with the pioneers on Mars? Have you followed the broadcast every hour, every minute? The moment has come for you to cross over to the other side of the screen, and add your own stone to the building of a Martian civilisation. The *Cupido*, now empty, has just embarked on its return journey to Earth. It will take off again in a year and a half, heading back to Mars, carrying twelve new astronauts ready to enter the history books – and you could be one of them!

You too can find Love with a capital L!

Kirsten and Alexei, Fangfang and Tao, Safia and Samson, Kelly and Kenji, Elizabeth and Mozart, Léonor and Marcus. These couples are already the stuff of fairy-tales. Their love is already legendary. But now it's time for six more couples to play their part in creating a new population. All young Earth people at peak fertility are invited to apply to join the Season One candidates, to find their soulmates along the way, and inspire billions of viewers back on Earth.

GENESIS PROGRAM – SEASON 2
Are you aged between 17 and 20?
Do you want to be the next Romeo or Juliet of outer space?
Send in your application today, and take your turn
writing the most beautiful love story of all time!

ACT I

1. Genesis Channel

Sunday 7 January, 8:15am

GENESIS PROGRAM – SEASON 2

SIX NEW GIRLS

SIX NEW BOYS

SIX NEW LOVE STORIES

AND EVEN MORE BABIES

APPLICATIONS OPEN TODAY

APPLY TODAY ON THE GENESIS WEBSITE!

2. Shot

Month 21 / sol 578 / 10:35 Mars time
[28th sol since landing]

Alone.

I'm alone, even if the people who've lived with me through the most important moments of my life are all around me: them, the Genesis pioneers – the space heroes – the condemned of Mars.

'Oh, Léo, I'm begging you: look at me!' cries Kris.

I hear my best friend's voice, overcome with anguish.

I sense the weight of her hands gripping the shoulders of my suit, which I've put back on to face the late summer storm.

I feel the caress of her ragged breathing on my cheeks, still damp with sweat since taking off my helmet.

But I can't see her.

I can't take my eyes off the boy who's standing a few metres away, in the living room of the seventh Love Nest – or rather the Death Nest, where the guinea pigs from the Noah experiment disappeared, the Martian year before this one.

The boy I thought was so close has become a stranger.

The boy who made me shiver with pleasure now makes me shudder with disgust.

When I think back to those intimate moments I've

known with him and only him, all those intimate first-time experiences . . .

Ugh!

It makes me want to throw up!

Suddenly Marcus's face seems horribly empty – a cinema screen when the lights come back on once the movie's stopped playing, a white page when you've finished the last paragraph at the end of a novel. How could I ever have read poetry in his eyes, how could I have lent them the silvery colour of the stars? They're silt-coloured, a greyish mud that conceals calculation, selfishness and contempt. How could I ever have believed they were looking at me with love? Marcus loves nobody but himself. He's sacrificed eleven lives without a moment's hesitation – mine and those of the other pioneers. He knew he was at the mercy of the deadly D66 genetic mutation, and he didn't hesitate to condemn us along with him just because that was the price to be paid for giving himself his little journey to Mars.

At that thought, I feel my guts twist between a laugh and a sob, my shoulders shaking like a robot malfunctioning.

'Léo!'

Kris holds my head in her soft hands – she's taken off her gloves – and forces me to turn my face towards hers.

Beneath her crown of blonde braids, slightly crushed by the helmet she too has just removed, her big blue eyes are wavering between anxiety and doubt. She can't understand. None of the girls gathered in a circle around me can understand – not Fangfang the Singaporean, who fixes me with her intelligent stare as though I were a tricky equation; not Liz the English girl, who is shivering all over even in her thick suit; not Safia

7

the Indian girl, whose forehead adorned with a blue bindi is creased with fine wrinkles; not Kelly the Canadian, chewing her gum till it looks like she's going to dislocate her jaw.

In every gaze, there is confusion. Hasn't Serena McBee, the executive director of the Genesis programme, just announced in front of billions of spectators that she's going to finance the self-energising space elevator that will allow us to escape from this base and its hidden flaws? And isn't this public announcement like an indelible pact, signed in her own blood? And do we not have two allies on Earth, our Survival Officers, Andrew and Harmony, who will make her keep her word? My dejection must seem ridiculous to my teammates: to them, it's all got to be for the best in the best of all possible worlds.

'What's up, darling leopard?' Kris asks me, fearfully. 'Why did you lock yourself in the seventh habitat with Marcus? What's come over you both? You can relax: the storm has passed. And you can celebrate a miracle has just happened. We're saved! *You*'re saved! The two of you will go back to Earth and start a family and grow old there, together, you and Marcus.'

Kris's enthusiasm – so innocent, but so clumsy! – tears me roughly out of my dejection.

There isn't, there never has been, a *me and Marcus*. I've been alone this whole time, and Marcus has always been alone too. From the moment he set eyes on me at our first meeting in the Visiting Room, he already knew he was looking at a corpse on borrowed time – a girl whose death sentence he himself had signed in advance, by choosing not to reveal his mysterious awareness of the Noah Report when we were boarding the rocket. But I had no idea I was condemned to die. I thought

8

I was in the process of writing the first chapter in a new life; while he knew all along this chapter would be the last.

Was that what excited him, knowing I was a thing that belonged to him?

Did he relish that feeling of power, keeping me in ignorance?

Bewitched by his magnetic words, I was like a little ewe a farmer was coddling as a pet, knowing full well he's going to take her to the slaughterhouse the following morning.

Suddenly dizzy, I cling to Kris's arms so as not to falter.

'Léo!' she cries.

'I'm sorry,' I manage to say.

My tongue feels horribly thick, like a dead organ in my mouth.

'What's the matter? Why aren't you celebrating like the rest of us? What did you and Marcus say to each other when you were alone in here?'

My heart is beating so hard it hurts.

(Tell her!) the Salamander whispers in my ear – the voice expressing the most intimate, most shameful, and also most fragile part of me. *(Stab Marcus right now, the way you'd lance a boil, so everyone can see the pus inside him!)*

It would bring me such relief to reveal to everybody the despicable way he's betrayed us. To explain to the other pioneers how he's lived alongside them for months, playing the innocent, when he really knew everything.

(You know that if you keep the secret to yourself, it'll poison you from the inside and end up killing you – so tell them. Tell them!)

'Have you lost the power of speech or what?' Kelly joins in, spitting her gum into the kitchenette sink. 'You're scaring us.'

(Tell them!)

'We can see something's wrong,' adds Liz gently. 'But we can't help you if we don't understand. You need to answer Kris's question: what happened between Marcus and you?'

(Tell them!)

'What did that jerk do to you?' yells Mozart suddenly, making me turn towards the group of boys at the other end of the room.

The Brazilian is standing there, trembling with anger in his suit, his thick brown curls twisting like snakes. Behind him, the other boys have also taken off their helmets. Instinctively they have surrounded Marcus, like a mirror image of the circle the girls have formed around me – the sexes separated once again, just like on the *Cupido*.

(For God's sake, tell them now, now's the time!)

The Salamander is right: I could tell them everything, right here and now, in this place where the cameras and mics have been destroyed, protected from the Genesis programme's viewers and organisers – yes, I could, except *I can't do it.*

'Did he insult you?' growls Mozart, increasingly on edge as the silence continues.

He grabs the collar of the American's suit and squeezes it so hard his knuckles go white.

'Did you hit her, asshole? If you dared lay a hand on her I swear I'll kill you!'

His furious black pupils flit from Marcus to me, then from me to Marcus, faster and faster, as if he was trying to read something between us.

But I remain totally dumb, unable to articulate a single sound.

Deep in my throat there's a knot that's stifling me.

10

I see Marcus as limp as a ragdoll in his attacker's hands. This guy I thought was so upright, so strong, is no more than a feeble, spineless puppet.

He doesn't even try to defend himself.

He's going to get himself slaughtered.

He deserves it.

'Just stop and think about it a second!' As Mozart raises his fist, Samson tries to stop him. 'Marcus would never hurt Léo, you know that perfectly well; he wouldn't hurt any of us!'

The blind confidence shining in the Nigerian boy's green eyes makes me feel ill. He doesn't know he's standing face to face with his killer. And Alexei suspects nothing when he grabs hold of Mozart's arm to make him let Marcus go.

'Calm down!' roars the Russian boy, in a voice that is anything but calm. 'We're not in your shitty little favela now, get it? You can't just play at being some big boss and impose your own rule of law however you want to.'

'Shut it!'

At that moment, a furious crackling comes out of the habitat's master bedroom, which unlike the living room is still equipped with working cameras and mics, adding to the general confusion.

'What are you all doing?' we hear Serena McBee's voice ask. *'Where are you? Is this how you thank me for offering you that self-energising space elevator, by disappearing from our screens without a moment's warning? Yet again I was forced to send out some commercials, and even the call for candidates for the second season of the Genesis programme, to keep the viewers distracted during your absence! But this can't go on, you understand? Return*

11

to the Garden at once, or I will no longer be held responsible.'

The youngest of the boys, Kenji, is frantically putting his helmet back over his suit, as if wanting to escape Serena's threats, and the girls' worries, and Alexei's provocations.

Because the Russian isn't done yet; he turns his steel-blue eyes, sharp as a pair of daggers, towards the group – and what comes out of his mouth is a dagger blow too.

'We all know it, all of us know Mozart hasn't gotten over Léonor choosing Marcus over him. I know it, the other guys know it, and the girls know it too. Even Liz knows it: his own wife isn't going to be taken in!'

Standing beside me, the tall English girl gives a hoarse moan, and lowers her big eyes towards the ground. This girl who once had everything she needed to succeed – beauty, gracefulness, talent – finds herself with nothing. Mozart never really belonged to her. Even if, one month on, they pretend to play the perfect couple, the way her husband looks at me whenever she has her back turned has escaped no one: his eyes always find their way to me.

As they do now.

Mozart looks over at me, though it's Liz he ought to be looking at to reassure her of his love, Liz he ought to be comforting, doing what he can to disprove what Alexei says.

But Alexei whispers a few more words to him, his voice cruel.

'You'd invent any old bullshit to drag Marcus through the mud, isn't that right, Mozart? But you've just got to face it: Léonor is never going to leave him, specially not to marry a bit of scum like you!'

Something metallic flashes in the spotlights of the seventh

12

habitat, and this time it's not just a killer look, or a sharp wounding insult.

A flick knife has appeared in Mozart's hand, pulled from the all-purpose pocket of his suit.

Kris gives a shrill cry.

At that same moment, the knot that was stopping me from speaking suddenly melts in my throat, taking the pressure off my vocal cords, freeing my tongue.

'Stop!' I yell.

Mozart's knife freezes a few centimetres from Alexei's throat.

All eyes are on me.

'Stop . . .' I say again, breathless.

(Tell them!)

'. . . I'll tell you what happened . . .'

(Tell them!!)

'. . . even if you'll think it's unbelievable . . .'

(Tell them!!!)

'. . . even if it tears me apart to admit it . . .'

(TELL THEM!!!)

'. . . me and Marcus, we're breaking up.'

Mozart's eyes widen; he slowly lowers the knife.

'What are you saying?' he asks in a low voice.

I feel tears coming to my eyes.

'Things haven't been working between us for a little while,' I manage to say. 'Actually – no – it's never worked, really.'

I force my eyes to rest on Marcus's distraught face, on his body, his swaying arms.

It would bring me relief to offer up that face to Mozart's

blade, to hand this body over to Alexei's and the other boys' fists, just as the Salamander had encouraged me to do. But what good would vengeance do me, apart from a fleeting moment of satisfaction that would leave a taste of ashes in my mouth? The damage is done. Whether we die on Mars or manage to get out of here through this providential – and hypothetical – space elevator, turning Marcus in wouldn't change a thing. He did end up confessing his crime to me, after months of pretence. Even if his admission was nothing to do with bravery, even if it was stress and weakness that finally broke him, he did still tell me the truth. And he spared me the humiliation of going on living side by side with a murderer.

Now it's my turn to spare him.

One day, one month or one year, it doesn't make much difference how long he's got left to live before the D66 mutation finishes him off: let him spend that time on his own, with his regrets, and maybe then, if he's capable of such feelings, with his remorse.

'We're not together any more,' I say, allowing my tears to flow freely, the sight of Marcus turning blurry. 'It's over. For ever. There's nothing else to tell. Let's go back to the Garden.'

Kris puts her arms round me.

'Oh . . . ! My darling Léo . . . ! Don't say that! You're made for one another, it's so obvious . . . ! All couples have arguments sometimes, even the most united ones, but it'll sort itself out!'

'No. It's not going to sort itself out.'

Kris suddenly stops comforting me to turn to look at the person who has just spoken: Kenji.

He's standing there, pale, holding his helmet, which he has just taken off again.

He knows!

I'm not sure how, but I can read it on his pale face, in his eyes ringed with tiredness: *he knows!*

'What are you saying, Tiger?' Kelly asks, walking towards him. 'Why won't things work themselves out between Léo and Marcus? I'm afraid you can still be just a touch too much of a pessimist, my darling little scaredy-cat.'

'I'm not a pessimist. I'm a realist. What Marcus has done . . . What Marcus has said . . . there's no possible going back from that.'

With these words, he crouches down at the foot of the sofa and from underneath it he pulls out a small black pad fixed with a suction cup.

'A mic,' murmurs Safia. 'From our comms kit.'

'Yes,' says Kenji. 'I've positioned them everywhere, even here in the seventh habitat the first time I came in here. You think I haven't been sleeping since we arrived on Mars because of my nightmares. But the truth is, most of the time I've been forcing myself to stay awake: I've wiretapped the base, to be able to hear New Eden breathing, and so guard against the worst. My mics pick up everything that happens here, everything that's said, twenty-four / seven, and transmit it to the speakers in my helmet, in real time or on delay.'

He clears his throat.

'I've just heard the recording of what Marcus said to Léonor before we came into the seventh habitat . . .'

My breathing catches in my chest.

'. . . and I think it's time the rest of you heard it too.'

15

3. Reverse Shot

Vice-presidential residence, Washington DC
Sunday 7 January, 08:15am

Alone.

Pale in her green suit, in the Ultra-libertarian party colours, Serena McBee is alone behind her large desk, at the centre of the study in the Observatory residence. The corded telephone sitting on the corner of the table doesn't stop ringing, but the new vice-president of the United States of America doesn't pick up. Opposite her is the aluminium gantry studded with spotlights and cameras through which she hosts the Genesis channel remotely. On the giant screen in the middle of the gantry, the multiple windows hooked up to the cameras on the Martian base all show deserted scenes. It's as though New Eden has been abandoned – or as if it had never been lived in at all.

The Love Nests – deserted.

The access tubes – deserted.

The compression airlock – deserted.

The Garden – deserted. Only the two robots, Günter and Lóng, are still there. They stand, motionless, by the covered plantations, under the supplementary spotlights which were turned down to a minimum to preserve the base's electrical energy while it was in thrall to the storm. They look like two pieces placed on a chessboard with its squares erased, like two pawns in a game nobody remembers any more. Behind the giant dome that encloses the greenhouse, a red fog, dark and viscous, prevents any visibility.

But the programme's executive director doesn't waste any time on these various windows. In the middle of this office, filled with the echoes of the ringing telephone, all her attention is on one view only: the last one, in the top right of the screen, identified as LOVE NEST 7, MASTER BEDROOM.

Serena's forehead, normally so perfectly smooth, is creased in a frown.

The smile has left her face. The corners of her lips have relaxed into a pair of bitter furrows that we haven't seen on her before, and which, for the first time, seem to make her true age visible.

Her hands are flat on the surface of the desk, one on each side of a small black box with a keyboard, at the centre of which gleams a red button above a screen which reports, in digital letters: PRESSURIZATION 100%.

All of a sudden, there's a white flash on the screen, in the corner window. Serena gives a jump; she brings her hands sharply to her blouse; her fingers close around the silk, over where her heart is; a network of veins throbs on her cheeks and temples.

'Idiot creature, you scared me,' mutters Serena when she recognises the silhouette of Louve, one of the on-board dogs, a crossbreed, half poodle and half unidentified other species.

Louve is wearing her canine spacesuit, but her helmet has

been taken off, revealing her head covered in little white curls, amid which a pair of big black eyes are shining with curiosity.

The dog is nosing about at the foot of the bed. She inspects this place, which is new territory for her, this habitat which has been kept out of bounds to the Genesis channel, where the pioneers go only rarely, only individually, for their one-on-one sessions with the psychologist.

'I don't know what's stopping me dispatching you all to hell, your masters and you animals too,' says Serena quietly, her voice out of tune, almost quavering. 'I'd only have to press . . . It would be so easy . . . Such a pleasure . . .'

Her index finger hovers over the red button in the middle of the remote control for depressurising the Martian base, freezing immediately above it. Each shrill ring of the telephone makes her finger tremble a bit more, makes her bring it slightly lower.

'It would be such a pleasure, yes,' she goes on, talking to herself like a woman on the edge of madness. 'But mostly it would just be stupid to give up everything so close to success. I've spent my whole life waiting. I can certainly wait a little longer.'

She draws her hand away from the remote control and rummages feverishly in the pocket of her suit. Eventually she pulls out a small pillbox, from which she extracts two white pills. She puts them between her lips, closes her eyes, swallows, takes a slow, deep breath.

She breathes in.

Her cheekbones and temples gradually stop throbbing.

She breathes out.

The protruding veins disappear back into her skin, like a picture on the shore erased a little more by each breaking wave.

She breathes in.

The corners of her mouth tighten again.

She breathes out.

The wrinkles on her forehead fill out again.

When she reopens her eyes, her face has regained its smooth, ageless surface.

She locks the button on the remote control by tapping in a code, and puts it carefully away into her snakeskin bag.

Then she picks up the telephone without answering and puts the receiver sharply back down on its base to bring an end to the call.

Finally, with the room now in silence, she turns on the microphone that allows her to speak to New Eden.

'This is a message for Léonor,' she announces in a voice that is calm, with no remaining trace of a waver. 'We need to talk.'

4. Off-screen

Abandoned mine, Death Valley
Sunday 7 January, 05:15am

'Are you ready to go, Harmony?'

Andrew Fisher is standing in the doorway, the potholer's lamp on his head and his rucksack on his back. His black-framed glasses barely conceal the bags that have formed under his eyes. His brown hair has long ago lost any trace of its former parting, back when he was still a brilliant student with a bright future ahead of him at Berkeley. Today he's no more than a fugitive, an outlaw. Behind him stretches the black gulf of night in Death Valley, with no public lighting to disturb it for miles around. In front of him is the narrow bedroom, the only room in the bungalow adjoining the abandoned mine on Dry Mountain, where he and Harmony McBee have taken refuge for the past month.

'I can't find the gold nugget you gave me,' the girl murmurs.

She's rummaging frantically in the yellowing bed-sheets she's slept in for most of her days and nights, prey to the drowsiness of the codeine which is supposed to help with her withdrawal from the most addictive drug in the world: zero-G. After weeks of this regimen, she looks more than ever like a slow-moving

20

ghost. Her long white hair, nearly transparent, sweeps across the mattress like a diaphanous veil.

'It's not serious, Harmony,' Andrew reassures her. 'I'll give you other things. It's been an hour since we hijacked the Genesis channel and revealed the plans for the space elevator to the pioneers on Mars and to viewers across the world. I don't know whether the Genesis guys have been able to locate the origins of our signal. I'd guess probably not– but still we shouldn't take any risks. We really need to go, put as many miles between us and Dry Mountain as we can.'

'But I was so sure I'd put the piece of gold in my locket,' says Harmony sadly, looking for the tenth time inside the little jewel she wears around her neck, where she keeps her most precious relics – the photo and the lock of hair belonging to Mozart, the Brazilian pioneer.

The girl turns over the pillow on the bed, shakes down the sheets, sticks her hands into the pockets of her grey lace dress – and her face lights up.

'Found it! It was right here in my pocket. I'm such an idiot!'

The moment she's about to get up to join Andrew, a flash of light bursts through the last window that still has panes of glass in it.

'What the . . . ?' murmurs Harmony, using a hand to shield her water-green eyes.

The window shatters, a hail of glass crashing onto the worm-eaten floor.

'Harmony!' cries Andrew, rushing towards her.

He grabs hold of the girl's wrist and pulls her towards the door, abandoning their belongings behind them.

Outside, the night is a chaos of beams raining down from shadowy shapes suspended in the air. It's impossible to make them out, or tell how many there are. But there's no question: they're drones, remotely piloted engines of death, their metallic blades whirring around silently.

'*CIA! Identify yourselves at once, in the name of the law!*' orders a synthesised voice from one of the machines, whose sides are illuminated with an inscription in red letters:

CENTRAL INTELLIGENCE AGENCY

- ROBOTIZED AERIAL BRIGADE -

By way of response, Andrew pulls the gun he took from the police officer in Wyoming a month earlier from his belt.

'Run over to the campervan and take cover!' he yells to Harmony, squinting behind his glasses.

The girl escapes the pitiless beam of the spotlights and launches herself towards the dust-covered vehicle parked not far from the cabin.

'*Identify yourselves!*' says the police drone again, moving lower and aiming its lights at Andrew's face.

With his eyes behind his glasses reduced to mere slits glistening with tears, Andrew raises his gun . . .

. . . and fires.

The explosion rips through the night, followed immediately afterwards by the noise of the bullet bouncing off the surface of the drone.

'*You are under arrest,*' announces the voice, impassive, while

Andrew empties his gun's magazine without managing so much as a scratch on the armoured surface.

Three pairs of pincer-tipped mechanical arms emerge from the drone. The machine dive-bombs towards the ground, followed immediately by its fellows:

Two . . .

Three . . .

Four . . .

Five . . .

A swarm of five giant insects, raised up on chrome legs, swoops down onto Andrew. The young man bolts towards the campervan where Harmony has already taken shelter. He opens the door and slams it shut behind him just before a pair of pincers closes over his jacket.

There is a metallic clang as something hits the roof of the vehicle – *bang!* The chassis resounds like a huge bell, making Harmony scream.

'It's one of those things. It's right over our heads!' she shouts.

'Not just one,' growls Andrew through his teeth, while the roof starts to shudder beneath a shower of monstrous hailstones.

The campervan sinks a bit further onto its shock absorbers each time a drone lands on it.

Bang! – two . . .

Bang! – three . . .

'We're finished!' wails Harmony, bringing her hand to her lucky locket in a reflex of desperation.

'We do still have one chance.'

The girl turns her startled eyes to the driver, who is tapping feverishly on the screen of his cellphone. His forehead creased in concentration, he doesn't even flinch when the fourth drone collides with the roof – *bang!*

'You'll have to do exactly as I say, Harmony,' he murmurs quietly. 'When I say "now", you have to throw yourself out of the campervan and run straight ahead, as far and as fast as you can.'

'But . . .'

'And wrap yourself in this,' adds Andrew, pulling a blanket from the back counter and holding it out to Harmony. 'The wool is fireproof.'

The girl's face freezes in an expression of horror.

'*Fireproof?* B-but you aren't really going to . . .' she stammers.

She doesn't get the chance to finish her question before the final drone lands on the hood, just beyond the windscreen – *bang!*

Harmony gives a terrified scream.

From this close, it's possible to make out the shape of the machine's body. It really does look like an insect. Its long, pincered legs resemble a spider's, just as the countless gleaming round cameras mounted on its 'head' conjure up spider eyes. Its four spinning blades, which are gradually slowing to a stop, are more reminiscent of the wings of a gigantic cricket. This nightmare vision is rounded off by a sort of steel jaw, which looks as though it would only need a few blows to cut through the panels of the hood, pierce the windscreen and impale the passengers.

But for now, the jaw is not moving.

Above it, a circular screen lights up, showing a human face, set into this bizarre body. It's a man in his thirties, with very dark hair, quite handsome . . . if you set aside the black cloth kerchief covering his right eye.

A voice emerges from the innards of the drone, synchronised with the lips of the man on the screen.

'*Orion Seamus, C.I.A.,*' he introduces himself.

The two powerful electric torches set on either side of the screen sweep across the campervan's cabin, flooding it with light.

'*I may not be able to see you through these tinted windows, but I know you're there,*' Orion Seamus continues. '*The drones' infrared sensors can pick up the heat from your bodies. The famous Andrew Fisher and his mysterious companion . . . ! Don't try anything stupid and you won't be hurt. Climb out of the vehicle, slowly.*'

Harmony wraps herself up in the blanket, trembling.

She throws Andrew a furtive glance. He still has the straps of his rucksack over his shoulders; his left hand is on the handle of the door; his right is holding his cellphone. Digital numbers scroll across the screen – 30 . . . 29 . . . 28 . . .

Realising it's a countdown, Harmony gives a barely audible moan. She in turn puts her delicate hand on the handle of her door.

'*Don't make me ask you again,*' Agent Seamus continues on the drone's circular screen. '*According to the files, you're a smart kid, Andrew. Top of the class at high school, gold medal for best young scientist in California, admitted to Berkeley with flying colours! You have a bright future ahead of you. You aren't really going to throw that all away, are you? Come out of that campervan without causing any trouble, and life will be able to go on as normal.*'

25

'As normal?' shouts Andrew. 'How could my life ever be normal after what's happened? My father disappearing, the hacking of the Genesis channel and all that?'

A smile appears on Orion Seamus's face, revealing sparkling white teeth. He can't see the numbers that are still scrolling across the screen in Andrew's hand: . . . 15 . . . 14 . . . 13 . . .'

'You needn't worry,' he says. *'You just need to apologise publicly for these provocative little actions of yours – youthful errors, easily explained as the distress of a young man dealing with the death of his father. The viewers will understand. Serena McBee herself has already understood. She has already forgiven you.'*

'Really? She's forgiven me?' asks Andrew, buying time.

'She has, I'm telling you. So go on, come out now. Come out, both of you.'

Andrew's hand tightens around the door handle.

It opens with a click.

'Excellent!' says Orion Seamus encouragingly.

But behind the tinted window, Andrew isn't paying him the least attention. His eyes flit between the cellphone in his hand and the girl sitting beside him.

8 . . . she looks at him too, with those water-green eyes that seem too big for her gaunt face;

7 . . . the sweeping beams of light through the windshield make her pale hair gleam, like glowing optical fibres;

6 . . . deep in this night, inside the cabin of this campervan, Harmony McBee looks stranger, more alien than ever.

The moment the number 5 appears on the screen, a sharp order bursts from Andrew's lips.

'Now!'

He kicks the door open and throws himself out.

Running straight ahead, he turns to glance towards the campervan: the second door, on the far side, has also opened; Harmony's silhouette is disappearing into the shadows in the opposite direction, the ends of the blanket flapping behind her like a cape. On the roof and hood of the vehicle, however, the drones remain in place. It takes a few seconds for their still blades to start turning fast enough to drag their heavy metal bodies up against gravity – seconds Andrew has accounted for in his calculations.

'*Stop!*' cries Agent Seamus, his voice distorted by the speakers in the drone. '*You have nowhere to go, Andrew Fisher, and you know it! Stop at once!*'

But Andrew does not stop.

On the contrary, he accelerates, leaping over the rocks sticking out of the ground of Dry Mountain, lit up by the beams from the drones.

'*Stop, or I promise you'll . . .*'

Agent Seamus is unable to finish his threat.

A deafening explosion swallows the end of his sentence.

The drones' headlights are consumed in a blaze ten times brighter than they are.

A squall of burning air slaps the back of Andrew's neck.

By the time he turns around again, the campervan is no more than a flaming inferno, its wild blaze swallowing up the night. Four of the drones are lying on the ground, blown back by the explosion. On their backs, their bellies on fire, legs twisted and still: they look like flies grilled on a halogen bulb. The fifth drone, also in flames, whirls erratically in the air, giving off a revolting buzzing. Eventually it goes into a spin, crashing in a spray of sparks.

'Harmony!' yells Andrew, heading back towards the vehicle. 'Harmony, where are you?'

He jumps over the shards of broken glass, weaves between the charred corpses of the drones, on the very edge of the inferno, paying no attention to the heat baking his cheeks.

'Harmony!'

'I . . . I'm here, Andrew . . .'

The delicate silhouette of Harmony McBee appears from the dark of the night, totally wrapped in the blanket. Beneath the fabric that falls down each side of her like a veil, her face is white as a statue.

'Harmony . . .' whispers Andrew, placing his hand on a blanket-covered shoulder – with infinite care, as if he were scared a rough gesture might make this apparition disappear. 'Forgive me,' he murmurs. 'I thought, for a moment . . . I thought I'd seen a ghost.'

A smile appears on the girl's bloodless lips.

'That's the first thing I ever said to you, when we met.'

'What?'

'You remember – when you knocked on my bedroom door at the Villa McBee, out of nowhere, I took you for a ghost. But you're all flesh and blood. Just like me, Andrew.'

She presses herself against the young man's body, and he in turn puts his arms gently around her. Floating in the air is a smell of petrol and burnt rubber. The sound of the campervan, still being consumed by fire, is like the purring of a wild animal digesting its prey.

'How did you do that?' murmured Harmony.

'My Taser, you remember, the thing I used to paralyse the cop in Wyoming? I attached it to the top of the campervan's gas tank, a few days ago, while you were sleeping, and connected it to my cellphone. So that I'd have a secret weapon in case things went badly. As a diversion, in case the police caught us. An electrical discharge in a tank filled with gasoline vapours – that's all it takes to start a remote-controlled explosion.'

Harmony shivers; Andrew holds her a little tighter; his lips brush against the girl's pale forehead, between her silky eyebrows, just above the bridge of her nose.

'Are you cold?'

'Cold? No. Hot actually, from the fire. And you're holding me so tight.'

Andrew relaxes his grip slightly, embarrassed.

'Sorry,' he says.

Their eyes meet – Andrew's dark and shining behind the lenses of his glasses, Harmony's flaming like fiery lakes where the blaze is dancing.

'More drones will be coming,' whispers Andrew, his heavy breathing lifting the strands of Harmony's hair that have come loose under her woollen blanket veil. 'We should go.'

But he doesn't move an inch.

It's as if he's paralysed, while Harmony raises herself up on her tiptoes and – light as a dragonfly – closes the few centimetres' gap still separating them.

Andrew shuts his eyes; though he never usually lets go, now he abandons himself totally to the magic of the moment.

But it's not on his lips that Harmony's come to rest – it's on his cheek.

29

He abruptly reopens his bewildered eyes, thinking, *Why did I get that kiss, a kiss of friendship, instead of a kiss of love?*

At that same moment, Harmony's scream explodes against his ear.

'Behind you!'

He turns his head: a ball of fire is scuttling horribly across the ground towards him on its six pincered legs.

'W-what the . . . ?' he stammers.

The drone's jaw rams into his foot. The white-hot metal beak pierces the plastic of his sneaker, his skin, his bones and cartilage, nailing the whole thing to the ground with a shriek of pain.

On the screen in the middle of the half-incinerated drone, between the disarticulated legs swarming about amid the flames, the face of Orion Seamus is grinning.

5. Shot

'It changes nothing – you're sure of that?' he says. *'Listen to me, before you go back naively to that old "an eternity to love" slogan.'*

Marcus's hoarse voice echoes weakly around the seventh habitat. It's coming from Kenji's helmet. The Japanese boy has placed it upside down on his knees and turned the volume on the speakers up to max.

'Does it still change nothing if I tell you I knew before we set off that the base was rotten, that I knew the animals that came before us had all died, and that we were headed for our deaths too?'

Marcus and I are the only people who haven't moved in to hear better. He knows the words in this recording: they are his. I know them too: they were for me. I'm just looking at him now, unable to take my eyes off his papier-mâché face; he can't take his off the floor. I don't recognise him. This contemptible creature who seems to want to disappear beneath the ground, who doesn't even have the courage to meet my gaze: who is he, really? And most of all: how could I ever have loved him?

'Does it still change nothing if I tell you I knew about the Noah

31

Report, and that I could have revealed everything to the world during the launch ceremony – but that I let you all board that rocket without saying a word?'

There are muffled exclamations from the group. Even more incredulous outbursts of stupefaction, rage and hatred.

'Marcus knew about the Noah Report?' says Fangfang tonelessly, repeating the words from the recording, as if rolling them on her tongue might help her to grasp their monstrous meaning.

Alexei, on the other hand, digs his heels in, refusing to understand.

'What the hell does all that bullshit even mean?' he protests.

Meanwhile Kris says nothing, but I can feel the full weight of her blue gaze on me, and I can hear the sob rising in her throat.

'Does it still change nothing if I tell you the only thing that mattered to me was getting to Mars, and doing it no matter what the cost?'

Tao is the first to accept the unacceptable. Perhaps because he's the most grounded, the one with the biggest supply of good common sense. I guess you need to be a realist if you're going to head off to conquer space in a wheelchair.

'We thought we were going to make up a cast-iron team,' he murmurs, gripping the wheels of his chair hard in his strong fingers, as if he were trying to twist them out of shape. 'We thought we'd be able to count on one another like brothers from the trenches. But the truth is, Marcus was never our teammate. He was never our brother. And if he fought, it was not on our side.'

In a sinister, chilling echo, the recording confirms Tao's accusations.

'I'm not a victim, Léonor. I'm a murderer who threw away your eleven lives, knowing full well what I was doing. Would you dare to say the same thing to them, that you will love me for all eternity?'

The very moment we hear that last word, 'eternity', Marcus snaps sharply out of his dejection.

Catching us all by surprise, he makes a dash for the gaping door that opens to the access tube to the Garden.

Liz gives a shrill cry.

Mozart's the first to react, this boy with reflexes honed in the most dangerous favela in Rio – as agile as a panther, he in turn launches himself down the access tube, in pursuit of the fugitive.

There are muffled sounds outside my field of vision – the pounding noise of boots stumbling? Or of punching fists? Or just the pummelling of my heart, as it threatens to burst out of my chest? – before the other boys emerge from their stupor and hurry down the access tube, followed by the girls.

I remain in the deserted habitat.

All alone, once again.

'This is a message for Léonor. We need to talk.'

The voice of Serena McBee, from out of the bowels of the seventh habitat, makes me jump. I'd forgotten she was still there, hidden in her screen like a moray eel behind her rock.

'Come on, then, Léonor,' the voice comes through the half-open door of the master bedroom. 'Just you, alone.'

Alone.

Always that same word.

Always that same curse.

Despite everything I've achieved these past weeks, despite everything I've said to convince myself that I was part of a greater indestructible whole, it was Serena who was right. She predicted that when it came down to it, at the most important moments in my life, I would always be alone. At this moment, there's no couple, no group to cling to. There is only me.

And Serena's voice.

'*We can find some solution . . .*'

I feel myself sliding towards the doorway, numbed by everything I've just taken in.

The door slides open noiselessly under the pressure of my hand.

The room appears before me, overlooked by a screen showing the executive producer's face, unruffled under her bob of silver hair.

I stand there for a long while, just looking at her.

She is alone too, there in the middle of her huge study. The difference is, she's never pretended otherwise. She's never pretended to be one of twelve, or even of two. She thought more clearly than I did . . . Or, in a way, she was more honest.

'*Woof!*'

The bark brings me sharply back to myself.

Louve is there, at the foot of the bed, looking at me with her big black eyes. They're only the eyes of an animal, but their intensity pierces me like an arrow. There's such trust in them, such conviction, that suddenly I'm so ashamed of what I was just thinking. Serena, that monster of duplicity, honest? I was feeling so sorry for my bad luck, I was ready to believe it!

I force myself to breathe and let my fingers run through

34

Louve's warm, soft fur, a contact that fills me with energy. The hammering of my heart slows. I feel myself gradually overtaken by a new strength. A determination that is raw, bitter. It's what's left when you have nothing to lose.

The past six months scroll through my head like a movie. Since the *Cupido* set off, I've refused the role of leader that the others want to bestow on me. By trying to play the love game like the others, I allowed my feelings to intoxicate me and weaken me, to turn me into a small trembling thing that collapsed pathetically like a house of cards at the first wounding words from Marcus. But it's no longer the time for me to play somebody else's game. It's no longer time to refuse the mission that destiny has assigned to me. Maybe at the beginning I was running away from it out of modesty; but if I go on, it'll be out of cowardice.

No way!

If I'm doomed to be as alone as Serena, then I'll have to be as tough as her too!

I'll live only to fulfil my duty, to the very end, like a machine that nothing would ever cause to seize up again: the machine I was supposed to be from the very first day, which I'll have to be for the rest of the crew: the Determinator!

The moment I take this steely resolution, the face opposite me lights up on the screen. It's been ten minutes since I entered the room: at the end of the communication latency separating Mars and Earth, Serena can finally let me know that she sees me.

'*Léonor! There you are,*' she says. '*What a relief! I need you to explain to me everything that's happened, everything that's happening right now. We can't stay off the air any longer, this can't go on any longer. Do you understand?*'

While Serena keeps spouting her demands, I hear the noise of boots again in the living room: the others are back. I also hear a muffled scraping across the aluminium floor, like the sound of a body being dragged.

'Just let us have a few more minutes and I promise you we'll be ready to go back on the air,' I say.

From the living room, behind the muted curses of the boys and the panic-stricken murmurs of the girls, I think I can make out a hoarse breathing, a gravelly wheezing, like the voice of . . .

'Once you've heard this message, just give us five more minutes after that!' I bark, turning on my heel.

I push open the sliding door and burst into the living room.

There's a body lying on the floor, held down by Mozart and Samson. There's a long red streak running down the white of the suit: it's blood flowing copiously from Marcus's nose. It bubbles at the edge of his swollen mouth, smashed by a punch, mixing with his saliva to form a pinkish foam. The moaning that comes out of his split lips turns into gurgling.

'Eeee-o-ooor . . .'

Alexei presses the sole of his boot down on his bloody mouth to close it again.

'Shut it!'

Kris gives a muffled sob; she doesn't dare look at me, or at Marcus.

'I just can't believe he kept that from us, something so immense,' says Fangfang, as white as a sheet.

'But you heard it just like I did, like Léo did, like all of us here did,' answers Kelly with a grimace. 'And you saw him run away like a frightened rabbit the moment he got the chance.

36

Shit, he should have opened the decompression airlock and just fucked right off into the Martian storm! The handsome boy with all those lovely tattoos is a filthy traitor crossed with a filthy coward. It's crap, but that's just the way it is.'

She throws another piece of chewing gum in her mouth and starts chewing furiously.

'What are we going to do with . . . with him?' stammers Liz.

No one answers.

Because it's too scary.

Because it's too painful.

Because in movies and in novels there's only one punishment that suits a traitor, and we all know very well what it is.

The terrible silence is disturbed only by the sobbing of my darling Kris, who is clinging onto Liz at the other end of the room, and the squeaking of the brakes on the wheelchair that Tao is nervously squeezing in his hands.

'I thought he was a pal,' says Alexei finally. 'But what did he think of me? A shitty extra in one of his magic tricks, the kind you make disappear with a wave of your wand or you saw in half? Some poor jerk whose life's so unimportant you don't even bother to warn him he's going to die?'

Alexei presses his boot against Marcus's cheek, and presses down with his eighty-five kilos of muscle, plus the thirty kilos of the suit – even at reduced gravity, it's a lot for a human skull to take.

'Stop it, you're going to crush his brains in!' shouts Samson, his voice hoarse with stress.

He grabs hold of the first thing he can lay his hands on – one of the living-room chairs – and brandishes it above his head to drive Alexei away.

'Samson, be careful!' cries Safia, her doe-eyes ringed with kohl looking at her husband, begging. 'The guy's a thug!'

Tao comes to the Nigerian's rescue.

'Alex, get off him!' he growls. 'Can't you see you're about to kill him?'

'And?' asks Alexei, squinting. 'You just said it yourself – he's never been our teammate. He's never been our brother. In his head, he's already killed us all!'

Alexei seems to be holding back tears – of rage, of spite, of sadness.

But he can't stop his eyes shining.

Marcus's, meanwhile, are dull, held down beneath that notched sole, so perfectly designed for treading on the Martian ground.

Samson stands as still as a statue, the chair in his hands, ready to strike Alexei. Leaning on one of the armrests of his wheelchair, Tao seems about to hurl his massive body forward. Mozart has slipped his hand back inside the pocket of his suit, where he kept his knife. Everybody is quite still, even Kelly, who has suddenly stopped chewing her gum, plunging the habitat into a deathly silence. I feel as though I've been shut up inside a canister filled with gas, which only needs a single spark to go up in a huge explosion.

I've got to do everything in my power to stop that spark being lit.

It's my responsibility: keep the group together, whatever the cost.

'Move your boot, Alexei! Now I'm the one who's asking you!'

Surprised at my roar, the Russian looks over towards me.

38

I force myself not to look down at Marcus at my feet, but to look him, Alexei, straight in the eye.

'If you kill him out of selfishness, just to calm your anger, you'll also be killing the one thing we have left,' I say, my voice hoarse, struggling to keep my emotion in check. 'You'll shatter that one precious thing Marcus himself almost managed to destroy: *us*.'

I catch my breath at that word: *us*.

I summon all my strength, all my being, to support me, and I repeat it in a voice that is suddenly much more certain.

'*Us*. Our cohesion. Our mutual trust. What has bound us to one another since the very beginning. What will maybe allow us to make it through this one day. We can't let Marcus's treachery divide us; just the opposite, we need to make it bind us even tighter together. If he has to die, it's up to the group to decide. And if the group decides he must, then I'll be the one to execute him. I swear it.'

Alexei glances around, at the nine other pioneers frozen in front of Marcus; then, slowly, he puts his boot back down on the floor and moves a few steps away.

'We are going to judge Marcus,' I say finally, a lump in my throat, without so much as a glance at the human wreck slumped on the floor. 'That's the only way we can survive what he's done to us. But not right away. We need to concentrate on the storm now, and on the space elevator, and on the fact we're about to go back on the air. We'll shut the accused in the seventh habitat, we'll return to the Garden and later we'll organise his trial.'

6. Off-screen

Abandoned mine, Death Valley
Sunday 7 January, 05:31am

Andrew Fisher's scream of agony tears through the night.

His foot is nailed to the ground, pierced through by the steel jaw of the police drone. By the light of the flames dancing around the machine's body, it's possible to see the blood flowing from the mutilated extremity, reddening the white plastic of the sneaker, soaking into the dry earth of Death Valley.

'Andrew!' wails Harmony, throwing herself at him.

She grabs his arm and tries to pull him towards her.

But the jaw has plunged in too deep.

The young man's face has become no more than a white circle, bloodless, in the middle of which is the open black hole of his screaming mouth.

Agent Seamus's face, meanwhile, is still smiling on the round screen set into the belly of the drone, in the middle of the flames.

'Let him go!' pleads Harmony, turning towards the spherical cameras that act as eyes. 'I'm begging you, let him go!'

'*So he'll just run away again?*' answers the agent's crackling voice. '*No, I don't think so.*'

'But he's going to die!'

'He would if I let him go, that's when he'd die. Same goes for you, little girl, you won't be going far, if you're as weak as you seem. You're going to wait here nicely, both of you – help won't be too long in arriving.'

Andrew's howling is dying in his throat – he no longer even has the strength to cry out. His eyes are rolling white under their lids.

Harmony lets go of the fire-retardant blanket, which slides from her delicate shoulders and slips down to the ground. Then she too collapses in the middle of the material and curls up into herself, sobbing.

One of the drone cameras turns on its axis and zooms in to get closer to her, while the beam from the last headlight still working blazes onto her forehead.

'Tell me something though,' murmurs Agent Seamus. *'Your face is real familiar . You aren't Serena McBee's secret daughter, are you? The one nobody but the Secret Service knows about? It's Harmony, right?'*

The effect of this name on the girl is like an electric shock.

'No!' she shouts.

Her hands grip the edge of the blanket.

Her nails drive into the pebbly earth, bone-dry now without even the faintest memory of rain.

'That's it! You're the spitting image of your mother! You have the same eyes . . . the same hair.' One of the machine's pincers reaches slowly towards her blonde locks. *'But when the vice-president told me a girl had run away with Andrew Fisher, I didn't know it was you!'*

The pincers close on Harmony's long hair; at the same moment, the girl's fingers close on a stone larger than the rest – a chunk of rock weighing several kilos, probably heavier than anything she's ever lifted in her over-protected life.

'Nobody but the C.I.A. knows of your existence, and even then, your file has almost nothing in it: your first name, a description, a few photographs stolen by aerial drones flying over the Villa McBee. Why does your mother hide you from public view? What's your secret? And most important, who is your father?'

Terror, rage and despair fuel Harmony's stunted muscles; she rips the stone out of its coating of dry earth . . .

'Answer me: who is your fa—'

. . . and hurls it with all her might at the cyclopean screen, before Agent Seamus has a chance to finish repeating his question.

The screen smashes into pieces. The pincer jerks back violently, pulling out a small clump of hair. The other five legs of the drone are overtaken by spasms. The metallic appendices clank in the void, then all freeze at the same moment. Finally the insect shape turns on its back, like a huge dead beetle in revolting slow motion.

Andrew gives out a hoarse moan at the moment when the jaw loses its power and detaches itself from his foot with an appalling suction noise.

Harmony rushes over to him.

'We've got to get back to the cabin! We need to get you lying down!'

'No,' he manages to say with a grimace. 'Other drones . . . will come soon. We . . . we should go . . .'

'But we no longer have anything to drive,' Harmony reminds him with a glance at the carcass of the campervan, which is still being consumed amid the defeated drones. 'We're lost in the middle of the desert, with nobody for miles around!'

'There's a little hotel . . . not far from Dry Mountain. And in that hotel . . . there's a woman who might help us . . .' He points a trembling finger at his cellphone that has fallen on the ground. 'We have to call her.'

7. Genesis Channel

Sunday 7 January, 8:47am

Open onto the Garden, which is plunged into near darkness.

Léonor is standing there, in front of the covered plantations.

Her thick red hair catches the scattered light that is pouring out of the supplementary spotlights. They glow like copper wires with an electric current passing through them. Her amber eyes have something electric about them too. Something magnetic.

Behind her stand the Mars pioneers, upright in their white suits, beside the motionless robots and the dogs as still as statues. Only two of the boys are missing: Alexei and Marcus.

A caption appears at the bottom of the screen: RESUMING LIVE BROADCAST FROM THE GARDEN OF NEW EDEN, 10:57 (MARS TIME).

It's Léonor who speaks, looking straight into the camera.

'My dear Serena, my dear viewers, we owe you an apology. On behalf of all the pioneers on Mars. And on behalf of Marcus in particular. He was taken ill a short while ago, just after the unbelievable news of the self-energising space elevator. Overcome by emotion, maybe, or possibly something more serious, some aftereffects of the accident that nearly cost him

44

his life in the New Eden airlock a month ago. I don't know yet, I feel so ill-equipped, I'm still just an apprentice in medicine.'

Léonor's eyes shine a little brighter, but she doesn't flinch, and continues stoically: 'Marcus went to take shelter in the Rest House. I of course followed him, and the others did the same. There he lost consciousness for a moment. He's come to again now. But he's very weak. The other Medical Officer, Alexei, has stayed there with him. I want to go back to his bedside now. I hope you'll forgive me for abandoning you on air, given the circumstances.'

Léonor takes a deep breath.

Her red curls rise slightly on either side of her face, moved by the swelling of her chest, then fall gently back onto her shoulders as she breathes out again.

She opens her mouth one more time. 'Marcus . . .'

But this time her voice stumbles, cracks, overcome by a sudden emotion.

She closes her eyes and squeezes them tight, as if to stop them tearing up any more.

Then Kris puts her hand on her shoulder. She is copied by Liz and Mozart, by Safia and Samson, Kelly and Kenji. Even Tao rolls over towards her and holds out his powerful hand to support her right arm, while Fangfang gently takes her left.

When Léonor reopens her eyes, they are dry. She has managed to hold back her tears.

Her voice no longer trembles when she resumes speaking, and she says in a professional tone: 'Marcus will undoubtedly have to remain confined to the Rest House for a time. Better not to move him for now. That's the advice we were given

45

by Dr Montgomery, our medical instructor, in case of illness. We will be asking for his long-distance help to try to reach an accurate diagnosis. We will of course keep you up to speed with the situation.'

No sooner has Léonor spoken these words than a ray of light falls on her face, illuminating the countless freckles scattered over her cheeks and the flecks of gold that speckle her irises. Instinctively the pioneers look up at the spotlights attached to the Garden ceiling.

But that's not where the light is coming from, its intensity growing with every second: it's coming from outside.

Beyond the glass panels of the greenhouse, the last red clouds are slowly fading.

The dust storm has cleared.

The sun is shining again.

8. Reverse Shot

Vice-presidential residence, Washington DC
Sunday 7 January, 09:35am

Serena McBee is met by a burst of flashbulbs the moment she steps out of the gates that enclose the Observatory residence.

Reporters have gathered here in their hundreds, microphones outstretched, cameras pointed.

'Madam Vice-President, what made you decide to bring forward your announcement and reveal this extraordinary project for a self-energising space elevator?' asks a man in a suit and tie, his cheeks pink from the cold. 'Should we be seeing this as an evacuation plan for the pioneers on Mars?'

'I've already answered that question live on the Genesis channel,' Serena McBee reminds him, with a shrug of her shoulders in their luxurious mink coat. 'I thought it sensible to make this announcement to give the pioneers some reassurance during the storm, to show them that we do have a solution in the event they really do want to return to Earth one day. This option allows them, let's say, some security, *a sense of well-being* – a bit like an airbag in a car. But in any case, it's not an evacuation plan. I'm certain the base will weather all future storms. This elevator will allow us – on the contrary – to accelerate the colonisation of Mars by making it easier to send people and materials into the planet's gravitational well. The human race has set foot on the red planet, and it's there to stay!'

'Yes, but who's going to pay for it?' asks a woman decked out in a pair of downy earmuffs. 'You've only just been elected on an Ultra-libertarian party platform and you're going to toss away all of President Green's electoral promises and increase contributions from American taxpayers?'

Serena swats the question away with a wave of her gloved hand.

'I've spoken on that subject too,' she says, not bothering to hide her irritation. 'It's Atlas Capital, a totally private fund, who will be financing this project. Taxpayers won't be paying a single extra cent.'

She clicks her fingers and gestures for her bodyguards to part the crowds to allow her access to the limo that is waiting a few metres away.

At the last moment, one final reporter manages to stick his microphone under her nose.

'Ms McBee, have you had any news on the health of Marcus, our own nation's pioneer? You're the only person on Earth who has access to the Rest House.'

Serena cracks a smile that is intended to be comforting.

'You heard Léonor as well as I did: she said he's regained consciousness. Let him have a bit of a break. He needs it. As do I.'

And with this, she makes her way through the crowd without stopping again and gets into the back of the limo. The door slams shut; the camera flashes and the journalists' shouts vanish as if by magic behind the perfectly soundproofed, double-glazed, tinted windows.

'Good morning, Serena.'

A man in a tweed suit is sitting on the black leather padded seat: Arthur Montgomery, the programme's medical instructor, the last surviving ally of silence since the others' disappearance in a plane crash a month earlier.

'Good morning, my dear!' exclaims Serena, all smiles. 'How kind of you to accompany me to the White House for my meeting this morning. The president has been asking me for further details about the self-energising space elevator too, it's becoming quite tiresome, but what do you expect? Ever since his re-election, the great man has considered the Genesis programme an affair of state!'

But Arthur Montgomery is not smiling. Beneath his perfectly shaped white moustache, his mouth is closed as tight as a fist.

'You know it's been forty-eight hours and you haven't given me any news at all,' he says at last, his voice heavy with reproach.

'There's no reason to take offence, my dear,' Serena replies airily, gesturing to the driver through the soundproof glass separating the front seats and the back that he can pull away. 'The preparations for the storm, the coaching I'm offering the pioneers, and finally the announcement of the self-energising space elevator: it's all kept me extremely busy, as you can well imagine.'

'But you still found the time to see *him*.'

Serena is silent for a moment.

'*Him?*' she then repeats, raising an eyebrow.

'Don't play the innocent. You know perfectly well who I'm talking about. I spent the night sitting in my car outside your house, watching all the comings and goings. I even tried calling you, again and again, but you never answered. You might have been too busy to see me, but that didn't stop Orion Seamus from coming in!'

The vice-president's lipsticked mouth forms a round O of surprise, which almost immediately transforms itself into a half-moon.

'You were spying on me like a teenager? You, Arthur – a man of your age and distinction?'

'The ingratitude! After everything I've done for you! Sherman Fisher, Ruben Rodriguez, Gordon Lock and his whole gang: I killed some of them, I lied to cover up the murder of the others. And this is how you thank me? You're no better than a –'

'That's enough!' Serena interrupts him with a voice as sharp as a razor blade.

The doctor's recriminations catch in his throat, while the woman beside him on the seat glares at him with those mascara-enhanced, water-green eyes.

'Have you gone out of your mind?' she whispers. 'Mentioning names, talking about murder?'

'You're the one who's driven me out of my mind,' pleads Arthur Montgomery, suddenly as gentle as a lamb. 'And anyway, there's no way the driver can hear me through the soundproof glass.'

'That doesn't make any difference! And I thought I was dealing with a man, a real man, a hunter of wild beasts, with nerves of steel. And now look how badly you've fallen short, letting me down like all the others before you. All because of a ridiculous attack of jealousy, completely baseless, because of some ordinary agent who – I might remind you – has been detailed to my personal security, and not because I asked for him. It's as if you'd gotten jealous of my dog!'

Arthur Montgomery tries to put his hand on his lover's, but she shakes it off.

'Oh, Serena,' he begs. 'Forgive me. It was stupid of me to think that some common lackey like that Seamus could ever have gotten between us. Of course he can see you, he can talk to you as much as you like, I won't get offended any more. Will you forgive me, my tigress? My heart is in your claws.'

At that moment, a bell sounds in the car.

Without answering the doctor's entreaties, Serena puts her hand into her snakeskin bag and takes out her cellphone. The name of the incoming caller appears on the screen: ORION SEAMUS.

Serena makes no attempt to hide it: on the contrary, she makes it quite visible so that her fellow passenger cannot be unaware of who is calling her.

'Hello – Orion?' she says, never taking her eyes off Arthur Montgomery, as if challenging him. 'I'm so glad to hear from you. Do you have good news? Tell me everything.'

'*They got away.*'

Serena McBee's face freezes.

'What?'

'*Andrew Fisher and . . . the girl. Their van was booby-trapped. They blew it up, and the police drones I'd sent to apprehend them with it.*'

51

The vice-president plunges her green nails into the leather seat, as if she really has metamorphosed into a tigress.

'Totally hopeless,' she says in a quiet, accusing voice. 'I give you their precise location, I offer them up to you on a platter, and you manage to let them escape.'

'*They can't have gotten far. Andrew Fisher is seriously wounded. It's only a matter of hours before we find them again.*'

'I strongly suggest you do, Agent Seamus, if you don't want your meteoric rise to be brought to an end with an equally precipitous fall.'

Serena hangs up sharply.

Sitting beside her on the back seat, Arthur Montgomery is smiling again.

9. Off-screen

Last-Chance Highway, Death Valley
Sunday 7 January, 06:36am

The pick-up stops with a loud screeching of brakes, tearing into the silence of the night.

A cloud of dust, disturbed by the tyres, rises into the beam of the headlamps. The door opens with a creak – it's an old vehicle, damaged by the years and by the coarse sands of Death Valley. A woman in an anorak gets out – she's fortyish, her face crumpled with tiredness, her red-dyed hair pulled hastily into a bun. She's holding a flashlight in her left hand, and an oblong shape in her right. As she makes her way forward in the beams of the headlamps, the shape of the object becomes clearer.

It's a shotgun, held out in front of her and pointed at the two shadows waiting on the verge.

'Was it you who called the Hotel California?' she says quietly, raising the flashlight. 'You said something about an accident on the road, but I can't see anything.'

Two faces appear in the dazzling beam.

The first belongs to Harmony McBee – it's gaunt, her eyes wide with distress.

The second is no more than a mask of pain: it's Andrew

Fisher's, leaning his whole weight on the girl's delicate shoulder; he's holding his right foot in the air, and a thick dark liquid is dripping from it.

'Oh God!' the driver of the pick-up exclaims.

Forgetting all her suspicions, she swings the shotgun over her shoulder and hurries to rescue this young couple.

'What's happened?' she babbles, holding out her arms to support Andrew. 'But . . . I recognise you! You're the ghost who comes around in the middle of the night to get supplies from the hotel minimarket!'

'And you're the kind soul who leaves the minimarket door open . . . every night . . . so I can help myself,' Andrew manages to reply.

In the distance, there is a muffled hooting.

All the way down at the end of the valley, the horizon is starting to turn white. Day will soon be breaking.

'Call me Cindy,' says the woman. 'Or rather, no, don't call me anything, don't say another word. Best save your strength. Looks like your foot is in a horrible state, and the nearest hospital is two hours' drive.'

'No, not the hospital.' Andrew resists her, but his voice is getting ever weaker.

'Why not? Have you done something wrong? This a gang thing, is that what it is? Are you going to get yourselves shot? Are your enemies still somewhere nearby?'

Nervously, Cindy sweeps the flashlight across their surroundings; but it finds nothing but loose stones, dry grass and thorn bushes.

'There are no enemies here – not for now, at least.'

Surprised at the voice of the young girl who has just spoken,

54

Cindy trains the flashlight on her. Harmony's moon-like face is lit up again.

'Please, ma'am, you need to take us far away, as far as possible,' she begs. 'You're right – Andrew can't talk any more, the state he's in now.'

For a moment Cindy looks at Harmony, and then at Andrew. Finally, she nods, with a sigh.

'OK. But as soon as we're out of Death Valley National Park, we're going to stop at a clinic to get that foot looked at. I don't want a death on my conscience – even the death of a ghost.'

A shadow passes across Harmony's face. 'We said no hospital, no clinic. We need to avoid anywhere he'd be asked to state his identity, show his papers, or –'

'The clinic I'm talking about won't ask you for any papers,' Cindy interrupts her. 'The patients who show up there don't have passports, or drivers' licences, or ID cards. Come on, help me get this poor kid settled on the back seat. What did you say his name was again? Andrew? Good to put a name to a ghost.'

Harmony stiffens.

'Please stop calling him that. I can assure you, Andrew's no ghost. He's not dead.'

Harmony's pale eyes are filled with a combative gleam, which doesn't come from the flashlight or the pick-up's headlamps, nor even the early dawn.

'. . . cos the truth is, he's one of the most alive people I've ever met,' she concludes in a whisper.

At that moment, Andrew's hand, which has been clutching onto Harmony's shoulder, relaxes, and his whole body sags against Cindy's: he has just passed out.

10. Shot

Month 21 / sol 578 / 15:34 Mars time
[28th sol since landing]

'Are you telling us Marcus lied not once, but twice?' asks Fangfang quietly.

All five of the girls are in the Rest House, squeezed together on the sofa: the pioneers of the Genesis programme, the girls I've spent the best days of my life with – and the most horrible days too. Officially they've come here to visit the sick boy, that's the version we offered up to the organisers and the viewers. In reality, I used the secrecy of the seventh habitat to tell them everything. So that they know and can make their decision in full possession of the facts, when the time comes to pronounce their verdict on Marcus.

He's been imprisoned for several hours, behind the steel door of the second bedroom, which we've locked from the outside with one of the base's skeleton keys, after having destroyed its cameras and mics with the welding gun.

I feel a shiver of pity, of disgust and sadness run through me, as if a thousand icy needles were piercing my spine all at once.

I bite the inside of my cheeks to force myself to swallow down the sobs that are trying to rise in my throat.

I have no right to show any sign of weakness.

I need to be strong, for my own sake and for the others.

That's my part to play.

That's my responsibility.

'Yes,' I say at last, in answer to Fangfang's question. 'Marcus lied twice over. Or rather, he hid the truth from me twice. I forgave him for the first time: it's not his fault he's the victim of a fatal genetic mutation.'

'Maybe not, but it's a hundred per cent his fault he hid it from you!' Kelly objects, fiddling nervously with her bleached locks. 'Just by boarding the rocket, he knew he was forcing a girl to marry a guy who was sick and likely to drop dead at any moment! He was careful not to warn you before the publication of the final Heart Lists; he only did it afterwards, when he was sure it was too late to get himself dumped. So there's no need to bring out the violins and start some pity campaign for orphan diseases. That isn't going to wash with me: the guy's a bastard all the way, period!'

'He conned us all, but you more than anyone, Léo,' Kelly concludes bitterly. 'I feel so sorry for you, my poor darling.'

I nod, but I can't find the words to answer.

Liz is first to break the silence.

'There's still one mystery though,' she murmurs. 'Marcus's second little secret. The one that's condemned us. We don't know how he learned of the existence of the Noah Report before everybody else.'

'And we don't give a crap how, either,' replies Kelly. 'It doesn't make any difference. The damage is done.'

Safia coughs quietly.

'I disagree, Kelly,' she says, seriously. 'It's important that we know.'

Beneath her red bindi, Safia's eyes are squinting slightly in concentration. Once again, it's the youngest among us who's displaying the greatest maturity: she's managing to overcome her anger and dread, to get beyond these immediate emotional reactions.

'Anything to do with the Noah Report is important,' she adds. 'It's about our survival. If Marcus knows something we don't, he absolutely must tell us during his trial, at 8 p.m. tonight.'

At 8 p.m. tonight . . .

That's the time we've chosen to begin the preliminary hearing. At that moment, we will all gather in the Rest House, unseen by the cameras, to decide Marcus's fate.

Kelly gives a mirthless laugh.

'Why do you still expect anything of that guy?' she says. 'He's already lied twice, what's to stop him lying a third time? Lying and running away, that's all he's good for. He'll do whatever it takes to save his skin. We aren't going to learn anything from the cross-examination, I'd bet my right hand on that . . .' She looks at each of us in turn with her unblinking blue eyes. 'And I can tell you – in my head, the verdict has already been settled.'

The cold determination in Kelly's voice makes me shudder.

But I stop myself from telling her off, from trying to calm her down, or from asking her exactly what she's thinking. The fate of the accused is in her hands as much as mine. The trial belongs to all the girls and boys Marcus has betrayed. Each of us will judge Marcus according to what she or he personally believes.

And when the verdict rings out and the time comes to enact the sentence, I'll be the one to execute the people's will, as I vowed to do.

All of a sudden, we hear a vague crackling from the master bedroom.

'Hello? Girls? It's me, Serena, I'm back. I was held up at the White House talking about your self-energising elevator – and I've got to get back there in a few hours to continue the meeting. As you can see, here on Earth we're keeping very busy, and we're all with you! But tell me, what are you all up to in the Rest House? Is Marcus doing better? Let me have some reassurance soon, I'm worried sick.'

Kelly rolls her eyes.

'Marcus and that woman could compete for who's the worst hypocrite, big time.'

'You think she knew that he knew?' asks Fangfang. 'About the Noah Report, I mean? According to what Léonor said, Serena's known about Marcus's illness ever since the selection rounds, and she still let him board without telling anybody.'

'My guess is she didn't know,' answers Safia. 'Hiding Marcus's illness, that's one thing, but she'd never have allowed a passenger to board who might let the cat out of the bag live on air at any moment.'

As if echoing the Indian girl's words, Serena's voice seeps in once again from the master bedroom.

'Do you read me, my dears? Ah, how frustrating it is not being able to see you ever since Léonor unfortunately damaged the living-room cameras! And those in the second bedroom seem to have been broken for a while now too, apparently. Probably worth

59

thinking about fixing them – what do you think?'

Kelly opens her mouth to let out a well-chosen swearword, but I get up off the sofa at that same moment.

'I'm going to answer her,' I say.

'Because you believe she's really going to stand up for Marcus, that snake, or for any one of us?' says the Canadian girl.

'Of course not. But I still get the feeling we need to keep the truth from her. Ever since she forced us to start playing this weird game, that's what it's all about. Pretence. Bluffing. Controlling the information. I'm going to try and figure out what Serena knows about Marcus, while telling her as little as possible. In the meantime, go join the guys in the Garden; while the viewers are watching, it has to look like everything's back to normal.'

The girls get up in turn, and one by one they disappear into the access tube that leads to the Garden.

Kris is the last to leave the room, and before she does, she turns and takes hold of my arms, gently. Her blue eyes stare straight into mine.

'It bothers me, leaving you alone with Serena . . . and with Marcus.'

She glances at the bolted door of the second bedroom.

'Don't worry, love,' I say. 'I'm not crazy. I won't open it.'

'Promise?'

'Promise.'

Kris smiles faintly.

Then she too disappears down the access tube, closing the airlock behind her.

For a long moment I just stand there, alone, unmoving in the silence.

The two doors are in front of me. Behind the first is the woman who sent us all to our deaths; behind the second, the guy who could have saved all our lives. Only minutes ago, I promised Kris I wouldn't open one of those doors. But the desire to do just that is niggling at me all of a sudden. Just to see Marcus's smashed-up face one more time and try to look beyond his injuries and recognise a memory that's already beginning to fade.

(What harm would it do, Léonor, to open that door for a moment?)

I step towards the second bedroom.

(Where's the risk in opening it just a little? You've got nothing to fear: the person we've dragged in there is no more than the shadow of a man, physically and morally destroyed.)

My hand comes to rest on the skeleton key that is still in the lock.

But at that same moment, I hear Serena's voice once again behind me.

'*Léonor? Are you there, Léonor? I've seen the girls back in the dome via the Garden cameras. Have you stayed behind to talk to me, my good girl?*'

My fingers instantly let go of the key, as if it was burning.

Just think what I had been about to do!

I turn away sharply from the small bedroom and rush to the large one.

This time, I raise the lever to open the door without a moment's hesitation and find myself standing opposite the mural screen displaying the face of the executive producer of the Genesis programme.

'Here I am, Serena,' I say. 'Sorry to have kept you waiting, a woman as busy as you are. You asked for news of Marcus. I can understand how worried you must be.'

Taking advantage of the communications latency, I breathe in deeply and have a good look at the silver bob, the smooth skin, the made-up lips.

'As I explained on the air not long ago, Marcus was taken ill,' I say. 'I was really, really worried about him. He stopped breathing . . . His heart stopped beating . . . I honestly thought he'd died.'

All lies, of course, but there's no way Serena could know that: she didn't witness what happened. What I've just described to her would match an attack caused by the D66 mutation – Marcus's secret illness, which we aren't supposed to know about, not me or the other pioneers or the rest of the Earth.

I swallow slowly, to get rid of the bitter taste still lingering in my mouth. Lying doesn't always come naturally to me, even when I'm speaking to the biggest liar of all time.

After long minutes have passed, Serena finally reacts.

Her face tenses up, a tiny amount that would be undetectable to most mortals, but I've had plenty of practice spotting it, and I can tell there's something bothering her – *I'm sure of it, she recognised the symptoms of the secret mutation.*

'Oh, my poor dear Marcus!' she cries. 'But . . . he's doing better now, isn't he? He's still . . . alive? You said on the air a moment ago that he'd recovered consciousness, isn't that right?'

Without waiting for me to formulate an answer and for it to reach her, she immediately adds:

'Did he . . . did he say anything when he came to?'

There it is.

Serena's scared that Marcus has talked.

But what is it she's afraid of, exactly? That he's revealed his illness to me, or that he knew about the Noah Report?

'Did he say anything?' I repeat, naively. 'I don't understand? Whatever do you mean?'

I let my question fly across the depths of space.

Total silence in the seventh habitat.

Behind the closed door of the second bedroom, Marcus might as well be a dream. And who knows, maybe that's all he is, maybe that's all he's ever been. Chasing those crazy thoughts out of my mind, I force myself to look directly at the woman facing me on the screen, and to think of nothing else.

She's had time to compose a skilful expression of concern, artificially sympathetic.

'Yes, well, what I meant was, so you could give him better treatment.' She tries to explain. 'I don't know, did he maybe say something about his symptoms, about what he was going through? About his medical history? Anything about his background? Just a random thought, really. I just wondered whether perhaps he'd said anything that might help us reach a correct diagnosis and find the right remedy. At the same time, if he said nothing . . . Well, I'm sure I can count on you to keep me up to date with developments, can't I?'

I understand now: what's really worrying Serena, behind those clumsy hints of hers, is the mutation. I can understand why she's freaking out: it's not exactly easy for her to reveal to the pioneers at breaking point and to the viewers all wired about the storm that she's dispatched a terminally ill guy into space and not told anybody about it. I'm sure she'd planned some other way of making the announcement – at a moment of her choosing, and in total control. And suddenly all this is threatening to turn everything against her and cause some real damage.

'The only thing I care about, as you know, is that you are all in the best of health,' she says. 'As united as possible until the self-energising elevator arrives, before the next Great Storm.'

I can't help clenching my teeth – even when I try to play Serena's perversely rational chess game, emotion ends up getting the better of me and overwhelming me. This woman who today is talking about uniting us, is the same woman who persuaded Marcus to come aboard without revealing his condition, on the pretext that the girls weren't really after love anyway but glory, and that as a result his future wife would get over her widowhood without any pain on the very same day he died. Today Marcus isn't dead, but I'm a widow all the same, and it does hurt. It hurts like hell!

Take it easy, Léo.

Breathe.

Assess the situation.

Draw your conclusions.

Conclusion number one: as Safia suspected, Serena seems unaware of Marcus's knowledge of the Noah Report prior to our departure – in any case, that's not what she's focusing her anxiety on.

Conclusion number two: while I'm face to face with her, watching her try everything to prove how eager she is to help, this is the moment to make my request – to ask for Marcus's confinement, which would allow us to organise his trial without anybody knowing, not even Serena herself.

'I will keep you posted, of course, Serena,' I say, unclenching my teeth. 'We need medical assistance from Earth to help us handle this situation. We won't be able to get through it without you. While we wait, I think it's best for Marcus to stay in the Rest House, where it's calm, away from all the media pressure. You do understand, don't you? And I'm sure the viewers will understand too. As you yourself put it so well, we need to be more united than ever and surround the patient with all the affection we can to get him better as quickly as possible. This is why tonight, at 8 p.m. Martian time, the other pioneers and I will be coming in to have dinner with him – just us, far away from the cameras.'

I breathe out slowly, while my words fly through space, across the millions of kilometres separating the sender from the recipient.

Was I firm enough for Serena to submit to our decision?

Was I neutral enough to stop her suspecting anything? My heart is thumping so hard I feel worryingly as though its thunderous beats can be heard all the way on Earth; a flush of blood inflames my cheeks – I'm sure I must be as red as a beetroot on Serena's monitor.

'So be it,' she says simply, after ten interminable minutes have elapsed. Her face is so unmoving it's enough to make you wonder whether there's a heart beating in her chest at all. 'We'll fill up the time by broadcasting the reports we filmed about each of the candidates before lift-off. It'll be encrypted, subscription only – a nice bit of extra income to help finance that elevator of yours!'

11. Off-screen

'That should stop the gangrene.'

The hand in a latex glove takes hold of a pair of sterilised scissors to cut the thread of the suture over the freshly sewn wound. The hand belongs to a woman in a green medical smock, her face hidden behind a surgical mask.

The patient stretched out on the operating table is unconscious, a breathing tube in his mouth. His black-framed glasses have been removed and there's a drip in his arm.

'But I insist, he absolutely must be taken to a *proper* hospital. I've dealt with the most urgent things first, in order to reduce any threats to his life, but there's a whole world of difference between this young man and the patients I usually operate on.'

A second woman comes up behind the surgeon.

It's Cindy, the waitress from the Hotel California, also wearing a green smock.

'Don't do yourself down, Kat – you did wonders for Marilyn when she punctured her stomach swallowing a chicken bone. It's only because of you that she lived so

66

many long years after her accident, before falling asleep so peacefully at last.'

'Marilyn was a miniature dachshund,' replies the surgeon. 'It's not the same thing at all . . .'

She puts the scissors back down on a metal tray, resting on a shelf amid a variety of flasks and implements. The wall behind her is covered in photos of cats, dogs, parakeets, hamsters and other animals. Also visible is a framed diploma, which declares: 'THE UNIVERSITY OF INDIANA HEREBY AFFIRMS THAT KATRYN PETERSON HAS BEEN GRANTED HER QUALIFICATION OF DOCTOR IN VETERINARY MEDICINE.'

The medic removes her mask, revealing the face of a fifty-year-old woman.

'After all this time we've known each other, Cindy, you're much more than a customer now,' she says with a sigh. 'You're a friend. That's the only reason I agreed to operate on this young man without asking questions. But as your friend, it's my duty to warn you that you're taking a terrible risk if you don't get him into the hands of qualified doctors. It's a very deep wound; if it ends up getting infected despite the antibiotics, you're looking at septic shock, and then death, no doubt about it. You'll be held responsible: failure to assist a person in danger.'

'If we take John to the hospital, that really would be putting him in danger.'

Cindy and Dr Peterson turn to look at the person who has just spoken, the fourth person present in the small operating room. Her colourless hair stands out against the green of her overall, which matches the green of her eyes.

The vet just looks at this strange girl for a moment. She

67

opens her mouth to argue, then stops at the last moment, contenting herself with a shake of the head and another sigh.

'This *John*, whoever he is, will be regaining consciousness soon,' she says finally, pulling off her gloves. 'I'll leave you with enough antibiotics and bandages to take care of him until the wound scars over, God willing. But of course, as far as I am aware, he was never on this operating table. We only take animals on here.'

'*John?* Seriously? You had to lie about his name?' Cindy asks, stepping on the gas. 'And more importantly, are you finally going to tell me what this whole crazy business is all about?'

From her place on the passenger seat beside the driver, Harmony glances nervously into the rear-view mirror. In it she can see the veterinary clinic gradually receding into the distance, and soon the small town surrounding it gives way to a motorway flanked by barren plains. There is a collection of rocket-shaped key-rings hanging from the rear-view mirror, swaying gently. Each of them is inset with the official photo of one of the pioneers from the Genesis programme: a proper fan collection.

'I'm warning you, if you don't tell me I'm going to drop you at the next bus station we pass. I don't even know why I'm doing any of this, specially as I'm way too tired to drive after spending the whole night awake in front of the TV. And anyway, you heard what Kat said: I'm risking being put in prison.'

By way of response, Harmony turns to examine Andrew's body stretched out on the back seat, his foot wrapped in a thick bandage. He looks like he's sleeping peacefully. His head is resting on one of the cushions piled up there: promotional items covered in red fur imitating the spherical shape of the planet Mars, stamped with the Genesis logo.

On the rear counter, behind the dozing patient, there are two dog figurines dressed in spacesuits, their articulated heads nodding to the rhythm of the highway bumps. It's not hard to recognise Louve's white curls and Warden's grimacing features. The two figurines bear the logo of *Best Friend Forever*, the pedigree dog food brand from Eden Food.

'And I'm supposed to start my shift at six o'clock to serve dinner at the hotel where I work,' Cindy goes on, unstoppable. 'Not to mention that you're keeping me from my favourite channel, just at the moment of greatest suspense! It's making me ill not knowing what's happening up there! God, I hope the self-energising elevator Serena announced will be ready soon, to go help the pioneers in the event of any problem!'

'It's all down to you . . . whether the construction can happen more quickly.'

In her surprise, Cindy swerves, before regaining control of the vehicle.

'What did you just say?' she asks, glancing in the rear-view mirror at the back seat, where Andrew has just woken up.

'I said you can help the pioneers on Mars,' replies the young man in a voice that is thick and sticky from the anaesthetic. 'You can help them . . . by helping us.'

'Andrew!' Harmony is alarmed. 'You're still in shock. Don't say another word!'

But Cindy's curiosity is well and truly piqued now.

She presses down on the brake pedal and pulls the pick-up roughly onto the side of the deserted road.

'Not another word? Then not another mile!' she declares, crossing her arms over the steering wheel. 'Tell me what this mess is, or get ready to continue your journey on your one foot!'

Harmony is just about to reply, but Andrew holds her back with a hand on her arm.

'This woman could have turned me in so many times, when I used to help myself from the minimart at the gas station, and she never did. We should trust her. Truth is, I don't see how we have much choice in the matter. We haven't got a car, or any money. There's a warrant out for our arrest. My family is under surveillance, and as for yours . . .'

'I know, but . . .'

'. . . and we're never going to be able to make it alone, Harmony. Cindy really does seem attached to the pioneers. We should make her part of the team. We have no choice.'

Annoyed by this conversation, which makes no sense to her, the driver wriggles around in her seat.

'Arrest warrant? Family under surveillance? You're worrying me more and more. Who are you, really?'

She can't help glancing nervously down at the floor of the pick-up on the door side, where she usually stores her rifle.

It's no longer there.

'Wha—?' she gasps.

She doesn't need to turn around again to know where the gun has got to – the cold touch of the barrel against the back of her neck is clear enough.

'Af-after all I've done for you . . .' she stammers.

'I'm truly sorry, Cindy,' says Andrew from the back seat,

the rifle trembling in his still weak hands. 'But like I said, we really have no choice. And nor do you. The fate of Mars is in our hands, along with that of my mother Vivian, my sister Lucy, and possibly the whole of the Earth. Even if I wanted to trust you without making threats, the stakes are too high to take even the tiniest risk. In the coming days, you're going to have to break more than one law and risk more than a speeding ticket. You can tell yourself it's to save your beloved pioneers from certain death, and to save the whole world from one of the foulest swindles ever perpetrated. You're going to send an email to your employer to tell him you're taking some unpaid leave. And for now, you're heading for Washington DC, to Georgetown, home of Professor Barry Mirwood – but taking the back roads, please.'

'Washington DC? But that's the other side of the country, three days' drive at least!'

'That'll give us time to tell you everything. Harmony, please empty our friend's pockets, and most importantly take her cellphone. Also, find out how much cash she has on her. You're going to be the one filling up the tank at the gas station.' He adds, in a whisper: 'If we succeed, and we come out of this alive, Cindy, I give you my word of honour I'll make amends.'

12. Reverse Shot

White House, Washington DC
Sunday 7 January, 3:27pm

'We're all ears, professor – tell us everything!'

From his seat behind the large desk, President Green flashes his famous ultra-bright smile at the old man with the luxuriant beard sitting opposite him.

For his meeting at the White House, Barry Mirwood has put on his 'best' attire: a striped suit, a checked shirt and a polka-dotted bow tie – which is crooked. This scarecrow outfit is in contrast with the elegant dress of the other people present in the Oval Office: not just Edmond Green himself, but also Serena McBee and a dozen other people including the president's inner circle, cabinet members or special advisers. They are all wearing small black badges pinned to the lapels of their jackets: the ribbon of remembrance, in tribute to the instructors from the Genesis programme who disappeared in a plane crash a month earlier.

'The idea behind my self-energising space elevator is very simple,' says Barry Mirwood eagerly. 'Microwaves emitted from a satellite in orbit around Mars, which would allow a transit capsule to travel up and down at will, just like a real elevator. It's all summarised in the diagram I emailed to my colleague, Professor Serena McBee, whose brilliant idea it was to broadcast it on the Genesis channel!' He turns to the woman with a Stanford psychiatry diploma, with a look of great admiration. 'You were right to bet on your viewers' intelligence, Ms McBee: billions of Earth's inhabitants were able to understand the principle behind it, even a child of five could do it, and . . .'

Serena stops the professor with a wave of her hand.

'You're the one we should be thanking for your invention,' she says with a friendly smile – but behind this pleasant façade, her voice is dry as dust. 'What we would like to know is what resources you require – isn't that right, Mr President?'

Edmond Green agrees with his closest associate.

'Indeed so, Serena,' he says, before turning back to the old man. 'I have total confidence in you, Barry, and I'm delighted to have named you special scientific counsel to the president on space matters. I'm relying on you to give it all you've got. Public opinion places so much importance on the Genesis programme. Now more than ever, as a second season's just been announced, with a new team of astronauts who will blast off in a year and a half! The first team have survived a little squall, but what will happen when the climate cycle goes around again? Because these storms are cyclical, if I've understood your explanations correctly?'

The scientist nods vigorously, sending seismic waves down his beard.

'Quite right, Mr President,' he says. 'Each Martian

year – which, I might remind you, corresponds to two Earth years – temperatures rise as Mars gets closer to the Sun. Driven by the heat, the winds blow harder and harder, raising up tonnes of dust. And so summer on the red planet is storm season: a period of increased disturbances culminating in month eighteen, the month of the Great Storm. That said, the New Eden base has been built to withstand atmospheric phenomena of that kind – it's already suffered countless spells of bad weather, over the course of many Martian years, before it was even inhabited.'

President Green coughs discreetly.

'I see,' he says. 'But it also suffered some damage, on at least one occasion in the past, going by the testimony we heard on air from that robot. I know the damage was all repaired immediately and automatically, but . . . could your elevator be ready before the next Great Storm? In case the base does encounter new damage, which might be more serious this time around?'

The most influential man in the world breathes out, slowly, resting his hands flat on his polished desk, his eyes boring into those of his interlocutor.

'I've given my support for the Genesis programme to go ahead and choose a second team of contestants. Because the spirit of conquest demands it. Because public opinion demands it. Because that's the way forward for history. But I'm putting one condition on this: a viable evacuation plan. We mustn't be content with a one-way ticket. It's cool for us to keep on sending pioneers, but if and only if we can bring them back again if the need arises. Without that guarantee, I'm vetoing any future departures from American soil. We need a return ticket, Barry: my image, and my government's, is at stake.'

The scientist opens his mouth to reply, but a brown-haired woman, in her thirties, her eyes shaped with glittering eyeshadow, is quick to add: 'We do indeed need a return ticket, Mr Mirwood, but without the Treasury having to spend a single cent. President Green is right to stress that the Genesis programme is vital to the image that won him his mandate, but I'd add that it's dangerous territory too. The opposition are waiting to catch us out. The slightest mention of any new public expenditure, given that we've just been re-elected on an Ultra-libertarian ticket, would be a communications calamity. By the way, I should introduce myself: I'm Dolores Ortega, and I'm the image secretary for the presidency.'

Serena McBee clears her throat.

'Don't worry about public expenditure,' she says decisively. 'I should remind you that Atlas Capital will be financing this elevator in its entirety.'

'If I may, Madam Vice-President: are you really totally sure?' replies Dolores Ortega quick as a flash, squirming slightly in her designer suit with overstitched seams, the latest trend on the catwalks. 'We haven't received any written commitment on their part.' She flicks back her asymmetrical fringe, then adds, 'Please don't misunderstand me, I'm not doubting your good faith, but my first duty is to protect President Green's reputation.'

'Do you have a card?'

The other woman hesitates for a moment.

'Pardon me?'

'A business card,' explains Serena McBee, never losing that smile she wears as a mask.

'I . . . uh . . . yes.'

Dolores Ortega rummages in the pocket of her suit, under the gaze of all the ministers and advisers, and finally pulls out a small visiting card which she hands to the new vice-president.

Serena McBee takes it with the tips of her manicured fingers and reads it out loud.

'*Dolores Ortega, Image Secretary for the Presidency.*'

'That's precisely what I just said, when I introduced myself to Professor Mirwood,' says Dolores Ortega, recovering her poise.

'I just thought I might have missed something, but apparently not, I heard you correctly: it says "*Image Secretary*", not "*Bank Manager*". When Atlas confirms its commitment in writing, President Green will be the first person to hear of it . . .' Serena nods slightly towards her superior. '. . . along with Treasury Secretary Lyndon.' She gestures towards a man with thick square glasses.

'Each to her own area of expertise, my dear, that's the key to success for a winning team,' she concludes, turning back towards Dolores Ortega. 'For us, that means the finances of the nation; for you, smartly brushed hair and neatly tied ties.'

The image secretary opens her holographic-lipsticked mouth to answer, but no sound emerges from her 3D-enhanced lips.

Flushed with shame, she fixes her eyes on the floor and doesn't look up again.

'Well, then, where were we?' Serena McBee continues. 'Ah

yes – resources! So tell us, Barry, how much are you going to need?'

The old scientist rifles around in his leather briefcase and pulls out a digital tablet, which he puts on the desk. Feverishly he scrolls through page after page covered in equations until he reaches a diagram showing his invention.

'I've carried out some further refinements to my preparatory work this morning, so this is the latest version,' he says, excitedly, zooming in on the image. 'As you know, the elevator is made up of two components: an energy satellite and an ultra-light transit capsule. The satellite will remain in orbit around Mars at the same altitude as the moon Phobos and will act as a giant solar panel. According to my calculations, the diameter of the satellite needs to be a minimum of two hundred metres if it's to store enough of the Sun's energy – it will also require four rotations for recharging in order to be able to emit enough microwaves to move the transit capsule between the surface of Mars and its outer orbit. Technologically there is a double challenge. We not only need to construct this vast piece of equipment in record time for it to be ready before the next journey of the *Cupido*, but also to transport it thirty-five million miles from our planet. But I think I have a solution to that.'

Once again, Barry Mirwood puts his hand into his briefcase. This time, he pulls out a small cylinder that looks like a roll of sticky tape.

'Here's my prototype – the home-made version,' he murmurs, his voice still excited, as he detaches a sort of very thin paper tongue from the side of the cylinder. 'Here, Mr President – hold on very tight to this.'

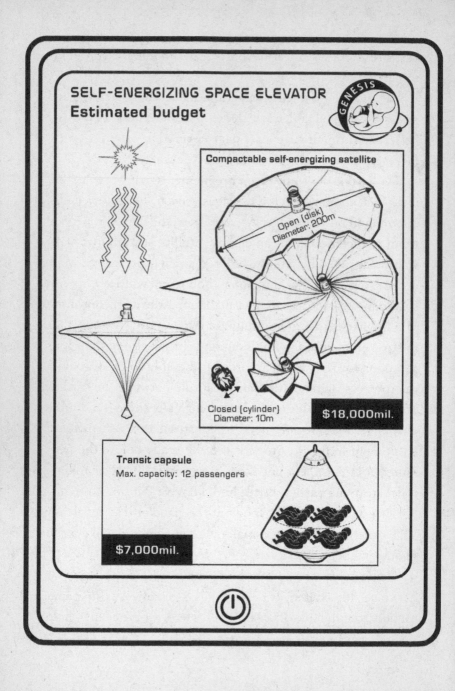

SELF-ENERGIZING SPACE ELEVATOR
Estimated budget

GENESIS

Compactable self-energizing satellite

Open (disk)
Diameter: 200m

Closed (cylinder)
Diameter: 10m

$18,000mil.

Transit capsule
Max. capacity: 12 passengers

$7,000mil.

Edmond Green, taken aback, glances at his staff, but nonetheless takes hold of the end of the slip of paper.

'Do you know much about origami, Mr President?' continues the scientist, detaching a second tongue, which he grips firmly between his fingernails.

'Origami?' repeats the president, tonelessly. 'It's a folding game for small children in Japan, right?'

'It's not a game, Mr President! It's a science! An ancestral science!'

Continuing to hold forth all the while, Barry Mirwood pulls his arm firmly away. The cylinder starts to unfold between his fingers and the president's, like a fan opening, gradually revealing its complex structure.

'For centuries the greatest Japanese minds have contemplated origami, and today the greatest mathematics researchers devote whole theses to it.'

The scientist takes a step back, then a second.

The reduced-scale model of the satellite continues to take shape over the desk of the dumbfounded president. The cylinder is transforming bit by bit into a huge disc of Bible paper streaked by an infinity of folds.

Moving aside to allow space for the scientist, the audience 'ooh!' and 'aah!' in wonder.

'And thanks to the science of origami, I have managed to reduce the dimensions of the solar panel by a factor of twenty, as you can see for yourselves, ladies and gentlemen!' says the professor, puffing himself up as if he was already delivering his Nobel Prize acceptance speech.

But just at the moment when he's about to take his final

step back, there is a long ripping sound: the paper disc tears all the way down, leaving half in the scientist's hand and the other half in the president's.

An appalled silence falls on the audience.

'I . . . uh . . . well, of course, it's . . . it's just a prototype . . .' stammers Barry Mirwood, hurrying back to his tablet to save face. 'There are still a lot of preliminary tests that need to be conducted. That's why I'm estimating the cost of developing the satellite at eighteen billion dollars. Plus another seven for the transit capsule.'

The silence changes from appalled to horrified, as the numbers appear on the screen.

But Barry Mirwood hasn't finished yet.

'And we also need to devise an escort module capable of affixing the compact satellite to the side of the *Cupido*: two billion dollars,' he says, moving to another page. 'But before we're even in a position to progress to the assembly, we'll need to send three hundred tonnes of payload into the Earth's orbit, with a dedicated super-launcher and a made-to-measure rocket head: one billion dollars. Of course, all the costs I'm giving you are for the materials themselves, very competitively negotiated from subcontractors the whole world over; it goes without saying that there will have to be men and women to bring the project to its completion. Atlas Capital will have to reemploy the NASA staff who were made redundant three years ago, and unquestionably more than them too. If we want the self-energising elevator to be operational before Mars's next Great Storm, that means the *Cupido* will have to head back to Mars with its precious cargo not in a year and a half, as had originally been planned for Season Two of the Genesis programme, but in fifteen months at the outside. Five brief trimesters during which thousands of highly qualified people are going to have to work overtime, non-stop, Sundays and holidays included. Estimated total salaries: two billion dollars.'

The treasury secretary looks pale, and loosens his tie.

"Thirty billion dollars altogether . . .' he says tonelessly. 'The costliest rescue operation of all time . . . Double the total budget of the last Olympic games . . .'

President Green himself is looking a little queasy: beneath his orange tan, his skin is turning ashen.

'I'm absolutely counting on you, Serena,' he says, turning towards his deputy, a slight tremor in his voice.

The vice-president cracks a gracious smile.

'And you are right to do so. You can count on me. You can count . . . up to thirty billion. Just let me negotiate with Atlas Capital to get them to put their hands in their wallets. I'll head over there right away. Mr President, ladies and gentlemen of the cabinet, if you would excuse me . . .'

Serena McBee gives a slight bow. Then she turns on her heel and walks out of the Oval Office, leaving behind her the most powerful man in the world, as helpless as any viewer of the Genesis channel at the moment when the programme is interrupted.

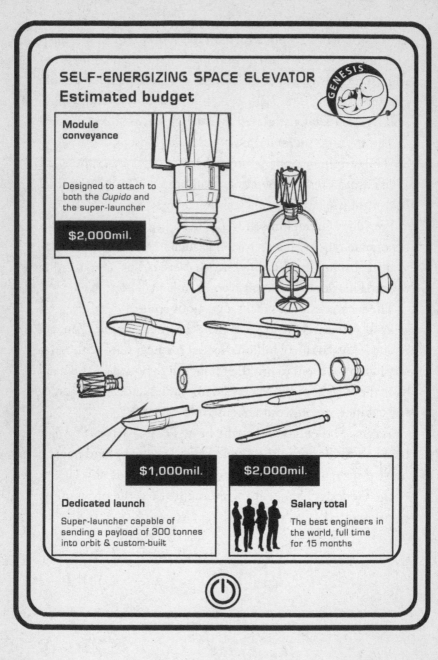

SELF-ENERGIZING SPACE ELEVATOR
Estimated budget

GENESIS

Module conveyance

Designed to attach to both the *Cupido* and the super-launcher

$2,000mil.

$1,000mil.

Dedicated launch

Super-launcher capable of sending a payload of 300 tonnes into orbit & custom-built

$2,000mil.

Salary total

The best engineers in the world, full time for 15 months

13. Genesis Channel

Sunday 7 January, 6:18pm

Long shot on the deserted dome.

Beyond the glass panels, night is falling.

The internal spotlights attached to the aluminium girders are all lit. They're shedding a bright light on the layered plantation that rises up in a pyramid in the centre of the dome, which is still covered in the tarps that the pioneers put in place the previous night to protect it from the storm.

A caption appears at the bottom of the screen: NEW EDEN GARDEN / 19:58 (MARS TIME).

Suddenly a light-coloured shape emerges from one of the access tubes leading to the Love Nests.

The camera zooms in: it's Kirsten, dressed in a sky-blue silk dress, her hands covered in thick oven gloves in which she is holding a large steaming dish.

The German girl crosses the Garden at a run, reaches the access tube leading to the seventh habitat, and slips discreetly inside.

Cut.

* * *

The screen goes black, replacing the view of the Mars base. A message begins to scroll up it.

DEAR VIEWERS,
THE GENESIS CHANNEL HAS DECIDED
TO GRANT THE PIONEERS
A FEW MOMENTS OF PRIVACY OFF THE AIR,
ENOUGH TIME FOR THEM TO HAVE DINNER
AT MARCUS'S BEDSIDE.

BUT DON'T GO AWAY!
TO KEEP YOU ENTERTAINED WHILE YOU WAIT,
WE ARE PLEASED TO SHARE WITH YOU
THE FIRST OF OUR 'ORIGINS' REPORTS
ON OUR PIONEERS' LIVES BEFORE THEIR JOURNEYS BEGAN.

(PROGRAM ENCRYPTED — ACCESS TO
PREMIUM SUBSCRIBERS ONLY.)

The message fades gradually, while a short jingle plays: the notes of the chorus to *Cosmic Love*, the official soundtrack to the Genesis programme.

Fade up onto a glass-walled room, on the top floor of a skyscraper.

The view spins three hundred and sixty degrees across a breathtaking panorama, bristling with steel towers, on which a tropical sun is reflected, blindingly bright. To the east, you can make out the sparkling sea, edged by magnificent white sand beaches; to the west, the favelas pour down the hillsides, encroaching on the city like streams of magma mixing sheet metal and plastic. The only furniture in the room is one single chair.

All of a sudden, somewhere, a door opens with a click.

A name appears over the picture, ringed by a space ellipse:

A silhouette comes into shot: it's the Brazilian candidate, now world-famous, but from a time when he was merely a seventeen-year-old unknown. He walks over and sits in the chair. His tanned skin stands out against the white cotton of his shirt; through the open collar it's possible to see a crucifix hanging on a gold chain. His eyes show the reflection of the spotlights trained on him.

A woman's voice, out of frame of the camera filming the scene, speaks. '*Hello, and welcome to the Brazilian offices of McBee Productions. It is my pleasure to notify you that you are one of the hundred thousand candidates from across the world who are through to the second stage in the selection process for the Genesis programme, among the many millions who sent in application forms. There still remain, of course, many stages to get through before moving into the final round that will determine the twelve contestants for travel to Mars, and which will be overseen by the Genesis programme's executive producer, Ms McBee herself. But all in good time. For today, I shall ask you a few questions – these will be in English, since this is the official language of the programme. You needn't worry – easiest thing in the world. At this stage, it's simply a matter of seeing how you look in the lighting, the quality of your diction, all those little things that do matter for producing a high-quality show.'*

The young man interrupts her. 'So how do I look, then, in the lighting?'

A smile appears on his full lips, partly teasing, partly seductive. You can guess that it's not the camera his ink-black pupils are focused on, but the woman who's standing behind it, facing him.

The casting woman's voice falters, clearly unsettled. '*Um ... well. V-very good, actually,*' she stammers, before regaining her professionalism. '*Just give me simple answers, looking right into the camera in fron*ZZZZZZZZZZZZZZZZZZZZZZZZZZZZZZZZZZZ ZZZZZZZZZZZZZZZZZZZZZZZZZZZZZZZZZZZZZZZZZ ZZZZZZZZZZZZZZZZZZZZZZZZZZZZZZZZZZZZZZZZZZ ZZZZZZZZZZZZZZZZZZZZZZZZZZZZZZZZZZZZZZZZZ ZZZZZZZZZZZZZZZZZZZZZZZZZZZZZZZZZZZZZZZZZZ ZZZZZZZZZZZZZZZZZZZZZZZZZZZZZZZ ...

Without any warning, a snowy curtain obscures the image, while a buzz of interference transforms the dialogue between the candidate and the recruiter into an incomprehensible blur.

The encryption has begun.

14. Shot

Month 21 / sol 578 / 20:00 Mars time
[28th sol since landing]

'Here you go, it's ready!' Kris's voice echoes through the access tube leading to the seventh habitat.

We're already gathered there, all eleven of us.

Two couples are wedged on the sofa, Samsafia and Mozabeth. Fangtao are just beside them, him in his wheelchair and her sitting delicately side-saddle on the armrest. Kenkelly are sitting on two of the chairs we've brought into the living room, making a strange sight. While all the rest of us have removed our undersuits to put on civilian clothes (I've put on my grey sweater and a pair of baggy jeans, my pre-Marcus gear), Kenji has absolutely insisted on strapping himself into his whole suit, helmet included, in case an accident occurs while we are all in the same room. I'm sure he's right: even if it's unlikely Serena would choose this moment to depressurise the base, with Andrew and Harmony still at large, you can't be too careful. Paranoid Kenji really is the only one of us pioneers who can show up for a dinner party in a helmet and spacesuit without raising eyebrows among our viewers.

Because that's what this is, at least officially: a dinner for friends, surrounding our dear Marcus, to bring him some comfort. No one on Earth would suspect that what's really going to unfold in this unseen room, away from the cameras, is his trial.

'Careful, it's very hot!' calls Kris, making her entrance into the living room, holding a steaming dish in her oven gloves.

She's seemingly cooked her famous mince, one hundred per cent vegetarian, one hundred per cent made from ingredients grown here on Mars, which is universally popular. But today my friend isn't wearing that proud smile she usually has when she's about to treat the team: beneath her crown of blonde locks, her face is expressionless, like a mask of cold wax. The truth is, tonight Kris has prepared a fake dish, just to pull the wool over the viewers' eyes. The truth is, none of us has the least appetite.

She drops the boiling dish onto the small round dining table, as if she were offloading some heavy burden; then she hurries to snuggle up against Alexei's shirt, as he wraps her shivering shoulders with a protective arm. And so Krisalex is now re-formed in turn, united like the two sides of a single coin.

The two robots, Günter and Lóng, are pressed close to one another, and for once even Louve and Warden seem willing to put up with each other.

I am alone in the seventh nest's one armchair – disunited and incomplete, for ever.

'OK, so anyway – how do we do this?' asks Alexei suddenly, while Kelly carefully closes the habitat door, chewing on the gum of the day. 'Do we get the noose out right away and have done with it?'

There is such anger in Alexei's words.

And such distress too.

'No,' answers Safia firmly. 'We've said we're going to organise a trial, not a mockery of justice.'

Alexei grimaces.

'OK, here we go! The great defender of lost causes! You're going to find some mitigating circumstances for him, you're going to do everything you can to save his filthy traitor's skin.'

'You shouldn't believe that,' the Indian girl interrupts him, with her natural authority that's always amazed me. 'I have no sympathy for traitors. Marcus must pay. But for his punishment to have any meaning, we need to do things properly . . . We need to follow judicial protocol . . .'

'What are you talking about? We don't know anything about all that stuff.'

'I do. I've been in court before.'

'Oh, right, watching from the viewers' gallery?'

'No, in the dock. And since I needed to handle my own defence, I made sure I got myself properly informed about it.'

There is silence in the habitat.

From the way the other pioneers are looking at her, I can guess that some already know and some don't: how in India Safia was brought to trial by the man who tried to disfigure her in an acid attack, after she'd refused to marry him – in the scuffle, he was the one who got the acid right in his face.

'Here on Mars there are no impartial jurors,' Safia continues. 'We're all victims. We should all be judges. That's the only way for us to proceed.'

The youngest in our group takes us all in with her gaze – the third eye attached to her forehead, matching her saffron-coloured sari, seems to be watching us too.

Nobody in the living room says a word, not even Alexei, who has momentarily set his aggression aside. A man's life or death will hang in the balance here, in just a few moments, and Safia is currently explaining the rules of the game. We're all hanging on her every word.

'Stage one: setting out the charges,' she says.

'Stage two: the accused chooses his plea: guilty or not guilty.

'Stage three: the prosecution present evidence and witnesses.

'Stage four: the case for the defence and the questioning of the accused by the court.

'Stage five: deliberation and judgement.

'Stage six: the final stage: the carrying out of the sentence.'

Six.

It's always that same number, which has been pursuing us since the start of the programme like a curse. The voiceover from the opening credits spools through my head, chillingly. '*Six girls on one side. Six boys on the other. Six minutes to meet. An eternity to love.*'

'So –' Safia continues seriously, yanking me from my thoughts – 'there are some roles to allocate. Even if we all need to be involved when it comes to the deliberations, some of us need to wear a different hat while the trial is underway. First of all, we need somebody to chair the discussions. We could vote on who that presiding judge will –'

'No need to complicate things!' Kelly interrupts her, briefly pausing in her gum-chewing. 'We've already found our chairman. Or should I say, our chair*woman*. I nominate . . . Safia.'

The Canadian girl turns to the rest of us and says to nobody in particular: 'Anyone not agree with me?'

There's total silence.

'There you have it. Done. Next role?' she says, and goes back to chewing.

Safia nods slightly to indicate that she accepts the responsibility that has been placed on her shoulders, the dignity of her movement in contrast with Kelly's feverish chewing.

'We need a clerk to take a record of the proceedings and all the testimony,' she continues.

'Is that really useful?' asks Kris, never daring to look up from the floor. 'After all, it's just us here. Do we really need to . . . leave any trace of all this?'

There's such discomfort on my darling Kris's face, it pains me. I can tell that what's about to happen here horrifies her.

But Safia replies in a firm voice, totally intransigent. It's a voice that sounds hard, but also, I know as soon as I hear it, that sounds fair.

'Yes, it's useful,' she says. 'Essential, even. Firstly, because when it comes time to deliberate, our memories might play tricks on us and that way we'll have the minutes of the trial right there to remind us precisely what was said between these walls. And then, and mainly, because if we're already too ashamed now of what we're going to do to *leave a trace of it*, as you say, what's the point of it? Whatever the outcome, whatever the sentence, everything must be noted down. So that none of us will ever dissociate themselves from this decision. So that we remain together, and we take responsibility together, right up to the end.'

Kris gives a barely audible moan, but does not answer.

'I'm prepared to be the clerk,' Fangfang volunteers, her face stony.

'Can I ask you something?' says Kelly.

As she does whenever the Canadian addresses her, the Singaporean girl digs her heels in and starts to defend herself.

'Why, what's the problem? You don't think I'm up to it? Because I took all those exams and competitions in Singapore, I learned to type fast, and . . .'

'I'm not questioning your typing skills. What I wanted to ask was just if you wouldn't mind sitting next to Tiger here. I know his helmet's connected to the mics in the living room, but in case he misses any scraps of conversation, he'll be able to read what you write on your tablet so he can follow the proceedings. Please?'

Fangfang straightens her glasses, then, without a word, she picks up her tablet and pulls a chair over to sit beside the Japanese boy.

'Next we're going to need to assign a prosecuting attorney to support the case for the prosecution,' Safia says, still on track with her unstoppable logic.

'Me!' says Alexei, leaping forward, so fast that he knocks into Kris without even noticing.

'Hang on a minute,' says Mozart. 'You aren't the only person who wants to take on this role.'

'Maybe, but I'd be the one to do it best. That Marcus – I'm going to annihilate him!'

'Oh yeah? I'm not so sure. You were such good pals with him, and not that long ago either . . . Krisalex and Léorcus,

92

Mars's star couples, always sticking together.'

'And? Are you jealous? You think you hate him more than me, just because he's nabbed the girl you wanted?'

'That's enough!'

I'm not the one who shouted, even if it feels as though the shout came from deep inside me.

It's Liz.

She's standing there, trembling, in one of her thick woollen polo-necks, clutching her Engineering Officer's tablet to her chest. Scorned once again: Alexei, who talks as if she wasn't there; Mozart, who's too enraged to think of defending his wife, and all the others who are looking at her, not knowing how to react.

'That's enough,' she says again, breathless, tears in her eyes. 'This trial is supposed to bring us together, not divide us.'

'Liz is right,' agrees Safia. 'We absolutely must remain united. Mozart, Alexei – if you want so badly to get involved, then do it together, not against one another. What I propose is that the two of you act as our police force. It will be your responsibility to ensure that the accused presents himself to the court when he's called, that he remains calm, that he stands up and sits down when he is asked to. Do you agree?'

Nods from the two boys in question.

'OK,' Alexei accepts, 'but who's going to take the part of prosecuting attorney?'

'I volunteer!' says Tao in a booming voice.

His broad forehead frowns up to the edge of his crew cut, marking a furrow of concentration over his almond-coloured eyes. I see an impressive determination shining in them, which reminds me that before boarding the spacecraft to Mars, before ending up in a wheelchair, Tao was a circus acrobat able to look life straight in the eye without trembling.

'I'm the guy who's studied the least,' he admits. 'I'm the one who speaks least well. But I'm also the person who has the most reason to blame Marcus – I mean, after Léonor, that is . . .' He swallows. 'There are things I haven't yet told anyone in this room. But the time has now come. I'll tell you everything during the trial. I'll be merciless towards him, just as he once was to me.'

There's such conviction in Tao's voice that no one dares question his nomination as prosecuting attorney, not even Fangfang, whose eyes are wide with amazement as she watches him from behind her glasses. She must be asking herself the same question I am, the same question we all are: what *things* does Tao want to talk about?

'Now we need a counsel for the plaintiff,' Safia continues, unperturbed. 'In other words, the person who will represent the victims: a lawyer for the eleven of us.'

Samson takes a step forward.

'I volunteer.'

'You?' Mozart asks him, suspicious. 'When you were the one who stopped us destroying Marcus this morning? You separated us when we came to blows, Marcus and me. You got between Alexei and him, even if it meant you risking getting a Russian missile to the neck. I do like you a lot, Samson, but you're just too kind. I'm not sure you're cut out for the role of our attorney.'

The Nigerian boy's green eyes light up.

'If you do *like me a lot*, as you say, you should trust me,' he

94

murmurs. 'You're right, I stopped you massacring Marcus this morning: because at that moment he was the victim, facing a furious mob ready to lynch him without thinking about it, without listening to what he had to say. But that's no longer the case. Now we've all recovered our cool. If Marcus must be punished, it won't be on a whim now, it won't be in a fit of blind rage. It will be in full possession of all the facts, and after having listened to him.'

Samson inhales quickly, never taking his eyes from the Brazilian boy's, before adding, 'He's not the victim any more. We are, I am . . . You are, Mozart. I want to defend *us*, this evening, just as this morning I defended Marcus.'

A moment of silence passes, behind which I seem to hear Samson's last words echoing still. That *us*, he really is talking about the eleven pioneers, isn't he? So why do I get the impression he's mostly talking to Mozart, from his blazing eyes that seem to see nobody else?

Instinctively I turn my attention to Safia, as if searching for an answer to my question, to try to see whether she's noticed something strange too. But no, there's nothing. She looks lovingly at her young husband, with a gaze that's filled with pride, no more than that.

'Very well,' she says, decisively. 'We have our counsel for the plaintiff. There's only one post that needs filling now, then. The counsel for the defence . . . who will be responsible for making the case for the accused.'

At these words, all eyes turn towards the sofa where I'm sitting, like the faces of piranhas enticed by the scent of blood.

Yes, they're turning towards me!

As if I'm the best person to defend the guy who stabbed me in the back!

'Don't even think about it!' I say hoarsely, feeling my skin bristle under my grey sweater.

Alexei crosses his arms over his broad torso and sizes me up from his great height.

'Why not? After all, you're the one who knows him the best, that little darling of yours. You didn't even want to turn him in this morning when we all showed up in the Rest House. You wanted us to think you were just going to break up. If Kenji hadn't recorded your conversation, we never would have known what a bastard the guy really is, and we would just have gone on living alongside him as if there was nothing wrong and this trial never would have happened. Just a few hours ago, you wanted to save his skin. So why not now?'

An uncontrolled bark comes out of my mouth – yes, the bark of a cornered dog who's desperately trying to find a way out.

'Shut it! Don't forget, this trial was my idea. Don't forget, I've committed to carrying out the sentence. So don't you dare accuse me of being on Marcus's side! There's no way I'm going to be his lawyer though, get it?'

Thrown by my aggressiveness, Alexei takes a step back and lowers his voice.

'OK, take it easy, I get it . . . But we do need somebody to defend that scumbag.'

'Me.'

At the back of the room, her eyes still shining with tears, it's Liz's turn to face the piranhas, those questioning eyes that only leave me to take aim at her.

'M-me,' she stammers. 'I . . . I'll defend Marcus.'

'Liz,' says Mozart gently, 'you're tired, you don't know what you're saying.'

He tries to put his arm around his wife's waist, but she pulls away, slipping like an eel between the threads of a fishing net.

'I know perfectly well what I'm saying,' she replies, forcing herself to control the tremor in her voice. 'Every role needs to be filled, as Safia has reminded us, or the trial can't go ahead. Somebody needs to defend Marcus, otherwise the condemnation will be worthless. It's my duty to sacrifice myself to this, to take on this task that nobody else wants.'

'But . . . why you?'

Liz runs her hand over her face, wiping away the rest of the tears under her reddened eyes. I can see how hard she's trying not to look away, to keep her eyes on ours. Her long legs folded under her chair like distorted limbs . . . the wild locks of hair escaping from her bun . . . it all makes her look like a broken mannequin. She looks so fragile, so alone – maybe even more than me.

'Like Marcus, I too have betrayed you,' she manages to say. 'Like him, I've cheated. I too have lied. Don't forget, Mozart: I stole Léo's sketching tablet and persuaded you she wasn't interested in you any more, to try and persuade you to choose me.'

As a reflex, I glance down at the small tablet resting on my knees – the same one that Liz took from my stuff without telling me, near the end of the *Cupido*'s journey, to show Mozart my drawings of Marcus's tattoos. I brought it along with me tonight to sketch on it – to escape into it – in case I need to.

'You're deluding yourself, Liz,' Mozart tries to reassure her. 'You have nothing in common with that guy . . . You're no traitor . . . Léo's forgiven you. And so have I.'

A sad, hopeless smile crosses the English girl's beautiful face.

'You're the deluded one, Mozart,' she says. 'If I hadn't meddled in the last speed-dating sessions, Léo and you might be together right now. And that's something for which I know you're never going to forgive me.'

Mozart should offer some protest, but he remains mute, unable to deny the evidence: deep down, he still bears a grudge against the girl he married. With a knot in my stomach, I realise I feel the same way. Even if I did indeed forgive Liz at the time, and in front of everybody, for having stolen my tablet, I'm now discovering that there's an acid resentment in me still, a bitterness that twists my guts.

And we thought we were going to stand united against Marcus!

There's so much still unspoken between us!

The revelations that Tao has promised his audience. Samson's strange glances at Mozart. Liz's nagging guilt. The whole thing is making my head spin, making me dizzy.

Safia coughs hoarsely.

'Ahem . . . I think the court is complete now,' she says amid the heavy, tense silence. 'Do you all want us to postpone the hearing to tomorrow, to have time to prepare, or . . . ?'

She never gets a chance to finish what she was saying.

The fervent expressions on the team's faces speak louder than any words. They want only one thing: to get it over with, as quickly as possible.

'OK, we're not going to wait till tomorrow. I suggest that the prosecuting attorney should sit with me on the sofa, and we'll push it up against the wall to make space. We'll use the dining table as a witness stand. Léonor, let us use your armchair, please: that's where the accused is going to sit, with the counsel for the defence next to him. The clerk, the counsel for the plaintiff and the victims will be opposite, on the kitchenette side, on two rows of chairs. No questions?'

The boys slide the furniture over the smooth floor of the seventh habitat, transforming the space into a courtroom.

Tao parks his wheelchair next to the sofa, onto which he hoists himself up with his strong arms, while Samson comes over to join Fangfang, Kenji, Kelly, Kris and me on the chairs positioned by the kitchenette that has never been used. Liz goes to sit opposite us in the area reserved for the defence. Alexei and Mozart position themselves on either side of the door to the second bedroom. The Russian boy's hand is on the opening lever, while the Brazilian takes out his flick knife from the pocket of his faded jeans.

'I hereby declare this session open,' declares Safia. 'Call in the defendant!'

15. Off-screen

'It's been half an hour now since the pioneers disappeared from the screens of the Genesis channel, to have dinner together in the Rest House and keep Marcus company. Speculation is rife about the state of the American boy's health. What caused the illness that has struck him down? Is it anything to do with the incident in the New Eden airlock shortly after the landing? Let's ask the medical opinion of Professor Herkel, from Mount Sinai hospital . . .'

'There's something fishy going on,' murmurs Harmony, not bothering to listen to the answer from the doctor on the radio. 'The fact they've all been taken off air at the same time isn't a good sign at all.'

She's focusing on the rocket-shaped key-rings that are swaying beneath the rear-view mirror, above the car radio. The small photo headshots of the pioneers clink against one another in a chaotic dance, knocked about by the bumps in the road. The girl brings her hand up to still them. Her finger pauses on the portrait of Mozart: smiling and relaxed, he seems to be looking at her.

100

'You're right,' says Andrew from the back seat. 'It's not normal. This idea of the whole group taking refuge in one room isn't like them at all. Normally they don't put all their eggs in the same basket, they make sure they're spread around the base so as to have a better chance to react in case of depressurisation.'

Cindy gives a disillusioned sigh.

'Again with this business of the depressurisation. It doesn't make any sense . . .'

'But it's the truth!' says Harmony, letting go of the key-rings and turning to the pick-up's driver. 'We've told you everything – what else do we need to do to make you believe us?'

'Well, maybe if you told me the whole story again but without the barrel of a gun in the back of my neck?' answers Cindy, not taking her eyes off the road. 'I really do want to believe Andrew is the son of Sherman Fisher. I could even get used to the idea that you're the hidden daughter of Serena McBee. But to go from there to imagining that the vice-president of America is the monster you're describing?'

'We showed you the screen caps of the Noah Report, the exact same ones the pioneers sent us from New Eden!'

Cindy allows a car to overtake the pick-up – the first in at least fifteen minutes, on this barely used stretch of road, away from the main routes. Beyond the windscreen, the winter sun is already very low in the sky, stretching out the shadows over the desert expanses of Nevada.

'Yeah, I did see those pictures,' she says, as the car moves off into the distance. 'But there's no proof that Serena McBee knew about it . . .'

'The names of her closest collaborators appear on the title page of the report – she couldn't not have known!'

'. . . and there's no proof that she has some way of depressurising the base remotely, even if she did want to.'

It's Harmony's turn to give a long, frustrated sigh.

'My mother ordered Balthazar to kill me. Balthazar, the man who raised me. Is that monstrous enough for you, or are you going to go on claiming there's no proof and call me a liar?'

Breathless, the girl slumps back into her seat. She's so pale, so fragile – if it weren't for the seatbelt holding her back, she looks as though she might take flight.

'Leave it, Harmony,' Andrew says. 'If Cindy doesn't believe us today, maybe she will eventually, given a bit more time. She hasn't gone through the same ordeals we have – in fact, no one on Earth has. We should see her reaction as a warning: when the moment comes to reveal your mother's true face to the whole world, we're going to run into a wall of resistance. Serena McBee's popularity rating has never been higher. People sometimes prefer to remain deluded, rather than admit they've been fooled . . .'

Suddenly, at a bend in the road, a carpet of sparkling lights rises up, its thousand colours drawing a kaleidoscopic pattern at the far end of a dull day.

The sight is so unexpected, in the heart of this arid, desolate region, that it seems to have something magical about it, something marvellous.

'It's like . . . a mirage,' murmurs Harmony, her eyes wide.

'It's not a mirage,' says Cindy coolly. 'It's Las Vegas.'

'Yes, it's a mirage,' says Andrew. 'What else would you call a place where spectators are hypnotised by a show that runs twenty-four hours a day, where billions of dollars pass through day and night, where it takes just one hour for people to marry a stranger they've only just met? Doesn't it remind you of your favourite TV show, Cindy, the Genesis programme? The problem – in Las Vegas, as in space – is the morning-after headache. When the Earth finally does wake up, I can assure you it will have the hangover of the century – I only hope it'll be able to recover . . .'

At that moment, there is a small beep.

Cindy looks into the rear-view mirror, frowning.

'What's that?' she asks.

'A notification,' replies Andrew, grabbing his cellphone. 'I've received an email in my anonymous inbox.'

His eyes fun feverishly down the screen, while Cindy remarks, sarcastically, 'An email? From who? You told me you'd burned your bridges to the whole world, including your mother and sister. A question of security, that's what you told me. So I'm guessing this is, what, your network writing to tell you that your prepaid card has expired?'

'No. It's a woman caught up in a plot that's devastated her family. It's a wife who's lost her husband in the tentacles of the Genesis programme. But tonight, she's mostly a survivor: the first to have escaped Serena McBee.'

Andrew looks up, his eyes shining behind his black-framed glasses, and reaches out to take Harmony's hand from the front seat.

'Cecilia Rodriguez has managed to leave America in secret

103

with her child, to take refuge in Cuba. She's safe and sound, outside your mother's jurisdiction, ready to testify against her when the time comes.'

The pick-up slides silently along the lonely road, while behind it the city that appeared out of nowhere sinks back into the desert.

16. Shot

Month 21 / sol 578 / 20:32 Mars time
[28th sol since landing]

I am hiding in the back row of the courtroom, on the victims' stand, next to Kelly and Kris. Fangfang, Kenji and Samson make up a barrier in front of me. Between the massive spacesuit of the Japanese boy and the Nigerian's shoulder, I watch for Marcus's imminent entrance like an animal at bay. To our left is the sofa where Safia and Tao – *the officers of the court* – are sitting, and in front of us is the still-empty chair which, in a few minutes, will welcome the defendant. As soon as I sat down, I powered up my tablet and started sketching out the scene. I'll leave writing the minutes of the trial to Fangfang – my own way of remembering has always been pictures rather than words. The court artist: I've decided that this will be my role today.

(Your role, Léonor? You should admit you don't draw to remember, but rather to forget.)

The tip of my stylus goes over on the barely sketched silhouettes nervously, over and over, as if that might carve them into the glass of the tablet . . . as if it might silence the Salamander.

(Admit that you draw mainly so you can feel you aren't a part of this trial, you're outside, just an observer.)

Suddenly, a slight click forces me to look up from my work. Alexei has just lowered the lever, opening the door to the second bedroom – *to the cell.*

Above the tablet, my stylus is suspended motionless.

At the end of the habitat, the door slides open without a sound.

Beyond it is total darkness, the lights all turned out like in an oven.

'Come out of there!' orders Alexei.

No answer.

An idea swoops down onto me like a bird of prey, digging its pointed claws into my brain: what if Marcus succumbed to his second attack from the D66 mutation – the one that is always deadly – while we were discussing how to judge him?

Immediately, in answer to this hypothesis, the Salamander manifests itself once again.

(What are you really afraid of, Léo? Be honest. That Marcus is already dead? Or that he's still alive?)

I try to focus with all my strength on my drawing, to muzzle the terrible reptile as I've managed to in the past. But today I can't do it. My hand hangs paralysed over the screen. My mind remains fixed on this insidious, inescapable, whispering voice, which pours its poisoned questions into my ear with nothing I can do to escape it.

(If Marcus is already dead, then it will all be over – this trial and the whole psychodrama that goes with it.)

Unable to draw, unable even to think, I keep my eyes riveted on the black, grimacing mouth that swallowed Marcus up ten hours ago.

(But if he is still alive, you will have to participate in the judgement. You will have to carry out the sentence. It would be better for the whole world if he's already taken his leave, right?)

'If you don't come out right now, I'm coming in to get you!' growls Alexei from the threshold.

The way his voice is trembling, I guess he's in the same state of expectation as I am, as we all are, shaken by doubt. Can Marcus see and hear us? . . . Is he dead or alive? . . . How can such a small room hold so much darkness? . . .

Mozart suddenly brings the unbearable expectation to an end: he slides his hand across the wall of the room, groping around till he finds the light switch.

Click! – all the spotlights come on at once, pouring their raw light onto the foot of the bed and onto the slightly curved white plastic walls.

Marcus is standing there, at the back of the room, up against the thermoform cupboard, in his black undersuit that had melted perfectly into the darkness. His white suit, stained with blood, is lying at his feet, like a sloughed-off skin, totally still, he's been watching us in silence the whole time.

'Why don't you come when we call you?' Alexei spits. 'Waiting for an embossed invitation? Or did I thump you too hard earlier and make you deaf?'

Marcus's face recalls that beating. He has nothing to clean himself with, so his blood has formed a brownish crust around his nostrils. His split lip looks like the grotesque make-up of the Joker. His eyes . . . I'd rather not look at his eyes.

'No, I'm not deaf,' he says in his gravelly voice, the voice that's cracked without needing to wait for Alexei's blows, as if it had been broken all along. 'I just wanted to see.'

'See what?' barks Mozart, gripping his knife in his fist.

'How you were going to react. Your expressions when you thought maybe I was already dead. Because you all thought it, didn't you?'

'What the hell do you care what we thought?!' rages Alexei.

But Marcus doesn't get flustered. When we left him, he was feverish, bloody and pathetic, but now he's strangely serene.

'Here in this room I was like Schrödinger's cat,' he says mysteriously, as if to himself. 'It was a strange, magical feeling: the feeling of being both alive and dead . . . outside of time.'

Unable to bear any more of this, Alexei bursts into the room and grabs Marcus by the arm. He drags him unceremoniously and forces him to sit in the chair opposite us.

'What did he mean with that business about the cat?' murmurs Kris very quietly beside me, her hands clinging onto Louve's curly fur.

Fangfang looks up from the tablet on which she's scrupulously recording the minutes of the hearing and replies immediately – the desire to parade her learning has always been stronger than she is.

'Schrödinger's cat is an imaginary experiment to illustrate the paradoxes of quantum physics,' she explains quickly. 'A cat is locked up in a box with a canister of poisonous gas, a radioactive source and a Geiger counter. As soon as the radioactive atom disintegrates, the Geiger counter is programmed to trigger a mechanism that breaks the bottle and releases the gas. However, at an atomic scale, it is actually impossible to predict when an atom will disintegrate. The result: as long as we don't open the box to see inside, the cat is considered both alive *and* dead.'

While the Singaporean girl, who spouted all her science in one go, pauses to catch her breath, Kelly holds her chewing gum in the hollow of one cheek to allow her to roar, 'What the hell is all this crap? There's no way we're letting the David Copperfield of Mars confuse us with his little tricks and his grand speeches this time! You *can't* be both alive and dead! That's impossible!'

'Yes, it is possible,' Marcus answers calmly from the chair where Alexei and Mozart are keeping him. 'A moment ago, when you were scanning the darkness of the bedroom, I could see my reflection in your faces: it was the reflection of a living dead man. To you I was neither completely one nor completely the other, and at the same time I was both at once. Alive and dead. I could see it in your eyes.'

Just as he's saying that last word, his own grey eyes catch mine before I get the chance to escape.

Two blades of icy steel – my breathing freezes in my chest.

Two streams of molten silver – my heart skips a beat.

Alive and dead. Yeah, he's right, that's what he was, just a moment ago, in the darkness of the bedroom. A ghost lurking in his vault . . . A creature straddling two worlds . . . A being half inside its tomb, whose magnetic, hypnotic eyes plunge into the depths of my being – real vampire eyes, come back from the beyond to haunt me!

There's a sharp noise; the shock allows me finally to disconnect from Marcus, to turn to Safia; in the absence of a judge's gavel, she's just clapped her hands.

'Silence!' she says with authority. 'The defendant will speak only when he's invited to do so.'

I look back down at my tablet, where my stylus has resumed its movement without my even being aware of it. The silhouettes are so dark now, their faces are unrecognisable. They look like shadows. Spectres. Them too: *alive and dead.*

'The defendant will rise!' orders the Indian girl.

'You can call me Marcus.'

'This evening I am not the Safia you know, and you aren't the Marcus I've been living with for six months. I am the presiding judge of the court in which you are being charged. Tao is the prosecuting attorney in charge of the indictment.' She turns to the Chinese boy, sitting to her right on the couch. 'Samson is the counsel for the plaintiff, representing all eleven of us.' She nods towards the Nigerian. 'Liz is the defence lawyer: your lawyer.' She gestures towards the English girl, who is sitting on a chair next to Marcus's armchair. 'If you wish, you can spend a little bit of time with her in private to prepare your arguments.'

A kind of fleeting smile crosses Marcus's face; but with that injury disfiguring him, it looks more like a grimace.

'So, a trial, that's what this is,' he murmurs. 'Well, if it might bring you a bit of relief . . .'

Alexei kicks his armchair roughly.

'Hey, stop pretending this has nothing to do with you! We swallowed plenty of your filthy contempt when you sent us all to the slaughterhouse, like animals! Add too much more on top of that and you're going to end up making us puke!'

Safia silences Alexei with a glance, putting him back in his place as a police officer – the role assigned to him.

'I'll ask you the question again,' she says, turning to the defendant. 'Do you want to consult Liz in private before we set out the charges?'

'I have nothing to say to her that I wouldn't say to you, Safia, or to anybody in this room. I no longer have any secrets to hide. I no longer have any account to give.'

Anger.

Sadness.

Frustration.

But more than any of these, urgency: to not let Marcus off the hook, to stop him from making himself disappear with one of his famous bits of sleight-of-hand trickery.

With my heart beating ten to the dozen, I meet his gaze for the second time.

'You'd better get over that idea,' I say. 'There are eleven people in this trap, to whom you owe a proper account. And if it was possible, there'd be eleven people with the right to carry out your sentence when the time comes. But that wouldn't be practical, so there's just going to be one executioner: she's sitting opposite you right now.'

This time it's Marcus who is the first to drop his gaze, a bitter victory that brings me no satisfaction at all.

'Go on then, Safia,' I say, breathing out what little air I have left in my chest. 'Let's get this over with.'

The Indian girl clears her throat, then she begins.

'Marcus, aged nineteen, is accused:

'*First*, of attempted murder, having knowingly concealed a piece of information that might have saved the other pioneers of the Genesis programme by preventing them from boarding.'

In the row in front of me, Fangfang the clerk is typing at full speed; at the other end of the room, Liz is also tapping away frantically on her tablet, doubtless taking notes on the accusations she's going to have to challenge.

'*Second*, of aggravated lying, having hidden his illness from Léonor before marrying her.'

The words Safia is using, such cool and abstract words for such burning, real emotions, chill my blood.

'*Third*, of running away, in a cowardly attempt to escape from justice and exit the base without taking the due decompression precautions.'

Marcus's eyes are fixed stubbornly on the floor, giving no indication of what's going through his mind, or that he's even heard what Safia has said.

'Does the defendant plead guilty or not guilty?' she asks.

As she asks this question, her gaze flits between Marcus and Liz, not altogether sure from which side she ought to expect an answer.

Sensing that she's supposed to step into her lawyer role, the English girl finally speaks.

'The confession recorded by Kenji perhaps shouldn't be taken totally literally – your words obviously went well beyond your thoughts,' she suggests in her client's ear.

113

She might have been whispering, but it's easy enough to make out her words: in the constrained space of this habitat, not even whispers can remain private.

'And anyway, you should consider the mitigating circumstances. You've got plenty of those, Marcus.'

'No,' he whispers. 'I have no mitigating circumstances to offer.'

'I forbid you from saying such a thing!' says Liz, grabbing hold of his arm, pleading aloud with him now, since she knows everybody is following their exchange anyway. 'Your past! Your illness! It all counts. It should all carry some weight in the court's decision. Do the words "sentence" and "executioner" not mean anything to you, Marcus? Don't you understand your life is on the line? You must defend yourself – if you don't, I'll do it for you, in spite of you. I won't let you throw away your chances like this, do you hear?'

Marcus looks up, his grey eyes coming to rest on Liz's hand, which is still gripping his arm.

'I haven't got any mitigating circumstances, Liz,' he says again, his voice gentle, as if their roles were suddenly reversed, as if he were the confident lawyer and she the defendant facing a possible death sentence. 'But there's one thing the court is wrong about. There's one of the charges that I do challenge. There's one crime of which I'm not guilty.'

Liz's slender fingers let go their grip.

'I knew it!' she babbles, hopeful now. 'You're not the unscrupulous monster Safia has described. 'You aren't a murderer.'

'Yes, I'm a murderer,' says Marcus.

114

He turns to the court.

'Yes, I'm a liar.'

His eyes pan across the habitat and, for the third time, meet mine; his torn mouth moves, a flower of red and violet blood.

'But I'm no coward.'

17. Reverse Shot

'I wonder what they can be talking about right now,' Arthur Montgomery muses out loud, smoothing his moustache with the tips of his fingers.

He's sitting beside Serena McBee's enormous desk.

She's in pride of place in her own armchair, opposite the aluminium gantry studded with dozens of gleaming lenses. Once again, the giant screen set into the middle of it shows only a deserted base. It's been nearly an hour since the Mars pioneers disappeared from view to gather in the seventh habitat, the only one that escapes the watchful cameras.

'And I also wonder what happened to Marcus,' the doctor is still murmuring, 'what with this illness he's had since the morning.'

Serena brings the palm of her hand down onto the desk, making her guest jump.

'You're not here to ask questions, Arthur, but to provide answers!' she thunders. 'You're in charge of medical matters for this mission. It's unacceptable that we should find ourselves reduced to speculating about Marcus's health!'

'You can relax, Serena. I promise I'll have a diagnosis for you as soon as possible – as soon as I get access to the patient's biomarkers. I've asked my students Léonor and Alexei to use their dinner time to take his blood pressure and carry out the necessary tests. One thing's for certain: his illness has nothing to do with the D66 mutation, or he would have died at once.'

'I hope you're right,' says Serena, fiddling nervously with her bracelets.

'Why are you so attached to him?' As an idea suddenly strikes him, he quickly lets go of his moustache and opens his eyes wide. 'Maybe he's the kamikaze candidate, the one you hypnotised to depressurise the base if necessary without needing the remote control?'

'If anybody asks you, you'll say you don't know,' answers Serena drily. 'The name of the kamikaze candidate must remain secret to the very end. I'm no more attached to Marcus than to any of the other eleven brats up there, but I do need to keep up appearances.'

The doctor scowls, hurt.

'Still, when you chose him, you knew perfectly well that you were taking a risk,' he reminds her in his chilliest British accent. 'You knew he was carrying the D66 mutation, and that he'd already had his first attack and so might die at any moment.'

'Some moments are more convenient than others. I hoped he might have the good taste to kick the bucket at some quiet moment – that would have been a perfect opportunity to give the ratings a great boost. The public would have been

117

grateful to me for having given a sick kid a chance, and allowed him to see the stars – an astonishing cosmic funeral would have been arranged by global satellite broadcast, we'd have organised a great *Goodbye, Marcus* operation inviting billions of the Earth's inhabitants to light their lighters at the same moment, in a final tribute to the young man we had lost.' Serena's eyes sparkle for a moment, as if the flames from the lighters were already reflected there, but she continues almost immediately: 'But that's no longer possible. If Marcus were to let us down now, just after the Martian storm, when all the viewers on Earth are on edge and the whole team on Mars seems to be in danger, it would be disastrous. We'd be accused of negligence, of cruelty, of ignorance for having sent a D66 up into space. Oh yes, Arthur, it's not the events themselves that matter, it's the moment they take place and the way in which they're interpreted. Timing is everything in show business. For now, we absolutely must conceal the existence of the mutation and the fact we knew about it when we selected the American candidate.'

Arthur Montgomery brings his hand to his heart. Despite the baseness of his actions, there's something pure about his devotion to Serena: a kind of sincerity, which sometimes shines through.

'Nobody knows except you and me, and I'll be silent as the grave!' he swears. 'I give you my word of honour!'

Softened by this unconditional pledge, Serena gives a winning smile.

'Very good, Arthur. I know I can count on you, as usual.'

At that moment, the corded telephone rings.

The lady in charge picks it up.

'Hello? Yes? Very well, I'll see him now. Send him in, please.'

She hangs up.

'An official visitor?' asks Arthur Montgomery, glancing at the telephone that links directly to the White House.

'You might say semi-official,' replies the vice-president. 'It's my security man.'

The doctor, who had managed to relax for a moment, tautens like a bow.

'You mean Orion Seamus?' he growls.

'Indeed. But this time I'm hoping you aren't going to make a fuss. We talked about it this morning, remember: no misplaced jealousy. You're going to greet one another like a pair of gentlemen. And you won't listen at the door once you've left the room, will you, my dear Arthur?'

Before the doctor has a chance to answer, the door opens to reveal Samantha, Serena McBee's personal aide, accompanied by a tall brown-haired man dressed all in black, one of his eyes hidden by a patch.

Arthur Montgomery gets up, standing to attention, a reflex from a distant military past – you can almost hear his heels clicking together.

'Sir,' he says icily.

The hand he holds out to the younger man is as stiff as a robot's, the smile he gives him as expressive as a cardboard mask.

Then he turns and leaves the room without a backward glance.

The door closes, leaving the vice-president and her security agent alone in the office.

119

'I'm sorry to have interrupted you, Ms McBee,' he says. 'That man who just left, that's Arthur Montgomery, who's in charge of medicine for the Genesis programme, isn't it?'

'Yes, that's him, but we'd just finished our meeting. Let's get right down to business, Agent Seamus: have you come to tell me you've found Andrew Fisher and the girl?'

'No, not yet, Ms McBee.'

The vice-president gives her hand a shake, making her bracelets clink together, as if brushing away a troublesome fly.

'Well, what are you doing here then? Go! Get out of here! Shoo!'

But Agent Seamus doesn't leave.

Quick as a flash, he grabs hold of his interlocutor's arm in mid-air.

A stunned expression freezes on Serena's face, which is usually so controlled.

'What's this?' she whispers. 'Do you dare to raise your hand against the vice-president of the United States of America?'

'Which is something you won't be for long,' replies Agent Seamus without loosening his grip, without blinking his single jet-black eye.

'You're threatening me too?'

With her free hand, Serena is about to move towards her bee-shaped brooch-mic, which connects her directly to her whole staff.

But before she gets the chance to press it, Orion finishes his sentence.

'Something you won't be for long, because if I reveal what I've discovered, the people are never going to forgive you.'

Serena's hand stops moving.

'But if I stay silent, there's nothing to stop you continuing your rise which, I know, is destined to take you to the very top. I've said it before, and I'll say it again: either way, you won't be vice-president for very long.'

Orion and Serena stare at one another, frozen for a few moments in this trial of strength.

'To the very top? What are you suggesting?' she whispers, finally.

'That the path that led you here owes nothing to chance and everything to your ambition.'

She gives a haughty little laugh.

'That's the devastating revelation you're threatening to go public with? That I'm ambitious? As if anybody who rises to this level in politics isn't? That's hardly a scoop! And I've certainly never hidden it from you.'

Framed by her impeccably cut silver bob, the face of the most powerful woman in America is impenetrable, back to its usual mask of self-control. The only movement is in her eyes, which are examining the expression on her interlocutor's half-hidden face as if trying to read it, to guess what he really knows. They look like two sphinxes, facing one another down.

'No, indeed, you've never hidden that from me,' agrees Agent Seamus in a silky voice that gleams like his thick black hair. 'You explained to me very clearly that you had your sights set on power and that money was just a means to an end for you. You let me see that the Genesis programme isn't a machine to make you rich, but a stepladder to raise you up . . . up to the highest office . . . up to the presidency . . . and higher still . . .'

'I didn't put it in those words. You're distorting my intentions. I'm here to serve President Green. Period. No more than that.'

'. . . but meanwhile you were careful not to reveal to me the identity of the girl travelling with Andrew Fisher. *Your daughter*, Serena, who you've been hiding from the public for ever, but whose existence is recorded in the C.I.A.'s files.'

'Let go of me at once!'

Finally Agent Seamus unclasps his fingers.

Serena quickly snatches back her arm.

'Yes, I hid her existence, what of it?' she says, rubbing her wrist under the edge of her desk, with a furious clicking of bracelets. 'I've got every right to protect my offspring from the unhealthy attention of the media. Discretion isn't a crime, as far as I know!'

'Not discretion, no. But human gene manipulation is.'

Serena freezes.

Instantly her bracelets stop clinking together and fall silent.

'I told you Andrew and Harmony got away from me this morning,' Agent Seamus continues, unflustered. 'But they left something behind them.'

He slowly slips his hand inside his jacket and pulls out a small plastic bag, at the bottom of which are a few strands of almost colourless hair.

'This lock of hair was left behind, caught between the pincers of a drone. I took the liberty of getting it analysed and compared to yours – which I took from your jacket at the cocktail party at the White House just after your election. I hope you'll excuse this somewhat unorthodox gesture . . .'

Not a word escapes from Serena's sealed lips.

Not a wisp of breath from her nostrils.

'According to DNA sequencing, the profiles are absolutely identical, to the nearest single gene,' Orion Seamus says slowly. 'It's not your daughter you've been hiding from the whole world, Ms McBee . . .'

He puts the small plastic bag down beside the telephone.

At that moment, Serena raises her hand from under the desk and points a small automatic pistol that she has retrieved from a hidden drawer.

'. . . it's your clone.'

18. Shot

'Yes, I'm a murderer.

   'Yes, I'm a liar.

   'But I'm no coward.'

With three clipped phrases, Marcus has just answered the accusations of the court, but I'm the one his grey eyes are fixed on. And I feel as though he's addressing only me when he explains in his hoarse voice: 'I've been a coward in the past, but not any more. It wasn't cowardice that made me try to get out of the base. On the contrary. That was my greatest act of bravery. This morning, I finally found the courage to go out and encounter Mars, the planet I so dreamed about on Earth and for which I didn't hesitate to sacrifice everything: morality, friendship and love. It wasn't an act of running away – it was an achievement.'

Sitting beside her undefendable client, Liz gives an impotent, hopeless sigh.

My own breathing stops as though my lungs were filled with treacle. However much I might rack my brains, I just cannot understand Marcus's defiant tone. Does he really have no remorse? Is he really proud of himself and his crappy 'bravery'?

124

'If you'd let me leave this morning, this trial wouldn't be happening,' he says, casting his eyes over us. 'But I would have been out of your lives for ever. Isn't that what you all want? Wouldn't it have been easier to end it that way: letting me disappear into the sands of Mars? There's that network of canyons to the west of New Eden, at the very western end of the Valles Marineris, whose name I've fantasised about since I first set eyes on a map of Mars. *Noctis Labyrinthus*. The labyrinth of night. A name that sounds like it's come right out of a dream. That's where I wanted to end up. That's where I wanted to lose myself. And maybe find myself.' A faint smile passes across his swollen lips. 'Statistically speaking, I've already survived well beyond expectation for those with D66 after a first attack – I haven't got long left. Give me my suit, a mini-rover, and I promise you I'll go quietly; you'll never hear from me again.'

A leaden silence greets his words.

So is that what he's asking for?

For us to open the New Eden door for him?

And how long does he expect to be able to survive, alone on this damned planet, in his labyrinth of woe?

Safia clears her throat.

'It is not up to the defendant to set his own punishment,' she says. 'The court has noted that he pleads guilty to the first two counts, and not guilty to the offence of running away. I call the counsel for the plaintiff to address the court.'

Samson, who was sitting in the row in front of me, gets to his feet. He gestures to Warden to remain seated, then he walks over to the table that's serving as the witness stand. In profile, with his long neck and his skin almost as dark as the fabric of his

125

short-sleeved charcoal shirt, he really is as handsome as a statue. I race to reproduce his silhouette on my sketching tablet. But while I'm doing this, I realise there's nothing mineral about him. The way he struggles to control his breathing . . . the trembling in his nostrils . . . He's alive, subject to high emotion like me, like all of us in this room – and maybe even more than most.

'I haven't got much to add,' he begins, a little awkwardly. 'The charges are clear enough. Marcus himself admits the facts.'

With an encouraging nod, Safia urges him to keep going; Samson gradually gains in confidence, as if his young wife's affection is giving him strength, as if the Indian girl's famous eloquence is being reflected onto him.

'He led us to believe he was our friend, but he deceived us,' he says, his voice a bit firmer now. 'If he'd revealed the Noah Report to us in time, we never would have boarded that rocket.'

His almost fluorescent green eyes sweep over us. When they come to me, it feels like they're piercing right through me.

'If he'd revealed his illness to Léonor from the start, she might not have chosen to marry him.'

I feel my lips open involuntarily, my shoulders tremble as if I was guilty too. Would I have chosen the same husband, if I'd known about his illness from the start? I've already answered that question. Marcus put it to me himself: '*Léonor, when I die, will you regret having married me?*' That was one month ago. It was in another life. And yet I remember perfectly the answer I gave then. It was totally obvious at the time. '*I say it again, what I said to you before, Marcus the Condemned: even if you have to disappear, right here and now, I will regret nothing. Nothing at all!*'

'I would still have put him at the top of my final Heart List,'

I say quietly. 'I think so, anyway.'

'You *think* so,' says Samson, his light green eyes boring into mine. 'But you don't know. You'll never know. Because Marcus stole the possibility of making that choice from you – of *really* making it, knowing all the facts.'

I can hear a tremble in Samson's voice. I can tell how hypersensitive he is. And I can sense his determination too, the way he's dedicating himself to playing his role of the lawyer defending me to the very best of his ability. Wasn't that what he said when he volunteered for the role, that he wanted to defend us all? But why did he only look at Mozart when he said that?

'The truth is, Marcus made you his prisoner,' he continues. 'He presented you with a fait accompli. He lied to you about what he really was, to take advantage of you. He treated you like a thing. And no doubt that's what he said to himself this morning too, when he tried to run away from New Eden, even if it meant risking opening the airlock in the middle of a storm.' Samson shoots a look at the defendant in the dock. 'He told himself we were all things. Not even animals, let alone human beings: just things, easy to sacrifice.'

Marcus, in his armchair, is totally still. The better to take it all in? Because none of this bothers him? Or because fear and remorse are winning him over at last? There's no way of knowing.

'As counsel for the plaintiffs, I guess I'm meant to seek reparation,' Samson concludes, calming his breathing and mustering his energy one more time. 'But nothing that Marcus broke can be repaired. Here on this desolate planet where we're all stuck because of him, there's nothing I can ask him for by way of compensation. I have only one task: to protect the

127

future, our future, all of ours. A new, fragile hope has recently been lit, with the news of the self-energising space elevator. We must prevent Marcus from putting out that flame with new lies, extinguishing that hope with more deceptions. We must make totally sure he cannot betray us any more, that he cannot hurt us any more – ever again.'

Samson comes and sits back down, in total silence, allowing each of us to interpret that terrible *ever again* for ourselves.

'It is now the turn of the prosecuting attorney to speak,' says Safia.

She turns to Tao, who is sitting beside her, and adds: 'Owing to his infirmity, the court will permit him to make his case from the sofa.'

The large Chinese boy nods solemnly.

'Making a case – I don't know if that's something I can do,' he says, apologising in advance. 'Samson's already spoken much better than I ever could. But I have things to say that nobody else would be able to reveal. Things I've experienced, and that I should have shared with you a long time ago. Things Marcus told me, and which I blame myself for concealing from you. My testimony will be my plea. I hope it will help you understand a little better the thinking and actions of the guy sitting in the dock.'

Tao takes a deep breath. He slips his hand into the collar of his white T-shirt and pulls out the chain he's been wearing there, hidden from view, touching his skin. Abandoning my half-done sketch for a moment, I lean forward and screw up my eyes to get a better view of this delicate jewel, so incongruous in the calloused hand of this former acrobat. It looks like a sun . . . yes, a golden sun, melding with a silver crescent moon.

'W-what's that, *baobei*?' stammers Fangfang, who has finally looked up from her tablet. 'I . . . I've never seen that before.'

She must have noticed the same thing as I did, as we all did: the necklace is definitely a piece of woman's jewellery.

'You've never seen it before, *tian xin*, because I've always kept it hidden at the bottom of my toilet bag,' explains Tao, embarrassed. 'When I boarded the rocket six months ago, I decided to stop wearing it. But this morning, when we were getting ready to face the Martian storm . . . This morning, when we got up long before dawn, not knowing whether we were going to see the evening . . . it was stronger than me, I needed to have this chain against my skin. In case I died. So I could die with it. With . . . her.'

Fangfang lets go of her tablet, which drops to the habitat floor with a dull slap.

'*Her* . . . ?' she says in a voice that sounds like a gasp.

'Xia. The girl this necklace belonged to. Who I was supposed to marry. I promised her we'd travel into space together.'

Tao talks all in one go, barely taking time to breathe. As if with the slightest pause, he would run the risk of stopping for good, this boy who claims to have so little eloquence yet who's keeping us all spellbound.

The habitat spotlights catch the small piece of metal in the palm of his hand, and all of a sudden it seems to shine brighter still.

'She died before I was able to keep my promise. Crazy with grief, I tried to end my own life too, allowing myself to fall from the summit of the big top one evening during my act. I almost managed it.'

Tao looks down at his unmoving, dead legs.

'The doctors were able to save me,' he continues. 'It was Genesis who paid my hospital costs: by that point, I'd already been selected for the programme. Serena convinced me to head out to the training camp in Death Valley in spite of my disability – I thought her encouragement was an act of compassion, though now I suspect she just liked the idea of having a cripple among her selection. Like the doctors, she believed it was an accident; she didn't know I'd wanted to kill myself, otherwise I'm sure she'd have changed her mind. To the organisers of the programme, only my legs were broken; they never suspected there was something else, on the inside – how would you say it, in English . . . ? An *abyss*, is that it?'

Tao swallows painfully.

'An abyss that's only widened day after day. And I just sank a little further into it every morning, with a desire to die that clogged up my brain and weighed my body down like lead.'

In the row in front of me, Fangfang is totally still.

At the other end of the room, Alexei rocks from one foot to the other, clearly uncomfortable.

'All those times I yelled at you for you to get a move on,' murmurs the Russian boy, recalling memories that I don't share, from that training year when the boys and the girls were still kept apart. 'All that abuse I shouted at you to get going . . . I called you a loafer, a worthless layabout . . . I thought you were just some guy making the most of your wheelchair to sit there twiddling your thumbs; I had no idea you were in an actual depression.'

Tao drops the chain back onto his chest and sweeps away Alexei's belated remorse with a wave of his broad hand.

'Nobody knew,' he says. 'Nobody . . .' His black eyes flick across towards the defendant in the dock. '. . . but him.'

In the single armchair, Marcus doesn't blink. How does he manage to hold it together, with those hostile glares from his jailers, Alexei and Mozart, burning into the back of his neck, and Liz's staring at him as if he was totally helpless?

'He's the only person in the group I told everything to, one month after we started training,' says Tao, softly. 'Because he seemed more in tune. Because it was too hard to talk directly to the production team. Because I was on the edge of an abyss. I . . . I told him that my guts were being gnawed at by guilt. That I felt responsible for Xia's death. That I'd already tried to kill myself. That I might try again. It was a cry of desperation. It was a cry for help. I put my shitty little life in his hands!'

As long as I've known him, Tao has hardly ever raised his voice. He's a kid in a giant's body. But now the child has fallen silent and it's the giant who roars, shaking the habitat to its foundations.

'When I asked you to go talk to the production team and tell them what a bad way I was in, do you remember what you replied?' he growls, challenging Marcus directly. 'You told me you wouldn't lift your little finger to help me, that I was just bluffing to make myself seem more interesting, that I'd never have the guts to kill myself. And you ditched me there – yes, just the way Samson described: you dumped me like a thing, like a bit of old trash, like a piece of shit!'

For a moment I think Tao is going to launch himself off the sofa and miraculously recover the use of his legs to hurl himself at the other side of the habitat. But he doesn't. He restrains himself. He contains himself. And he finishes his summing-up in a quiet voice, never taking his eyes off Marcus.

'As the months went by, I forced myself to forget our conversation. I did everything to try and see you in the best light I could, since after all we were fated to go through this Martian expedition together as teammates. Even this morning, just as a reflex, I defended you alongside Samson when Alexei was about to smash your head in. But this afternoon, I thought about what you've done to Léonor. I thought about what you've done to all eleven of us. And this evening, I did look, but I can no longer see anything positive about you. I see only a selfish liar, unable to put himself in anybody else's skin, and it's even worse than that: taking pleasure in other people's misfortune. Because with hindsight, I'm sure you loved throwing my distress back into my face, making you feel so powerful, standing so tall next to this guy who's down on the ground. You aren't just pathetic, Marcus – you're dangerous. Samson's right. We need to make it so you can no longer do any harm. Right now. And for good.'

Tao takes one more deep breath, the deepest so far.

'Someone's got to say it, even if it has to be me,' He breathes out again slowly. 'I call for the death penalty.'

There it is.

The words have been spoken.

The terrible, fateful words I feared more than any others.

'*The death penalty?*' says Samson, tonelessly, half rising from his chair. 'That wasn't what I meant when I said "ever again"! There has to be some other solution!'

Safia makes him sit back down with a glance that is both tender and firm.

'Deciding on the sentence isn't up to you, Samson. It's up to the prosecuting attorney to call for it. You're here to defend the victims; he's here to make sure a price is paid for the crime. Is the price a fair one? It will be up to the jurors to decide that.'

I feel my throat tighten as if it is trapped in a slipknot, even as the invisible corset that's seemed to have been gripping my belly for hours is miraculously loosened. It's an incomprehensible mixture of anguish and relief. As if Marcus's death was the thing I feared most in the world. As if Marcus's death was the thing I most wished for in the world. I no longer know what I want. My stylus starts to tremble uncontrollably in my hand.

'It's the defence's turn to speak,' Safia continues, relentlessly.

What possible defence could there be against such overwhelming charges?

Liz puts her tablet down on the chair and makes as if to get up, as hesitant as a dancer being pushed onto a stage when she knows neither the score nor the choreography; but Marcus takes her gently by the arm to hold her back.

'I'm supposed to – to defend you . . .' she stammers.

'Sit back down. Even if Tao claims I take pleasure in other people's misfortune, I want to at least spare you this. I'll answer for myself.'

'But –'

'To begin with anyway, Liz. Please.'

She drops back into her chair.

Marcus steps up to the witness stand, facing Safia and Tao – the girl who read out the charges against him and the guy who has just called for his death.

'You claim I treated you like shit,' he says, looking the

Chinese boy in the eye. 'It's true. Even worse than that.'

Tao's broad face is lined with tension.

A feverish muttering runs down the rows of victims.

At the back of the room, Alexei lets out a curse. 'Asshole!'

Safia squirms on the sofa. 'What does this provocation mean – are you trying to damage your own case?'

But Marcus is still staring straight into Tao's eyes, still addressing only him, unmoved.

'I talked to you as if I didn't give a crap about your mood, as if I really did want you to try and do the deed a second time. A real bastard, just like Alexei says: that's what I was. But what about you? You haven't revealed your whole story to the court yet, have you, Tao?'

'What?'

'You haven't told them why you actually didn't try a second time. You haven't told them how you held out until lift-off. You haven't explained why you didn't swallow the pills.'

For a moment, Tao is silent.

His eyes dart about for help, coming to rest on Fangfang who is looking at him from behind her square-framed glasses as though seeing him for the first time. Finally he looks back at Marcus.

'The pills . . . ?' he says, uncertainly. 'What are you talking about?'

'You know perfectly well. The sleeping pills.'

Tao's forehead relaxes. His eyes open wide. The look he gives the defendant now is something quite new, his contempt now replaced by astonishment.

'Playing the bastard was the best way of keeping an eye on you without your suspecting anything,' Marcus goes on. 'Every

134

evening for weeks I saw you ask for a sleeping pill from the infirmary – a pill you'd hide under your mattress instead of swallowing it, waiting till you'd have enough to take them all at once and never wake up again.'

Tao's body seems to sink several centimetres deeper into the soft thickness of the sofa.

'The numbers n-never added up . . .' he stammers. 'I thought I was going nuts.'

'I stole enough pills from your stash to stop you committing the irreversible act before lift-off.'

Marcus gives a faint smile, which despite the pitiful state of his mouth is no longer Joker-like at all.

'Yeah, I did treat you worse than a piece of shit,' he concludes, 'but it was only so I could help you. Yeah, I did behave like an asshole. But it was to save your life.'

A turnaround in the situation, a totally unexpected occurrence: it's Tao who's unable to hold it together.

His heavy head tips into his enormous hands, which swallow up his face shaken by spasms.

'Tao!' cries Fangfang, her voice trembling, still turned upside down by these revelations about the past of this person she thought she knew so well, but about whom there was so much she didn't know at all.

'Marcus sacrificed himself for him!' says Kris beside me. She takes my hand and squeezes it hard in hers. 'Just as he sacrificed himself for you, Léo, when he threw himself into the New Eden airlock the day we arrived, to save you from the depressurisation!'

But Alexei isn't ready to forgive as quickly as his wife.

'Don't get carried away, Kris!' he says. 'We have no way of

confirming what Marcus has just said.'

'But my love,' the German girl pleads, 'Tao's pills . . . Marcus didn't invent those, so it must be true!'

'For once I agree with Alexei,' says Mozart, who is still holding his knife in his fist. 'Marcus didn't "save Tao's life" just out of altruism. If you ask me, he did it to prevent a suicide that would have delayed the mission and the flight to Mars. His whole story only proves one thing: that he's every bit as manipulative as Serena herself!'

'Exactly!' says the Russian. 'They're exactly the same! And I'm sure it was Serena who told him – that she was the one who told him about the Noah Report! Who else would it have been?'

Instantly the atmosphere in the habitat feels like it's changed, the blind scales of justice tilting back towards vengeance after just a moment leaning towards forgiveness.

'Alexei is right to ask the question,' says Safia, who is trying to keep her composure next to Tao, who is curled up into himself. 'The court must know. The defendant must answer. How did he learn of the existence of the Noah Report?'

'Just this once, Serena had nothing to do with it,' says Marcus in a voice so calm it's almost alarming.

From his place at the witness stand, he turns towards the victims. Instinctively I drop my gaze to my tablet. But this time, it's not me he's speaking to – it's Samson.

'You remember, the day before we left, just before our final night in the accommodation block in Cape Canaveral?'

'That doesn't answer Alexei's question,' the Nigerian boy answers.

'We went off, the two of us, to the animal store, to fetch

our animals, while the other guys waited in the van. You: for Warden, the on-board dog; me: for Ghost, my trained dove.'

Ghost – I remember Marcus talking about him once. Telling me he hadn't been allowed to bring him on board the spacecraft. Where's he going with this? I raise my head slightly, to peer at him through my hair.

'You were able to collect your dog, but Archibald Dragovic told us my dove had escaped,' Marcus continues. 'I found that hard to believe, since a bird raised in captivity doesn't just fly away like that. I gave you the slip to go off on my own looking for Ghost in the winding corridors of the animal store.'

'I remember all that – what about it?' asks Samson, impatiently.

Warden, at his feet, starts growling, as if he could understand the words exchanged by the two boys and the mention of the animal store had reawakened dark memories in him.

'I didn't find Ghost. But I did come across a computer, open on old Dragovic's desk at the back of the store, in a shadowy corner where I wasn't supposed to go – where there was no one around.'

Warden's growl is transformed into a long high-pitched wail, a song or a sob stretching out unceasingly from his gargoyle throat.

I look up properly now, taking in the whole habitat that's been transformed into a kind of tableau: each person has frozen, waiting for the thunderbolt. For the first time, Marcus is about to reveal the moment when everything changed. The moment we could have been saved, but when we were condemned. The moment he could have become a hero, but instead became a traitor.

'The computer screen showed graphs, figures, dates. And a heading, in red, which you now all know about: *Noah Report – strictly confidential*. While Dragovic was looking for me, yelling my name through the labyrinth of cages, I scrolled through the pages. The further I went, the more I understood the trap we found ourselves in. I just had time to return it to the first page and run off, and found Dragovic only a few steps away. I apologised for having gotten lost. Then I went to meet Samson at the entrance to the animal store, before joining the others back in the van.'

There is silence in the habitat.

I think we were confused, all expecting some Machiavellian conspiracy, a plot hatched in the tiniest details, a demonic Marcus who is the spiritual son of Serena McBee and Satan himself.

Instead of which, there's just chance, a coincidence, hardly anything at all: if Marcus had taken another route through the animal store, if his steps had led him a little further to the right or a little further to the left, he would have remained as ignorant of the Noah Report as the rest of us..

'That doesn't make any difference,' mutters Samson, finally.

I can see he's as shaken as the others, but he's making an effort to stick strictly to the actual accusation, in the name of the victims he's representing, now that Tao is basically out of action.

'It hardly – it hardly matters how you discovered the report –' he stammers. 'You knew and didn't tell anybody! The deception's the same, if you ask me . . . I hardly think that changes the seriousness of the crime . . . or my duty to protect the group from any harm you might still do them, since you appear to have no sense of morality at all . . . Not once in this hearing have you expressed the least bit of regret, or even simply said sorry . . .'

While Samson gets tangled up in his thinking out loud, there is a scraping noise from the back of the habitat.

It's Liz, who has pushed back her chair and found the strength to get up and walk over to the witness stand, beside Marcus.

Through her polo-neck it's possible to see the emotion making her chest rise and fall, while the stress flushes her cheeks. She puts her hands flat on the table, as if to steady herself.

'Madam president, ladies and gentlemen of the jury, I would like to speak for the defence,' she begins, taking support from those set phrases just as her body takes support from the table.

Safia nods, inviting her to continue.

'Has this person who's talking about deception really looked at himself in the mirror?' asks Liz, turning sharply towards Samson.

The Nigerian boy stiffens.

Warden suddenly stops growling, and presses quietly up against his master's legs.

'What do you mean by that, Liz?' asks Safia.

She looks like she's stiffened too, all of a sudden, perched on the edge of the sofa like a small doll in a sari seated on the edge of a shelf, almost ready to fall over and break.

'I mean that Samson knows a thing or two about lying,' Liz continues, undaunted, forcing herself to control her hurried breathing.

'What does that mean?' the girl who is chairing proceedings asks again. 'Samson isn't the one on trial!'

'The truth is on trial. Because that's what you all want, isn't it? That's what you're all shouting for? The truth! All the truths! So I don't see why there are some truths that mustn't be spoken!'

Mozart takes a few steps forward to try to calm his wife.

139

'Liz – please . . . Don't say any old thing just because you're trying to defend Marcus. Samson has done nothing wrong.'

'Oh, really? You're so sure about that? And the stolen glances he's been giving you ever since we arrived on New Eden?'

The Brazilian frowns.

'What?'

'All that time he's spent with you, on excursions outside, or inside the Garden dome, or even in our own habitat, where he seems to pitch camp every evening?'

'As Navigation Officer, I'm supposed to accompany him when he goes out, just as I would with any other member of the team, And I don't see what's the problem with meeting up to play cards in the evenings in our habitat – he's not the only person taking part in our poker games, as far as I know?'

'For God's sake, are you blind? All of you, are you all blind?'

Kelly gives a whistle.

'Phew, well, I don't know what she's been smoking, but if it's something that grows in New Eden I want some for myself! Be a team player, for once, Liz: pass it around!'

The English girl ignores the sarcasm, and stands right in front of her husband.

'Each time Samson comes to visit, he brings little fritters cooked just for you,' she says accusingly.

'What's this madness about, Liz, seriously?' asks Mozart. 'Samson cooks *acarajés* like a pro, even better than the girls in the favelas. I think the Nigerian recipe might be even better than the Brazilian one. And anyway, I don't know why you say he makes them *for me*: he does it for all the players – you eat them too – admit it, they're to die for!'

I won't be the one to contradict Mozart: after Kris, Samson is definitely the best cook on Mars. He uses the potatoes from the Garden, which he's in charge of growing as one of our Biology Officers, and he's managed to recreate many dishes from his country – and particularly those delicious fritters he often serves us before dinner.

Liz doesn't let it go.

'During the games, he spends all his time staring at you as if you were the eighth wonder of the world.'

'The eighth wonder of the world? What crap! He's just eyeing me to see if I'm bluffing, that's all. That's the whole point of poker . . .' He turns to Samson, seeking approval. '. . . isn't that right, pal?'

The Nigerian boy does not answer.

He sits as still as a man struck by a magic spell, as silent as the dog sitting at his feet.

Safia tries to fly to his aid.

'That's enough now, Liz! I'm ordering you to be quiet. You must do what I say, I am chairing these proceedings, and –'

'And I'm the counsel for the defence,' Liz interrupts her, breathless. 'I'm going to defend my client to the very end. I'll show you he's far from being the only liar in New Eden. And I'm going to make you all see what you insist on ignoring – you give me no choice.'

With these words, she hurries back to her chair, grabs the tablet she'd left on the floor, and with a trembling finger scrolls through what it's showing.

'There!' she says, her voice shrill, turning the screen to Safia. 'There it is: that is the truth!'

19. Reverse Shot

The barrel of the pistol is just a few centimetres from Orion Seamus's chest.

Serena McBee is holding it out at point blank range, her arm stretched out over her desk, her eyes beneath her silver fringe absolutely focused.

'Who else knows about Harmony?' she asks slowly, enunciating each syllable with care.

'Nobody,' replies Agent Seamus.

He sits perfectly still in his chair, in the middle of the enormous, silent room, beneath the gantry covered in cameras, all of them turned off.

'Nobody?' repeats the vice-president icily. 'You think I'm going to buy that? There must be other people who know, even if it's only the scientists who analysed the hair you stole from us, from Harmony and me.'

'I don't have to say where exhibits come from when I submit them to the C.I.A. lab for testing. In this case, the report concludes that the two hair samples belong to the same person:

at no point did the experts suspect I had taken hair from two different women.'

But Serena does not seem ready to be satisfied with these explanations.

'You'd have me believe that if I shoot now, right away, you'll take the secret of this discovery to your grave? I'm sure you've made a copy. Some file that would be disseminated automatically if you disappeared.'

'Even if I were to swear the contrary, would that change anything? What's the point of a promise if you aren't obliged to keep it?'

Serena is silent.

'Your silence is most eloquent,' he continues. 'Such a promise is indeed worthless. This morning, for example, you promised to keep me closely connected to your political future; you predicted I'd go far and that the two of us were made to lead our fellow men and women. But just a few hours later, you call me incompetent and threaten me with a rapid fall just because I let a couple of fugitives get away. It isn't very pleasant, you know, to feel like you're sitting on an ejector seat . . . especially when we know that almost all your former partners in the Genesis programme disappeared in a mysterious plane crash.'

Serena doesn't even try to deny Agent Seamus's thinly veiled accusations.

'So that's it,' she says, gripping the butt of the pistol between her ringed fingers. 'Common blackmail.'

'No, Serena, not blackmail. On the contrary. A partnership. *An alliance*. Of equals, and for the benefit of both.'

Agent Seamus leans forward in his chair, his one eye never

leaving the woman opposite him.

'Nobody needs to know about Harmony,' he says.

The pistol's metallic mouth brushes the cotton of his shirt.

'It was my only way of having a child,' says Serena, without weakening her voice, without moving her arm.

Orion Seamus keeps moving forward; the barrel presses into his chest, level with his heart.

'You don't need to justify yourself,' he murmurs. 'It's not your fault if you're infertile.'

'I'm not infertile. I'm demanding. Why mix my genes with those of some other inferior creature? If I've chosen to reproduce myself identically, it's because I've never yet met a man who was my equal . . .'

'. . . until today.'

This time Serena's arm does tremble imperceptibly.

Her voice quavers slightly, somewhere between unease and irritation.

'Don't be ridiculous. I could be your mother!'

'I like accomplished women.'

'And I don't like arrogant brats.'

'Are you scared of me, Serena?'

'You think too highly of yourself.'

'Even if I tell you I've been watching you for a long time? Since well before your swearing-in as vice-president? For years?'

He slips his hand, very slowly, into his jacket, looking for the pocket from which a few moments earlier he'd taken the bag of hair samples.

'Stop!' says Serena. 'I'm going to pull the trigger!'

'No, I don't think so. You'd have too much to lose. And more than that, you have too much to gain from having an ally beside you, ready to do anything to help you . . .' Orion Seamus's hand comes back out of his jacket; he's holding a small black velvet case. '. . . for better, for worse . . .'

Serena's eyes, their lashes sharpened with mascara, open wide like a pair of carnivorous plants.

'. . . for richer, for poorer . . .'

Her lips open in an expression of disbelief.

'. . . in sickness and in health . . .'

Her fingers grip the pistol so tightly that the skin around her polished nails turns white.

'. . . till death do us part.'

'You don't seriously mean . . .'

'Yes, Serena, I do. When I was talking about an alliance, that was what I was thinking of. As the high priestess of marital relations, having counselled so many couples, bound so many unions, it's now your turn to sacrifice yourself to the goddess you claim to serve.'

Agent Seamus drops to one knee beside the desk; the tip of the pistol slides from his chest up to his face; he opens the case with his fingertips, to reveal a diamond solitaire ring, its setting shaped like a single eye.

Like this, kneeling, with the gleaming barrel positioned in the middle of his forehead, he makes his marriage proposal as one might challenge somebody to a duel.

'Serena McBee, will you be my wife?'

20. Shot

Month 21 / sol 578 / 21:13 Mars time
[28th sol since landing]

'The truth!' says Liz once again, holding the tablet in front of her and brandishing it at the court, the way you'd brandish a shield, a trophy, a severed head.

Safia presses her nails into the armrest of the sofa to steady herself. A denial escapes from her lips, but it's no longer an order given by the chair of a tribunal, it's more like an entreaty from a condemned woman.

'What truth?' she groans. 'What does he have to do with it? That's just Samson on the screen, and nothing else.'

'Yes, it's Samson. Alone in my habitat. Or at least, so he thought.'

Liz steps away from the witness stand and takes two paces sideways towards the jurors – towards us. It's like she's dancing, channelling her feverish feelings into inch-perfect movements that she controls perfectly. With a ballet dancer's gesture, she holds the tablet out to us so that we can all see.

The screen shows Samson, standing in the middle of the poorly

146

lit living room of one of the habitats. He's holding a salad bowl filled with still-steaming fritters. At first, it's like I'm looking at a photo, but bit by bit I realise it's a film. The bowl is trembling slightly in Samson's hands; his eyes blink nervously; he seems both embarrassed and at the mercy of somebody else, as if he were ashamed of being there but there's some invisible force preventing him from turning around. His eyes are on a partly open door, from which some light is streaming out. I can't see what's behind the door, but I can guess. It's the bathroom, and the noise of the running water means there's somebody taking a shower . . .

'I'd suspected for quite a while,' explains Liz, her voice breathless as she presses the 'stop' button to bring the video back to the beginning, 'so I decided to get to the bottom of it once and for all. When you're preparing to compete for a place at the Royal Ballet, you learn to mistrust everybody, to expect low blows, to spy even on your friends. I'm not proud of it, but those are the reflexes that allowed me to catch Samson out.'

The video starts again from zero, a long shot on the empty living room with the ceiling light switched off, lit only by the glow escaping from the bathroom. Suddenly there's a tap-tap *out of shot, as somebody knocks on the habitat door. 'Hey, guys, it's me, Samson! Are we meeting at six, like Liz said? The others haven't arrived yet. Am I the first?'*

'Usually poker games start at six thirty, before dinner,

everybody who plays knows that,' says Liz. 'But that morning I told Samson to come earlier, at six, exactly the time Mozart always takes a shower after his day's work.'

The sound of footsteps. The door was already open. Samson appears in frame. Despite the dim lighting, it's possible to see the broad smile on his face, as he holds out the bowl of acarajés *as an offering. 'Liz? Mozart?' he calls. 'Are you hiding? Is this a joke?' The hissing of the shower swallows up his words. His eyes sweep across the room in search of somebody there. They settle on the room where the light's coming from. They freeze.*

'That evening,' Liz goes on, 'as soon as Mozart got into the shower, I turned off the living-room lights, leaving the bathroom door half-open, and I propped my tablet up on the sofa, programming it to start filming at the first sign of any movement. I laid a trap for Samson, and he walked right into it. I'd planned to keep these pictures for myself and never show them to anybody. Because it didn't bother me knowing it. Because I still consider Samson a great friend. Because I didn't want to hurt him. But today, regrettably, things have changed.' Liz breathes out with a whistle, her face twisted by a mixture of guilt and determination. 'And yeah, I know it's disgusting to attack somebody because of their private life, but this video is my only way of taking the charges apart, of showing the court that nobody's perfect and by doing that, just maybe, I can soften Marcus's sentence a bit.'

On the screen of the tablet, the video is back at the moment we'd already seen: the image of Samson standing immobile at the sight that is invisible to us, unable to turn around and yet trembling with fear at being discovered. Yes, caught in Liz's trap. But more than this, caught in the trap of his own feelings – of that secret love he's managed to repress somehow or other for all these months, but which is bursting out of this video, on that face, in those eyes . . .

Liz does a three-hundred-and-sixty-degree turn in the middle of the seventh habitat, holding her tablet up high to be sure that there's nobody who can't see what she's showing – not the jurors, not the bench, not Alexei . . . and not Mozart.

I feel a terrible awkwardness spreading all around me: some people's silence, the way others squirm on their chairs; the back of Samson's neck bends in the row in front of me, as if he were trying to disappear back into himself, to sink into the ground, to vanish for ever.

Suddenly there's a voice from the tablet. 'Samson? Is that you? Sorry, I messed up on the time.' Liz comes into frame, entering the habitat from the access tube that leads in from the Garden. 'It was six thirty as usual, not six. I went round to your place to let you know, but you were already here – we must have just missed each other.' On the screen, Samson spins around, as if he's been stung by a wasp, turning to face Liz. The bowl in his hands is shaking furiously. The fritters are knocking into one another. Several of them fall on the habitat floor. 'I . . . I've just arrived,' he stammers. 'I realised there was nobody here, I was about to leave.' He bends down to pick up the squashed fritters, tosses them in the bowl then rushes out as if he were a burglar caught in the act. 'Come back at six thirty!' Liz calls after him through the door, innocently. Then she walks over to the sofa – towards the tablet she'd concealed there. Her shape gets bigger and bigger as she approaches, and within a moment it has become a giant's silhouette; then she stretches out her hand and with an abrupt movement presses the button that brings the recording to an end.

The screen goes black.

There's a whistling from the far end of the seventh habitat.

It's Alexei, his cheeks flushed, his eyes rolling upwards.

'I don't believe it! Did you see that, Mo? You see how Samson was checking you out for three minutes? Like . . . Like . . .'

Mozart's face darkens.

'Yeah, I saw,' he spits. 'Like a homo. And I always thought of him like a brother.'

Samson looks up sharply.

'I can explain everything, Mozart,' he begs.

'There's nothing for you to explain. It couldn't be clearer. The worst thing about it is you having the nerve to accuse Marcus of lying so he could use Léonor.'

'But I never lied!' says Samson, enraged. 'I never used anybody!'

But the Brazilian isn't listening to him, not any more.

'When I think back to all your fucking *acarajés*, which I stuffed myself with without suspecting a thing, it makes me want to puke. I need to get some air.'

Angry and ashamed, he turns around, lifts the habitat lever and disappears down the access tube, ignoring the shouts from Kris and Fangfang who are trying to stop him going.

'Whoa, guys!' says Alexei, still stunned. 'We spent months with the guy, sharing a dorm in Death Valley – doesn't that creep you out? It does me! No wonder Mozart's disgusted! And Safia should be even more!'

All eyes are on the Indian girl now. She's been up on her feet since Mozart left the room, effectively stopping the trial and bringing the hearing to an end.

'Safia, the guy betrayed you!' Alexei says, furious. 'He betrayed all of us, just like Marcus! He's a liar, an impostor! He shouldn't be sitting with the other victims, he should be in the dock too!'

'Hey, you suddenly spying for the Russian secret service now or what?' says Kelly, getting up in turn. 'It's not a crime to be gay, as far as I know! At least, it isn't in Canada, and it sure as hell isn't going to be on Mars!'

'Lying is a crime in any country,' snarls Alexei. 'You've got to be seriously twisted to join a programme of space procreation when you're a homo!'

Ignoring everybody's shouts, Safia walks silently across the living room and stops next to Samson, who is sunk in his chair, his head in his hands.

She puts her hand on his shoulder.

She stands with him.

Alexei stops ranting suddenly, to exclaim in astonishment: 'What? You're not surprised? You . . . you knew?'

Safia meets his accusing gaze.

'That'll do,' she says. 'That's enough. There's nothing twisted about Samson – morally speaking, he's straighter than you.'

The words she spoke to Alexei that time when he was having one of his paranoid attacks, when he accused Samson of flirting with Kris, come brutally back to my mind. *'There's no reason for jealousy between Samson and me. I could explain why, but I don't think you'd understand. Nobody has betrayed you, Alexei – if you're wearing horns, it's not because you're a cuckold, but because you're dumb as an ox!'*

Watching Alexei's eyes get wider and wider, I can guess he's remembering the same thing, those words that now make perfect sense.

'You knew about Samson and you didn't say anything? You covered up his lie! Why? How? No – wait – I don't want to know. You . . . you're his accomplice!' He walks over towards Safia, threatening. 'So you've betrayed us too! You have no business presiding over this court. Give up your place!'

An indescribable commotion takes hold of the habitat – the boys and girls getting to their feet, shouting, chairs being knocked over, the dogs starting to bark at the tops of their lungs. The trial that was supposed to bind us closer together is turning into a fist fight. The bond between us dignified victims has been left in tatters.

Only Liz and Marcus remain calm, not reacting, in the centre of this hurricane, bound to the witness stand like two sailors on a ship that's taking in water from all sides.

ACT II

21. Genesis Channel

Monday 8 January, 6:33am

Long shot on the deep valley of Ius Chasma, at the heart of the Valles Marineris, in the depths of night.

A huge black cliff, several kilometres high, blocks off the image on the left. At the top, at the upper edge of the frame, there is just a tiny squeezed square of space. The stars of the Martian sky are shining there, pale and distant like gravel at the bottom of a deep well.

All the winds have gone quiet.

Total silence.

Suddenly, a caption appears at the bottom of the screen: WESTERN VIEW OF IUS CHASMA, EXTERIOR CAMERA, NEW EDEN GARDEN / MARS TIME 08:13 – SUNRISE.

Within a few moments, a pinkish glow appears at the top of the cliff and carves out the jagged silhouette of the canyon, a witness to billions of years of erosion, against the night sky. The crevasses, the cracks, the fissures in the rock are gradually illuminated, revealing this ancestral skin – the ageless leather of the planet Mars – to the new dawning day.

Eventually the anaemic-looking stars disappear altogether,

chased off by the Sun that is creeping up to the very edge of the canyon. When it finally falls, its rays plunge harshly over the precipice, pouring in deep red cascades: an infinity of dust particles still float in the air, the vestiges of the previous day's storm – as it strikes them, the light transforms them into crimson globules, into torrents of blood.

Cut.

22. Shot

It's been a quarter of an hour since the lights came on in my bedroom.

A quarter of an hour since the cameras started rolling again.

A quarter of an hour since I should have got up.

But this morning, I can't do it.

My body feels like it weighs several tonnes. It's a lump of cast iron wrapped in a silk nightie, crushed against the mattress of the double bed I've occupied alone for the first time since my arrival on Mars. I barely shut my eyes all night. No sooner had I dozed off than Marcus's face came back to me – his face from *before*, when his mouth had not yet been deformed by avenging fists, when I saw only promises of the future in his smile, and stars in his eyes. I woke with a start twenty times, only to rediscover the terrible emptiness in the bed next to me; and twenty times over, I lost Marcus again.

After so many hours, I'm too exhausted to go back to sleep, and too exhausted to get up.

Being awake is even worse than being asleep. When I'm conscious, there's nothing that can distract me from the countdown in my head: this evening at 8 p.m. we're gathering yet again in the seventh habitat to complete the trial – and I still don't know what I'll have decided when my turn comes to say my piece.

'He made me suffer worse than I ever thought possible – I want him to die.'

No, I could never say such a thing, because it isn't the whole truth, because Marcus didn't make only me suffer, and the idea of his being executed still seems unbearable.

'I loved him more intensely than I ever thought I could – I want him to live.'

Impossible and inept: love has never been enough to redeem a crime. What right would I have to forgive Marcus for what he subjected the others to, that despicable behaviour for which he seems to show no remorse, in the name of a story that only I experienced?

'My head's going to explode. I don't want to think about Marcus any more. I want to forget him for ever. I want to go back to being the girl I was before I met him. Decide without me.'

What? Would I really dissociate myself from the group, a group that's already set to explode, just to give myself the comfort of not having to choose? Too easy and too cowardly!

'Léo?'

There's someone at the door, three short knocks that pull me from my thoughts.

'Are you awake, Léo?' The voice that comes into the room is Kris's.

I feel my muscles contract, my nerves regain control of my body. Kris shouldn't see me like this, prostrate on my bed like an invalid. I have to be strong, for her, for them.

'Yes, I'm up!' I call, jumping to my feet. 'Just give me five minutes to have a shower.'

I come out of my habitat wearing my black undersuit, my hair tied back, my eyes underlined with concealer from Chez Rosier. Putting on a determined face: that's my duty.

Beyond the Garden's glass dome, the morning is turning red, countless suspended particles filling the air. I can see the other ten pioneers standing out against the bright backdrop. At first they're only silhouettes, but as I get closer I can make out their features – eyes locked in position, forcing themselves not to look at the closed door of the seventh habitat, lips sealed shut so as not to speak of the trial that is haunting all our thoughts. All around us, on the dome's metallic frame, between the leaves of the plantations, the cameras are filming us, watching us. The microphones can hear us. We have to act as though there's nothing going on.

'Have you had time to get breakfast already?' Kris asks me shyly. 'I had trouble sleeping so I . . . I made some oat cookies with dried apples. Günter helped me.'

She holds out two still-warm cookies.

Though I'm not hungry, with a knot in my stomach, I take them delicately from her hand.

'Thanks, Kris.'

As I nibble on the cookies, without even tasting them, I look at my teammates. Can the viewers on the other side of their screens see what I see, the tension that reigns in the dome, all the cards reshuffled now? Sure, Kris is still pressed close to Alexei, one hand on her husband's shoulder, the other on Günter's 'head', with Louve lying obediently at their feet – the picture of a model family. Sure, Kenji and Kelly are holding hands, a gesture that is tender and touching. But to my eyes, the other couples look quite different to how they did yesterday.

For the first time, Fangfang is not standing next to Tao's wheelchair, but a few steps behind him. It's as though a ghost has come between them, that faceless girl Xia who died mysteriously before our lift-off, who might have been a member of our team in the Singaporean girl's place.

After yesterday's skirmish, Mozart and Liz also seem to be doing anything they can to keep their distance from each other.

Safia and Samson, meanwhile, are stuck closer together than ever, withdrawn into themselves as if they were scared somebody was going to try to force them apart.

It's Alexei who finally breaks the silence.

'Plans for the day?' he asks, reminding us all that we're going to have to fill it up somehow, this whole shitty day, while we wait for this evening's fateful meeting.

'Protocol demands that we check the integrity of the base on the day after any major bad weather,' says Liz. 'Do you remember, there was that strange clanging we heard during the storm, as if there were something knocking into the dome?'

Of course we remember! There's no way we could have forgotten that persistent noise, coming to us from those dark clouds: *Clank* . . . *Clank* . . . *Clank* . . . There's no way we could have forgotten the shock revelation from Günter, live on air, about the seventh habitat having been pierced by '*an unidentified body . . . from the outside*' at the time of the last Great Storm, before our arrival. I suspect viewers all over the world must be wondering whether it was the same *thing* that was banging against the walls of the base yesterday. Oh, those fine folks would be even more on edge if they knew that just over a year ago, at the moment when the shell of the seventh habitat was breached, all the secret guinea pigs from the Noah experiment disappeared at once.

'We'll have to go out to check on any possible damage,' says Liz. 'I'm the Engineering Officer – it's natural that the task should fall to me.'

'There's still dust floating around,' says Kris, worried. 'It might still be dangerous.'

Fangfang, the only Planetology Officer we have left, shakes her head.

'I consulted the exterior gauges when I got up this morning: the dust that's still floating about isn't sufficiently concentrated to create any risk of abrasion to the suits. In theory, a mission outside is possible.'

'But all the same,' Kris objects, 'we really don't know what caused those strange noises. Maybe there's still something there, outside . . .'

Liz cuts her off.

'Visibility is back to normal. We can clearly see for ourselves there's nothing out there. I'll go. It's part of my job description. And I do need to get out of this glass jar for a few minutes.'

'Me too,' says Kris, giving her mane of peroxided hair a shake. 'I don't know about you, but I'm feeling kind of cooped up in here. I could do with breathing some different air – even if it's only the air in my helmet!' She takes Kenji's hand. 'What about you, Tiger?'

Without a word the Japanese boy follows her to their habitat, where their exterior spacesuits are waiting for them.

'I'll get on with lifting the tarps,' says Samson, gesturing towards the terraces. 'I'll check on the condition of the plantations.'

He talks quickly, like somebody who's afraid of being interrupted.

His eyes seem to be deliberately avoiding everybody else's, but also, I think, the fixed stares of the cameras.

His whole body is tense, uncomfortable – ready to receive blows and to return them.

'I'm in charge of the crops too,' says Kris softly. 'I'll help you.'

Instinctively she glances up at Alexei, no doubt expecting some kind of reprimand – in the past her husband would never have put up with her spending hours in the plantations in the company of another man. But today he just responds with a superior smile, and an ironic comment.

'You may go, my angel. And call me if you need *a real guy* to help you lift those heavy tarps.'

Samson clenches his fists when he hears this veiled provocation, which the viewers will have no way of understanding.

What must he be feeling now? Fear? Shame? Rage? A desire to rip Alexei's head off?

Whatever his emotions, he can't express them: the public knows nothing about his outing by Liz yesterday in the privacy of the Rest House. For the billions of Earth's inhabitants, Samson and Safia are still a couple just like every other, a family from who they're expecting a run of babies in quick succession.

'While Liz checks on things on the outside, I'll go over the integrity of the base internally,' says Tao.

He turns to Fangfang to say something, but she doesn't give him the chance.

'I'm going out,' she says. 'I'm going to do a recce of New Eden's surroundings, to see whether the storm has caused any alterations to the topography. I need one of the Navigation Officers to drive me. Mozart, since Kelly's going to be with Liz, would you take me in the maxi-rover?'

The Singaporean girl and the Brazilian boy leave the Garden, in their turn, to put their suits on.

Soon there are only three people left beneath the dome: Safia, Alexei and me.

'The communications signals seem to be working normally, but I'm supposed to do a whole battery of tests just to check,' says the Indian girl.

In the morning light that makes her long black hair and kohl-lined eyes gleam, she looks so fragile – so young! Hard to believe that only yesterday she was presiding with such authority over a courtroom – and impossible to imagine how she'll be doing it again, this very evening.

'I'll leave you then,' she says.

Her slender fingers brush across my arm, then grip for just a moment to pass me a bit of her energy, to communicate her unshakeable desire always to do what is right. I sense that this – this gesture to replace all the words she can't say in front of the cameras – is her way of telling me to stand firm until tonight.

I'm left alone with Alexei.

'And what about you, what plans have you got?' I ask the team's other Medical Officer, in no more than a murmur.

'How about we go to the infirmary to see if we can find something to take care of Marcus?'

There's no aggression in Alexei's voice, no provocation. Just seriousness and – amazing as this may sound – a kind of gentleness.

Unable to say a word, I just follow him to the entrance to the panic room beneath the Garden's central pyramid with the plantations layered above it. We plunge into the dark den; the movement sensors set off the artificial lighting, illuminating the case of the 3D printer and the infirmary area; the cameras start rolling.

Alexei confidently pulls several boxes of medication off the glass shelves: aspirins, anti-inflammatories, antibiotics . . .

'Based on the symptoms we described to him,' Alexei says out loud, 'Dr Montgomery thought it might be a bacterial infection. With all this stuff, we should be able to get Marcus back on his feet in a couple of . . .'

I know that this speech, as well as the prescription he's assembling, is only designed as misdirection in front of the cameras.

There's only one thing he's really interested in: the hearing in a few hours' time when we will decide on Marcus's sentence.

Only one thing he's really come here to find, on the morning of this day when a man might die.

'Oh, and while we're here, I'll get a bottle of sedative too, just to calm the dogs. They've been so unsettled since the storm. A little shot will help them sleep better, won't it?'

23. Off-screen

Grand Canyon National Park, Arizona
Monday 8 January, 10:50am

'It really does feel like we're on Mars . . .' murmurs Harmony, her forehead glued to the pick-up window.

The vast, arid, red expanses of the Grand Canyon unfurl before her eyes.

'This is certainly the closest landscape to it we have on Earth,' says Andrew from the back seat where he's stretched out, his leg immobilised. 'Though the Valles Marineris canyon is four times as deep.'

The highway turns a tight bend and the vehicle moves behind a heap of rocks that temporarily hides the view.

'I've never seen anything this big in my whole life, anything so huge, so . . . Argh!'

Harmony gives a cry of fright when Cindy turns the steering wheel sharply to bring them around the last rock. The view that opens up in front of them is dizzying – the strident blue of a cloudless sky, the dazzling red of the sun-splashed stone, the black shadows of the gulf.

'You . . . you nearly killed us!' stammers Harmony, her heart

165

racing, nails gripping her seat.

'I'm in total control of this truck and I'm not suicidal,' answers the driver, never taking her eyes off the road. 'Which is really the only reason I haven't yet tried to give you the slip: I'm too afraid of taking a rifle shot. I have no intention of reenacting *Thelma and Louise* today.'

'Thelma and Louise?' repeats Harmony, recovering her breath. 'Who are they?'

Cindy shoots her a look in the rear-view mirror.

'You claim to be the daughter of one of the most important producers of all time, and you don't know your classics?' she mocks. 'Geena Davis and Susan Sarandon! Brad Pitt's first appearance on the big screen! Oscar for best screenplay in 1991!'

'You mean they're characters in a movie? Mom never allowed me to watch them. She said I was too suggestible, too easily influenced. I was only allowed nature documentaries . . . and the Genesis channel, of course.'

Cindy stares at the strange girl with a mixture of suspicion and astonishment. She seems so different, so out of place, so unsuited to the situation in which she finds herself.

'So who are they?' Harmony asks again, the words from her pale lips like a petition to grab hold of any part of this world that she might lose at any moment, on which she closes her fingers but which keeps slipping away.

Another bend.

Cindy turns her attention back to the road.

But when she next looks in the rear-view mirror, her expression has changed – it's softer now, almost maternal.

'Thelma and Louise are two women who want to be free,' she says.

'Free? From what?'

'From men. Society. The past. Everything.'

Harmony's eyes widen; a delighted smile plays on her lips. 'That's wonderful!'

'It's tragic.'

'What do you mean?' Harmony is alarmed. 'They don't make it?'

Cindy sighs; she tucks a lock of her red-dyed hair behind her ear.

'Yes, they do. At the end of a road spattered with fire and blood. Because the world didn't want to allow them that freedom, they had no choice but to grab it for themselves, to hurtle into the sky leaving everything behind them.'

Harmony is smiling again.

'So if Thelma and Louise managed it, maybe I'll be able to free myself completely one day too – from this society that's so alien to me, from this past that crushes me despite my knowing so little about it.' She turns around in her seat to share her enthusiasm with Andrew. 'Did you hear that, Andrew? Hurtling into the sky! What a gorgeous image! I've really got to watch that movie!'

But Cindy stops her.

'You don't understand. It's not an image. Thelma and Louise *literally* hurtle into the sky, right here in the Grand Canyon. This is where the movie ends. They're surrounded on all sides by the police, with no possible way to escape, so they press down on the accelerator and hurl their car into the void.'

Harmony turns pale, gasping as if she's just been slapped.

Cindy looks away from her and gives a long sigh.

'This world is full of disappointments for people who just want to dream. I used to adore the Genesis programme, but you'd have me believe that it's really a monstrous plot hatched by the very worst aspects of humanity. I thought I'd found my soulmate in Derek, the soldier from Connecticut I met at the marriage ceremony in Cape Canaveral a month ago, but two weeks ago he stopped calling. Seduced and then abandoned . . . I feel like my life is a dead end, just like Thelma's and Louise's.'

An abrupt beep sounds from the back seat.

'Another message to your anonymous inbox?' asks Cindy wearily, looking at Andrew in the rear-view mirror. 'Yet another secret?'

'No,' replies Andrew. 'This time it's not my cellphone. It's yours: the one I confiscated so you wouldn't be tempted to call for help. Can I read it to you?'

Cindy nods, lifts her foot from the pedal, and Andrew starts to read aloud the message on the small screen.

'*Dear Cindy, I hope you'll forgive me for not giving any signs of life earlier. My cellphone broke during some exercises, and like an idiot I hadn't saved my contacts in the Cloud. I called all the hotels in Death Valley and the surrounding area, until I found the one where you work. Your boss, Bill, told me you'd taken some unpaid leave to clear your head a bit. I confess I did try to geo-locate you thanks to the technology we have in the army, but seems your cellphone is scrambled. Answer me, I'm begging you – I'm so scared I've messed everything up! – Capt. Derek Jacobson.*'

Andrew looks up from the screen, a genuinely pained expression on his face.

'I'm sorry, Cindy, but you're going to have to write to Captain Jacobson and tell him to stop looking, and explain that you're just not ready for a big love story right now.'

24. Shot

'So, your verdict?' asks Alexei.

'Oh, nothing to report from me,' answers Liz. 'I've checked all the external walls – no visible damage.'

She turns her tablet to face us and scrolls through the pictures she took on her recce: she's carefully photographed the shell of each habitat, each of the panes that make up the Garden walls. That's where the eleven of us have gathered again, at the close of the Martian day.

'Nothing to report from the inside of the base either,' adds Tao. 'All indicators green. Whatever it was that made those noises yesterday during the storm, it hasn't caused any damage.'

I imagine this information must reassure the viewers. And they're probably expecting us to look relieved too. But the truth is the opposite: ever since this morning, each hour that passes brings us closer to the fatal outcome. On the surface, we're pioneers taking back control of their colony, a united team working together; but deep down, we're jurors turning our thoughts over and over, individuals who are hopelessly alone with our consciences. I've been over the arguments so many times in my mind that right now my head feels as if it's spilling over.

On the very threshold of our decision, I no longer have any idea what I want to happen to Marcus.

'Well, it'll soon be time to get back to our invalid for dinner,' says Alexei, looking at his watch.

We all exchange strained, wordless glances.

There's no going back now.

There's only a leap forward.

'Time for a shower,' adds Alexei, 'and we meet in the seventh habitat in half an hour.'

25. Genesis Channel

Monday 8 January, 6:20pm

DEAR VIEWERS,
TODAY, ONCE AGAIN, WE WILL BE LEAVING THE PIONEERS
IN PEACE TO HAVE DINNER WITH MARCUS.
BUT DON'T GO AWAY!

TO KEEP YOU ENTERTAINED WHILE YOU WAIT,
WE ARE PLEASED TO SHARE WITH YOU
THE SECOND OF OUR 'ORIGINS' REPORTS.

*(PROGRAM ENCRYPTED — ACCESS TO
PREMIUM SUBSCRIBERS ONLY.)*

Open onto a huge windowless room, with smooth concrete walls.

A thick crimson carpet covers part of the floor, which is also concrete. Breaking up this minimalist décor, some pieces of traditional Chinese furniture, in lacquered wood, are artistically arranged around the room. Two red varnished chairs are facing the camera. On one, we recognise Tao. On the other, there is a slender girl, as delicate as her companion is imposing, wearing a simple white linen dress.

The couple look indestructibly united, and yet only one name appears on the screen.

A man's voice is heard, off-screen, sounding worried. '*So, there are two of you? I think there must have been some mistake filling out the application form . . . We read* Tao Xia, *we thought that was just one person.*'

Tao forces himself to smile. His large face, his square jaw, his dark hair cropped very short – all this might make him look a little intimidating. And yet the shyness in his smile eclipses everything else. 'Uh, it's – it's not a mistake,' he stammers, uneasy. 'My name's Tao, and my friend is called Xia. We're applying – both of us.'

There's a cough, off-screen. '*Right, but in that case, you should have filled out one form apiece.*'

Tao's cheeks flush slightly. He's embarrassed, overwhelmed at being there, a little lost for words.

The girl looks up – beautiful black almond eyes rimmed with fine lashes – and comes to her friend's help. 'Yes, sir, you're right,' she says in a melodious voice. 'The rules did say one form per candidate. But we shouldn't be separated, Tao and me. Because as you can see, one of us without the other would dZZZZZZZZZZZZZZZZZZZZZ ZZZZZZZZZZZZZZZZZZZZZZ ZZZZZZZZZZZZZZZZZZZZZZZZZZZZZZZZZZZZZZZZZZZ ZZZZZZZZZZZZZZZZZZZZZZZZZZZZZZZZZZZZZZZZZZZ ZZZZZZZZZZZZZZZZZZZZZZZZZZZZZZZZZZZZZZZZZZZ ZZZZZZZZZZZZZZZZZZZZZZZZZZZZZZZZZZZZZZZZZZZ ZZZZZZZZZZZZZZZZZZZZZ . . .

26. Shot

Month 21 / sol 579 / 20:05 Mars time
[29th sol since landing]

'The time has come for us to decide,' announces Safia.

It's hard to believe twenty-four hours have passed.

The scene that's playing out before my eyes is identical to the one from the same time yesterday, the drawings on my tablet can testify to that. Each of us is back in their place, in the same clothes, like actors on a theatre stage, like figurines in a dolls' house.

The only thing that's changed is the dishes prepared by Kris for our pretend-jolly dinner. Today she was satisfied with reheating some frozen food in a big family-size dish, the very last of our stock left over from the *Cupido*. The sickly sweet, vaguely chemical smell of the *Astronaut Meals*, as Eden Food called them to entice their customers, make me nauseous. Next to the dish are the syringe and the bottle of sedative that Alexei took from the infirmary – apparently to calm the dogs, actually to have the means at hand to carry out the sentence, depending what it ends up being.

'You will have to speak with complete honesty, based on the testimony and the pleas that you heard in yesterday's

175

session,' explains Safia. 'I should remind you, there is no right or wrong answer. It's not a question of us judging each other: we're here to judge Marcus. The only thing that matters is your private conviction, each of you, while always respecting other people's convictions.'

Kelly shifts in her chair, ill at ease, making the big golden hoops hanging from her ears sway.

'*No judgement, respect for one another,*' she repeats bitterly. 'Everybody is beautiful, everybody is kind, it's like we're at an A.A. meeting! But who's going to speak first? Who's going to speak last? How – practically – are we organising this? It's not like this was just some common opinion poll or something: we're deciding on a guy's life or death, for Christ's sake!'

No one answers her.

No one dares speak.

We can't take our eyes off the flask of sedative sitting on the table, drawing us in like an evil magnet. Through the thick brown glass, we can see it's filled to the brim, untouched. There's enough there to take care of the dogs for weeks, for months. There's enough to kill a man with a single injection.

'Does anybody have a piece of paper and a pen?' I ask sharply.

Kelly turns towards me, abruptly, and there's a pout on her glossed lips.

'Hey, Picasso, this isn't the time for one of your little artistic whims,' she says. 'You can just use your tablet for now.'

'It's not for drawing. It's for writing. Our eleven names. On eleven bits of paper.'

Kelly's pout is transformed into a smile.

'Oh yeah, I get it, we're going to draw lots!' she says. 'Smart!'

If Kelly suspected I'd used the same process to select the first boy to invite to the Visiting Room, six months earlier, when I refused to choose . . . If she discovered that on that occasion fortune had chosen Marcus . . .

'I've got what you need,' says Tao.

He leans over to his wheelchair folded up against the sofa, rummages in the storage pouch fixed to the backrest and pulls out a notebook with a pencil attached to it.

'Protocol requires that the Engineering Officers always have some paper to hand, to take notes in case a piece of electronic equipment breaks down.'

He holds out the notebook.

I rip out a page and tear it into eleven pieces. The others watch me in silence, while I write their names on these miniature slips. Then I fold them in four and jumble them up in one of the empty dishes Kris brought with the dinner.

'We're just missing one more thing,' I say, 'an innocent hand. Who volunteers?'

Once again, nobody answers.

I know the others feel the same way I do: the time for innocence has gone, for all of us, for ever.

'There might not be any innocent hands in New Eden,' Kris says suddenly, 'but there are innocent *pincers*.'

Alexei flinches.

'You don't really mean . . .'

'Yes, Alex. I'm talking about our son.'

The Russian boy grimaces.

'I've already told you, my angel, that heap of scrap metal is not our son . . .' he begins.

But Kris doesn't listen.

She's already on her way into the access tube, calling: 'Günter!'

A few moments later, the robot butler appears, sliding in silently on his four all-terrain wheels. He's still wearing the bow tie that Alexei wore for his wedding and which Kris tied affectionately around his neck. Not long ago she also put one of those black woollen hats that came with our equipment onto his round head. To humanise him? To persuade herself this machine is her 'son', as she stubbornly insists on calling him?

'Günter, darling, could you do a little something for us?' she asks, enunciating each syllable as if addressing a small child.

'*Affirmative,*' replies Günter in his artificial, strangely toneless voice.

Kris's face is reflected in his single eye – that round, huge, gleaming lens. I know that behind that glass eye there's no brain, no soul, no identity. There's only a network of printed circuits, with short electrical impulses passing through it. Is Kris aware of this too?

'Pull out a piece of paper from that dish, Günter, and read the name written on it aloud, please – be a darling.'

Programmed to respond to his owner's orders, the robot stretches one of his long, articulated arms out to the dish. His pincers close on one of the slips, like those machines at the funfair where for a bit of small change you can try to catch yourself a stuffed toy. Except that today, nobody wants to win.

The small piece of paper rustles as it's unfolded in Günter's pincers.

The synthetic, inhuman voice announces coldly: '*Léonor.*'

For a second, perhaps two, I'm perfectly still, unable to react, a cold sweat sticking my jersey-top to my skin. Then Safia makes a slight gesture with her hand, gently inviting me to approach.

I drag myself off my chair and walk with heavy steps over to the table that is acting as witness stand.

'Welcome, Léo,' says Safia, encouragingly. 'You were Marcus's first victim, and tonight you will be the first to speak. It's a heavy task – but it's also a privilege. To be the person to open the debate, and no doubt to influence it. Sometimes chance does get things right. We're listening.'

I thank her with a nod. At least I can express myself without having to look the defendant in the eye – will it be easier like this, in his absence?

'*Marcus's first victim,*' I repeat. 'I know that's how you all see me now, isn't it?' I look at the other ten jurors, forcing myself to calm my breathing and the beating of my heart. 'But I'm not just that poor little girl who got betrayed, deceived, duped. I'm also the fighter who, once, filling out her application form to join the Genesis programme, told herself that she was going to conquer the vastness of space and win eternal glory.'

The speech that had been spinning round and round my head all night and all day until it was no more than a mash-up of contradictory meaningless words gradually starts to make sense again as I speak it.

'Today the question we're being asked isn't only about Marcus's future. It's also – it's mainly – the question of *our own* future. Personally, I want to go back to being the girl I really am, the girl who boarded the rocket without giving love a second thought. I want to rally all my strength to face the months we still have to come, to resist Serena, to hang on until the self-energising elevator arrives. If you think our journey to Mars was demanding, I can assure you that our return to Earth will be a thousand times harder. I want to turn the *Marcus* page. Once and for all.'

As I talk I realise I'm breathing more easily, each word I speak carrying a bit of my distress away with it.

'Yes, we could execute Marcus, like Tao asked us to in his summing-up speech, and maybe that's what he deserves. But by killing him, I think we'd be killing ourselves a bit too. To judge him a murderer would be to admit that he has fatally injured us. It would be to admit that the past has condemned us. It would be to define us permanently as the thing I refuse to be: *a victim*.'

There's no more tension left in me now. There's just a confidence, a certainty of taking the straightest road for me, for us.

'There's another way of seeing things. We could turn our backs on the past and look only at the future. We could do better than punish Marcus: we could forget him, rather than have the memory of his execution weighing on our consciences for ever. Let's allow him to disappear alone into the deserts of Mars, like he asked us. Let's allow him to disappear into his Labyrinth of Night – not to do him a favour, but to preserve ourselves. To continue this adventure not just without him, but without his ghost either. I propose that we banish him, for evermore.'

I return to my seat in silence.

It may sound strange, but I feel at peace. It's not like the excitement I felt when I learned I'd been chosen for the Genesis programme, nor is it like the whirlwind of emotions that carried me away at the beginning of my story with Marcus. It's just the opposite: not the feeling of losing myself in a happiness that overwhelms me, but the sense of finding myself in the certainty of what is right.

'The court notes the sentence proposed by Léonor,' says Safia. 'It's time for the second juror to speak.'

Once again, Günter plunges his pincers into the bowl of small pieces of folded paper.

This time it's the name of his 'mother' that he reads in his emotionless voice.

'*Kirsten.*'

My beloved friend walks shyly towards the stand, her eyes flicking between Alexei and me. I can tell instinctively that she wants to make us both happy, and not to disappoint her husband who's certainly given her voting instructions, nor her best friend who has just spoken.

'Alex and I talked about the trial a lot last night in our room,' she says, confirming my hunch. 'We talked about what justice means and how Mankind can deliver it down here. Alex thinks that for justice to be done, it should always be equal to the crime. But I . . .'

Kris breathes out slowly. Her golden hair that's escaping from her crown of braids trembles slightly. The fine silk of her blue dress shivers like a wave. Her eyes go out of focus – they're no longer looking at Alexei, or at me, or at anyone: she's completely turned in on herself.

'. . . but I . . . I don't think human beings are always able to make justice happen. I think as a last resort there is someone greater, and wiser, who will judge us for our acts, for what we've done or failed to do. I believe there is . . . God.'

God – of course!

That was the weight I'd forgotten to put on the scales, the factor that would make Kris's conscience tilt further one way than the other: her profound faith.

'*Thou shalt not kill.*' She focuses again, to address the court. 'It's one of the Ten Commandments that every Christian should obey. If I voted for Marcus's death, I'd be damning myself. Léonor is right to say it's too heavy a decision for us to take . . .' She turns her blue eyes on me – I've never seen her so determined. '. . . and I also think we must demonstrate charity towards somebody who's sick and could die at any moment. I also vote for Marcus to be banished.'

Kris leaves the stand and walks back to Alexei. From the way his jaw is clenched, I suspect he's furious. But the moment is so solemn that he has to control himself and respect the process. It'll be his turn to speak soon enough.

'Two jurors have spoken in favour of banishment,' says Safia, with nothing in her voice to suggest whether she approves or disapproves of the direction the deliberations are heading.

Günter's voice is similarly toneless when it announces the name of the third pioneer who will be invited to speak.

'*Tao.*'

From his place on the sofa beside Safia, the large Chinese boy sits bolt upright as if he's suddenly awoken with a start.

Ever since he collapsed in the middle of yesterday's session, his face has shown some distress, something blurry like the surface of a lake disturbed by a swell that doesn't want to settle.

'It was me who called for Marcus's death, on behalf of the whole group,' says the guy who yesterday played the role of prosecuting attorney. '*The death penalty* – those were the words

I spoke myself. And when I said them, I promise I really did believe in them, that they were words spoken genuinely. But now . . .' Tao lowers his head slightly, as if it was suddenly too heavy even for his muscular neck. '. . . now I'm not sure of anything any more. I'm not sure what's good, and what's bad. Suddenly it feels like Marcus is beyond those . . . categories. He's betrayed me, as he betrayed you, letting me leave on a voyage to my death. But he also saved my life, secretly stopping me from killing myself. So I don't know what to say.'

Tao's mouth twists slightly. His shoulders tense up nervously under his white T-shirt. He searches for the words, he tries to hang on to the ideas that keep escaping. It pains me to see him like this, it reminds me of the moral torments I went through myself all night and all day long. I'm about to stand up and tell him to stop torturing himself, when he raises his head.

'In China, where I come from, we have a symbol – the Yin and Yang. You know the one – those two shapes that combine to form a single circle.'

He picks up his notebook and starts scribbling furiously, then turns it towards us.

'The Yin is black, the Yang is white,' he explains, showing us on the sketch. 'Yin and Yang are as different as night and day, empty and full, cold and hot . . . evil and good. But look – there's a white spot in the black part, and a black spot in the white part. Because nothing is ever totally black, or totally white. Because nobody is ever totally bad, or totally good.' He looks up from his picture at us. 'I'm not sure if I'm making sense? Sometimes I find it so hard to express what I mean.'

Yes, it makes sense, at least to me.

'Marcus is like that symbol,' I say. 'That's what you mean, isn't it?'

'Yes!' says Tao. 'He's done bad things, but he's also done good. The two things are inextricably mixed up in him. He doesn't deserve to be acquitted, or executed – not *white*, and not *black*. What he deserves is really *grey*. And that's banishment.'

Safia nods gravely.

My idea seems to be gaining ground, and it's even getting stronger as other people speak. Kris's Christian charity and Tao's Chinese wisdom both point in the same direction as my conscience: banishment really is the moral solution, the only humane way of us getting through this test.

'*Fangfang*,' Günter says suddenly, having just read another slip.

The Singaporean girl in the row in front of me stands up and walks mechanically towards the table.

She pulls nervously on her skirt and straightens her square glasses.

Behind their lenses, her eyes are careful to avoid Tao's, even though she seems to be addressing him.

'I'm sorry, Tao,' she says, 'but you're wrong. Even though you think you know about the Yin and Yang symbol, you're interpreting it wrong. The *taijitu* – that's what the symbol's really called – has nothing to do with good and evil.'

So far, Fangfang has always made a point of insisting on the cultural links between her and Tao – she's from Singapore, and he's from China. That's even why she chose him as her partner, right after the first speed-dating session in the Visiting Room. But today, for the first time, she's calling this link into question. Something between her and Tao has cracked beyond repair.

'Connecting the *taijitu* with some second-rate morality is a mistake that uninformed people often make,' she continues, somewhat coldly. 'The truth is, the Yin and Yang are just illustrations of opposing and complementary forces at play in the universe – forces that aren't themselves intrinsically good, or bad.'

She reaches over the table and picks up the notebook Tao has left there.

'The only thing that matters in the *taijitu* is the equilibrium between the forces,' she says, pointing to the two interlinked petals. 'There must be enough justice to amend the injustice. Someone who truly understands the *taijitu* would never start a war. But once a war has been started by somebody else, he will do anything in his power to end it, to win it and restore harmony.'

Fangfang breathes out slowly and, for the first time, meets Tao's gaze.

'Marcus started this war,' she murmurs.

The moment she says these words, I wonder what war she's

really talking about. The one between Marcus and the rest of the team? Or the one that seems – since yesterday's discovery of Tao's past – to have been declared between her and her husband?

'Marcus has broken our harmony.'

Who does that 'our' refer to? To the eleven jurors gathered in the seventh habitat? Or to Fangtao alone?

'Marcus should die.'

Fangfang's choice falls like a cleaver. I can't help thinking that, by condemning Marcus, it's Tao she's really trying to get to, and even more than him, the girl who has appeared between them: that girl Xia, who he's never forgotten.

'Three votes for banishment, one for death,' says Safia gravely, while Fangfang returns to her place and sits back down.

I feel a slight dizziness that sends me back several weeks to when we were still on board the *Cupido*. The craft had just reached the orbit of Mars, we'd all just learned of the existence of the Noah Report, and we needed to vote on whether to come down to land or turn straight around. Right now, a new vote is taking shape, and Safia has just laid out the possible outcomes. It was naive of me to think that all my teammates would come together unanimously behind my proposal.

There really is a choice.

There really are two possible outcomes.

Banishment or death.

'*Alexei*,' says Günter, tearing me from my thoughts. The Russian takes his turn to step up to the stand. With his perfectly ironed shirt and his impeccably combed blond hair, he looks like he's straight out of a fashion catalogue, a picture designed to seduce. But looking at the ferocity shining out from his too-blue eyes, I can guess that he won't be following my recommendation either. He won't be lining up with the choice already expressed by his partner.

'So religion doesn't allow us to kill killers . . . ?' he begins, turning on the digital tablet he's brought with him to the stand.

He's addressing Kris directly as much as the court, just like Fangfang addressed Tao as much as the rest of us – but unlike the Singaporean, Alexei stares straight into his wife's eyes from his very first words.

'You talked about the Ten Commandments. You asked us to have pity. You claim that men can't administer justice. You explain that it's all written in the Bible, and I know you must be saying all these things in good faith because you are goodness incarnate.'

In Alexei's words there is a quiet threat, the sweetness of his speech contrasting with the coldness in his eyes.

'Let me read you a brief passage, my angel. This tablet I have here is yours – the one with your file of the Bible. So you can't accuse me of falsifying the text. The extract I've chosen is from right near the beginning. In Exodus, chapter 21, verses 23–25 to be exact: "*But if an injury occurs, you will pay with a life for a life, an eye for an eye, a tooth for a tooth, a hand for a hand, a foot for a foot, a burn for a burn, a wound for a wound, a murder for a murder.*"'

Alexei looks up from the tablet.

'The *Lex talionis*,' he says simply.

Kris stands up, shaking.

187

'But that's such an ancient law!' she says.

'It is. It's the oldest law in the world. It's also the simplest, the most indisputable, which even a child of three could understand.'

'It goes totally against the message of the Gospels, which teach us about mercy and forgiveness!'

'And yet that law's written right here in black and white in your Bible, whether you like it or not. It hasn't lost any of its relevance. It was enforced scrupulously back where I used to live before I came onto the Genesis programme.'

Back where he used to live . . .

Alexei's mysterious Moscow past has never worried me as much as it does now: an unclear, shadowy universe, peopled by damned knights, by deadly revenges and inflexible laws. Every time I've talked to Kris about it, she's seemed to believe that with enough love and understanding she would be able to close up her husband's wounds. But today this past is catching up with her, overwhelming her. Crushing her. Lost for words, she sits quickly back down.

'If Marcus's betrayal has taught us anything, it's that New Eden needs rules,' says Alexei, turning towards the court. 'No human society can function without them – and the harder the conditions for survival, the tougher the laws must also be. Those are the conditions for order to reign and to save us from chaos. Marcus wanted our deaths. He deserves to receive his death in turn. Like it says in the Bible:

'An eye for an eye.

'A tooth for a tooth.

'A life for a life.'

* * *

'*Kelly*,' says Günter's digital voice soon after Alexei has returned to his place.

The Canadian girl wraps her chewing gum in a bit of paper and steps up to the stand.

Finally the nightmare is going to end, and the group will come back to its senses!

Two votes for death – well, that's definitely two too many, but they won't count for anything against the other nine!

'You all know me, I'm not the kind of girl who's going to swallow all the nonsense that's coming out of Fangfang's mouth,' Kelly begins. 'And I'm also not one of those girls who's going to get all hormonal whenever a guy like Alexei starts showing off his muscles. Eggheads don't impress me, and fascists even less ...'

Go, Kelly! You're one of us! I call out mentally.

'. . . but this time, I agree with them.'

What?

I blink, unable to believe the scene playing before my eyes. But there's no possible doubt: Kelly the libertarian, the rebel, the insurgent, is lining up alongside the reactionaries!

'Like all the rest of you, I thought about this a lot last night,' she says, fiddling nervously with her long blonde hair. 'I thought about our future, about the uncertain time ahead which according to Léo is the only thing we've got left, which we should bet everything on by wiping our past clear. Well, I know it's shitty to say it, but I can't do it. I can't forget the past. Whenever I close my eyes, I see my brothers' faces ... my mother's face. Yeah, I see all four of them, stupefied by that fucking zero-G, in the shabby little caravan where I grew up.

I remember all the times I tried to move them, to shake them out of it, and never managed to do it.

'I remember how frustrated I got when I was faced with that human trash, but they were still my only family, the people I loved more than anyone in the whole world.

'And most of all I remember my hatred when the dealer used to knock on the door and finally they dragged themselves off their sorry asses to hurry over to him. Like dogs running to meet the master who feeds them, too stupid to remember that it's him who beats them too.

'If I'd stayed on Earth, I know I'd have ended up running into that scumbag who thinks he's a living god, who played with my family's lives without giving a damn. Last night in bed I realised that must have been why I left: so I wouldn't end up with blood on my hands. I didn't sign that stupid application form for the Genesis programme to be a hero or because I had a taste for pushing my limits. The truth is, I deflated like an old tyre. I preferred to play the clown in dumb commercials and in a lame TV show than face up to my reality.'

A grimace twists Kelly's shining lips – anger, remorse, guilt. At the back of the room, Mozart stares at his feet, not daring to look up. But he – the former Aranha dealer – isn't the target of Kelly's bitterness tonight.

'Don't you think this is ironic?' she continues with a bitter smile. 'Today, at the far end of space, I'm in the same situation as my bros in their caravan. I'm facing a guy who's totally happy to let me die, with complete impunity. So yeah, I know, you're going to tell me he's also done nice things, Marcus, that he saved someone suicidal and all that crap. But those small actions are like a master who tosses his mutt a hunk of fat, like a dealer who lets his junkie have one free hit. It doesn't change all the blows, or the fact that finally the junkies and beaten dogs all end up dying. It just makes things worse. More *grey*, to use Tao's word. Fuzzier. More *disgusting*.'

Kelly snatches her hand quickly away from her hair.

'I don't want to lie down at my master's feet,' she says softly. 'I don't want to lick his hand. I'm going to bite it so hard I'll tear it apart. In my mother's name. In my brother's names. In the name of all the mutts in the world.'

27. Genesis Channel

Monday 8 January, 6:45pm

Open onto a huge snowy forest. The sound of barking coming from between the frozen tree trunks. All of a sudden, a sleigh pulled full-speed by huskies appears in frame.

Bundled up in her animal skins, the driver is wearing a beaver-fur hat on her head, from which windblown strands of long blonde hair are coming loose.

Zoom in: it's Kelly, her cheeks red from the cold, her lips vibrating with loud cries of encouragement: *'Yee-hoooo!* That's it, dogs! Faster! Faster!'

Eventually the sleigh disappears behind the pines, while instrumental music strikes up, mixing the warm rusticity of the harmonica with the modernity of the electronic organ.

A man's voice, big and deep, starts talking off-screen. *'We were born in Canada, where the wide open spaces have given us a taste for conquest . . .'*

Crossfade.

We're once again in a landscape that's covered in white, but this time there isn't a single tree in sight: it's an ice floe.

The purring of an engine, accompanied by a cracking of the ice.

The metallic prow of an icebreaker ship comes into frame, carving a path through the vast whiteness. Standing at the helm, a hat on her head, Kelly looks out at the horizon, inspired. Here and there, on the ice floe, polar bears follow the vessel's progress, cavorting happily.

The music rises in crescendo, while the voiceover continues. *'On Earth, in the sea and in the air, for a century we have pushed back frontiers . . .'*

Crossfade.

A dizzying effect transforms the prow of the ship into the deck of a spacecraft, and the bar in Kelly's hands becomes a steering lever.

The melody climbs to an epic summit, really trying to grab its listeners by the guts.

The voiceover has to struggle slightly to be heard above the enthusiastic tones of the harmonica. *'To this day,* Cruiser *is at the forefront of progress: it's our engines that power the* Cupido, *taking us further than ever before!'*

Kelly – in her space undersuit now – turns to the camera for the first time since the start of the commercial and speaks directly to the viewer. 'Whether you're travelling by boat, by train, by plane or by spaceship, do what I do – choose a piece of Cruiser equipment.' She gives the camera a wink. 'So – are you coming?'

High-speed zoom out.

The camera pulls out of the craft, which, using the effect of a blazing nuclear burst, disappears off into the stars.

The final logo appears in sparkling letters in the middle of the cosmos.

~~CRUISER~~→
Are you coming too?

Cut.

28. Shot

'*Samson,*' says Günter like a metronome.

Yes, that's what the robot has become – just like a metronome, unstoppable, motionless, marking out the time of our deliberations. Each time his metal pincers unfold a slip, each time his invisible mouth speaks a name, we get a little closer to the verdict.

Three votes for banishment and three votes for death: a dead heat. There's no way to predict how this match is going to end, after I was so quick to think I'd won it already.

Which team will Samson join?

What's going on behind those green eyes of his – as he takes his place at the stand – what train of thought, what private beliefs? I can't make him out. None of us was able to see who Samson really was, even after all these weeks we'd spent with him, and like everyone else I was astonished at his surprise outing.

'Yesterday, at this same stand, I insisted that Marcus had deceived us about himself,' he begins. 'I remembered how he'd

195

hidden behind a mask, that he'd lied to us all. And straight after that I got whacked by Liz's video.'

A drop of sweat forms on Samson's forehead, catching the gleam from the spotlights. His charcoal shirt is sticking to his back.

I can see he's just as nervous, just as uncomfortable, as I am right now.

Since the revelation of his homosexuality last night he hasn't had a chance to come back to the subject – with the cameras permanently rolling, he's had to keep playing straight in every way. But now, here in the privacy of the seventh habitat and in the beam of the eyes on him, he's once again the gay kid, the intruder, the homo who has no place in the Genesis programme.

I feel myself overtaken by a feeling of sympathy, rising up from the depths of my guts. It's a feeling that comes to me from very far away, drawing from my most painful childhood memories, feeding on all the insults I received because of the Salamander, because I was different – or rather, because I was *'monstrous'*, *'disgusting'*, *'freakish'*, *'only good for being put down'*, to use the words of the other kids who thought of themselves as 'normal'.

'Yesterday, when Liz started sharing the video, I first of all wanted to disappear,' Samson goes on, his nostrils flaring with emotion. 'If I'd been able to vanish, on the spot, I'd have done it. After that deadly shame came rage, when Alexei accused me of being a liar like Marcus. But the feeling I was left with the moment Mozart ran out of the habitat, making no effort to hide his revulsion, was injustice. Me – who for months had been doing everything I could to be a perfect friend, a model husband and an exemplary teammate, I hadn't deserved that!'

Samson's breathing is racing.

The drop of sweat trickles down his forehead, leaving a gleaming furrow from his brow down to his cheekbone.

'I hadn't deserved that,' he says again, a little quieter now. 'Or at least, that's what I thought yesterday when I left the trial. The night came, and with it came doubt. Like Kelly, I wasn't able to sleep, I couldn't stop thinking over the past. I watched my life spool past from the very beginning – my childhood in Nigeria, signing up to the Genesis programme, the trip to Mars . . . And the more I thought about it, the more I realised that that jerk Alexei was right about one thing: yeah, I was a liar. And the first person I'd lied to, for years and years, was myself.'

Samson bravely confronts the eyes all fixed silently on him – including Mozart's.

'At middle school and high school, when my pals started looking at girls, it was them I was looking at – but that's not something you talk about, specially not in Nigeria, and you'd have had to tear my eyes out before I'd have admitted it. Much later, I was gripped by last-minute doubts before we boarded and I told Serena McBee I wasn't sure about my sexuality – but she explained to me that I was imagining things, that I would recover from this passing phase, that speaking as a psychiatrist she was totally able to confirm that I was a completely regular straight guy. She didn't have to work too hard to persuade me. I wanted so badly to believe it. I preferred to live in denial rather than face up to myself, and so I boarded the rocket.

'The problem is, who we really are always ends up showing

197

its face. What I felt about Mozart may have been born in Death Valley, but it was in the closed environment of the spaceship that it exploded and burned through my brain. The forced intimacy of the boys on board the *Cupido* was real torture – specially when Mozart went up to the gym bare-chested to do his push-ups! Not to mention those gales of laughter, those lips always ready to hum a song, those eyes shining in the artificial glare of the spotlights – each of these missiles struck me a hundred times a day, without anything I could do to escape them. In those few square metres of our spacecraft, I couldn't run away, I couldn't lie to myself any more, I was forced to face up to the truth!

'And that truth became too big a weight for me to carry alone. The mask became too heavy, specially when I was facing the girl who might one day put me at the top of her Heart List – Safia deserved the very best, definitely not a liar like me. In despair, I asked Kenji to teach me his sign language, the code that the organisers taught the Communications Officers to allow them to exchange visual information in the event of the radio transmitters not working. That's how one morning, halfway between the Earth and Mars, I asked to see Safia in the Visiting Room and told her everything.'

Samson's eyes meet Safia's for a long moment, from her place on the sofa in front of him. I remember all those times they used their sign language between them, sometimes making Alexei furious. But today they don't need it to communicate: more than ever, we can sense a bond between them that is almost palpable.

With a nod, she encourages him to continue.

'It was in the glass bubble, with billions of people watching from Earth,' Samson remembers. 'But nobody seems to have paid any attention to our gestures, not even those who knew the sign language for the deaf that the Genesis code was based on. To the viewers, they must have been just the clumsy movements of first-time astronauts not yet used to weightlessness. They must have been totally focused on our words too. While my mouth poured out banalities to distract the public, my hands revealed my most deeply buried secret to Safia. Using the signs, I laboriously admitted to her that I was gay. I thought maybe she was going to get angry, or worst of all she would laugh; there would have to be a price to pay. But she didn't get angry. She didn't laugh. With a few simple gestures she answered, using her own hands, that it wasn't serious. Then – in full view of our audience, this time out loud – she said again that she wanted to marry me.'

For the first time since he's started speaking, Samson's face relaxes. His full lips show a tender smile, with a flash of his white teeth. Safia smiles back, sweetly, as though in a mirror – yes, that's it: like two soulmates, reflected in one another.

'Over the course of the speed-dating, using a combination of sign language and words with double meanings, we came to an agreement about keeping up appearances. We agreed to submit to the Heart Lists, to the marriages, to everything about the Genesis programme. Nobody but us was to know – not the viewers, not the pioneers, and especially not Mozart. Ever since arriving on Mars, we've played the perfect couple. I think I could have gone on playing that part till the end of my days, protected by Safia's love – because what we have between us is love too, even if there's no sex.'

The way Samson and Safia look at one another, it's impossible to have any doubt about the strength of the bond that holds them together. A platonic love? A loving friendship? What do words matter, anyway? When you come down to it, only actions matter.

'Last night, faced with Liz's tablet, everything I thought I'd managed to conquer collapsed on top of me,' says Samson finally. 'Like I told you: shame, anger, a sense of injustice. But when I got up this morning, after a sleepless night, I was actually relieved. Since the sharing of the video, I can finally be myself with all the people I spend all my time with every day. Thanks to Liz, the person I care for the most in the world no longer has to carry the weight of a secret that isn't really hers.'

Samson's smile shines a bit brighter, as he turns towards the English girl. She stammers the beginning of an apology.

'I-I didn't show the film to hurt you – I was just trying to save Marcus.'

'I know, Liz. And I should thank you, not only for him but for myself too.'

He speaks his final words to the whole gathering.

'As counsel for the plaintiff, it's not my job to find mitigating circumstances for the defendant; but as a human being, I can feel sorry for him. For years, he's felt he had to hide his mutation – maybe because he desperately wanted to forget about it himself, maybe because he was afraid that other people would see him only through that one thing. I can understand that. And I'm sure his life would have been totally different if he'd dared to speak earlier, instead of shutting

200

himself up, alone and in secret. Please understand: whatever cards we're dealt at birth, each one of us is responsible for our actions. Marcus's suffering in no way excuses his crime. But we have the right to sympathise with that suffering. And we also have the right to think that – for him, as well as for any one of us – some redemption is always possible.

'I don't vote for execution, nor for a banishment that would really be no better than a brief reprieve. I vote for detention. We'll keep Marcus prisoner in this habitat, until he's served whatever sentence the court decides on, or until his illness takes him naturally.'

After this long speech, Samson steps away from the stand under the dumbfounded stares of the jurors. Even Mozart himself is looking at him with a mixture of astonishment and admiration, so differently from the way he looked at him yesterday.

Detention?

Is that really a possibility?

All that matters, right now, is that Samson didn't vote for death, and that the scales are tipped towards survival once again.

'*Safia*,' Günter calls out, as if luck itself was powerless to separate this couple – so unlikely and yet so united.

For the first time since the start of deliberations, the Indian girl gets up from the sofa where she's been presiding, and she walks to the stand where she is to speak as a juror.

'I can back up everything Samson has said,' she says confidently, determined. 'And I should warn you, I won't put up with any sarcastic comments, any criticism of the bond we have, Samson and me. We aren't a couple like the rest of you.

201

But we're still a couple. Just as good as yours. And I won't let anybody spoil what we've got. '

It would never have occurred to me to question the strength of that relationship, which I've witnessed so very clearly just now. More surprisingly, Alexei and Mozart hold their tongues too, and listen reverently to Safia.

'Samson is a person I admire enormously, a fundamentally good guy, with a rock-hard sense of morality. I'd give my life for him, and he would give his life for me. But today it's not our lives we're talking about, it's Marcus's. And I'm not sure I can support Samson in his suggestion.'

Everybody in the habitat seems to be holding their breath.

Even the fabric of Safia's sari seems to freeze in the air, totally still.

'Yes, detention might perhaps seem like the most humane sentence in theory, but it's not something we could do in practice. So far, we've been able to keep Marcus away from the cameras by claiming he's ill, and that it was best not to move him from the place where he collapsed. The organisers and the viewers seem to be content with those explanations right now, but their patience won't last for ever. In a few days, they're going to start insisting on seeing the American boy. The sponsors will demand that. So there's no way we'll be able to hide it. We'll have to bring his confinement to an end and let him out of the seventh habitat.'

Safia's reasoning is impossible to argue with, and she knows it, and I know it, and we all know it.

Detention just doesn't hold water. We'd have to release the prisoner almost immediately.

But Safia will choose banishment, then, won't she?'

'As for allowing Marcus to go out alone into the Martian desert, towards the Noctis Labyrinthus, that's a solution that speaks to my heart but it does violence to my brain. If we let him go as he's asked us, we'll need to construct some story to pull the wool over the viewers' eyes, a solo planetology expedition that ends badly because he never comes back. But for the few hours in which Marcus will be in the view of the New Eden cameras, how's he going to behave? Who in this room can predict with any certainty what he'll be like?'

At first, the response to Safia's question is silence.

Then, feeling like there's something important at play, I speak out.

'He's promised he'd disappear quietly,' I say. 'Those are the words he used, remember: *I promise you I'll go quietly; you'll never hear of me again.*'

But Safia shakes her head softly.

'If we know one thing about Marcus,' she says, 'it's that we don't know anything. He's totally unpredictable. He's a friend who can save Tao one day, then only weeks later betray his teammates, letting them get tangled up in a deadly trap; he's the Genesis contestant who can lie to his wife-to-be, and then risk his life for her. By letting him out of this habitat, whether it's after a period of detention or at the start of his exile, we'd be taking a huge risk: what if he throws everything away as soon as he's in view of the cameras? Whether it's out of resentment, out of revenge or just madness, thinking his final hour has come, it'd only take him a few words to reveal the existence of the Noah

203

Report to the whole world, to break our pact with Serena and cause the base to be depressurised.'

Safia takes a deep breath.

'I couldn't sleep last night either,' she says quietly, her voice suddenly sounding tired and very far away, as weak as an old lady's voice crushed down by the years. 'I went over and over the problem in my head, turned it around and around, trying to find the fairest solution. I've come to a conclusion that's cruel, but clear. What's at stake in Marcus's trial isn't only his sentence. It's also, and mainly, our survival. And if we have the moral obligation to judge a guilty man fairly, we have an even greater duty to protect the lives of eleven people who are innocent. That's what my conscience tells me. Even if a part of me revolts against the conclusion, I know it's the fairest one – or the least unfair one anyway.' Her voice is little more than a murmur, as she ends: 'We must kill Marcus off-screen, and when we present his body to the cameras we say he succumbed to his illness: that's the only way to avoid the risk of all eleven of us dying.'

'*Elizabeth.*'

I barely hear Günter summoning the defence attorney to the stand.

I'm stunned, speechless.

Eight jurors have already said what they think, and half of them have voted for death. I'm sure Liz won't be joining them, but after her? There are only two more voices to be heard: Mozart and Kenji.

'Yesterday I defended Marcus as best I could, with some

methods I'm not proud of, but they were the only things I had,' Liz begins. 'The fact that you're thanking me, Samson – that's just wild! I'm glad enough that you're even forgiving me!'

I'm listening to the English girl's voice, but not looking at her. My eyes are flicking back and forth between Mozart and Kenji, Kenji and Mozart, as if I were trying to read their thoughts. Waste of time. The Brazilian's bronze face is impenetrable. The space helmet on the Japanese boy's head is just a mirror reflecting the room – can he really hear everything that's being said, through the speakers in his helmet? There's no way of knowing.

'I'm not going to drag the suspense out unnecessarily,' Liz goes on. 'I'm adding my voice to Samson's, and voting for detention, even if it has to be short. It's the most lenient sentence, I'm aware of that. I'm also aware that some of you wouldn't be satisfied with that. The thirst for revenge that's grabbed some of you by the guts, which Kelly was talking about . . . The need to set up clear laws so that order can reign, as Alexei says . . . I can understand those things. And I can understand Safia just as well, when she explains pragmatically that the survival of eleven people weighs more in the balance than the survival of just one. But the issue we're facing isn't just a question of arithmetic, I'm certain of it. What counts isn't just the number of people who survive, it's also the quality of that survival.'

I'm touched by the poignant sincerity that makes Liz's voice tremble, and I finally manage to look at her. And I realise she's no longer addressing the rest of the court but Mozart and Kenji, the two who haven't yet voted – like me, she understands that the outcome of the trial is going to depend on them.

'What matters isn't just that we satisfy our desire for revenge,' she says, her eyes shining – suddenly back in her role as defence attorney. 'It's also the aftertaste the revenge leaves us, the bitterness that we'll have in our mouths until our final breath.

'As for establishing the order without which no society can exist . . . We also need to know what kind of society we want to create on Mars. Because ultimately, that's the real question we need to deal with. We have this unique opportunity: to build a utopia on this untouched land, starting from scratch. Even if this utopia only lasts a few months or a few years before we're saved or killed, the responsibility for what we've created will be ours alone.'

Liz really has all my attention now.

With her dancer's bearing, her majestic natural grace, she seems to rise above the rest of the group, even above herself – and what she says raises the debate above the grim facts of the trial too.

Her calm eloquence is in such contrast to her hesitation last night, it transforms her.

Her words aren't just beautiful, they're also profoundly true.

Liz is right, I can feel it in every fibre of my being: our responsibility goes beyond our own personal survival.

'We're the first Martians in history,' she goes on, 'the first inhabitants of this planet. In the name of the Earth and of humanity, we have a duty to dream of a new world, just like in the Dvořák symphony.

'Personally I dream of a world where the death penalty is never a solution.

'I dream of a world where everyone is allowed a second chance.

'I dream of a world where redemption is possible.

'Yes, the world I dream of is one that offers all those things I had no right to on Earth myself.'

Liz's voice pauses in mid-flight. She won't say any more about her past, which – I suddenly realise – we all know nothing about. Instead she ends her plea with a question, looking first at Mozart, then at Kenji.

'What about you? What kind of world do you dream of?'

'*Kenji*,' says Günter, unfolding one of the two remaining slips.

The thick white suit gets up from the chair in front of me and moves slowly towards the table. There's something surreal about this swollen astronaut shape in the middle of all of us in our civilian clothes. More than ever I can't help feeling Kenji is somehow separate, different from all the rest of us. It's not just his sick paranoia, the suspicion that led him to wiretap the base, the caution that makes him keep his helmet on whenever he can. It's his mystery, my sudden and painful awareness that I know nothing about his past, no more than I know about Liz's. I'm unable to predict which side he's going to take, and this uncertainty grips my throat tight.

The astronaut gloves rise up silently in the space in front of Kenji, like the white hands of a mime artist – his helmet may have earphones, but it doesn't have a loudspeaker. Sign language is the only way he can communicate with the court.

'*Marcus . . . has asked . . . us to banish him . . .*' Safia

207

translates out loud, deciphering the coded gestures of her Communications counterpart.

I breathe a little more easily.

Kenji is going to vote for banishment, adding his voice to Kris's and Tao's voices, and to mine. Including the two votes from Samson and Liz, who chose detention, that will be six out of eleven against the death penalty: an absolute majority.

'. . . *which means . . . he's asked for . . . a reprieve of thirty-six hours,*' Safia goes on translating.

My diaphragm clenches again.

What did she just say?

Did she interpret Kenji's gestures correctly?

'*Thirty-six hours . . . that's the capacity the spacesuits have to survive independently . . . during external sorties.*'

Beneath the living room's spotlights, Kenji's helmet gleams like a crystal ball in which the future is starting to take shape before my eyes, all too clearly.

'*By choosing to leave . . . Marcus has chosen suicide . . . It's a noble and honourable way out . . . like that chosen by the . . . the . . .*'

Safia hesitates, gesturing to Kenji for him to repeat a word she doesn't understand, which perhaps isn't a part of their sign language.

The Japanese guy plants himself heavily on his boots, legs bent, and mimes the movements of a martial art as if he had an invisible sabre in his gloved hands. With his helmet and outfit looking like a suit of armour, you'd think he was a . . .

'*Samurai!*' cries Safia, understanding at the same time I do. '*It's the path that the Samurai would choose . . . committing*

suicide . . . when they'd lost a battle. We should allow Marcus . . .
the thirty-six hours he is asking for . . . but he should spend them
here . . . in the seventh habitat . . . without cameras.'

Like the conductor of an orchestra, Kenji raises his hands
one last time, a little higher than before, for the conclusion.

'Marcus should die . . .' Safia translates, '. . . thirty-six hours
after his sentence has been proclaimed.'

Kenji's arms drop back down to his sides.

Without any more gestures, he returns to his seat.

Mozart steps forward before Günter has even spoken his name.

He gets to the witness stand just as the metallic pincers pick
up the last piece of paper – the robot continues mechanically
to do the task he's been assigned, even if there's no longer
any point, even if we all know the final juror's name already.

The Brazilian's jaw clenches and relaxes in turn. His thick
black hair rises over the back of his neck in time with his
breathing. The veins bulge on his muscular forearms, under his
rolled-up sleeve: I imagine that in the pocket of his jeans he's
gripping onto the handle of his knife like an amulet, a talisman.

'Mozart,' Günter's monotone voice says at last, not quite
keeping up.

Only now does Mozart open his lips and begin to talk.

'So it's all up to me then, right?' he says. 'Five votes for
execution – if I add mine, that's it – game over.'

His eyes fall on the table in front of him.

In its large family-size dish that Kris brought in with her, the
dinner has stopped its fragrant steaming. The béchamel sauce
has solidified on the frozen Astronaut Meal, forming a waxy

beige crust. The flask of sedative looks horribly like a little bottle of wine, placed there to accompany this repulsive meal.

'Since I met Marcus, we've had some great moments of friendship,' Mozart continues. 'We've had our rivalries, too, our differences . . .'

No need to explain that Mozart is referring to me when he says this.

On the table the sharp needle of the syringe is gleaming almost magically – like the spinning wheel where Sleeping Beauty pricked her finger before falling into a very long sleep.

'. . . but today I've got to forget all that. Today I'm not a friend any more, or a rival. I'm a judge, because the responsibility for settling the argument falls to me.' An ironic smile, painful as a graze, passes across Mozart's lips. 'Jesus – a judge!' he says again. 'Me, the little thug from the favelas! Me, the pedlar of illusions, the bastard, the scumbag! What am I supposed to do? Show some understanding for a guy who – like me – sent loads of people to their deaths? Or be pitiless, like the judges would have been with me in Rio if they'd caught me? There's only one thing that's certain: I've screwed up enough lives as it is, from the days when I was palming off the Aranha's shit on Ipanema Beach. I can try anything to persuade myself that it wasn't my fault, that I had no choice but to deal, that I wasn't responsible – but I know it's not true. Like Samson said, each one of us is responsible for his actions. I could have refused to keep distributing Zero-G, even if it meant getting a bullet in my head.

'It's just like that today. If I let Marcus go and he spills everything in front of the cameras, I'll be the only person responsible. Personally, it doesn't matter very much if I die, but adding another ten victims to my tally, that's not something I can let myself do. That's why I have to vote for Marcus's death – because it's my responsibility to do that.'

At first I feel a buzzing in my ears, like when you've just heard a cannon firing, or when you come out of a club where the music was too loud.

Then bit by bit I become aware of the little voice that has reawakened at the back of my neck and is whispering to me.

(So there it is, Léo . . . the sentence has been decided . . . a sentence that is unavoidable, irreversible, chosen by the majority: death . . .)

I open my mouth to speak, but no sound comes out.

I already know that any words will be pointless.

I've immediately submitted myself to the group's will, and I spontaneously offered to be the person who carried out the sentence, whatever it may be.

'The jury has spoken,' I hear Safia's voice far away. 'It has voted for death, six votes out of eleven, a sentence which – according to Kenji's request – will be carried out thirty-six hours after it has been announced. Call in the defendant.'

(Take a good look at that syringe . . .)

The lever of the door to the second bedroom clicks open.

(Imagine that sharp needle, going into Marcus's arm . . .)

The sound of footsteps against the aluminium floor.

(Imagine yourself at the other end, your finger on the plunger . . .)

A figure in a black undersuit comes to a stop at the stand, flanked by Mozart and Alexei whose silhouettes look blurred, as if I'm seeing them through a filter.

(Will you take your time, or press it all in one go . . . ?)

'Marcus, you have been found guilty of murder and aggravated lying, crimes you have already yourself acknowledged. The jury has turned down your request for exile and condemns you to death by lethal injection. However, the court will grant you a reprieve of thirty-six hours before the sentence is carried out.'

'That won't be necessary.'

The defendant's answer pulls me harshly back into the here and now.

The habitat resumes its shape all around me – terrifyingly real.

Marcus's face looks like it did on the first day. His mouth has almost healed. His relaxed features show no sign of disappointment, or fear, or even anger. His eyes gleam as if they were already reflecting some other sky.

'I've had all night and all day to prepare myself mentally for this outcome,' he says quietly, in that hoarse voice. 'I would have preferred if it had been different, of course, but that's how it is. Please, don't make me stew any longer, spare me another night of waiting in that cell. Since you've made your decision, I'd rather the sentence be carried out now.'

29. Genesis Channel

Monday 8 January, 7:30pm

Open onto a modern interior.

A black leather sofa decorated with cushions attached with Velcro, a ceramic-tiled kitchen area, a holographic fireplace: at first sight, you'd think you were looking at the living room on the *Cupido*. But looking closer, you see it's only a trick. The sofa is not the same shape as the one on the spacecraft, which has become as familiar to fans of the Genesis channel as if it were a part of their own homes; the kitchen area doesn't display quite the same range of implements; the colour of the holographic flames dancing in the hearth is just slightly different.

It's a set that was constructed in a studio for filming a commercial, long before the rocket's lift-off.

But still a caption appears at the bottom of the screen inviting viewers to pretend that these are images taken from the programme: VOYAGE OF THE *CUPIDO*, 4TH MONTH IN SPACE, BOYS' QUARTERS.

An astronaut enters the frame, wearing a spacesuit. He removes his helmet, to reveal the smiling face of Marcus, who

213

then rubs his belly, saying: 'Missions into space can be hungry work! I'm ravenous! Let's see what we've got in the pantry.'

He turns around and opens the first cupboard in the kitchen area: it's empty.

He opens the second cupboard: also empty.

He exclaims, with a grimace: 'Aargh! We're running really low on provisions! There's only one thing for it: magic.'

With a theatrical gesture, he turns his helmet upside-down like a magician's top hat, puts his hand inside . . .

. . . and pulls out a large transparent bag full of brown seeds.

Marcus's thick brown eyebrows frown as he puts the bag on the brushed-steel dining table. 'Sunflower seeds? They're fine for a snack, but a man can't live on them.'

He puts his hand inside his helmet once again . . .

. . . to pull out a second bag even larger than the first, this one full to bursting with yellow seeds.

'Grains of wheat? If I have to wait for these to grow, I'm not likely to get any dinner!'

For a third time, he rummages in his seemingly bottomless helmet . . .

. . . and pulls out a huge bag of white cuttlefish bones.

Marcus's famous half-smile appears on his lips. 'Oh, OK, I think I get it now!' He puts the third bag down next to the first two and calls down into the depths of his helmet: 'Hey, Ghost, old pal, I think you've stored up enough for a whole year! I'll let you keep your seeds and your grains of wheat, but, say – haven't you got a little something for me too?'

At these words, a white shape appears out of the helmet. It's a dove.

In its beak, instead of an olive branch, the bird is carrying a small packet covered in stars and multi-coloured writing.

Marcus's face lights up. 'Yum! A frozen *Astronaut Meal* from Eden Food! Easy to store in even the smallest freezers, and it fills out all on its own in the microwave: a perfect individual portion for bachelors who haven't yet found their perfect partner!'

He takes the packet, and the dove flies around to perch on his shoulder.

Marcus turns to the camera for a final shot. 'Thank you, Ghost . . . and thank you, Eden Food!'

The camera zooms in on the product, and the brand wording appears beside it:

✦Astonaut meals: ✦
Compact, low-cal and delicious!
Taking bachelors to seventh heaven!

A tag showing a very recent offer appears by the commercial's final image – a cartoon character inspired by Ghost, the dove, which flaps its wings while saying in a nasal voice: '*Special MAGIC offer! Right now, every Astronaut Meal you purchase will entitle you to a fifty per cent discount on your first Leorcus gastro dish!*'

Cut.

30. Shot

Mozart leads Marcus to the armchair at the end of the room, and with a slight pressure on his shoulder, an almost friendly gesture, he makes him sit down.

'Your arm, pal . . .' he murmurs softly, the way you murmur a prayer.

Without a word, Marcus pulls the right-hand sleeve of his black undersuit up to his elbow, revealing his forearm covered in tattoos and veins.

There's a small sharp noise: it's the stopper of the phial of sedative coming out in Alexei's hand. He sticks the syringe needle into it and pulls gradually on the plunger, sucking the colourless liquid up into the barrel. It looks like water, that basic thing on which life depends, not a poison that can bring death – just pure water.

Because that's the impression I get right now, in the middle of this silent room, with nobody speaking: what I sense is a great purity. A perfect innocence. As if we were at the beginning of the world.

Alexei turns towards me and holds out the filled syringe. In his elegant hands – real pianist's hands – the syringe looks like a sparkling glass slipper.

Abandoning my sketching tablet, I get slowly to my feet. The Salamander chants a refrain, which, for the first time, has nothing aggressive about it at all.

(Tonight, you're going to be Cinderella . . .)

This familiar voice cradles me, carries me, as I move towards Alexei.

(Tonight, you really will go to the ball . . .)

Maybe, deep down, I've always been wrong about the Salamander, thinking it's an evil genie when it's really been my guardian angel, my fairy godmother, all along.

(Tonight, you'll leave all your worries and your problems behind you . . .)

My fingers brush against Alexei's, closing on the smooth glass of the syringe. I take hold of it. There's something about its weight in my hand, something . . . reassuring?

(You are the queen of the night, tonight . . .)

I move away from Alexei and turn towards the chair where Marcus is waiting, unmoving.

He too is handsome.

More handsome than ever.

My steps carry me effortlessly towards him.

I crouch down beside the chair, next to the armrest where his arm is lying. He is totally offering himself to me. And I feel I'm offering myself totally to him.

My finger strokes the curve of his elbow, snakes around the calligraphy brambles, seeking the most prominent vein. I find it. Beneath the pad of my index finger I can feel Marcus's blood flowing, his heart beating.

I look up.

My eyes meet his.

He's been watching me unblinking from the start, his eyes the colour of a storm.

The colour of a cloud.

The colour of cinders.

(Yes, you're the queen of the night, but at the moment the clock strikes midnight that queen will go back to being a kitchen maid – cinders, cinders, Cinderella!)

My hand starts trembling.

I let the syringe slip between my sweaty fingers.

Suddenly I become aware of Kris's stifled sobs, of Liz's constrained breathing, of the dreadful sound that some kind of spell seems to have been masking from my ears.

My eyes fall onto Marcus's arm: the needle has gone in without my even noticing. A drop of blood beads on one of the raised stems covered in thorns, like a red berry.

There are also letters tattooed between the brambles and leaves around it. One of those quotations that Marcus's body is covered in: *I can't change the direction of the wind, but I can adjust my sails to always reach my destination.*

And even higher up, in capital letters, one single word: *CHOICE.*

My choice.

What am I doing?

Oh God, what am I doing!

'I can't . . .' I murmur.

(You can't what, Léonor?)

(Press down the plunger and inject the deadly drug into Marcus's body?)

(Let go of the syringe, and go back on your promise to carry out the sentence?)

(Don't kid yourself – you haven't got any choice!)

The Salamander is right. I swore to abide by the group's decision. I know that if I shirk that responsibility, the group will tear itself apart and it'll never be put right. Marcus has to die.

(There's no alternative: he has to die.)

The thorny tattoos start to wave in my field of vision.

(He has to die.)

A figure appears from amid the interlacing of sharp lines.

(He has to die.)

It's a picture of a cat, its shape melting into the leaves.

The moment I recognise Schrödinger's cat, which is dead and alive at the same time, an idea shoots through my brain and a cry bursts from my throat like a thunderclap.

'Take him back to his cell!'

The pioneers look at me with a mixture of surprise and horror.

'Take him back to his cell!' I shout again, jumping to my feet, yanking the syringe from Marcus's arm and leaving a trickle of blood. 'The court has decided that Marcus has to die in thirty-six hours. We don't have to do what he asks and execute him at his request. He's the one who has to obey our sentence!'

Cruel words, I know, but essential for saving what can still be saved. I say them with such authority that Mozart and Alexei

jump into action without asking any questions, and force Marcus to his feet. I keep my eyes fixed straight ahead while the jailers drag the prisoner over to the second room. *Whatever you do, don't catch his eye.* When I hear the door lever clicking shut at last, I immediately carry on, my heart racing.

'Listen to me! I needed to get the condemned man out of here before speaking to you. The court has decided he's got to die: so be it. But the most important thing is that he dies in the eyes of the whole world, that's the cost of our security. That's why three of you chose capital punishment, isn't it?'

My burning gaze moves between Safia, Kenji and Mozart, the three who voted for execution not out of revenge but to ensure our survival.

'Marcus *should* die as far as the viewers are concerned,' I say. 'But hidden from them, he can pay a different penalty. A penalty that will sit more easily on our consciences. Like perpetual confinement, for example. I've just had an idea. An idea I'd like to propose to the court, now that the defendant's back in his cell.' I gulp down some air, but there's no time to breathe out again, the words are crowding into my mouth. 'We have the unique possibility of killing him without making him die. He can be both dead and alive at the same time. Like Schrödinger's cat in its box. Dead to the Earth. Alive in the secret world of Mars.'

Clinging onto the sofa, Safia echoes my words.

'Dead to the Earth? You mean you want to announce Marcus's death without us executing him?'

'Exactly,' I say, breathless. 'We can say he's died from symptoms of the illness, just as predicted.'

'But the viewers are going to want to see the body.'

'With the 3D printer and my Rosier make-up kit, I'm certain I can pull off the illusion. I'm sure I can sculpt a doll to look like Marcus, which we'll bury in his place beneath the Martian soil. After that, nobody on Earth will ever ask to see him or hear from him again, because officially he'll be dead and buried.'

A leaden silence falls after I say my piece.

I know I'm playing for high stakes, really high: the unity of the group, my word of honour and a man's life are all at risk. If the others don't follow me, I could lose everything.

'He'll be locked in this habitat for months,' murmurs Mozart. 'We'll have to bring him his meals on the quiet. It's going to take one hell of an effort, to keep up the illusion that he's really dead.'

I suddenly have a terrible urge to hug Mozart tight in my arms.

This boy who voted for Marcus's death, he hasn't yet said he agrees with my proposal but he's thinking the possibility through realistically.

'Yes, Mozart, it's going to take some effort!' I say. 'But together we can all do it!'

'Hang on,' Fangfang interrupts me. 'What are we going to do in one Martian year's time when the *Cupido* and the candidates for Season Two arrive?'

'We'll persuade the new crew not to land. We'll evacuate the base to join them on the orbiting craft. We'll leave Marcus behind us – neither the new pioneers, nor the viewers, nor even the organisers are ever going to know. Once we've left for good, that'll be the end of the Genesis programme and the New Eden cameras will stop rolling: Marcus will be left alone here, and no one will suspect a thing.'

'If he's alone, he'll end up dying,' says Kelly. 'Even if the next Great Storm doesn't do him in, there's no way he can keep the base operational without his teammates and the logistical support from Earth.'

'Yes, Kelly, you're right. He will die. But it won't be us who killed him: it'll be Mars. And that makes all the difference.'

The Canadian and Singaporean girls don't answer.

Because they are running out of objections?

Or because they, both of them, can see the virtues of the solution I'm suggesting?

'Hey, what the hell's going on?' asks Alexei suddenly. 'What are we talking about? I thought we'd all voted! There's no reason to go back on a legal decision. If Léo isn't able to press the fucking syringe then I can do it myself!'

He moves towards me – no doubt to grab the syringe out of my hands – but Liz positions herself between us.

'Everyone, stop!' she cries. 'I . . . I'm appealing the sentence. As defence lawyer I've got every right – it's just as much part of the legal process as the sentence itself.' She turns to Safia. 'I ask the court for a new phase of deliberations, in the light of this new information.'

The presiding judge nods.

'Granted. We'll vote. Raise your hands if you agree with the adjustment to the penalty as proposed by Léo.'

As she speaks these words, Safia herself raises her own henna-painted hand.

It's no surprise that all those who were against the death penalty during the trial copy her immediately: Liz, Kris, Tao and Samson.

I'm filled with a feeling of relief when I raise my fist that is still gripping the syringe: I know that my voice, the sixth out of eleven, will be enough for us to carry a majority.

But what I feel when Mozart, Kelly, Fangfang and Kenji raise their hands in turn, and in doing so move from the side of death to that of life, is much more than relief: it's a feeling of infinite gratitude that swells my heart and makes me warm inside.

A group.

We are – once again – a group. Bonded, united, together.

With one exception: Alexei, arms folded over his chest, his face frozen in an expression of hatred that is aimed entirely at me.

31. Reverse Shot

Vice-presidential residence, Washington DC
Tuesday 9 January, 2:45pm

'Here I am, Mr President,' announces Serena McBee as she enters the Oval Office in the White House.

Today she is wearing an elegant Asian-inspired pant suit, in purple raw silk, accessorised with a variety of jewels.

Her cheerful tone of voice is in contrast with the gloomy expression of President Green, wedged in his armchair, shoulders slumped. Sitting on the opposite side of the desk are Dolores Ortega, responsible for the president's image – she lowers her eyes as soon as Serena enters the room – and a man aged fiftyish in a light-coloured suit, whose mid-length blond hair and pug nose make him look slightly leonine.

'Thank you for answering my call so quickly,' says Edmond Green, gesturing to a third chair which stands empty.

'But of course, Mr President, I'm always happy to hand over my work producing the Genesis programme to my team in order to fulfil my vice-presidential duties – and in any case, there's not much interesting happening just now. The pioneers have all been attending to their routine activities since this morning.'

'The programme is the very thing I wanted to talk to you about,' says President Green, with a worried look.

'Oh!' says Serena. 'You aren't still fretting about the costs of the self-energising elevator, are you? I've already given you my promise that Atlas Capital will pay for the lot.'

'I'm not talking about a financial problem on this occasion, but a diplomatic one. I'd rather let Secretary of State Sunfield explain the situation. Milton, over to you.'

The blond man nods.

'Thank you, Mr President.' He turns to Serena. 'Madam Vice-President, the Russian and Chinese delegations to the United Nations are proposing a resolution this morning calling the Genesis programme into question.'

The vice-president raises an eyebrow.

'Calling it into question? What do you mean? I don't see how a bit of entertainment broadcasting is anything to do with the U.N.?'

The secretary of state gives a kind of purr that makes him sound more like a hoarse old tomcat than the king of beasts.

'According to the Russian and Chinese governments, the Genesis programme is a lot more than a bit of entertainment broadcasting. It is – and I'm quoting the Russian ambassador to the U.N. here – "*an imperialist project for conquering Mars to the exclusive benefit of the United States, flaunting all the rules of international law.*"'

Serena McBee bursts out laughing.

'An imperialist project?' she scoffs. 'What a ludicrous idea! The Genesis programme is a commercial undertaking, it's totally apolitical.'

'Yes, but the rockets lift off from American soil.'

'So?' responds Serena with a shrug. 'They could lift off from Timbuktu or the North Pole, I don't see how that would make any difference. The launch platform, the spacecraft, the New Eden base – it all belongs to an international investment fund. And the make-up of the crew is just as diverse, there's something for everyone. Pioneers from all those different countries are helping one another to survive on Mars – a beautiful image of solidarity among nations. The U.N. should award us a medal instead of trying to pick a quarrel with us.'

The secretary of state sighs deeply.

'You're right, Ms McBee, that's the spirit in which the Genesis programme has been run, and that's how the whole world thought of it when it began. But something's changed lately . . . I think, since you entered the government, our counterparts have struggled to see the programme as an *apolitical undertaking*, to use your words. They see the hidden hand of the United States of America behind it.'

Serena McBee folds her arms, indignant.

'What's your point, Milton?' she says, looking her interlocutor up and down. 'Do you want me to resign from the vice-presidency, is that it?'

'No, no, not at all!' says the secretary of state, appalled. 'That's not the idea at all! On the contrary, we need you, now more than ever.' He is wriggling around in his chair, like a naughty kid forced to admit he's done something wrong. 'In their draft resolution, Moscow and Beijing are claiming sovereignty over a part of the New Eden base and of the territory discovered over the course of the programme. Moreover, the Russians

227

and Chinese are asking to be able to make contact with their nationals: they demand direct communications access to Alexei and Tao, in such a way that they don't need to go via the Genesis network.'

'I see,' says Serena McBee icily. 'Yesterday I was being asked to squeeze billions of dollars out of Atlas Capital to fund the self-energising space elevator. Today, I'm supposed to go meet the board and tell them that the installations they purchased at exorbitant expense are being requisitioned by other countries.'

'We can ask the Russians and Chinese to contribute towards the costs,' the secretary of state hurries to point out. 'At least relating to the purchase of the habitats of their nationals? Um . . . a, uh, rebate would be a welcome gesture, of course, and would contribute towards good relations with our dear neighbours.'

Serena is about to reply, but at that moment her bee-shaped brooch-mic beeps loudly.

'My apologies,' she says, rifling through her handbag to pull out her cellphone. 'I put my phone on silent, but this alert can only mean it's something urgent. I'll have to take the call.'

Pressing on the touchscreen she turns the phone on.

'Hello, Samantha? I'm in a meeting in the Oval Office. Can't this wait?'

Hurried words escape from the phone, but they're too muffled for the other people in the room to be able to understand them.

'I'll be there right away, Samantha,' says Serena McBee. 'I just need to get back to the residency. Tell the pioneers I'll make contact with them in the Rest House in no more than thirty minutes.'

She drops the phone back into her handbag.

'Something wrong?' asks Edmond Green.

'Russia and China can offer support to their pioneers, Alexei and Tao, if they want to protect their interests in Mars, but it's going to be a lot harder for America, I fear,' says the vice-president gravely. 'Marcus, who represents our nation, is dead.'

32. Off-screen

'*The whole planet's in shock!*' The journalist's voice is coming from the radio in the pick-up. '*From New York to Toronto, from Paris to Istanbul, Mumbai to Tokyo, the announcement of Marcus's death has taken the whole world by surprise. Ahead of the funeral service that will be broadcast tomorrow at twenty hundred hours Martian time – that's seven forty p.m. Eastern – spontaneous tributes have been pouring in. Especially in Los Angeles, where the American pioneer lived before setting off on his journey, and where emotions today are running particularly high. Our special correspondent is there . . .*'

The atmosphere in the cabin of the pick-up is stifling, as it sits unmoving in a small area on the edge of a highway where Missouri meets Illinois. On the front seat, Cindy and Harmony are frozen still like wax statues. Their gaze is lost in the outer suburban landscape that stretches beyond the windscreen, as it is gradually overtaken by the falling night. The only sound comes from the back seat: Andrew is tapping feverishly at the keyboard of his laptop, trying to find some information about the tragedy that has just been announced.

'*As you say, here on Hollywood Boulevard, things are incredibly emotional,*' says a man's voice, as he struggles to make himself heard against a background that mixes the traffic roar with funeral laments. '*Before he got chosen for the Genesis programme, Marcus often used to come stroll down this Walk of Fame, this famous stretch of sidewalk bearing the names of the biggest stars of American cinema. At the time, he was no more than an anonymous kid, with no fixed address, lost in the crowd; but tonight, he himself is the reason the crowds have come out onto the streets, their arms filled with flowers. All around me, people are crying, hugging, trying to console one another as best they can. There's a petition going around to get a new star put into the sidewalk bearing Marcus's name – in less than an hour, it's already gathered tens of thousands of signatures.*

'*But who really was the pioneer all of America is mourning tonight, commonly considered one of the most mysterious and fascinating characters in the Genesis programme? Exclusive to our listeners, we've found one of the deceased boy's former companions in misfortune. Ladies and gentlemen, allow me to introduce you to Tomás, aged nineteen, who knew Marcus well at a time when the wider world didn't yet know him at all!*'

Suddenly some street lighting on its last legs comes on beyond the windshield, silhouetting the distant profile of dilapidated houses, between which stand several neglected buildings – this old industrial area has suffered particularly badly from the crisis, and the rise to power of the Ultra-libertarian party has done nothing about it, despite their electoral promises.

Cindy blinks, slightly dazzled by the artificial light of the street lamps, even if every second bulb has blown.

'Dead . . .' she murmurs. 'I just can't believe it . . .'

In her hand she's holding one of the rocket shaped key-rings that hang from her rear-view mirror. Marcus's official photo is shining from the middle of its yellowish halo, wearing that half-smile absolutely unique to him.

'*Good evening, Tomás,*' says the reporter on the opposite side of the country, direct from America's dream factory, very far removed from the post-industrial melancholy of St Louis.

'*Good evening,*' replies a young man's voice, with a marked Latino accent.

'*So like I was saying, you were close to Marcus?*'

'*Yeah . . .*' Tomás hesitates a moment. '*. . . as much as you can be close to somebody so elusive. He's a pretty secretive guy, Marcus. A good guy, generous, but secretive.*'

'*Did he often come here, to the Walk of Fame?*'

'*Yeah, this was the corner where I met him the first time. I was begging; he'd just come for a stroll. He really liked this place, it was like he was at home here, kinda.*' Tomás cuts himself off – thinks for a moment. '*Yeah, that's it: even when he was still on Earth, he was already living among the stars.*'

'*But he was a . . . um –*' the reporter is struggling to find the right word – '*he was a beggar, like you?*'

'*A beggar? No way, man, he was an artist! When people used to toss him a few bucks it wasn't out of pity, but gratitude, because he dazzled them with his magic tricks. He taught me two or three of them, to help me get myself off the street. He was one of those guys you could always count on. A good guy.*'

Cindy lets the small portrait of Marcus fall back among the other immobile key-rings.

'I c-can't understand it,' stammers Harmony. 'Last night he was working so hard trying to get the base ready for the imminent storm, he looked like he was in great shape. What could have happened to him?'

Andrew snorts on the back seat, looking up from his laptop.

'The official version on the Genesis site has referred to cardiac trouble connected to his accident a month ago,' he says in a strained voice, the light from the screen reflecting in his glasses. 'But the people on the forums aren't all convinced. Some are calling for a more advanced diagnosis, to find out what actually happened in the seventh habitat.'

Harmony half-turns in her seat to look straight at Andrew.

'The pioneers themselves know!' she says quietly. 'We could ask them directly! We could establish contact with the team by hacking into the Genesis interplanetary network! You've done it before, Andrew, when you sent them the plans for the self-energising elevator. You could do it again!'

But Andrew shakes his head.

'I've checked, it's impossible. The broadcast codes I unearthed from my father's files were changed after the hacking . . . We no longer have any way of contacting the pioneers. All we can do now is go to Washington to secretly check on Professor Mirwood and confirm that the construction of the elevator really is going ahead as planned. We'll be there tomorrow night.'

Harmony has no answer to this.

She knows Andrew is right.

Along with the billions of others on Earth, they're both condemned to remain in the dark about what really caused Marcus's death.

The reporter on the radio is bringing his interview to an end.

'It's time for you to leave us now, Tomás, my friend. Thank you for this moving evocation of sadly missed Marcus. I won't keep you any longer – I guess you must have come to gather your thoughts on the stars of the Walk of Fame and commune with all these people here, who . . .'

'But what does Marcus mean, really, to all these people?' the young man interrupts him. *'A TV star? A face on the Genesis posters and a name on the boxes of Eden Food processed meals? If I'm here tonight, it's only because I was hoping she might be here – because of* her.'

The reporter can't help a short gasp of surprise.

'Her?'

'Marcus's mysterious friend. The tall brunette, with the very pale skin and very dark eyes, who he used to meet every evening on the Walk of Fame, in front of James Dean's star. I never knew her name. And unfortunately I haven't seen her in the crowd. Too bad: I really would have liked to exchange some memories of a pal who's gone with somebody who really knew him.'

33. Shot

I take a deep breath, and press the button on the 3D printer.

The enormous machine is set in motion with a slight humming sound.

Behind the huge glass walls, on the floor of the construction chamber, the printer heads start to mark out a large rectangle. As they go over it, again and again, superimposing one layer of grey matter on another, the rectangle rises slowly. A human-sized box is taking shape before our eyes . . . a coffin made of specially treated Martian sand, the substance we use as the raw material for anything that comes out of the 3D printer.

'There you go, we can leave the printer running now,' I say aloud, aware of the cameras filming us all around the panic room where the printer's set up. 'According to the print file I've fed into the machine, the coffin will be ready in four hours.'

The print file . . .

I insisted on making it up myself on my sketching tablet. Serena herself thought it would be OK to let me have free rein to pay one final tribute to my dead husband – '*Sure, it's a bit morbid, but you are an artist, after all,*' she said, on the air.

I withdrew into the seventh habitat for all of yesterday and a good part of last night to produce my piece of work on my tablet's 3D app. I designed the object with care, decorating the lid with a bas-relief of stars and roses, moulding the handles in the shape of brambles, every detail a reminder of Marcus's tattoos. As I did this, I noticed I didn't even need to refer to my sketches to remind myself: they were all so fresh in my mind that it was as if I was staring right at them. But for the dead boy's face I didn't want to take any risks: I based my work on a whole lot of photos Liz took of the prisoner in his cell, until my 3D model was a perfect replica down to the tiniest feature – I've never been so grateful to fate for having given me a gift for drawing, and I've never before held my stylus with such devotion . . . But will it be convincing enough?

What the organisers and the viewers don't know is that the print file I've just loaded into the machine doesn't only contain the shape of the coffin, but also of its occupant: an effigy of Marcus, which is supposed to take his place for the official funeral scheduled for 20:00 Mars time.

'So, shall we go?' asks Kelly. She's tense, in a hurry to get out of the place before the real shape being printed becomes too obvious.

She and Samson helped me to carry in the bags of sand and tip them into the machine's tank. The nerves in the Canadian girl's voice might be mistaken for the distress of somebody who's just lost a close friend, just like the black circles under my eyes are well suited to a tearful widow. Even Warden, who's pressing himself against Samson's legs, is somehow looking miserable.

'Yeah, let's go,' I say, turning on my heel.

The lights go out.

The panic room disappears into the darkness.

Veiled by the shadows hiding it from human eyes and the camera lenses, the 3D printer continues to hum gently.

34. Genesis Channel

Wednesday 10 January, 3:20pm

DEAR VIEWERS,
IN A FEW HOURS' TIME,
MARCUS'S FUNERAL SERVICE WILL BEGIN,
BROADCAST ACROSS THE WORLD
EXCLUSIVELY ON THE GENESIS CHANNEL.

TO HELP TO SWEETEN THIS PAINFUL WAIT,
WE INVITE YOU TO TAKE A LOOK BACK
AT THE STORY OF THIS REMARKABLE YOUNG MAN,
IN THE THIRD OF OUR 'ORIGINS' REPORTS.

*(PROGRAM ENCRYPTED — ACCESS TO
PREMIUM SUBSCRIBERS ONLY.)*

Wide shot on a huge film set with a black parquet floor, like a theatre stage, lit by dazzling spotlights.

A candidate all dressed up to the nines has just walked off to the left of the frame; before he's even completely out of shot, a man's voice shouts: '*Next!*'

A new candidate appears in the frame, entering from the right, while the title of the episode is superimposed on the screen.

MARCUS
USA

The newcomer is indeed Marcus, from his bohemian days. He's wearing jeans with torn knees, and a denim jacket that also looks like it's had a lot of use. The material is so faded that it's turned grey, the same shade as the large cotton scarf tied around his neck. Under his thick brown hair, carefully smoothed down for the audition, his light eyes complete his almost monochrome look, the colour of asphalt, or of clouds.

A script girl announces to nobody in particular: '*Marcus, aged eighteen . . .*'

You can hear a certain tiredness in the young woman's voice. It's the end of the day and the end of the week, the conclusion of a five-day marathon of intensive interviews.

The man in charge of casting invites the newcomer to sit down on the only chair, placed in the centre of the set. '*Take a seat, let's not waste too much time. You see that clock on the wall?*'

The camera pans briefly onto the dial showing 4:24, then frames back on the candidate.

'You have six minutes to convince us, just like in the speed-dating sessions that await the winners when they're on the spacecraft. At four thirty, it's all over, and you disappear.'

Marcus sits without saying a word.

Cut.

Close-up shot of the clock hanging on the studio wall: the big hand is moving at high speed while a piece of frantic music gets louder, the kind of music that accompanies countdowns in movie thrillers.

Cut.

The picture is showing Marcus again.

His lips are moving, we can tell that his interview is taking place, but we hear neither the questions nor the answers – the music, which is getting faster and faster, drowns everything out.

Cut.

New close-up shot of the clock: the big hand is now on the number twenty-nine, while the second hand is finishing its final cycle.

Cut.

The picture shows Marcus, in extreme close-up now, his sidelong gaze turned upward, staring intently at an object located somewhere out of shot.

The alternating edit and the dramatic intensity of the music leads us to deduce that it's the wall clock he's looking at while he continues distractedly to answer the questions.

Cut.

Third close-up shot of the clock: the big hand moves onto the number thirty at the exact moment the music reaches peak intensity.

Cut.

Wide shot on Marcus's chair, alone in the middle of the deserted setting. He grabs hold of his scarf, and with an abrupt gesture flaps it in front of him like a cape.

For a moment, the picture is filled with a fog of grey fabric.

The next moment, the scarf falls back down, coming to rest on an empty chair.

Cries of surprise echo around the set. *'What? Where the hell's he gone?'* *'He's just . . . vanished!'* *'But that's impossible, the door to the set was locked!'*

The disoriented camera spins around a full three hundred and sixty degrees, searching for the candidate. The camera crew appear in shot: the guy in charge of casting is wide-eyed, the continuity girl stands unmoving with her hands full of index cards, the technicians are suddenly electrified by this unexpected occurrence. *'Where is he? Where? Where? Where?'*

But the dumbfounded team must face up to the evidence: Marcus has truly dematerialised from the set, as if by magic.

Letting go of her stack of cards, the continuity girl approaches the chair.

She grabs the end of the cotton scarf with the tips of her fingers, simultaneously fascinated and sort of intimidated. 'He's only left his scarf . . .'

Slowly she lifts up the large piece of fabric.

Underneath it, on the empty chair, there is a sheet of paper covered in handwriting.

You asked me to disappear at 4:30.
I'm a very polite & well-behaved boy.
Have a good weekend.
Marcus

ZZZZZZZZZZZZZZZZZZZZZZZZZZZZZZZZZZZZZZZZZZZ
ZZZZZZZZZZZZZZZZZZZZZZZZZZZZZZZZZZZZZZZZZZZ
ZZZZZZZZZZZZZZZZZZZZZZZZZZZZZZZZZZZZZZZZZZZ
ZZZZZZZZZZZZZZZZZZZZZZZZZZZZZZZZZZZZZZZZZZZ
ZZZZZZZZZZZZZZZZZZZZZZZZZZZZZZZZZZZZZZZZZZZ
ZZZZZZZZZZZZZZZZZZZ . . .

35. Shot

Month 21 / sol 581 / 16:40 Mars time
[31st sol since landing]

'Even in our reduced gravity, this thing weighs a tonne!' pants Mozart, as he enters the seventh habitat, unseen by the cameras. 'My shoulder's killing me.'

He and Kenji are each carrying on their shoulders one front corner of the coffin that's just come out of the 3D printer.

'Ready to dump the coffin?' asks Alexei, who's carrying the back end with Samson.

The two bearers in front bend their legs – but the Japanese boy stumbles, maybe because of the spacesuit he's still wearing: the coffin slips out of his hands and crashes heavily onto the floor with a gloomy thud.

'Watch out!' shouts Alexei, jumping to one side, only just managing to avoid getting his feet crushed by the coffin.

I get up from the sofa where I've been waiting for hours along with Kris and Liz, with anxiety gnawing at me, and walk over to my 'work of art'.

The 3D printer's done its job well – bas-reliefs, mouldings, handles: everything is just right, according to the design I'd planned on my sketching tablet. But the most important thing isn't what the coffin looks like on the outside. What matters most is what the printer heads managed to make in the panic room with the lights off, under cover of darkness, before closing the whole thing up with a lid. The most important thing is something neither the organisers nor the viewers suspect, since they're convinced we're carrying an empty box into the seventh habitat in order to place Marcus's body inside it.

'Open it up,' I murmur.

Mozart takes hold of one side of the lid, Alexei the other.

They lift.

The light from the spots slips into the sarcophagus, illuminating the human shape that's stretched out inside.

Kris can't help letting out a horrified little cry.

'Oh, God help us!' she says, crossing herself. 'That's terrifying.'

She's right.

It's truly terrifying.

Because the resemblance is absolutely perfect: Marcus's face looks so real you'd almost expect to see him open his eyes. Only the greyish colour breaks the illusion – that's the colour of the printing material synthesised from the Martian soil.

'OK, get him dressed, girls, while I pretty him up,' I say.

Kris and Liz head for the table where a few clothes have been laid out, taken from the condemned man's wardrobe: a pair of jeans, a shirt, a pair of shoes.

For my part, I open up my Rosier make-up case.

I take out a foundation I've selected in advance, with the colour that best matches Marcus's complexion, and I start spreading the liquid over the statue's mineral cheeks to make them look more like human flesh.

36. Off-screen

The streets of Washington DC
Wednesday 10 January, 7:30pm

'It's like the whole city has fallen asleep,' murmurs Harmony, her forehead pressed against the glass of the pick-up window. 'Like in Sleeping Beauty's castle.'

Beyond the window, the streets bathed in public lighting roll past, deserted. At this time of day, the city's inhabitants are usually coming out of their offices, but there isn't a single passer-by on the sidewalks. Even the wind seems to have dropped, and the branches of the trees, emaciated by winter, have stopped moving.

The girl opens her eyes wide to try to see into the shadows beyond the halo of the street lamps.

'Where's everybody gone?'

No sooner has she said these words than a majestic area opens out at a bend in a broad avenue, a huge park stretching out beneath the starry sky, the Greek columns of the Lincoln Memorial to one of its sides, the white dome of the Capitol to the other. It's the National Mall, one of the most famous views in the world. Tonight it's so crowded with people that it's impossible to see even a patch of grass, with even the central pool crammed to bursting point with hundreds of little rowboats, rafts, canoes. But the most astonishing thing isn't the extraordinary number of people – it's the total silence coming from this endless crowd.

Some way down, an enormous screen has been set up in front of the Washington Monument, the grand obelisk placed in the middle of the mall. The broadcast from the Genesis channel is being screened there, dozens of metres wide, hypnotising the crowd.

'The f-funeral . . .' stammers Cindy, agog. Instinctively she lifts her foot from the gas to slow the pick-up down. 'The funeral's about to start.'

On the giant screen, there are seven solemn figures in spacesuits, motionless as statues in some forgotten temple, their faces eroded by the passing centuries. The reflection from the Garden spotlights makes it impossible to see through the helmets, but the names on their chests allow us to identify the pioneers.

Slowly the camera runs across the embroidered letters: LÉONOR (FRA) – SAFIA (IND) – FANGFANG (SGP) – ELIZABETH (GBR) – KIRSTEN (DEU) – KELLY (CAN) – and finally reaching the last pioneer, sitting in his wheelchair: TAO (CHN).

BOOM! The bang of a drum suddenly pierces the silence, making the liquid surface of the central pool shiver.

Spotlights mounted on tall pylons come on, revealing the temporary set-up that has been arranged at the foot of the obelisk, directly beneath the giant screen. There is a full-sized symphony orchestra, all of its members dressed entirely in black. The drummers strike their instruments one more time, a thunderclap amplified by the speakers, whose echo seems to make the full height of the obelisk tremble.

BOOM!

The camera pulls in, onto the access tube leading to the seventh habitat.

At the very moment the drums on Earth sound for the third time – BOOM! – the airlock opens onto four astronauts carrying a coffin by its handles.

BOOM!

The first two astronauts – the shorter of the four – enter the Garden.

The camera zooms discreetly over their names: KENJI *(JAP) and* MOZART *(BRA).*

BOOM!

The bearers bringing up the rear – the taller two – emerge in turn from the opening.

The camera identifies them at once: ALEXEI *(RUS) and* SAMSON *(NGA), then it pulls back, taking in the entirety of the funeral cortege.*

At that same moment, it becomes clear that the coffin is open and that there is a man inside.

'Oh!' cry Cindy and Harmony as one – as do the tens of thousands of people, just outside, who are unable to contain their emotion any longer.

Andrew just clenches his jaw.

The pick-up comes to a complete stop right in the middle of the deserted street.

'He looks so . . . so . . .' Harmony stammers, lost for words.

'So alive,' Cindy says, quietly.

On the screen, the camera zooms in on the dead man's face.

The rosiness of his cheeks . . .

The freshness of his lips . . .

He looks like he's asleep.

And yet the beating of the drum doesn't wake him – BOOM! – and the bearers continue their inexorable walk towards the airlock that leads out of the Garden.

'We've got to go,' says Andrew gently, dragging his fellow passengers away from the spectacle.

'But it's just so poignant,' complains Harmony. 'It's a once-in-a-lifetime moment.'

'Exactly. We've got to take advantage of the one moment when the whole of Earth has its eyes on space, when the whole Genesis team is busy worrying about whether the funeral's going well. We're only a few city blocks from Barry Mirwood's house. This is an unexpected chance to try and make contact with him without anybody realising.'

He puts his hand on the driver's shoulder – a hand that is gentle, the hand of a friend, not a hostage-taker.

'Start it up again, Cindy. Please.'

37. Shot

Month 21 / sol 581 / 20:15 Mars time
[31st sol since landing]

BOOM!

The sound of the drum, through the speakers of my helmet, makes me jump. It might be the sixth one, but I'm not used to it. Nor have I gotten used to the sight of hundreds of thousands of people gathered in silence under the cover of night, which is the picture currently being projected onto the Garden's glass dome.

FUNERAL SERVICE: LIVE.

That's what Serena McBee asked for when we notified her about Marcus's death. She shed her little crocodile tear – no doubt relieved he'd taken the secret of the D66 mutation to his grave. She was happy enough with the phoney diagnosis from me and Alexei, that Marcus's heart had given out. Dr Montgomery hurried to confirm our conclusions to the press, referring to theoretical symptoms following from the accident in the airlock. He didn't even ask for additional tests or an autopsy.

The fervour of all these people who've gathered tonight to

pay a final tribute to Marcus makes me feel queasy. Not only did the person they're crying over not die of a heart attack, *he isn't even dead at all.* At this very moment, while we're processing in front of the cameras with his effigy, he's festering away in the shadows in his cell. But the illusion we've created is perfect. It's a poignant spectacle.

Suddenly I'm stabbed by a horrifying thought: if Serena knew, she'd be proud of me!

BOOM!

The door of the airlock of the base opens with a purr, moved by the invisible jacks that almost crushed us, Marcus and me, the day we arrived.

The four bearers enter the airlock first, then we follow them.

The door closes behind us.

With her gloved hand, Liz presses the red button that starts the equalisation procedure.

The numbers on the digital gauge start to scroll up as the tube is cleared of its air to attain the same low-pressure conditions as on the surface of Mars.

EQUALISATION 10%
EQUALISATION 20%
EQUALISATION 30%
EQUALISATION 40%

Behind the outer door of the airlock, which will open in just a few moments, the belly of Mars is getting ready to swallow up our offering.

From the speakers in my helmet, which are still broadcasting an entire planet's emotion, the drums never stop thundering.

BOOM!

38. Off-screen

The Georgetown neighbourhood, Washington DC
Wednesday 10 January, 7:58pm

'It's here,' says Andrew. 'The last house, right at the end.'

This street too is deserted.

The row of houses are pressed tightly against one another. Most of the façades look a hundred years old, ancient by American standards: we're in Georgetown, one of the oldest parts of the city and of the country. Among the ivy-covered bricks, the windows are shining with cathode-ray gleams: the residents who haven't gone out to the National Mall are all sitting in front of their TV screens.

The pick-up truck stops silently outside the professor's house. The shutters are already closed, but there's light filtering out between the slats: Barry Mirwood is home.

'So what now?' asks Cindy, turning off the ignition.

'Now's our only chance,' replies Andrew. 'I've got to go talk to this guy.'

He looks down at the screen of his cellphone.

'According to aircontrol.com, there are currently no police drones in the vicinity – Aircontrol is this illegal geolocation site that a lot of motorists use to avoid getting caught for speed violations,' he explains. He holds his cellphone out to the passengers in front. 'Look: tonight all the robotised police forces are gathered around the funeral ceremony.'

But the map with all the little red dots clustered around the National Mall doesn't seem to reassure Harmony much.

'It's much too dangerous, Andrew! And what if the site isn't a hundred per cent reliable? What if a drone shows up out of the blue? I'm scared you're going to get yourself caught. Why run the risk?'

'There are eleven human beings up there who're running the risk of dying at any moment. They're counting on us, they've only got us, nobody else. The self-energising elevator, and through it the future of the pioneers we've vowed to save, depends entirely on the expertise of Barry Mirwood.'

'Exactly! The elevator's going to be built, they've already announced it on the Genesis programme! The organisers can't back out now!'

Andrew sits up, unable to hide a grimace of pain – the wound in his foot is still raw – then puts his hand on the girl's arm.

'You know your mother better than anyone, Harmony,' he says. 'And you know better than anybody that she'd take any opportunity to go back on her promises. Right now, we've got a chance to reveal the truth to the one man on Earth able to bring the Mars pioneers to safety. If we don't grab this chance, we might never get another, and Barry Mirwood will be at the mercy of Serena McBee's lies. That's an even bigger risk than me getting myself arrested tonight.'

This time, the girl does not answer. On her pale face, panic is replaced by a grave expression.

Andrew takes his hand off her arm, to pass her the rifle he's kept with him on the back seat.

'At the first sign of any threat, and anyway if I'm not back in half an hour, get out of here,' he says. 'Leave, to save whatever can still be saved. Both of you . . .' He catches Cindy's eye in the rear-view mirror; she's been following the conversation silently from the start.

'. . . like Thelma and Louise.'

The door of the pick-up closes with a muffled click.

Andrew limps away, the hood of his sweatshirt over his head, rucksack on his back.

One by one he climbs the front steps. Here and there a small strip of ground is planted with evergreen bushes, among which somebody has stuck plastic windmills the shape of stars. In one corner there's even a garden gnome in an astronaut suit: no question, this is where the quirky old scientist lives.

Andrew presses the doorbell.

Something moves in the depths of the house, there are muffled footsteps behind the door, and the latch lifts with a click.

The door opens, letting out a halo of dim light, with the silhouette of the owner of the house appearing cut out against the brightness. The distinguished professor has knotted a big checked napkin over his abundant beard. This addition makes him look somewhat like an ogre at the door to his castle. In the background, coming from an invisible living room, it's possible to hear the drum beats to which other instruments have now been added in a funeral march: the professor has been eating dinner, watching the Genesis channel.

'If you're just selling something . . .' he begins, already preparing to close the door on the strange hooded visitor.

Before he's able to say anything more, Andrew gives him a sharp shove.

Barry Mirwood is surprised, and stumbles backwards. When the door closes again, Andrew is with him inside the entrance hall decorated with framed astronomical charts.

'Yes, I'm here to sell you something, Mr Mirwood,' says the young man quickly. 'According to our organisation's customer files, you have not yet been fitted with a multi-jet ionised shower, and we've currently got an offer on that you can't refuse.'

While he's starting this unlikely speech, Andrew takes his cellphone out of his tracksuit pocket and holds it under the nose of the alarmed old man.

On the screen, there's a message he's written there in advance, offering a quite different explanation for his visit:

I AM THE SON OF SHERMAN FISHER,
WHO YOU KNEW AT NASA.
I HAVE SOMETHING IMPORTANT TO TELL YOU
BUT I SUSPECT YOU'RE BEING BUGGED.
CAN WE GO TO THE BATHROOM
AND RUN THE WATER LOUD?

Andrew pulls back his hood.

Barry Mirwood opens his eyes wide and suddenly stops struggling.

255

'You . . . you look like . . .' he stammers.

'. . . like a young Tom Cruise?' Andrew interrupts him loudly, to make it clear his interlocutor isn't to say another word. 'Yeah, I get that a lot.'

Recovering his wits, Barry Mirwood points a trembling finger at the staircase.

'Very good. I'll show you the bathroom. If you'd just like to follow me, Mr . . .'

'. . . Smith. John Smith.'

The two men make their way up the stairs in silence – Andrew is still limping, and needs to hold onto the banister to reach the upper floor.

Once they get to the bathroom, Barry Mirwood closes the door behind them and turns the mixer tap of the shower till there's water gushing out. To be extra careful, Andrew does the same with the tap of the washbasin.

Only now does he allow himself to whisper.

'We don't have much time, professor. I can only stay a few minutes. The broadcast of the funeral is going to end soon and I've really got to be out of here before the streets start filling up again.'

'You're – you're the spitting image of Sherman,' stammers the scientist, visibly moved. 'I mean, from when he started at NASA, more than twenty years ago. He was such a brilliant guy, with such an amazing future ahead of him, a true scientist with great ideas. He was also a real self-made man, with a scholarship to Berkeley, who rose up the ranks at NASA through hard work. He and his charming wife, Vivian – your mom – made an impressive couple. Such a shame he met with such a tragic end.'

This recollection of his father makes Andrew shiver, but he gathers himself again quickly.

'We'll talk about him some other time,' he murmurs. 'There's something else I've come to tell you . . . and show you.'

With these words, he hurriedly pulls his laptop from his rucksack and opens it; the screen comes on automatically to show the first page of the Noah Report.

39. Reverse Shot

National Mall, Washington DC
Wednesday 10 January, 8:40pm

'It'll be your turn soon, Ms McBee,' says Samantha, coming into her boss's dressing room, which has been set up in a van parked at the foot of the Washington Monument. 'Everybody is already in position on the platform.'

Serena McBee tears herself away from the brushes of the two make-up artists who are busily evening out her skin tone. Tonight she's wearing a mourning dress in black lace, which she has already worn twice before, first to mark the passing of Sherman Fisher and then for the whole of the Genesis programme's team of instructors. On her collar, alongside the bee-shaped brooch, the black remembrance ribbon is coming slightly loose. Through the armoured windows of the van, it's possible to hear the drums and brass of the orchestra, the funeral march at its height.

'I'm ready, Samantha,' she announces gravely. 'Let us pray I can find the words to console our grief-stricken people on Earth and on Mars.'

She straightens her dress, gets up, and walks past her assistant and out of the dressing room.

But no sooner has she entered the narrow corridor leading to the rear doors of the van than a hand closes over her arm.

'Arthur?' she says with a start, recognising the doctor amid the shadows.

'I've got to talk to you.'

Arthur Montgomery's voice is strained, his eyes shining like embers in the gloom. Although he's still wearing one of his stiff tweed suits, he no longer looks anything like an unflappable gentleman.

'Later, Arthur,' says Serena, trying to free her arm. 'I've got a date with History.'

But the doctor doesn't let her go.

'Earlier today I was the one you had a date with, for lunch,' he whispers. 'After my press conference confirming the cause of Marcus's death. But you stood me up. Yet again.'

'Still at it with your adolescent moaning – it's getting quite tiresome!' replies Serena sharply. 'Can't you understand I'm busy preparing my speech? Billions of people on Earth are counting on me, and I'm not going to make them wait on account of just one person.'

'I wonder how the billions of people would react if I told them what you really are?'

Serena McBee freezes, all her senses alert, then glances over her shoulder down the corridor to be quite sure they are alone and nobody has heard.

'You've got no proof, Arthur,' she says in a low voice. 'No proof of anything.' A smile appears on her lips, and her voice turns sweeter. 'Don't spoil the beautiful thing we have. Silly old fool. Let me go now. I promise you, tonight after my little speech, we'll have dinner together.'

With her free hand – the one on which she's wearing her new diamond ring with the eye-shaped setting – she strokes the doctor's cheek.

The man shudders at her caress.

He opens his mouth to say something, his fingers uncurling at the same time.

Serena takes advantage of the moment to escape his grasp and slip away towards the doors of the van.

The doors open onto a pathway marked out by security barriers, dappled by the light from the spotlights, leading to the platform beneath the obelisk. A dozen bodyguards are posted along the route, jaws clenched, eyes scrutinising the mall from which the music of the symphony orchestra is surging. Only the first of them is not wearing infrared glasses: Agent Seamus, in his eyepatch, holds his arm out to Serena to help her down from the running board.

The diamond sparkles on the vice-president's finger as she gives her hand to the leader of her security detail.

Deep inside the darkness of the van, far from the spotlights and the public's gaze, Arthur Montgomery gives the quiet groan of a fatally injured animal, which is immediately swallowed up by the sound of the orchestra.

40. Genesis Channel

Wednesday 10 January, 8:50pm

Long shot on the valley that stretches out beyond New Eden, lit by the floodlights attached to the top of the dome.

Ten of the pioneers are positioned there, like skittles, their shadows stretched out infinitely by the beams. In front of them is the coffin, which is now closed. The eleventh pioneer is at the controls of the maxi-rover, whose integrated digger is moving slowly: it's just finished making a hole in the Martian soil.

The articulated arm plunges one last time into the black pit, pulling out a final pile of sand, and falls still. The driver gets out of the vehicle – zoom in: from the label sewn onto the chest of the spacesuit, we see it is Mozart.

Alexei, Samson and Kenji help him to pick up the coffin.

With ropes gripped firmly in their gloved hands, they lower it into its final resting place.

Then they return to join the others by the side of the grave.

Split screen:

On the left: the lonely Martian night. Caption: VALLEY OF IUS CHASMA (TEN MINUTES' DIFFERENCE FROM EARTH TIME)

261

On the right: the night-time crowd on Earth. Caption: NATIONAL MALL, WASHINGTON DC.

On both sides, the same silence – the orchestra has stopped playing.

Tracking across the front of the platform at the foot of the obelisk.

Serena McBee is standing here, dominating the crowd with her dark silhouette. Just like on the day of the marriage ceremonies, she is surrounded by representatives of different religions. We recognise the cardinal, the Orthodox priest, the pastor, the monk and the Brahman who officiated a month ago, as well as an imam who has come along to join the ecumenical ceremony. There are also a number of dignitaries and representatives of the platinum sponsors, in mourning clothes, who have come especially to pay a final tribute to the lost pioneer.

The mistress of ceremonies leans in towards her mic. 'Ladies and gentlemen, my dear citizens of America, and all of you, inhabitants of the whole world – thank you for being here with the pioneers of Mars tonight.'

She pauses briefly, just long enough to allow a pained expression to pass across her face – then after this moment of contemplation, she gestures towards a woman in the first row of sponsors, wearing an elegant maternity dress in black velvet, whose face is hidden by a dark veil. 'To begin our farewell to Marcus, I'd like to ask for a few words from a representative of those people who believed in Marcus from the start. I'm talking about Phoebe Delville, the daughter of Henry K. Delville, the founder and CEO of Eden Food International – she has been responsible for the group's partnership with the Genesis programme. Miss Delville insisted on being here in person, and I'm so grateful to her.'

The camera follows the pregnant woman on her long silent walk up to the microphone, her shape emphasised by the shimmering reflections of the velvet – to judge by the roundness of her belly, she must be at six or seven months. Then it zooms slowly in on the veil, as if trying to penetrate its secrets. What kind of face is hidden behind the narrow webbed stitching? A woman in her thirties who's made her whole career in her father's business? An heiress who's ready to work right up to the last day until her labour, a firm-handed woman who's going to be taking over from the patriarch in just a few years?

No – as she raises the veil with her black silk gloves she reveals a face that is smooth, youthful – a young woman aged barely twenty. An inky-black bob frames her alabaster forehead and marble cheeks, which the pregnancy has barely swollen.

Her mouth – made up with a red lipstick that is dark and matt, reminiscent of the movie stars of yesteryear – opens to speak. 'Eden Food International couldn't have wished for a better ambassador than Marcus to be the bearer of its image,' Phoebe Delville begins. 'He was honest and transparent, a perfect match for our group's ethical charter.'

The young heiress's voice changes slightly, blending the words of this funeral eulogy with the promotional jargon borrowed from the Eden Food brochures. 'He was the perfect "All-American Boy", as simple and generous as the recipes of our individual frozen meals to suit every pocket, our *Astronaut Meals*.'

Her dark eyes start to shine; a thin line of mascara breaks out from the corner of her right eyelid down to her cheekbone, while she keeps reciting mechanically. 'He was the perfect gentleman, as intense and refined as our top-of-the-range *Leorcus* gastronomic collection. He was . . . he was . . . No, he wasn't any of that at all!'

The camera pulls back slightly, surprised at the vehemence of the expression that has just passed across Phoebe Delville's face – an expression of genuine pain, a thousand miles away from corporate rhetoric.

With the back of her hand, the girl brushes away her mascara-coloured tear.

'The boy who let us use his image had nothing transparent about him at all,' she declares, contradicting the appropriate words she said a moment ago. 'He was as mysterious as the night. There was nothing simple about him – he was as complex as the movement of the stars. As for his intensity, it wasn't like a frozen meal, top-of-the-range or otherwise: he was like a poet haunted by the allure of space!' She grabs the mic with both hands, fixes her eyes directly into the camera. 'That's the boy Marcus was. Let's remember him too, and not just as a living advertising billboard.'

She pulls her veil back down, turns on her heel and walks back over to join the other startled sponsors.

But it will take more than this unexpected speech to put Serena McBee off her stride. With an elegant gesture, she walks back up to the mic and turns towards the camera, all smiles.

'Very well said, Miss Delville! Marcus was a poet, a visionary! At this moment when we're getting ready to say our goodbyes to him, we shouldn't be sending him off with sadness, but with hope that we might build a better world together. On this day when discordant voices are rising up to accuse the Genesis programme of harbouring imperialist ambitions, we shouldn't be hanging onto division, but the unity of the human race, all gathered together around one single dream. This dream of universal comradeship was Marcus's dream, I know it.'

41. Shot

Month 21 / sol 581 / 21:15 Mars time
[31st sol since landing]

'*This dream of universal comradeship was Marcus's dream, I know it.*' Serena McBee's voice resonates from my helmet speakers.

Universal comradeship, for the most solitary boy I've ever met?

Those definitely aren't the words I'd have chosen for Marcus's funeral eulogy – the ones from the Delville heiress seem fairer to me: the mystery, the complexity, poetry, yes, but not comradeship.

Weird how perfectly that girl had Marcus all figured out though.

Could it be that watching the Genesis channel has meant the viewers all know him better than I do?

Or is it just her, Phoebe Delville, who got to know him on Earth, when each of the sponsors was prepping their protégé?

No time to think about that now: on the outer walls of the New Eden dome, on which the ceremony on Earth is being broadcast, Serena continues her shameless hijacking.

'. . . *it falls to us today to grasp the torch held out to us by Marcus, to continue his dream. Yes – we must remain united,*

266

overcoming our selfishness and our national demands, to aim further, higher.' Serena clears her throat. *'Our Russian and Chinese friends have recently staked a claim to the sovereignty of a part of the New Eden base and the planet Mars . . .'*

Ah, so that's it!

Vulture diplomacy!

I suspected Serena was going to take advantage of Marcus's death to wring out a few tears, but I never guessed she was going to make it into a political statement!

'Tonight, if you will allow me, I would like to ask my counterparts in Moscow and Beijing a question. Not as vice-president of the United States, not even as executive producer of the Genesis programme. Merely, humbly, as a woman who means well.'

Serena turns slightly more towards the camera – towards the foreign leaders she's hoping to convince.

Her smile widens across the whole surface of the dome.

Her eyes blaze with the reflection of hundreds of spotlights.

'My dear brothers, my dear sisters, are you willing to dream Marcus's dream with me?'

There is a moment of silence, as if Serena really was waiting for an *Amen* in Chinese and in Russian.

The only answer she receives to this angelic question is a loud explosion, which bursts through my earphones – *BOOM!*

Has the orchestra started up again?

No.

This drumbeat was no such thing, and no other note came after it.

Instead of a choir, I hear the sound of mumbled confusion rising from the crowd.

The smile on Serena's face disappears, replaced by an expression of shock.

She looks down at her chest and in the same movement the camera zooms in: something new has appeared there, above the remembrance ribbon – a big red hole.

The mumbling gives way to screams of horror the moment the most adored woman on the planet collapses and rolls to the edge of the platform. Her own weight pulls her down three metres to crash onto the grass with a thud.

ACT III

42. Genesis Channel

Wednesday 10 January, 9:05pm

Split screen.

On the left-hand half of the screen, the Mars pioneers have all turned away from the grave where the coffin is lying to look at the New Eden dome, on the surface of which the pictures from Earth are being broadcast. There, on this giant screen stuck in the middle of the desert, a lonely source of light in thousands of kilometres of darkness, Serena McBee has just collapsed.

On the right-hand half of the screen, utter chaos has overtaken the National Mall. Ten minutes have already passed since the vice-president was hit – the communication latency means that the Earth side of the report is ten minutes ahead of the Martian side. Yells, gunshots, deafening sirens: an infernal din fills the soundtrack. The crowds are in a panic and stumble, colliding, trampling one another. Hordes of people surging in various directions shake the mall, like human waves breaking against one another in the midst of a storm.

All of a sudden, the two parts of the screen turn blurry.
Cut.

The screen is black. No message, no logo. Empty.

43. Off-screen

Georgetown neighbourhood, Washington DC
Wednesday 10 January, 9:06pm

At the exact moment that Andrew Fisher emerges from Barry Mirwood's house, the sound of thunder explodes over his head.

He looks up, peering into the night. Four military helicopters are bearing down towards him, their blades tearing through the sky, their searchlights sweeping the city.

Out of reflex, Andrew crouches down and pulls the hood of his tracksuit low over his face.

But the blinding beams of the searchlights pass him without stopping, slide over the pick-up parked a few metres down the road and continue on their way towards the centre of the city.

Andrew jumps back to his feet, hurtles down the front steps – ignoring his injured foot – and runs for cover at the back of the vehicle where Cindy and Harmony are waiting for him.

'Those choppers . . . !' he exclaims, slamming the door behind him, out of breath, his face twisted in pain. 'I thought they'd come for us.'

There's another thunderclap.

Andrew presses his distraught face against the glass: there are more helicopters approaching from the south.

'What the hell's going on?' the young man demands, turning back to look at the two passengers in the front seats.

By way of response, Cindy turns up the volume on the car radio.

'. . . *right in the heart!*' yells a journalist. '*Just when she was preaching a lesson of peace and fraternity! Utter confusion has overtaken the National Mall, where the army has just been deployed. The gunfire has now stopped, at this moment when I'm speaking to you, but the killer has not been caught. Initial numbers are suggesting dozens injured, crushed by the panicking crowds. It would appear that even in that first exchange of gunfire a few members of the public might have been struck – Arthur Montgomery, the doctor in charge of medicine for the Genesis programme, was among the victims. Meanwhile President Green has been evacuated from the White House and taken for his safety to a secure location. The whole country is in shock tonight . . .*'

Andrew turns pale.

'Arthur M-Montgomery . . . ?' he stammers, his eyes flitting between Cindy and Harmony. 'And who else? Who's the person who was hit right in the heart?'

As if he'd heard the question via the radio waves, the journalist announces the news, his voice shaking with adrenaline.

'*To recap, for those of you just joining us: Serena McBee, vice-president of the United States of America, has just been brought down by an unidentified sniper in Washington tonight.*'

Cindy turns sharply towards the back seat.

'What now?' she asks.

Andrew doesn't answer immediately, stunned by what he's just heard. Harmony, in the seat in front, is as still as he is.

'The woman you claimed was responsible for the plot is dead,' Cindy goes on, her voice hoarse. 'The woman who apparently had the power to depressurise the Martian habitats is out of action once and for all. That's what you guys wanted, isn't it? This Professor Mirwood is going to be able to continue his work on the self-energising elevator without any risk of interruption. You're going to be able to send your famous Noah Report to the press without any risk of repercussions. You no longer have to fear Serena taking revenge on your mother and your sister. You no longer need to stay on the run . . .' She takes a deep breath. 'You no longer need me.'

Her gaze drops to the rifle clenched in Harmony's fingers – the girl is literally clinging to it. Cindy's words seem to slide over her without the slightest effect.

'The game of cat and mouse is over – don't you see?' says the driver again, overcome with emotion. 'Let me go free, I won't say anything to anyone, I promise! Please . . . Connecticut's just a few hours' drive from Washington . . . I'm dying to go meet Derek. I need it. He thinks I've moved on, and he'll move on too if I don't answer his messages. I'm not that young any more, I may never get another chance like this – don't make me give up the one guy who could be the love of my life.'

Finally a sob comes from Harmony's lips, a poignant mixture of pain, guilt and despair.

'Mom . . . Mom's dead,' she stammers, unable to digest the news. 'The only person I had in the world.'

When he hears these words, Andrew finally recovers his wits.

He takes Harmony's hands gently.

'No,' he says. 'She wasn't the only person. You have me too.'

He turns towards the driver, pointing the gun at her.

'Start it up again, Cindy.'

'But . . .'

'You're right, Professor Mirwood's continuing his work on the self-energising elevator, now that he knows about the Noah Report and the danger the Mars pioneers are in. But the time hasn't yet come for us to reveal our secret to the rest of the world. It wouldn't be wise before we get absolute official confirmation of the death of Serena McBee.' Andrew places the gun down on his knees. 'I'm sorry, Cindy. I can't let you go, not yet. The game of cat and mouse might not be over just yet – because we all know, cats have a lot of lives.'

44. Shot

Blackout.

The broadcast of the Genesis channel on the surface of the dome has stopped abruptly, casting the plates of glass into shadow. The only things disturbing the Martian night now are the spotlights illuminating us, we eleven Martian pioneers, at the edge of the chasm into which we've pretended to lower the twelfth of us.

In the earphones of our helmets, the humming of the Genesis channel goes off at the same time as the images.

Total silence.

Deafening.

Someone's shot Serena McBee.

I heard the gun firing, I saw the red hole in her chest, I watched her body collapse onto the ground like a mannequin that's disjointed – and lifeless.

'*You think she's . . . dead?*' I hear Safia's quiet voice in my earphones as if far away.

There's a jerky noise in the background.

Interference?

No – I turn and see Kelly's face, twisted into an expression of total joy, behind the visor of her helmet. She struggles to contain the nervous laughter that seems to rise from the very depths of her being, shaking her spine and filling the radio network with gasps.

My heart skips a beat.

I pounce on her and grab her shoulders with my astronaut-gloved hands, to force her to stay still.

'*Calm down!*' I order her through my mic, looking straight into her eyes, the visor of my helmet pressed against hers. '*I know we've just seen pictures that are hard to bear, but now isn't the moment to crack, not in front of the cameras.*'

It's my way of reminding her that, even if the Genesis broadcast onto the dome has come to a sudden end, there's no evidence the cameras have stopped filming us. So long as Kelly keeps control of herself, her trembling could be taken as a symptom of shock; but if she reveals her delight live on camera, then all the appearances we've been struggling to preserve since we arrived will be done for.

'*Be strong,*' I say. '*Be dignified. Be worthy of Serena.*'

Through her tears of joy – which I hope the viewers will interpret as tears of horror – the Canadian girl does finally seem to register my presence. I squeeze her shoulders even harder, until her breathing steadies.

'OK, *cap'n,*' she says, though her voice is still wavering, and she still has a rigid expression on her face. '*I'll be calm. I am worthy.*'

She breathes out slowly and grabs one of the shovels planted in the heap of Martian sand that's been piled up beside the grave.

Then she throws all her undeniable delight into the task of covering the coffin with large shovelfuls of sand.

Everybody watches her, stunned, their own dazed state contrasting with her frantic activity. For more than a month their whole lives have been about Serena, thinking only in relation to Serena, against Serena, tightrope walkers balancing between life and death. And now, all of a sudden, Serena has disappeared – the rope has been brutally cut.

I can tell that at any moment, any one of us might crack and reveal everything on air.

I've got to keep everybody's hands and heads busy – and fast!

'Let's all help Kelly!' I cry. 'Let's finish burying Marcus, while we wait for more news from Earth!'

I grab hold of the shovels and start to hand them around, never stopping, pushing my teammates towards the pile of sand.

Alexei is the first to come out of his stupor to join Kelly. He's soon imitated by Mozart and Samson, then Liz and Kenji join in. The shovels rise and fall in rhythm, moving quantities of sand it would be impossible to lift on Earth, where gravity is three times stronger than on Mars.

Tao grabs a tool in turn and leans his broad shoulders out of his chair to help fill the pit, like a soldier with his legs caught in a trench, using his bayonet to push back a surging enemy and conquer, conquer, conquer!

Yeah, that's what they all look like – not gravediggers in mourning, but angry warriors, who are attacking each other on the sand, blood-red as if they were attacking the body of Serena herself!

I feel a wave of pure adrenaline rising in my chest and I grab a shovel to let off steam with the others.

But the moment I push the cutting edge of the tool into the soft sand, a muffled sob echoes in the headphones of my helmet. I look around me, amazed, until my eyes find Kris.

My Kris, who never lies, who can't cheat, who shows all her feelings. She's standing there, motionless at the edge of the grave, her cheeks furrowed with tears behind the visor of her helmet.

'*It's so horrible,*' she sobs in a voice that chills my heart, because it sounds totally sincere. '*Our dear Serena is dead. Now we really are all orphans.*'

45. Reverse Shot

'Well?'

'Still nothing, Mr President. Serena McBee is still in a profound coma.'

Edmond Green's sigh sounds like the whistle of a pressure cooker just about to explode. The harsh neon lighting of the most sophisticated military hospital in the country, directly connected to the White House, makes his face look hollow. You would think he'd aged fifteen years.

'But I've been without a vice-president for forty-eight hours!' he says. 'Forty-eight hours with the country in a state of emergency, and deprived of the best among us! Serena McBee is the key figure in all the most pressing issues of the moment: the colonisation of Mars, even after we've just lost the American pioneer; the government's relationship with Atlas Capital; and playing for time with China and Russia. We can't function without her. When's she going to come out of this coma?'

The man standing opposite the president is greying, in

a white shirt, accompanied by half a dozen nurses wearing concerned expressions. The badge on his chest reveals his identity: Dr Olaf Spitzbergen, Head of Department, I.C.U.

'We're doing everything in our power, Mr President,' he says, in a level voice that betrays his military background. 'And we're using the most modern medical equipment to keep the patient alive. But she's in critical condition. Her rib cage was punctured. The sniper was aiming for her heart, and would have got it if that small jewel hadn't slightly deflected the bullet on its trajectory.' He pulls a small plastic bag out of his shirt pocket, at the bottom of which is a bee-shaped silver brooch. 'Instead, the bullet ended up puncturing the left lung. Since then, Ms McBee has been in respiratory distress. She can't survive without assistance. To be quite frank with you, her cerebral condition is a cause for concern too; I'm afraid her brain might have been oxygen-deprived for too long, which would mean her cognitive abilities being irretrievably damaged.'

Edmond Green sighs again; then he glances over his shoulder, as if trying to find a way out of this desperate situation. But his eyes find only the anxiety-creased brows of his closest staff, who have been following him everywhere during this crisis – Dolores Ortega, the inescapable woman in charge of the president's image; Milton Sunfield, the lion-maned secretary of state; and a third man with a troubled brow, who is mostly bald: Roy Berck, the secretary of homeland security.

As a last resort, it's Berck to whom the president speaks.

'Have we at least identified the shooter?'

'He got away, and nobody's claimed responsibility, Mr President. However, given the moment when Serena McBee was struck, in the middle of a speech about the sovereignty of the Martian base, there are some who ascribe responsibility for the attack to the Russians and the Chinese.'

Milton Sunfield jumps in, trembling with indignation to the very tips of his fingers.

'Moscow and Beijing have both formally denied any involvement!' he says. 'Your unfounded accusations could be calamitous for our bilateral relations!'

'I'm accusing no one,' replies the secretary for homeland security soberly. 'But people talk, they imagine things. Social media networks are getting very animated. Journalists are sharing theories to fill their columns.'

'I can confirm that,' Dolores Ortega interrupts him, consulting her digital tablet. 'If you look at what's trending on the search engines, the phrases "Chinese attack" and "Russian attack" are the ones growing the fastest. Directly followed by "Arthur Montgomery" – the public are trying to find out who the Genesis doctor was, the man whose body was found at the other end of the stage. The fact that he was gunned down at almost exactly the same time as the executive producer has seemed to confirm the suspicions of those people who see this as an attack by foreign powers against the programme.'

Milton Sunfield sighs, exasperated.

'All the more reason to be careful with the language we use, and not make any uncontrolled slip-ups, which could just feed this preposterous psychosis!' he says. 'This man, Arthur Montgomery, must have taken a bullet during the confusion, like so many other people did that evening: it was so dark, it all happened so fast. Law enforcement tried to counterattack without knowing where exactly the threat was coming from, there were some stray bullets, it's regrettable. But I beg you, let's not imagine this is some kind of international plot! The most likely scenario is that the assassination attempt on Serena McBee was the work of a madman working alone, just like Oswald against Kennedy.'

The image director puts away her tablet.

'That is indeed the most likely scenario,' she concedes reluctantly. 'But in the meantime, the shooter is still on the run. As long as the police don't formally identify him and arrest him, the public's imagination will keep working away – this is a democracy, and we can't stop people expressing themselves on the internet.'

The secretary of state is about to add something, but the president is impatient.

'Russians, Chinese, madmen or worshippers of the Flying Spaghetti Monster: for now, everything's just talk! I've always been a believer in realpolitik. While we wait for proof, I won't be making any public accusations or denials – but I am going to be maintaining the state of emergency in force.' He turns to the head of the I.C.U. 'Would it be possible for me to see Serena McBee before returning to the White House?'

'Of course, Mr President. She's in a secure room, as you requested. Only medical personnel and the security services have access.'

The group follows the doctor down a series of lino-floored corridors, up to an armoured door flanked by two dark-suited bodyguards.

These two men step aside to let the president and his

entourage past. Edmond Green pushes the door gently, as if he was suddenly afraid of waking the woman sleeping inside.

But Serena is plunged into a sleep from which nobody can wake her: there she lies, stretched out on a huge hospital bed, in a dim light. There is an intubation tube in her trachea, blowing into her body the oxygen that it's no longer able to take up for itself. There's a slight whistling sound each time her chest swells beneath the sheet, raised artificially by the machine. Her bare arms, stripped for the first time of their jewels and bracelets, are stuck with catheters pumping a variety of medical fluids into her veins. This woman who has always lived surrounded by screens now has just one monitor beside her: the one registering the rates of her cardiac and respiratory functions.

'She looks so peaceful,' murmurs the president, making his way slowly towards the pillow on which the patient's silver hair is splayed. 'So . . . *serene*.'

'Doesn't she, Mr President? She's never suited her name better.'

Edmond Green jumps – he hadn't seen that there was somebody else in the room: a man dressed all in black, whose shape seated on a chair blurs into the gloom.

'You might not recognise me, Mr President,' says the man, getting to his feet. 'I'm Agent Orion Seamus, in charge of Ms McBee's security detail. I guard her day and night. I feel so terrible for not having been able to protect her.'

Edmond Green forces himself to smile at this man with a black eyepatch.

'Absolutely, I do of course recognise you,' he says. 'I'm sure you did your best.'

'I feel so guilty, like Kennedy's bodyguards must have felt in '63. I can't help thinking about how it was here, the Walter Reed military hospital, that JFK's body was brought for its autopsy.'

'Uh . . . yes, of course,' replies Edmond Green, uncomfortable at the reference to his assassinated predecessor, whose memory is being evoked for the second time in just a few minutes. 'But tell me, Agent . . . um . . . Remind me?'

'Seamus. Orion Seamus.'

'Tell me, Agent Seamus: since you were at the scene of the crime, just a few metres from the vice-president, have you any idea who the killer is?'

With his one visible eye, the young C.I.A. agent holds the illustrious older man's gaze.

'No, Mr President. It all happened so quickly. It was chaos.'

Suddenly inspired, the president says a few words in a deep voice, a phrase intended for posterity.

'Chaos . . . is the great enemy of all politicians worthy of the name. Serena paid the highest price for facing up to it. May her spirit guide us in the days to come.'

While the woman in charge of the president's image hurries to jot down the quote on her tablet so she can pass it on to the press, the president gives the patient one final glance; then he leaves the room, whose grim atmosphere seems to weigh heavily on him.

Only Orion Seamus remains behind.

He pulls his chair up to the huge bed, in the silence disturbed only by the whistling of the artificial ventilator.

He delicately takes the patient's lifeless hand – the hand which, just forty-eight hours earlier, before it was stripped of all its jewellery for transfer into the theatre block, was wearing an engagement ring.

'Life's ironic, isn't it?' he murmurs bitterly, as if she could hear him even from the depths of her coma. 'A week ago, you were one of the most influential people in the world, and today you're no better than a vegetable. I should have suspected earlier . . . I should have known where the blow was going to come from . . . I saw Arthur Montgomery raising his gun from the shadows of the trailer just a moment too late; if I'd fired a second earlier, I would have got him before he pulled the trigger.' He lets go of Serena's hand, which falls limply onto the mattress, then his head sinks into his hands. 'We were just about to win everything, but instead we've lost everything and it's my fault!'

46. Shot

Month 21 / sol 587 / 08:00 Mars time
[37th sol since landing]

I wake up the moment the lights in my habitat start to come on. As it does every morning, my brain immediately starts counting the days, like an automatic calendar.

Already a week since Serena was brought down.

A week since Marcus died too.

Or at least, that's the official version presented to the viewers of the Genesis channel, those billions of invisible human beings, hidden behind the cameras that have been reactivated at the same time as the halogen spotlights studding my bedroom ceiling.

But I know that Marcus is still alive.

And I find it hard to believe that Serena is dead either – or in an irreversible coma, which comes to the same thing. That woman is so fake, so sly . . . How can we know this isn't just another of her twisted traps?

I get out of bed thinking about these unanswerable questions. Regular as an automaton, I go through all the daily motions that the whole world expects of me:

288

- showering (not thinking about the person who, just one week ago, was showering with me);

- drying my hair (focusing on the hum of the hairdryer, to try to forget the silence of the empty room);

- brushing my teeth (seeing *his* toothbrush sitting on the edge of the sink, wondering why I haven't thrown it away yet);

- getting dressed (using a system with bits of string I've had to come up with in order to close the zip at the back of my undersuit, now there's nobody here to help me);

- make my bed (mechanically feeling around beneath the mattress to make sure Ruben Rodriguez's phone is still hidden there).

Fifteen minutes later, there I am, ready to leave this habitat that's suffocating me, this one-time 'Love Nest' which has now become a nest of pure anguish.

But outside in the Garden my anguish is greater still. I'm alone beneath the vast glass dome. The other couples are still in their homes – presumably curled up together, those who are most in love; perhaps arguing, for those not getting along so well any more – but all of them *together*.

Easy, Léonor.

Breathe.

Everything's going to go fine today, and tomorrow, and every day that passes between now and the arrival of the self-energising elevator. We've been given assurances – live on TV – that with or without Serena, work is going to continue. Holding firm while waiting for the elevator, the key to our survival: *that* is my goal now, the horizon I'm aiming for, and I must never forget it. I don't have the right to relax.

Partly calmed by this mantra I repeat to myself every morning, I do a few stretches in front of the plantations. Then I do a series of exercises, push-ups and pull-ups on the Garden's girders, as recommended by the protocols for preserving our muscle mass in reduced gravity.

After a good twenty minutes of physical exercise, I'm already feeling better, almost relaxed. That's when I hear a voice behind me.

'Hi, Léo! How are you doing today?'

I turn around – it's Kris.

She's holding a cup of coffee and a dish on which I can see a slice of strudel made with the Martian apples. Every morning for the last week, she's been the first person to join me in the Garden, and she absolutely insists on bringing me a little home-made breakfast. My darling Kris, goodness incarnate.

'How could I not be doing well with a breakfast like that?' I say.

'Careful, it's hot!' she warns me, holding out the plate.

I sit down at the bottom of the plantations to taste the pastry with my friend, our eyes on the day that's breaking outside the glass dome.

'It's delicious, but you really don't need to, I'm fine with just a bowl of oats,' I say between mouthfuls. 'Alexei is going to start blaming me for stealing his wife from him every morning.'

'Oh, don't worry. I'm sure he understands I want to spend time with you, especially just now, after everything that's happened. He's really shaken too, you know. He hasn't been the same since the attack. Sometimes he'll spend a whole hour just sitting on our sofa, deep in thought. And he talks in his sleep, words in Russian I can't understand. I can tell he's got something on his mind . . . like we all do.' She hesitates a moment, then continues: 'Say, Léo, since you've been up for a bit – have we had any news about Serena?'

The taste of the strudel turns bitter in my mouth.

Serena again, always Serena.

Ever since the attack, Kris's thoughts have never been far from our TV godmother. More than once I've spotted her interrupting her work on the plantations to mutter a silent prayer Earthwards.

'No, they haven't said anything,' I reply, swallowing.

I finish my breakfast in silence, while one by one the other couples emerge from their habitats. Mozabeth and Fangtao are the first two pairs to come out – but those composite names we've always used to refer to them have never felt less well suited. On either side of the dome, the two couples split apart without a word. Mozart goes to hang from a girder to do his morning pull-ups and Fangfang unrolls a mat onto the Garden floor for her yoga exercises. As for Liz and Tao, they meet at the entrance to the access tube leading to the seventh habitat and walk inside, silently. Officially our two Engineering Officers are supposed to check the status of the module every day, to ensure that everything is properly functional and doesn't pose any threat to the integrity of the base. The organisers and the viewers seem satisfied with this explanation – they do know, after all, that the seventh Nest has suffered some damage in the past, after Günter's on-air revelation.

But the real reason for Liz and Tao's regular visits is something else entirely. The English girl is secretly using her toolbox to transport Marcus's daily rations. The Chinese boy uses his wheelchair to block the access tube for long enough to allow the prisoner to receive his food and tip the bucket he uses as a chamber-pot into the toilet. The operation takes twenty minutes in all: twenty minutes in which Marcus can stretch his legs in the camera-less living room, before returning to the tiny bedroom that serves as his cell.

This morning, at the exact moment Liz and Tao return to the Garden, the glass dome is covered by streaks, then an image takes shape on the surface: it's Samantha, Serena's assistant, who has taken temporary control of operations for the programme in her boss's place.

'My dear pioneers – good morning,' she says.

She seems troubled, as she has done every time she's spoken to us since the Washington attack. She radiates a kind of seriousness, reinforced by her black suit and her severely pulled-back hair. She no longer even wears the permanent earpiece through which she used to receive instructions from her employer – it's a sign, a sign that Serena has not yet woken up.

'Once again, I have no miracles to report today,' she says, confirming what I'd suspected. 'Ms McBee is still in a coma. But we must keep praying. We mustn't lose hope. We must never lose hope.'

These past days I've often asked myself how much Samantha knows about Serena's true self, if she was aware of the Noah Report . . . But when I see the genuine sadness glistening in her eyes, when I understand the real despair that makes her voice quaver, I tell myself it's not possible, that she can't be complicit in such a repellent plot: she and Kris are two of a kind, creatures who are profoundly good – making them particularly easy prey for a predator like Serena.

'We mustn't lose hope, we must keep forging ahead,' she continues, using a phrase that is a timid copy of her boss's language – we know how hard she's trying to live up to her role model, without ever feeling she's worthy, but she's doing her best. 'It's what Ms McBee would have wanted: for her work to live on. For the conquest of space to continue. The doctors claim that in her hospital bed her cerebral activity has been reduced to zero, but I do believe she's keeping watch over you at this very moment.'

Samantha's voice cracks. After a moment's hesitation, she manages to get herself together and continues.

'Now, as you know, the selection process for the programme's second season has begun. Our engineers have confirmed the date for the *Cupido* to set off again from Earth, carrying twelve new contestants and the self-energising space elevator: this will happen in precisely fifteen Earth months, on the seventeenth of April next year. The new colonisers will help you to build our Martian civilisation – they, and all those who follow them, twelve every two years, as the Genesis programme's schedules have always anticipated. The addition of the elevator is the only change to the original plan: it will now be possible to leave the planet, returning to orbit and ultimately travelling back to Earth, for those who wish it. This time, the *Cupido* will be carrying enough provisions, oxygen and water for this to be possible, even if everybody needed to be brought back.

'But you still have time to think about that. For now, the most important thing is to start work on expanding the base in order to increase its capacity to twenty-four people.' Realising she's just made a blunder, she blushes all the way to her ears and corrects herself at once: 'Well, I mean, *twenty-three people*, since poor Marcus has left us.'

Her embarrassed expression is replaced by a plan of the base as it currently stands, with its large central dome and the seven habitats arranged around it. Gradually six more Nests appear in dotted outlines.

'*You're all familiar with the extension protocol, from your training year in Death Valley,*' the interim executive producer's voice continues. '*Using the 3D printer with Martian sand, you can produce the separate parts from which you'll be able to assemble the six additional habitats. During the course of the work, which will take a little over a Martian year, you will be able to take advantage of our engineers' support at all times. They will always be there to answer the most minor questions you may have. And I'm here today, to answer any you might have now.*'

The plans vanish and Samantha reappears on the glass surface. Smiling kindly, she ends with the most Serena-esque of expressions.

'So I'm all ears. You can tell me everything – nothing's off limits.'

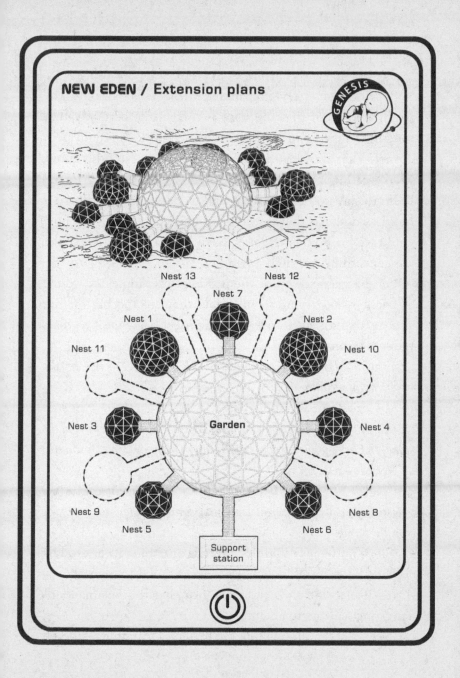

NEW EDEN / Extension plans

GENESIS

Nest 13
Nest 12
Nest 7
Nest 1
Nest 2
Nest 11
Nest 10
Nest 3
Garden
Nest 4
Nest 9
Nest 8
Nest 5
Nest 6
Support
station

Tell her *everything*?

She has no idea what she's talking about, poor thing.

Because that *everything* includes the Noah Report, the irrefutable proof that the base is rotten, the certainty that sending a new team out into these conditions would be a crime! What are we going to do when they're in orbit above Mars, getting ready to join us? Are we really going to tell them to stay up there and to send us down the elevator? I'd bet they'd refuse, that they'd want to come down – and how could we blame them, if they have no reason to suspect the danger waiting for them down here?

On the giant screen of the inside of the dome, the young assistant who's trying to fill boots that are too big for her suddenly seems so close to me. She must be, what, five years older? Ten, max.

(It would be so easy to reveal EVERYTHING to her, as she asked so innocently.)

My legs start to tremble beneath me.

(It would be such a relief to confess EVERYTHING in front of the whole of Earth, while Serena's really not in any position to harm us.)

My tongue is on fire.

(Go for it, Léo: let EVERYTHING out. They'll cancel the recruiting of the new team and just send the elevator to bring you all home.)

'Since nothing's off limits, there is one thing I want to talk to you about.' I suddenly hear Alexei's voice, to my right.

It's like a rifle shot suddenly bringing the Salamander's tempting whisper to an end.

'No . . . !' I cry, turning quickly, my heart thumping – there's a horror movie racing through my head: Alexei letting the cat out of the bag live on the air; Serena suddenly rising from her hospital bed like a vampire from his coffin; her claw-like finger pressing the red button on her damned remote control; the Garden dome collapsing in a huge crashing of broken glass; my teammates' skulls shattering like watermelons from the sudden depressurisation. 'No . . . shut up . . . you shouldn't . . .'

The words get jammed in my mouth. The way Alexei looks at me, as if I was a wild, crazy girl, makes me see it's a false alarm: he's not about to talk about the Noah Report.

'You shouldn't . . . um . . . you shouldn't worry about the building of the new habitats,' I say, pathetically, trying to save face in front of the cameras. 'Samantha said the engineers will be there to help us.'

'I'm not worried about that at all,' he says, shrugging.

He turns towards Samantha's enormous face.

'When Serena was targeted, she was talking about a claim being made by the Russians and the Chinese to do with the programme, isn't that right? If I understood correctly, my country and Tao's were claiming their part of the New Eden base and of the planet Mars.'

The other pioneers throw questioning looks at Alexei.

Kris takes his hand gently.

'Why are you talking about that, Alex?' she murmurs. 'Serena also said in her speech that everyone would have to remain united, don't forget.'

The big Russian guy puts his arm around his wife's shoulders.

'I remember what Serena said, my love. I remember every

word. Actually, I've been thinking about the whole thing for days.'

'Oh, my darling Alex!' sighs Kris, pressing tenderly against her husband's chest. 'I know how sad you are, I know how much Serena was counting on you – but like Samantha said so encouragingly, we mustn't lose hope!'

Kris can't see Alexei's expression. It's not sadness that's taken over the young man's features, that makes them seem so rock-solid: it's determination.

'For the last few days, I've been thinking about my country,' he says, raising his firm, blue gaze towards the dome. 'I think about my homeland. I think about my duty towards Mother Russia. As her son, I'm ready to represent her here, on Mars; to conquer the land that is her due, in her name.'

47. Genesis Channel

Wednesday 17 January, 1:30pm

DEAR VIEWERS,
WE ARE PLEASED TO BE ABLE TO INVITE YOU
TO WATCH THE FOURTH OF OUR 'ORIGINS' REPORTS.

*(PROGRAM ENCRYPTED — ACCESS TO
PREMIUM SUBSCRIBERS ONLY.)*

Open onto a hall whose white walls are decorated with elegant mouldings. Through the window at the far end, it's possible to see the illuminated towers of the Kremlin rising up in the night sky.

A young man in a black leather jacket enters the frame.

His broad shoulders are covered in half-melted snow, his cheeks flushed. Beneath the woollen cap that has been pulled down to his eyebrows, we recognise Alexei's face, and at that same moment, the name of the report appears on the screen:

ALEXEI
RUSSIA

Alexei turns towards the camera. 'I'm sorry I'm late.'

A woman's voice out of shot answers, slightly irritated. *'We were actually about to shut the studios for the day, what with the snow blocking the roads. You're only just in time. Have a seat.'*

Alexei sits in the chair opposite the lens.

He blows on his frozen fingers – the camera catches the flash of a silver signet ring on his right ring-finger. Then he takes off his cap, revealing his wheat-blond hair. His eyebrows are the same colour, but it's not their blondness you notice first: it's the black stitches that cross them, lined with bruises.

The casting woman is shocked. 'My word, you've really taken a bit of a beating!'

The young man raises his blue eyes towards his forehead. 'Oh, that? That's nothing! It'll heal soon. I fell over in the street, a couple of weeks ago. Crazy how slippery it can get, when the sidewalk's frozen over.'

He gives the camera a smile, somewhere between a bit of banter and a challenge.

A ruffling of papers can be heard off-screen, the sound of documents being consulted. *'Two weeks ago? The exact moment you sent in your application to the Genesis programme, according to my records – yours is one of the last files to have been entered into the system. Strange coincidence, um . . .'* – the casting woman reads the candidate's name – '. . . *Alexei.'*

The young man swings casually on his chair. 'Actually, it was my fall that clicked things into place,' he claims. 'Like Newton when he got an apple on his head, you see? I decided I'd had enough of gravity. Apparently on Mars it's three times weaker than on Eart*ZZZZZZZZZZZZZZZZZZZZZZZZZZZZZZZZZZ ZZZZZZZZZZZZZZZ ZZZZZZZZZZZZZZZZZZZZZZZZZZZ ZZZZZZZZZZZZZZZZZZZZZZZZZZZZZZZZZZZZZZZZ ZZZZZZZZZZZZZZZZZZZZZZZZZZZZZZZZZZZZZZZZ ZZZZZZZZZZZZZZZZZZZZZZZZZZZZZZZZZZZZZZZZ ZZZZZZZZZZZZZZZZZZZZZZZZZZZZ . . .*

48. Off-screen

A motel in the suburbs of Washington DC
Wednesday 17 January, 3:03pm

'*For the last few days, I've been thinking about my country. I think about my homeland. I think about my duty towards Mother Russia. As her son, I'm ready to represent her here, on Mars; to conquer the land that is her due, in her name.*'

Freeze frame: the video footage pauses on a close-up of Alexei's face. Cut.

*The TV newscaster reappears on the screen to provide a commentary on those pictures that have just been shown, which have been played over and over on every TV channel for the last almost four hours. '*Shockwaves run through the world of diplomacy! Echoing the claims made earlier by the Russian Federation at the U.N., Alexei has announced his wish to secede from the rest of the base. A dramatic turn of events happening in the midst of this state of emergency, only a week after the attack on Serena McBee – an attack for which nobody has yet claimed responsibility, but which public opinion didn't take long to connect to the air crash that cost almost the whole Genesis team their lives, little more than a month ago, over the Caribbean Sea . . .*'

The newscaster catches his breath, before looking straight into the camera and saying the next word with great emphasis. 'Ruxit: that's the word cropping up everywhere since this morning in the headlines of the world's newspapers.' A red banner appears beneath the presenter, showing the word RUXIT in capital letters. 'Will Russia – through their pioneer – break away from the Mars programme? Under what circumstances? At what price? And what is their involvement in the dramas that have devastated the Genesis staff? As we try to answer these thorny questions, I'm joined this morning via live link-up by the Russian ambassador to the United States, Ieronim Sokolov.'

The screen splits, to reveal a pleasant-looking diplomat, tastefully dressed.

'Good afternoon, Mr Ambassador.'

'Good afternoon, and thanks for having me on your programme.'

'What did you feel when Alexei made this announcement that caught everybody by surprise?'

'First of all, a sort of admiration – I'm sure it must take a lot of courage to speak like that, defending your convictions in front of the cameras. But it made me rather afraid too, I must admit: afraid that Alexei's words might be misinterpreted – and through them, the intentions of the country I represent.' The ambassador pauses briefly, looking straight into the camera now. 'The public have no reason to worry, especially at this difficult time for our American friends – by the way, I send them all my condolences for the loss of Marcus and for the hateful attack on Ms McBee, which naturally I condemn vehemently. There's no "seceding", as you put it in your introduction – I'm sorry to correct you, but words

303

are important. The term "Ruxit" is similarly quite excessive and inappropriate. Please understand, Russia has no desire to leave the Genesis programme. On the contrary, we are eager to play a prominent role in it: one befitting a great people in the union of nations.'

'It's ridiculous,' mutters Harmony, her eyes glued to the TV screen as she sits curled up on a hotel-room sofa. 'Why did Alexei say something like that if he knows the base is faulty and that he's going to evacuate with all the others anyway as soon as the self-energising elevator arrives?'

'I'm sure he has his reasons,' answers Cindy tersely from the other end of the sofa.

But Harmony is letting herself be overtaken by a growing indignation, a nervous excitement made worse by weeks on the run with no way out.

'The whole world should be uniting to save the pioneers, but instead they're going to start arguing about who owns a base that isn't worth anything! Maybe that's why my mom was targeted. I don't know, no one knows, but I've got a bad feeling about it all. I'm so tired, and I'm afraid of this whole madness getting much worse.'

'Me too, Harmony, I'm tired too . . .' murmurs Andrew, eyes fixed on his computer screen.

He's sitting on a chair positioned near the door of the room, laptop on his knees, rifle at his feet. Opposite him, the windows have their curtains drawn – a precaution for avoiding the curiosity of the drones that have been patrolling the streets since the beginning of the state of emergency.

'. . . and I also can't wait for it to be over. It's all ready, right here in the laptop – the press release with the summary of the Noah Report; the complete document; the international mailing list for all the major press groups on the planet. I just need to hit a few keys for the whole thing to go, both by email and onto a *Genesis Piracy* mirror site.'

'No!' cries Harmony, in great distress.

It's only been a few days since Andrew, in a rush of adrenaline, nearly sent the Noah Report racing through the fibres of the internet, and it was in her struggle to stop him that Harmony accidentally revealed the email with the self-energising elevator.

'Don't worry,' answers the young man, looking Harmony straight in the eye. 'This time I won't be doing anything till I'm totally sure Serena McBee really is beyond hurting anyone, and that she can't activate the depressurisation of the base remotely. I won't be sending any emails till I've gotten a green light from Barry Mirwood . . . which shouldn't be too long now.'

'Barry Mirwood?' says Harmony, not very reassured. 'I don't understand.'

Andrew looks back at the screen; behind his black-framed glasses, his eyes are sharper than ever.

'The professor sent me a message just a minute ago,' he says, not bothering to try to hide his excitement. 'He's confirming that he has finally managed to get permission to visit the Walter Reed Army Medical Center, after several days' waiting. In one hour's time, he's going to be walking into the vice-president's secure room. If he really does find her unconscious, like the media are claiming, he'll send us a coded message to tell us we can drop our bomb without fearing for the pioneers' survival.'

Harmony turns off the TV. The remote control in her hand is trembling slightly.

'So you trust this man completely, even if you've only spent a few minutes with him?' she asks, torn between excitement and doubt.

Andrew nods, quite certain.

'He was my father's mentor at the start of his career – before Dad was recruited by the Genesis programme, before he got corrupted by money, when he was still a young man filled with ideals. Your mother had Mirwood kicked out at the time of the Atlas Capital purchase, because she understood he'd be impossible to corrupt. She only kept the weak ones. She kept my father . . .'

A melancholy smile passes across Andrew's face, a mixture of sadness and happiness.

'. . . but now the time's finally come for us to redeem Sherman's mistakes and put right Serena's crimes.'

49. Reverse Shot

Wednesday 17 January, 4:00pm

The armoured door of the hospital room opens.

'Professor Barry Mirwood,' announces one of the bodyguards, moving aside to allow the scientist in.

The old man, wearing his smartest striped suit, hesitates for a moment in the doorway, still as a statue.

He's clutching a lush bouquet of sweetly scented flowers, so tightly he's crushing the stems in his fingers without even realising it.

He seems to be having trouble breathing – is his polka-dot bow tie perhaps a little too tight?

'Come in, professor,' says a voice from the back of the room.

Barry Mirwood is overtaken by nervous shivering when a human shape emerges from the gloom. With one eye hidden behind its black patch, his face as unmoving as if it were moulded out of wax, Orion Seamus reminds him of grim Charon: the ferryman between two worlds.

'I'm responsible for Ms McBee's security,' he says. 'You must have seen me several times when you've had meetings

307

with her at the White House. I know she has a high opinion of you. She'd be glad you visited, if she knew.'

'R-really?' stammers the scientist.

He flinches the moment the heavy door closes behind him with a muffled sound like a stone slab sealing a vault.

'Are those for her?'

'What?'

'The flowers.'

Barry Mirwood looks nervously down at the bouquet, as if noticing it for the first time.

'Oh – uh, yes. They're greenhoused, of course, this time of year . . . I just thought, to liven up her room . . . But in this aseptic environment maybe they're not such a good idea, I don't know if they're allowed, anyway I just thought –'

'I'll allow them.' Agent Seamus interrupts the old man's stammerings.

He solemnly takes the bouquet and sticks it into a glass pitcher of water, which is standing on the bedside table.

'They smell nice. Maybe the scent will get through to Ms McBee's nostrils, who knows?'

The two men's eyes fall on the patient.

One week after the attack, her body, which has been fed only on a drip, is totally transformed. Arms as thin as reeds, collarbones sticking out like mountain ridges: with such horrifying thinness, it looks so fragile that it might almost shatter with each breath of the artificial ventilator. But the most striking change is in her face. Above a neck which is now so thin that a single hand might wrap around it, the cheeks have sunken in completely, the lips deflated. The closed eyes are hollow, revealing the sockets in the skull beneath skin that's as fine as cigarette paper. Only Serena McBee's hair remains thick and apparently in good health, like the hair archaeologists sometimes find on shrivelled mummies long after their death.

'It's . . . horrible,' whispers Barry Mirwood. 'A woman who was so energetic, such a force of nature . . . It's crazy how much she's changed in such a short time . . .'

He rummages nervously in his jacket pocket and starts to fiddle with something.

'She didn't wake up again at all after the attack?' he asks.

'Not once,' replies Agent Seamus gravely.

'And she hasn't given any signs of being conscious? None at all?'

'None at all.'

Barry Mirwood's fingers are moving more and more hurriedly inside his pocket. A drop of sweat forms on his brow and rolls down his cheek to his white beard.

'I don't dare to imagine we might have lost her for ever,' he finally manages to say, in a choked voice. 'Such a loss to science.'

'What's that in your pocket, Professor Mirwood?'

The old man freezes.

'In my pocket?'

'Yes. You heard me. In your pocket.'

'It . . . it's just my phone . . . my cellphone . . .'

'Take it out at once,' says the agent, threateningly.

The visitor reluctantly extracts the device from his jacket pocket and holds it out, trembling, for his worrying interlocutor to see.

The other man just sighs.

'Sorry if I was a bit sharp,' he says, a sudden weariness in his voice. 'I just wanted to be sure it wasn't a weapon – just a bodyguard's reflex, not that it's much use now. I'm afraid we might never get Serena McBee back. She's gone too far away, for too long. If you have an important call to make, it's fine. Don't worry about me, or about the people out in the corridor – no one will be able to hear you, it's a soundproof door.'

Orion Seamus takes a few steps back, half-disappearing back into the gloom.

'I . . . I just wanted to see if an email had arrived, from the teams I've got working on the elevator,' says the professor. 'It's about the simulations we're carrying out for deploying the satellite . . . I need to send them my instructions so they can proceed . . . It'll only take a minute.'

But the agent doesn't seem to hear him.

Barry Mirwood starts to tap feverishly on the touchscreen of his phone.

50. Off-screen

FROM: BARRY MIRWOOD (BMIRWOOD@USA.GOV)

TO: SISYPHUS (SISYPHUS077@GMAIL.COM)

SUBJECT: SIMULATED DEPLOYMENT OF SELF-ENERGISING SPACE ELEVATOR

CONFIRMED: SAFE TO PROCEED WITHOUT RISK.

That is the coded message that has just appeared on the screen of the computer on Andrew's lap, using wording that imitates the Genesis engineers but whose meaning is totally clear to anybody who knows its real subject.

'We've got the go-ahead from Mirwood,' murmurs the young man quietly.

Harmony gets up from the sofa to rush over to him.

Even Cindy rouses herself from her persistent daze and gets up, letting the blanket slip to the floor at her feet.

'So it's really true?' she says, unable to believe it. 'You're finally going to send out the damn report? You're finally going

311

to let me go free?' Then she adds, quickly: 'And if I see Derek again, I promise I won't tell him anything about what's been going on for the last few weeks!'

Andrew nods, and taps an instruction onto the keyboard.

'Just five more minutes, time for my software to load up all the contacts so the information can be shared all around the world at the same moment.' The light from the screen on which the thousands of email addresses are scrolling is reflected in the lenses of his glasses. 'Just five short minutes.'

51. Reverse Shot

'Is it your phone making that noise?'

Barry Mirwood jumps, almost dropping the device.

'What?' he asks.

'That buzzing,' says Orion Seamus, coming closer to the bed. 'Can't you hear it?'

Struggling hard to calm his hurried breathing, the old man listens.

A buzzing?

Yes, there's a buzzing! But it's not coming from the phone, which is in silent mode.

'Sounds like it's coming from the flowers,' murmurs Orion Seamus, walking over to the bouquet.

His long fingers separate the roses and the hawthorns, the lavender and the hyacinths.

That's when it appears: *a bee.*

A lone nectar gatherer lost in the middle of the bouquet, a summer insect that's adrift in the midst of winter.

It buzzes across the room clumsily.

Trying to chase it out, Agent Seamus only manages to confuse it further – 'nasty little creature!' – and it finally dives down to rest on the dry lips of Serena McBee, just above the intubation tube.

'No!' cries Orion Seamus, raising his hand to swat the insect away.

Too late.

Taking advantage of the small space between lips and tube, the bee takes refuge in the patient's mouth as if it were an alveolus in a hive.

The man with the eyepatch freezes, unsure for the first time in his life how to react.

'Oh God, how horrible,' says Barry Mirwood, shocked, his eyes rolling in disgust.

A little bubble of flesh is protruding from Serena's thin neck, sticking out from under her skin and moving down towards her chest: *it's the bee, trying to clear a path down her windpipe.*

Suddenly a guttural cough rises from the patient's insides.

Her body, which has been motionless for a week, is shaken by violent spasms.

The lines on the hospital monitor start to go wild.

'It's a miracle!' shouts Orion Seamus at the moment when Serena springs like a jack-in-a-box up from her pillow.

Shaken by a coughing fit that makes the whole bed tremble, she spits out both the tube and the bee, covered in saliva, blood and bile.

Her eyes open, tearing the crust of secretions that have dried into their lids over the past days.

A voice from beyond the grave comes out of her throat – really a screeching more than a voice, the screeching of an ancient door, rusted over by the centuries.

'My baaaaag!'

Orion Seamus drops to his knees beside the bed, his one eye shining with emotion.

'Serena, you're – you're alive!' he stammers.

'My baaaaag!' she croaks again, her black pupils seeming to spin furiously in the middle of her water-green eyes.

The C.I.A. special agent recovers his cool.

He rushes past a stunned Professor Mirwood to the cupboard where the vice-president's effects are being stored, takes out the snakeskin handbag and runs back to the bed to give it to her.

With fingers that the long fast has reduced to mere twigs, Serena rummages frantically in the bag. She burrows over and over, among the lipsticks and the powder compacts, as if her fragile survival depended on it, as if her entire lengthy coma had been filled with this single obsession, as if she had come back from the dead for this purpose alone. With a hoarse gasp, she finally pulls out a small black box with a keyboard and a red button: the remote control that allows her to activate the New Eden depressurisation at any time of her choosing.

At this sight, Professor Mirwood is suddenly yanked out of his daze and he starts tapping away at full speed on his cellphone.

But he's so terrified, his hands are shaking uncontrollably.

His fingers fumble and the phone drops onto the floor.

Orion Seamus bends down to pick it up, and his eyes fall on the screen, to read the message that has just been sent.

FROM: BARRY MIRWOOD (BMIRWOOD@USA.GOV)

315

STOP SENDING REPORT! SERENA AWAKE!

'I-I can explain everything . . .' stammers the alarmed professor, backing away towards the reinforced door as Orion Seamus walks towards him.

From her hospital bed, the zombie who used to be one of the most elegant women in the world gives a yell that nobody can hear outside the soundproofed room.

The poor man feels around tremblingly for the doorknob.

The agent's firm hand comes down on his forehead in a movement that is precise, surgical.

Barry Mirwood collapses onto the floor, stunned.

52. Off-screen

A motel in the suburbs of Washington DC
Wednesday 17 January, 4:14pm

'What's that?' asks Harmony, pointing at a small icon that has just appeared at the top of the computer screen, in the messenger window.

Temporarily turning his attention away from the email software, which is still syncing the thousands of addresses, Andrew clicks on the incoming message.

The words flash onto the screen in capital letters.

'*Stop sending report,*' a horrified Harmony reads. '*Serena awake.*'

Quick as a flash, Andrew starts typing on his keyboard to interrupt the sending of the mail.

Faster still, Cindy races for the motel room door, turns the lock and disappears down the corridor.

53. Reverse Shot

Serena McBee gives a guttural growl, to clear the phlegm that has accumulated in her throat during her coma.

'Where am I?' she manages to say, in a voice that is weak but comprehensible – while still gripping the remote control with her vice-like hands.

'You're somewhere safe,' replies Orion Seamus, who is standing close to the door at the foot of which lies the lifeless body of Barry Mirwood. 'You're at the Walter Reed hospital. And most important of all, you're with me.'

Serena looks down at her famished body, at her needle-pricked arms, at the white sheets on which the tracheal tube left long red streaks when it came out of her mouth.

She decides to detach one of her hands from the remote control to lift the hospital gown covering her torso: and there, just above her heart, she finds a thick bandage.

'The National Mall,' she remembers now. 'The funeral service . . . That explosion in the middle of my speech, and the red hole in my chest . . . I remember.'

'You shouldn't tire yourself,' says Orion, coming towards the bed. 'You're only breathing with one lung at the moment. I'll tell the doctors that they need to replace the breathing tube, and . . .'

'No.'

Despite her extreme weakness, Serena is stunningly authoritative. Agent Seamus freezes.

'Who . . . who shot me?' she asks.

'Arthur Montgomery. I suppose he must have guessed, about you and me.'

The patient is shaken by a contemptuous, violent laugh, which comes out in a bloody spluttering.

'More of his childish jealousy . . . so ridiculous . . . I'll make him pay dearly for this!'

'He's paid already. I took him down myself. Nobody knows that however: in the chaos of gunfire, the media assigned blame for his death and your injury to an attack by obscure Russian activists.'

A smile appears on the streaked lips of the creature sitting up on the bed.

'An attack by the Russians?' she asks, delighted. 'Against me?'

'Yes, that's what people believe. Out there, people are ready to build a statue to you as a martyr, a saint.'

'Well, there's no need to disabuse them, those pious souls! Arthur might have failed in his life, but at least he made a success of his death. He's handed me public admiration on a silver platter, even more than before, if that's possible.' Serena's alarmingly gaunt face freezes, as if she has suddenly been struck by a doubt at the thought of her popularity rating.

'But tell me, while I was unconscious . . . did the pioneers say anything about me on the air?'

'Anything about you?'

Serena casts a suspicious glance around the room, which the agent immediately understands.

'You can speak in here, you needn't worry, there are no mics, I've checked the place myself.'

'Did they mention any *Noah Report*?' says Serena, who can't help lowering her voice and glancing down at the remote control in her hands. 'I'll tell you what it is, but answer my question first.'

Agent Seamus's eyelid crinkles over his one eye.

'No, I don't think they've mentioned any report . . . but Professor Mirwood did.'

He bends down to pick up the scientist's cellphone, which is still open on the last message he sent, and holds it out for the patient to read: *STOP SENDING REPORT! SERENA AWAKE!*

The vice-president smiles again.

'I see,' she says, moving her fingers from the remote control's red button.

She gives a sigh of relief, which, with her one lung, sounds like the air escaping from a punctured inner tube. Then she adds: 'This traitor Mirwood is in cahoots with Andrew Fisher, I'm sure of it – I'll explain all that to you too. But they haven't managed to sink me, not this time. I regained consciousness not a moment too soon!' Another gurgling from her throat, which sounds like a sink emptying. 'And surely by some miracle? Those people must be right: I must indeed be a saint. There must be a God, somewhere, keeping watch over me.'

320

'In that case, the God in question has pretty tiny angels,' says Agent Seamus, pointing at the dead bee lying on the sheets. 'That's the insignificant creature that woke you up. It presumably came from the greenhouse where the flowers Barry Mirwood brought you were grown.'

Serena's eyes widen, her pupils dilate.

'*The emblem of the McBee clan,*' she murmurs, with a voice that for the first time is tinged with genuine emotion, coming from someplace very far away. 'The bee I've had around me since my childhood . . . It's a sign . . . The moment I've been waiting for my whole life is finally here.'

Overcome by this dramatic gleefulness, she's seized by another coughing fit that sounds as harsh as an attack of tuberculosis. The lines on the medical monitor oscillate dangerously.

'Calm down!' cries Orion Seamus, rushing to her bedside. 'Don't forget, you've got a perforated lung! I really think I've got to call the doctors now.'

Getting her breath back with some difficulty, Serena throws him a bloodshot glance.

'The state I'm in, there's not a lot the doctors could do. The bee is a sign, I'm telling you. I need to get back in secret to my place in Scotland, the remote home of my ancestors – a place I've never mentioned in any interview, which the media don't even know still exists: McBee Castle. And there, behind the ramparts believed to have been abandoned decades ago, I'll be able to get better. There, in the melting pot of my blood, the final phase of my destiny can begin.' She pants. 'Yes, of my coronation . . . of my universal consecration . . .'

A light has come on in Serena's eyes, which might be taken for wild megalomania were it not for the fact her words suggest such mastery, such utter, cold control.

'And you can be my prince consort,' she whispers in a voice whose whistled breathing sounds reptilian. 'But to do that, you'll need to kill. A lot of people, and some in the highest places. You'll need to lie. More shamelessly than anybody has ever lied before. You'll need to surrender your soul to the devil. Can I count on you? I mean, *really* count on you? Or are you just like all the other men, as weak and unreliable as Arthur Montgomery, a pathetic creature enslaved to sensuality, ready to do anything for a pretty face?'

Serena is forced to stop for a moment to cough some bloody clots up onto the sheets – she's done a lot of talking. The moment she looks back up to continue with her questioning, she freezes suddenly: she has just caught her own reflection in the small mirror on the shelf of her bedside table.

Total shock.

She brings a trembling hand to her gaunt cheeks, to the bones visible beneath the surface of her wrinkled skin.

'My . . . my face . . .' she stammers.

Orion Seamus starts to move towards her, but she stiffens against him.

'Turn around!' she screeches, hiding her face behind her skeletal fingers. 'Don't look at me! I'm monstrous!'

'No, you're not monstrous. You're magnificent.'

Serena's fingers part slowly.

'Magnificent?' she says. 'So, you're mocking me now?'

'When I look at you, I see a survivor. I see a force of nature.

I see a woman who has come back from everything, who has borne everything, and who's still here today. I see a determination that can make the entire world bend to her will.'

Orion comes closer to the bed and this time Serena does nothing to stop him turning the mirror away.

'You're right, a pretty face may inspire a temporary infatuation,' he says. 'But *power*! Only power can feed a passion that's eternal. Its beauty never fades. The desire that power inflames never stops burning.'

He puts his hand in his pocket and pulls out the engagement ring he recovered after the attack, and returns it delicately to the patient's emaciated finger as if renewing a vow – like a pact that nothing will ever break.

'I'll take you to Scotland in secret, without leaving a trace,' he swears. 'I'll kill again for you, every last human being if necessary. I'll lie till I've forgotten what *truth* even means. And as for surrendering my soul to the devil, that's done already: it's in your hands.'

54. Shot

Month 21 / sol 587 / 16:05 Mars time
[37th sol since landing]

'Is Alexei being serious when he says he wants to take possession of a part of the base?' I ask quietly.

I can just make out Kris's face between the tightly packed branches of the apple trees. They're loaded down with those strange, enormous fruit that only grow in the reduced Martian gravity. It's ironic: it was here, in this orchard whose foliage is so dense that the cameras and microphones can't get inside, that Alexei led me the night of our arrival, to *make peace*. At the end of this Martian day, when we've started setting about the plans for extending the base, it's Kris's turn to join me in here – officially to collect apples for her to make another strudel, but really to talk about what's looking very much like *a declaration of war*.

'I don't know,' she replies. 'I told you Alex had been acting strangely since the attack, that he's been talking Russian in his sleep . . . He even sings, sometimes. They sound like battle hymns . . . It's like all his memories are coming up to the surface. Maybe by putting himself in the hands of Moscow, he's trying to find a way of clinging onto the past? Or maybe he's already thinking about the future, about our return to Earth, and he just wants to keep up good relations with his country? Either way, what can it matter to us, if a part of the base does belong on paper to the Russians? In practice, it's not going to change our everyday lives.'

As so often, Kris's affection for her husband amazes me. Even when he totally goes it alone, she's always ready to defend him. She's genuinely, totally smitten with him – and I know he's very much in love with her too. The thought gives my heart a pang: my own days of love are behind me.

'New Eden is supposed to be international territory, belonging to a private firm,' I reply, not completely convinced, and besides, knowing that's not really the point.

'You aren't seriously going to defend the interests of Atlas Capital, are you?'

Oh, it's nothing of the sort – there's no way I'd do that.

'Just try and calm Alexei down, try to focus him,' I say gently. 'Whatever he decides to do, he can't forget what we're all aiming for: holding firm till the elevator arrives. OK?'

Kris nods her agreement, her blonde locks brushing against the lush foliage of the trees.

'Thank you for being so understanding, darling Léo,' she says with a radiant smile. 'You've earned yourself a double helping of strudel! I think we've collected enough apples. We can go.'

The moment we emerge from the orchard, at the top of the plantation pyramid, the inside of the dome lights up. Down on the ground, the other pioneers who are busily putting away the day's gear all stop what they're doing.

Earth is contacting us.

To give us new instructions about the work on extending the base?

To respond to Alexei's declarations of independence?

What's Samantha going to come out with today?

But it isn't Samantha's youthful face that appears on the giant glass screen. It's that of my worst nightmare, yellow and bony, more hideous than ever.

55. Genesis Channel

Wednesday 17 January, 8:30pm

Open onto Serena McBee's face, in close-up.

Gaunt from illness, with no artifice or make-up, it would be unrecognisable – and yet the two water-green eyes in this thin face are impossible to mistake: they're the eyes of the executive producer of the Genesis programme.

The mouth opens slightly to let out a reedy little voice, amplified by the lapel mic pinned to the collar of her hospital gown. 'Your Serena is back . . . I nearly didn't come at all . . . I nearly passed on to the other side for good . . . But something gave me the strength to return.' A smile forms on the chapped lips, then widens, making a network of wrinkles. 'The love I feel for all of you, the pioneers of Mars, my dear children!'

The camera pulls slowly back, revealing the black remembrance ribbon pinned below the mic, and then the hospital bed on which the patient is sitting upright.

She is not alone.

There's a whole crowd squeezed around the bed, standing shoulder to shoulder with her.

We recognise the tanned face of President Green, to Serena's immediate right, a friendly hand resting on his vice-president's fragile shoulder. There's Secretary of State Milton Sunfield too, his mane of hair brushed especially for the occasion; and Roy Berck, Secretary of Homeland Security, his brow more creased than ever; Edgar Lyndon, the treasury secretary, serious behind his square-framed glasses; Dolores Ortega, in charge of the president's image, perched on her high heels; and the other members of the cabinet, in its entirety. All of them, like Serena, are wearing the emblematic black ribbon in their buttonholes.

The patient looks up at the man standing to her left, who is wearing a long white coat. 'Dr Spitzbergen here has been very frank with me,' she says, her voice weak but quivering with life. 'I've been incredibly lucky not to have succumbed to my injuries, but I won't be the way I used to be before. I'll probably be disabled for the rest of my life, unable to move myself around, short of breath from any exertion. I insisted on telling you this myself – you, the pioneers of Mars, the citizens of America, and all the viewers who over these past months have done me the honour of watching the Genesis channel.'

The tracking backwards continues.

In addition to the members of the Green administration and the hospital staff, we also see Jimmy Giant and Stella Magnifica, the official performers of *Cosmic Love*; Samantha, Serena McBee's personal assistant; and some twenty of the most senior members of the Genesis team, all of them in the grey jackets with the programme's red foetus logo – only Professor Barry Mirwood is missing.

* * *

The frame continues to widen, revealing the foot of the bed in the foreground, which is surrounded by children. We recognise the little kids from the New Jersey orphanage who were used back in December for the Genesis channel's Christmas broadcast. Their presence in the hospital room seems to serve no other function than to increase the emotion the picture evokes. They've all been dressed in white, and they're holding bouquets of white roses in their hands; the dark remembrance ribbons stand out, pinned to the children's chests.

At the far end of the frame that now encompasses the entire room, Serena McBee's bruised body seems smaller and more fragile than ever. And yet she's the focal point of this tableau. Invisible lines are converging towards her, as in an Old Master painting – the eyes of all the adults and children physically present in the room, but also, it would seem, those of all the viewers around the world too.

There's something religious about the scene, and Serena's voice does have a prophetic note when she speaks again: 'This is my body,' she says, in an almost direct quote from the Gospels. 'Delivered unto you, and to the Genesis programme . . .'

She holds out her scrawny arms, the better to offer herself up to the camera. '. . . sacrificed for the cause of a humanity that is united, happy and at peace. That was Marcus's dream. That was the dream of those who died in the Caribbean plane crash. And that is my dream – and it's still very much alive. I make you this solemn promise, here and now: I will never stop dreaming it! The Genesis programme will never end! In the name of this ribbon that adorns my chest, over my still beating heart!'

Overcome by her rush of lyricism, Serena is shaken by a

coughing fit that sends feedback from her microphone.

The camera swings violently towards Dr Spitzbergen, who rushes over to the patient to help her, delicately placing an oxygen mask over her emaciated face to help her recover her breath.

Close-up on President Green's reaction to the poignancy of the situation – he's genuinely moved.

He turns to the camera to continue with the speech, while his vice-president is getting her breath back. 'Serena absolutely insisted on addressing the viewers personally tonight,' he says, slightly emotional. 'Yet more proof, if proof were needed, of this exceptional woman's courage and devotion. A woman I'm proud to have nominated to be by my side at the head of government . . . A woman I'm honoured to be able to call *my friend* . . .' He pauses a moment, confused, then continues in a voice that is harder and more determined – the voice of a wartime leader: '. . . a woman the enemies of freedom wanted to silence for ever. But they will not succeed. The United States of America will not let them. Mars is international territory, according to the space treaty ratified by the U.N. in 1967, and it must remain so. We will not surrender to terrorism. As of this week, the whole Genesis staff will be gathering back at Cape Canaveral, under the protection of the U.S. Army, to continue to work undisturbed for the success of the programme. We will fortify the launch site to make it a real citadel, a beacon against obscurantism, a symbol every bit as strong as the Statue of Liberty herself. The state of emergency will continue right across the country until further notice – not because we are giving in to fear, but because we know we must remain vigilant.

As for dear Serena, she has asked my permission to withdraw temporarily from public life and media scrutiny to rest and recover her health. I have agreed, of course. She will spend the next few months in the tropics, in a climate well suited to her recovery, living in a location that will remain secret. In her absence, Milton Sunfield will take her place in the vice-presidency.' The secretary of state nods gravely, seized by the new responsibility that now falls on him. 'As for the Genesis programme, Samantha, whom you all know, and who knows our brave pioneers so well, will continue to look after it during Serena's absence.' The young assistant forces herself to smile, hiding her nerves.

From somewhere out of shot there's a slight moan.

The camera pulls back. It's Serena in her bed, gesturing to Dr Spitzbergen to remove the respiratory mask so she can speak again.

'Do not be afraid,' she says, her voice quavering, her eyes tearful, once again adopting a Biblical turn of phrase. 'I am not leaving you for good. You will not see me on your screens any more, but I will still be among you, from my place of retreat, following the Genesis channel, the destiny of the United States of America and of the Mars pioneers.'

She turns her angular face towards the camera as if to address those pioneers more directly, and concludes her speech in barely a whisper: 'I will continue to watch over you day and night, my little friends, I swear it – like a guardian angel, invisible but always there.'

Fade to black.

56. Shot

It's like a really horrible hangover.

That's what I felt when I woke up, a feeling that followed me to the Garden where, like every morning, I was the first to show up.

Only yesterday I was living in a world without Serena McBee; even though I never stopped being cautious, I can tell now that there was a kind of crazy hope making my heart race. That hope is dead today. Serena is alive – horribly diminished, sure, but alive. If she's decided to disappear from our screens – the biggest media freak in the history of the world – it's so that she can keep a closer eye on us from the shadows.

What's she cooking up now?

What's her next move going to be, in this game she's playing against us?

The final phase is about to start, I'm getting a grim foreboding of that. It'll be the longest, most vicious, most mysterious of all: twenty months for us to hold out until the self-energising elevator arrives. None of the rules I thought I understood apply any more: how can you fight an enemy who is silent and invisible?

'Sleep well, Léo?'

I shiver.

That warm, melodious voice can only belong to one person.

'Like a baby,' I lie, turning towards Mozart.

He's an early bird this morning, up even earlier than Kris. To look at his tired, drawn features, I can guess his night was no better than mine. The truth is, the Mozabeth habitat is no longer anything resembling a Love Nest, but more like a torture chamber where two people have to live who are becoming more distant from one another with each day that passes.

'I wish I could say the same, but I no longer have anyone tucking me up in bed at night, and I don't like sleeping on my own,' he admits, with a disillusioned smile, which lights up his face a little and reawakens that kind of incorrigible seductiveness he used to have about him. 'Liz and I are sleeping in separate rooms; she's in the master bedroom and I'm in one of the guest rooms. Not to worry – I'm still going to be delivering the materials for the work to go ahead – I'll be out all day, escorting the Planetology and Engineering Officers: they've got to carry out the topographical mapping for the extension of the base. I know you're supposed to stay inside in your role as the doc, but . . . if you wanted to get out of the Garden for a bit, take your mind off things . . .'

He's hesitant all of a sudden, and looks down at the floor with those brown eyes whose recent gleam has already been extinguished again.

And he ends his speech, not really believing it himself:

'Anyway, there'll always be a place for you in the maxi-rover. I could even teach you to drive it. Today. Or tomorrow. Or, you know . . . whenever you wanted.'

I feel my heart clench.

Without warning, memories from the *Cupido* come crashing back in deafening waves.

All those moments of fake intimacy, when we were pretending to forget about the cameras in the bubble of the Visiting Room . . .

All those casual songs he hummed to me as if we were alone in the world . . .

All those long looks we exchanged, when everything was still possible . . .

But nothing is possible now, not any more.

After the weddings, the secrets, the trial, there's nothing left of that innocent time. There's nothing left of love. There's nothing left but a furious desire to survive.

And nothing should distract us from that goal. Mozart needs to understand that. But the words that come out of my mouth, cold and sharp, bring me no relief.

'It's like you said: I've got to stay in here to ensure medical care is always up to scratch. Today. And tomorrow. And always. Just pretend I don't exist. If you've got a free spot in your rover, offer it to somebody else.'

ACT IV

57. Off-screen – One Year Later

Alphabet City, New York
Monday 31 December, 4:20pm

A stealthy figure is rushing through the snowy streets.

It is wrapped up in several layers of shawls, wraps and scarves, in a whole palette of greys, that cover its head like a thick veil. Its face is just a void, black and impenetrable. You might mistake it for a spectre.

The area is bathed in a dusky half-light. Although the sun has almost set behind the half-dilapidated red-brick façades, the street lamps are off. The truth is, it's been a long time since they've been on at all: by privatising public lighting, President Green's Ultra-libertarian government has cast entire neighbourhoods into the shadows, those neighbourhoods which are not sufficiently profitable for the private firms that have hijacked the market. Every night, little spots of the United States are in darkness, right alongside the areas of light, a map of wealth and poverty – often in the heart of the same city, like here in New York. The working-class neighbourhood of Alphabet City, at the eastern edge of Manhattan, has been hit hard by the crisis. After a fleeting period of gentrification at the

337

start of the twenty-first century, it reverted under the Green administration to what it had been previously. To libertarian dropouts, fringe artists and other anarchists who take refuge there, it's a haven; to everyone else, which is to say for the majority of people: a no-go area.

The grey spectre undoubtedly belongs to the former category. Its gait is nimble and quick, almost airborne despite the bundle of rags weighing it down. Totally unlike the hesitant, troubled steps of those people venturing bravely or accidentally east of First Avenue, to the enclave named for its alphabetised avenues.

Avenue A, you're All right, goes the old saying repeated by generations of New Yorkers.

The grey spectre passes cars that have been abandoned to poor weather and rust, brushing past other ghosts walking the snowy sidewalk. Some of them are wandering in the dark with no apparent goal, like grieving souls, their eyes fixed weirdly straight ahead of them; others, however, carrying paraffin lamps with a flame wavering inside, are hurrying towards some mysterious meeting, pushing shopping carts filled with sundry bits and pieces; all of them, whether druggies in withdrawal or fences for stolen goods in a hurry to end their day, are covered in layers of old clothes, shells to help them withstand the winter. Most of the squats in Alphabet City have no heating.

Avenue B, you're Brave.

Plastic sheeting is stretched over the smashed windows of the buildings' façades, in an attempt to keep in a little heat; but the December gusts have detached several of them and they're flapping in the north wind. The posters put up a year earlier to promote the call for applicants to Season Two of the Genesis programme are also coming unstuck, the red of planet Mars has faded, bits of graffiti have blossomed around the edges. This isn't vandalism, however: the graffiti artists have just written their own names with great care, as if this superstitious, almost magical ritual might help them get selected.

Avenue C, you're Crazy.

All of a sudden, a slight glow washes over the far end of the street. The grey spectre picks up the pace, ignoring the passers-by who stop to look up at the sky with red-cheeked, cracked faces: a squadron of police drones is passing, a daily sight since the establishment of a state of emergency one year earlier. On this New Year's Eve, the machines are passing at such an altitude that the beams of their headlights barely reach the ground – it looks like an aurora borealis.

Avenue D, you're Dead.

From Avenue D over to the dark banks of the East River, even the sky itself disappears: rickety gangways and platforms, all made from salvage materials, have been thrown up between the roofs of the squalid buildings to take over another little bit of space – or is it to bury Alphabet City's terrible secrets away even more deeply? The grey spectre enters this labyrinth where the squats spill out onto the streets, under the sheet-metal porches that annex large portions of the sidewalk from around the doorways to the buildings. Here and there, neon bulbs give off a white, flickering light – there's no doubting the ingenuity of Avenue D's residents when it comes to hijacking the city's electricity network. The murmur of TV sets has replaced the whistling of the wind, most of them playing the familiar notes of *Cosmic Love*, the Genesis programme's theme tune. The New Year's broadcast from Mars is about to begin.

The spectre stops at a ground-floor window through which a screen is visible, one of the few that is not tuned to the Genesis channel. But the headlines on the TV news broadcast, with the serious-looking reporter, are still about that same programme.

'. . . *on this final night before the New Year, the U.N. Security Council, more divided today than ever, has decided to extend the moratorium on Martian sovereignty. Among the permanent members, Russia and China are both claiming parts of the New Eden base, while France and the UK are standing by the United States in a belief that the planet Mars should be considered international territory. This position is considered hypocritical and imperialistic by Moscow and Beijing, who claim that in reality the base is* de facto *under American control through the Genesis programme. The representatives from Nigeria, India and Brazil had already backed the Russian and Chinese view, and to everyone's surprise, they were tonight joined by Singapore. Which means that six of the twelve nationalities represented on Mars are now in favour of dividing up the site. Experts believe this represents a sizeable challenge for the Green administration, and a potential crisis situation for international organisations . . .*'

The spectre walks on past the window, letting the reporter's voice fade into the night, and continues on its path as far as an iron plate set into the ground: a heavily locked trapdoor, such as one sometimes finds above New York cellars.

A hand in a patched fingerless glove emerges from the bundle of faded clothes: it's holding a large key, in fingers that have turned blue with the cold.

The lock opens with a click.

Somewhere – a few metres away or a few streets away, it's impossible to tell in the strange echo chamber of Avenue D – there's the sound of an explosion. A gunshot or a firecracker? The last crime of the year, or the start of celebrations?

With some effort, the spectre lifts the trapdoor, revealing a dark flight of stairs.

'Hey, pal – something to cheer you up for the New Year?'

The spectre freezes, as a man – his face split by a wide scar – appears in the glow of the nearest neon light.

'I've got coke, crack, uppers . . .' he says, opening one side of his anorak.

Dozens of little transparent plastic sachets are sewn into the lining, containing powder or pills of all shapes and sizes.

The guy's smile widens, showing yellowing teeth.

'I'm selling it all off cheap, to end the day with a bang. It's kind of my good deed for the New Year: twenty per cent off the whole range.' From his pocket, he extracts a sachet glimmering with powder that's brighter than the rest. 'Even on Zero-G, if you want to fly to the stars like the lucky little bastards on the Genesis programme!'

With a start, the spectre turns sharply around, shoves past the dealer and disappears down the stairs that plunge into the belly of the city.

'Hey, asshole!' shouts the dealer, getting down onto all fours in the snow to recover his precious merchandise. 'What the fuck you think you're . . .'

The trap slams shut on the end of his phrase.

'Harmony?' calls Andrew, sounding worried.

He looks up from the computer shell that he was in the process of tampering with by the light of a torch attached to a stand. On the edge of the circle of light, on the workbench covered in tools, screwdrivers, electric wires and printed circuits, lies a folded, yellowed page from a newspaper. In the photo, an elegant woman and a serious-looking girl are sitting beside a pair of black-and-white greyhounds. The headline: *A MOTHER'S APPEAL*. The text reads: *Following the tragic disappearance of Sherman Fisher, Communications instructor for the Genesis programme, Vivian Fisher has now spent months without any news of her elder son. From the Cape Canaveral base where she and her younger child Lucy are now living, she is launching an impassioned appeal to Andrew in these pages, begging him to return to them . . .* (The rest of the article is hidden in the shadows.)

'Is that you, Harmony?' asks Andrew again, getting up from his chair and turning towards the unlit staircase from which he can hear the echoes of hurried footsteps.

Without waiting for an answer, he hurries over to one of the makeshift bookcases covering the cellar walls, where he keeps the rifle he took from Cindy a year earlier. But one year on, his reflexes seem dulled; he no longer moves like the young athlete who leapt the fence of the Villa McBee in the middle of a snowstorm, who outran the C.I.A. drones sent after him deep in Death Valley. His one-time champion's body has atrophied, his chest has hollowed, his shoulders are stooped under the old sweatshirt that's covering them. Each time his right foot comes down on the damp stone, it makes a metallic sound, as gloomy as a prisoner's chains on the floor of his cell.

'Whoever you are . . .' he calls out, turning the barrel of the gun towards the staircase.

'Andrew, it's me!'

Harmony bursts into the cellar, pulling off the shawls covering her.

She's changed in a year too.

Her hair, which used to come down almost to her waist, has now been cut to shoulder-length. Its strange paleness has been disguised by a dye that's very dark brown, almost black. Her eyebrows have been similarly coloured to support the illusion. Is it this new colouring that gives the girl her air of confidence, a thousand miles from the timorous creature she was one year earlier? Hasn't her whole face become stronger, more determined, and doesn't she even seem several centimetres taller?

'What's going on?' asks Andrew, worried, not taking his eyes off the staircase, not lowering the gun. 'Have they tracked us down? Do we need to escape through the sewers?'

'No,' replies Harmony, her breath forming a small cloud of steam in the cold air of the cellar. 'It's nothing . . . just an unpleasant encounter.'

She removes one of the layers of clothes covering her and puts it on a rickety coat-rack – a piece of salvage furniture like everything piled up around here.

'Here's the day's delivery,' she says, putting a packet she's been carrying wrapped in her old clothes onto the workbench.

'Half a dozen cellphones to unlock.' She lines the phones up under the flashlight. 'We won't get much for most of them, but at least there's a latest generation Karmafone Virtual 8, which a lot of people are after on the black market these days.'

Andrew is finally ready to put down his gun, and he limps over to Harmony – while she looks like she's grown taller, he seems to have stooped.

His right leg comes into the light, revealing the reason for his limp: a metal prosthesis has replaced the foot that was injured a year ago.

'You came back in such a hurry I got worried,' he explains, his voice a little calmer now. 'Ever since we had to get my foot amputated, I've felt less sure of myself. My muscles have wasted away, I crawl around all day alone like I'm dragging a ball and chain. I really feel like a dead weight. If it does happen one day, and we have to use the city sewers to escape, I'm scared I'm going to slow you down. Every morning when you go off to get the merchandise I blame myself for letting you risk your skin – I'm so afraid you'll be recognised . . . And every evening I wonder if we've done the right thing coming to live here in secret in New York – you, the daughter of Serena McBee, and me the resident invalid . . .' Suddenly doubtful, he asks, 'Do you remember how to get access to the Noah Report, in case I suddenly disappear?'

'I remember perfectly, Andrew,' Harmony reassures him. 'The location in the Cloud that can be accessed from any computer . . . The seven levels of passwords . . . And I also remember all the computing know-how you've been teaching me for a year, how to get a file through despite any firewalls or barriers, the secret short-cuts that make it possible to bypass the walls of the internet . . .

'And as for New York . . . this is the best place we could have hidden, disappearing into the crowd, while making some money from your skills on the black market to cover our costs. We're taking a lot fewer risks here than on the highways where there have been police blockades since the state of emergency started.' She walks over to him, her eyes shining with gratitude. 'You're the exact opposite of a dead weight, Andrew,' she murmurs. 'You're the hero who's the reason why the Mars pioneers are still alive. You're the saviour who weaned me off drugs. You're the messenger who – one day, soon – will make the truth burst out into the world!'

A pale smile passes across the young man's emaciated face.

'Make the truth burst out into the world,' he murmurs. 'A year ago that's what nearly happened, and then the explosion would have blown everything up from Earth to Mars; a few more seconds and my mail would have gone out to thousands of journalists.'

'But fortunately you managed to stop the software running the moment my mother woke up!' says Harmony. 'You saved the pioneers from depressurisation, at the last possible second!'

Andrew sighs.

'I saved them? Maybe. But at what cost? It's been a year our political leaders have spent tearing each other apart over a base they don't realise is worthless. A year when we haven't seen Professor Mirwood again . . .' He looks down. '. . . or my family.'

Harmony puts her hand on his arm – a gesture she's made often in the past, to comfort him. But this time, does she notice that instead of calming him, the touch seems to provoke extra agitation?

No.

The cellar is too dark, and Harmony herself is too enthralled by what she's saying to notice Andrew's pupils dilating, his nostrils trembling, the hair standing up on his arms.

'We haven't seen Barry Mirwood since he secretly warned us about my mom waking up, but he still writes to us every week from the fortified base at Cape Canaveral,' she reminds him. 'Through his coded messages, he's been able to confirm that your mother and sister are there with him, as is everyone connected to the Genesis programme. The government has brought them all together as a security measure, and they have everything they need there – anyway, there's no way Vivian could have kept paying the bills on the Beverly Hills house without Sherman's salary, could she?'

Andrew lowers his eyes.

'Hanging onto that salary was why he became a criminal,' he mumbles, once again rehearsing the bitterness gnawing at him. 'So he could get his hands on some Genesis money. So he could pay for the house with the pool, the two Mercedes, his family's lifestyle . . . his son's college fees.'

Harmony closes her hand over Andrew's arm to tear him away from his morbid thoughts.

'Don't think about all that any more. What matters is that Vivian and Lucy are safe. President Green has promised to protect all the Cape Canaveral guests, he's made it a point of honour. Nobody would ever dare to hurt them . . . not even my mom.'

Andrew looks up again, but he doesn't seem totally convinced.

'We haven't seen her for a year either,' he murmurs. 'Has she succumbed to her injuries? Did she end up dying in that mysterious tropical retreat she was going to? We don't know any more than the general public do. Radio silence. I think that's really the worst part: not knowing if she might come back one day.'

He gestures with his chin towards a low rickety table, next to an old sofa with broken springs, on which magazines published over the last twelve months have been piling up. Serena McBee is on all the covers, omnipresent and yet unreachable, accompanied by sensationalist headlines that disguise the journalists' total failure to track her down.

February: a photo of Serena smiling, from her glory days, in front of a map of the world: OUR GLOBAL INVESTIGATION IN THE FOOTSTEPS OF VICE-PRESIDENT MCBEE.

April: another mystery story, this time with a picture from her hospital bed a few hours before she disappeared, with an alarmist claim in big red letters: WHAT THEY'RE HIDING FROM YOU: SERENA MCBEE STILL AT DEATH'S DOOR.

June: the tone has turned lighter again, a Serena who's been Photoshopped into a summer dress against the backdrop of a beach and palm trees. SERENA MCBEE FOUND ON THE ISLAND OF SAINT BARTS! is the fanfare on the cover of this one, which then adds, modestly, in its subheading: OUR CHOICE OF THE BEST V.I.P. TROPICAL DESTINATIONS.

September: the limits of Photoshop are tested once more, this time to show Serena accompanied by Elvis Presley from his Las Vegas days, white satin cape and sideburns included. A large bold headline, a punch aimed right at the reader's critical faculties: CARRIED OFF BY ALIENS!

'If you ask me, I don't think she's coming back,' says Harmony suddenly. 'Even if she is still alive.'

She blinks – there are brown contact lenses over her water-green irises, but there's still something unreal about these eyes, a kind of gap between her and the rest of the world.

'I hardly know my mom, even after eighteen years with her,' she admits. 'But I remember, when I was a little girl at the Villa McBee, those whole afternoons she used to spend in the gardens, taking care of her bees and flowers. Those were the moments I thought she was happy, cut off from the rest of society, from chasing money and power. Today my instincts are telling me she's found herself a new garden, someplace secret, a retreat where she'll stay hidden for ever, to avoid prison. Wherever she is, she knows there's nothing that can stop the progress of the self-energising elevator now. She's understood that the pioneers are going to be able to get out of New Eden, to escape Mars's gravitational well and return to Earth – and then her depressurisation remote control will become useless, and there's nothing then to stop us revealing the Noah Report. All of the world's leaders will realise that the base is corrupted and that there's nothing worth claiming up there; the struggles between nations will stop and the terrorist threat with it; the state of emergency will be lifted and the guests staying at Cape Canaveral will be allowed back home.'

There's such confidence, such enthusiasm in Harmony's voice that it's almost impossible not to go along with her idyllic vision. Andrew drinks in her words, consuming her with his eyes.

She's so close!

He so wants to believe her!

And he also so wants . . .

'It's just a matter of months, Andrew. Eight, to be exact,' she says. 'The new crew will soon be completing their training in Death Valley. In April, the *Cupido* will leave the Earth, in August it'll arrive in Mars's orbit. There it'll deploy the self-energising elevator, load up the pioneers and return home. These eight little months are going to fly past, I promise you. The worst is behind us. Before the New Year's up, you'll be back with your family, the best surgeons will have taken care of your leg, you'll be back in Olympic shape and you can finally go to Berkeley. You'll be back to the life you had before, and I . . .'

She pauses for a moment, her eyes on the future she's already thinking about, failing to see Andrew's that are shining just centimetres away and which seem to be crying out: *No, Harmony, I'll never go back to my life before, because you're in my life now!*

'. . . and I, I will get Mozart back,' she concludes with a smile, taking her hand off Andrew's arm and bringing it to the locket she's wearing around her neck.

58. Shot

Month 10 / sol 258 / 20:30 Mars time
[377th sol since landing]

'Champagne!' cries Kelly, brandishing a bottle labelled *Merceaugnac 1969*.

Fangfang tells her off at once.

'Careful what you say on the air. Technically it's not champagne, let alone Merceaugnac. Léonor's sponsor might reprimand us for misusing their brand.'

The Singaporean girl is right: it's been ages since we finished most of the bottles given to us by Merceaugnac, and the only two that are left now are being kept for two very special occasions: one of them to give us courage the night before the next Great Storm, which will happen eight months from now; and the other to celebrate our being saved, if we do manage to get up into the Martian orbit thanks to the self-energising elevator.

That hasn't stopped Kelly from taking one of the empty bottles and filling it with a liquid of her own invention. She's been working on it every evening for weeks, after her long days outside transporting the material needed for the extension of the base. With the help of Samson's biology equipment and the

3D printer, she's constructed a sort of home-made still in her habitat – apparently inspired by her brother's bootleg distillery back in Toronto. After various unsuccessful experiments, she seems to have managed to brew a drinkable alcohol from the oats in the plantation – and tonight, New Year's Eve, she's finally decided to let us taste it.

'You're kidding, Fangfang, right?' she laughs, pulling out the stopper. 'If the guys at Merceaugnac got a chance to taste this divine nectar, I bet they'd write me a cheque pronto with a load of zeroes to allow them the rights to use my recipe. The know-how of Canadian beer-making, the exotic flavour of Martian oats, and just a pinch of my own particular madness: it's art! Tell me what you think!'

Without another word, she pours the sparkling liquid into the glass that's closest to hand: it's Kenji's.

'Here's to you, Tiger!'

A year after our arrival on Mars, the sense of complicity between the two of them has never faded. They're still so different – the most extrovert girl on the base and the most repressed boy – and yet they're still so complementary. After all these months, they've improved in contact with one another, with Kelly gaining in stability and Kenji letting go slightly of his existential anguish – he sleeps without a suit these days: a great achievement. There really is something magnetic between them, something playful, a kind of loving friendship that sparkles like Martian 'champagne'. Their joyful, relaxed relationship is the total opposite of the serious, symbiotic passion that binds Kris and Alexei, and which makes them withdraw further and further into themselves every day.

Seeing the two of them at the end of the big aluminium table we've set up in the Garden for New Year's Eve, I'm struck by the resemblance between them. In a year, Alexei has let his blond hair grow, and it now comes all the way down his neck and makes his face look like a medieval knight, a crusader. Today Kris has unwound her crown of blonde locks and her hair is worthy of a Rapunzel – the distant look in her eye reminds me of that princess kept up in her tower too. Krisalex are both dressed in natural unbleached silk tunics – among the first ones Kris made thanks to the silkworms being raised here, which she was responsible for as one of our Biology Officers. She never leaves Günter's side these days, and he is wrapped in a kind of pyjama made to measure for his robot body. Krisalex and their unlikely pageboy seem to be somehow outside the group, belonging to a different time and space, to the world of fairy-tales.

As for the other 'couples'... Nothing has gone as the Genesis advertising leaflets promised it would. Fangfang and Tao are sitting at opposite ends of the table: that speaks volumes about their relationship, which is now in shreds. The Singaporean girl has never forgiven her husband for the other passion he experienced before her; and since the trial, he's never hidden the fact that he's still in love with his now departed ex-fiancée. Today, Fangfang and Tao are like strangers to one another, as if they'd never known each other at all.

Liz and Mozart don't make any effort to present a united front to the viewers any more either. The English girl, who's sitting next to me tonight, has never lost my respect. Not once in these past twelve months have I heard her grumble.

But she's always the first up in the morning and the last to bed, always volunteering for all the most disagreeable chores: she's supervising the extensions to the base, going to all the places where the other Engineering Officer is prevented from going by his disability; she's the one who every morning and evening goes into the seventh Love Nest, officially to check the status of the habitat. More than once I've been tempted to take her into the orchard, hidden from view of the cameras, to ask her for the latest on Marcus. But I've never done it. Because deep down it's best to pretend he really is dead; it's just simpler that way.

Mozart, meanwhile, is very lively, but he acts as though I'm the one who's died. He avoids looking at me, or talking to me. How can I blame him? He's just obeying the command I gave him a year ago: *Just pretend I don't exist*. No matter how painful it is.

And the final two pioneers . . . Admittedly, Safia and Samson are sitting side by side at the table, inseparable as ever, and I'm sure both the viewers and the organisers are totally in the dark. But the thing that unites them isn't exactly what Serena McBee was trumpeting when she promised the audiences 'the marriages of the century'.

At the thought of the executive producer, I feel a knot in my stomach, an old reflex. But it's not the sharp cramp I used to know so well, that took my breath away – over the months the feeling has lessened, till it's now no more than a slight, fleeting pinch. Serena's features are less clear than they were even in my photographic memory, the smooth face from her glory days mixing with the death mask she was wearing last time she appeared on screen. Crimson dawns follow dust-filled dusks, the daily medical tests on the team members, the monitoring of the building site for the base extension: the routines of Martian life, in other words, have gradually replaced things from Earth. I might know very well, rationally, that the Serena threat is always present, but I don't feel it so deep inside my flesh any more – and that's probably the most dangerous thing of all.

'Can I pour you some?' Kelly asks, completing her circuit of the table. 'As our representative of Merceaugnac and the classy French lifestyle, I'm counting on you to tell me what you really think!'

'I'll be totally impartial,' I promise her, holding out my glass.

The alcohol streams in, fizzing, a rich pinkish colour that reminds me of the most beautiful Martian days, when the sun is shining brightly enough to make the fine powder floating in the atmosphere sparkle.

'There's nothing in it except oats, so why's it that colour?' I ask. 'What have you added to it?'

'Aha, that's my famous little pinch of madness – you've got to try and guess.'

I bring the glass to my lips.

The bubbles roll across my tongue, prickling slightly.

Beyond the bitterness of fermented oats, I can detect a fruity, sugary note. I recognise that taste.

'Have you added some kind of artificial flavour? I thought we'd used up all the Eden Food factory produce a long time ago.'

'No, that's not it, there's nothing artificial at all. My drink's guaranteed one hundred per cent organic!'

'Organic or not, I have no intention of poisoning myself,'

says Fangfang, pushing away the drink that hasn't so much as moistened her lips.

'If you don't like it, that's no reason to put the others off.'

Leaving those two – the best of enemies – to their little verbal sparring, like an old married couple, Kris takes a small sip from her glass.

'I . . . I think I've got it!' she says with a childish smile that briefly replaces the picture of an inaccessible princess with my dear old friend.

She points towards the fenced-in container at the far end of the Garden, set aside for the cultivation of silkworms.

Fangfang can't help but grimace in disgust.

'Yeuch – the worms?'

'No! Mulberries!'

Of course – she's right! It does taste of mulberries! Kelly must have collected the berries from the mulberry bushes whose leaves are used to feed the insects.

One by one the intrigued pioneers taste the drink – even Fangfang brings the glass up to her nostrils for a sniff.

The weary faces are all smiling now.

'It's really not that bad at all,' I admit. 'You have my word as the resident one hundred per cent genuine Frenchie.' Silently I thank Kelly from the bottom of my heart for bringing us this little ray of sunshine – we so deserve it.

'You mean it's totally delicious!' says Samson, his beautiful eyes sparkling like the drink itself.

'I only hope my cooking will be up to scratch,' says Kris, glancing worriedly at the dishes around the table which she's spent the afternoon preparing.

'I'm sure it'll be awesome,' says Kelly. 'Some fine Martian dining, accompanied by a bit of the Martian vintage: we've invented a whole new gastronomy, my friends. And the good news is, I decided those four empty champagne bottles wouldn't be enough, so I've also filled two ten-litre barrels. OK, it's a bit less posh than Merceaugnac magnums, but like the poet says: *Who cares about the bottle, so long as it'll get you drunk!*'

She raises her glass and drains it dry, and the rest of the table do the same.

'Cheers to you all, my dear pioneers. Cheers!'

Huh? What?

Who's talking to me?

I open my eyes and then close them again right away, blinded by the brightness in the room.

Is it already morning?

What time is it?

'The whole Genesis team joins me in wishing you a beautiful and happy New Year.'

This headache!

My brain has turned to mush and the voice that's coming into my right ear pulverises it a bit more with every word!

As for my left ear, it feels like it's glued to a time bomb that's going *tick-tock . . . tick-tock . . . tick-tock . . .*

'Even if we are of course going by the Earth calendar rather than the Martian one to send you these greetings.'

There's a slurred groan from somewhere near me, and I think I recognise Kelly.

'Hey, Earth? What say you turn the volume down a bit?'

I force my eyelids open, fighting the desire to close them again.
Tick-tock . . . tick-tock . . . tick-tock . . .

Samantha's gigantic face appears on the surface of the dome, rotated ninety degrees, a bit blurred by my hangover – unless it's something to do with the long-distance interference, since Mars is currently almost at its greatest distance from the Earth: four hundred million kilometres.

'You had a lot of fun last night – what a lovely New Year's Eve!' says Samantha with a smile, as I realise I'm lying on the floor, right in the middle of the Garden; she adds, slightly embarrassed: 'Though it's true it did get a little nutty at one point, and we had to cut away from a few segments in order to stay on the air, as the Genesis programme charter requires.'

Cut a few segments?

What does she mean by that?

And most of all, why can't I remember anything that happened after Kris's carrot cake?

Tick-tock . . . tick-tock . . . tick-tock . . . goes the bomb against my ear, the ear that's pressed down against the aluminium floor.

The floor? Really? So how come my cheek feels like it's touching something soft and warm instead of something cold and hard? Am I really hearing a *tick-tock*, or is it a *boom-boom, boom-boom*?

I lift my head, slowly . . .

. . . and what I see sobers me up at once.

My head was on somebody's chest.

Mozart, who's still asleep lying on the floor, his white shirt half open over his golden chest: the thing I was nestled against as I slept was not a time bomb, but his beating heart.

357

I want to get up and move away as quickly as possible, but something's stopping me. A powerful desire from somewhere deep inside me: a wish to let my head fall back, to rest it again in the crook of Mozart's shoulder and go back to sleep, just go back to sleep, as if nothing else mattered.

It's the Salamander giving me this crazy idea, right?

That's got to be what makes me stay there, motionless beside Mozart, while the others wake up and all the viewers in the world have a good laugh at us from behind their screens.

But if it's the Salamander, why can't I hear its voice?

'On this January first, we've decided to give you some time off duty,' announces Samantha. 'The building site for the base extension has been progressing well – in the absence of babies, which the viewers are still waiting for impatiently, might I remind you. In any case, you're going to need this rest day to recover your strength before the final straight, the last eight months between you and the arrival of the new pioneers.'

'One day off after twelve months of work – oh, you're too kind!' scoffs Kelly, struggling to her feet, her blonde hair all in a tangle. 'How did you expect us to even have time to make kiddies with a schedule like this?'

There's no point waiting for the interim executive producer to reply: the distance means that the current communication latency has reached forty minutes (so between a question and its answer that's the length of a feature film). Besides, Kelly's jab is totally dishonest: we secretly forbade ourselves from procreating when we landed on Mars, given what we knew about the base.

'We've also got a second gift for you,' Samantha continues, cheerfully. 'But this is for just one of you guys – one of you *girls*, I should say, to be more exact. Léonor . . .'

Hearing my name is the trigger that allows me finally to tear myself from Mozart's body and jump to my feet.

A gift from Genesis, just for me?

Nothing could worry me more.

'. . . your widowhood has lasted one Earth year now. Without wanting you to forget Marcus, it's time for you to move on. You're young, beautiful and intelligent. And you're one of the future mothers of Mars. But to fulfil this maternal role, you'll need a new husband.'

A few metres away, Mozart opens his eyes, and it's his turn to get up now. Does he remember what happened last night? Is he aware of whatever it is that Samantha's announcing now live on the Genesis channel?

'In just over three months, the candidates who've been secretly chosen for the second season of the programme will complete their training in the camp at Death Valley. They will be introduced to the public at the launch ceremony, just as you were when it was your turn. But this time, there's going to be a little difference . . .'

Samantha's beaming; she really thinks she's making me happy even as she's tearing my heart open. 'We've chosen seven new boys and only six new girls. The male team will include an American to replace the Eden Food candidate, plus six other nationalities. Among the seven, there will be somebody for you, Léo, and you'll be able to choose him by taking part in speed-dating sessions by live link-up to the bubble on the *Cupido*!

59. Genesis Channel

Sunday 17 March, 10:00am

Long shot on a dry, red landscape. At first sight, we think we recognise the settings that are often seen on the Genesis channel: the Ius Chasma valley, at the heart of the Valles Marineris canyon, with the gleaming Garden dome.

But we quickly notice a number of differences: the rocky ground is less red; the sun is shining much more strongly, in a sky that is much bluer; in the place of habitats, this glass dome is flanked by a sheet-metal shed with windows in it.

A caption appears at the bottom of the screen: GENESIS TRAINING CAMP, THE BOYS' DOME, DEATH VALLEY.

Crossfade: we are at the foot of the dome in semi-close-up.

Somebody is standing beneath the crushing heat. It's none other than the Canadian singer Jimmy Giant, dressed in jeans, cowboy boots, a cowboy shirt and a black waistcoat; all the way up to the Stetson covering his blond hair and keeping his face in shadow, he's a perfect replica of James Dean in his third and last movie, the one he filmed shortly before dying and which inspired this star's pseudonym: *Giant*.

Raising the brim of his Stetson with a brief flick, with a

nonchalance also borrowed from the late actor, Jimmy Giant turns to the camera. 'My dear viewers, I'm sorry to be stealing a few moments of broadcast from you, and to be tearing you away from the Mars pioneers for just a few minutes. But it's in a good cause.' He half turns towards the dome that rises up behind him, on which the sun is so strongly reflected that it's impossible to see through it. 'Inside there are the seven male contestants who in just a month are going to be flying to the stars in the company of six new girls. With the exception of a few members of Genesis programme staff, nobody knows their names, their faces or their nationalities. I've never met them myself. And they, naturally, have not seen one another. But that's the lovely thing about it – these guys and girls all united by a shared vision of the future, far beyond their origins. United by a shared dream. Serena's dream. Marcus's dream. In these politically troubled times, it seemed important – to me and Stella – to remind ourselves of that . . . so it's our pleasure to introduce you to the official anthem of Season Two of the Genesis programme: 'Star Dreamers'!

The camera pulls back quickly, revealing a figure perched at the very top of the dome: it's the American singer Stella Magnifica, in one of her elaborate holographic dresses, whose vast blue train speckled with stars is floating like a banner in the burning wind of Death Valley.

An electric harp melody grows slowly in crescendo, somewhat reminiscent of John Lennon's 'Imagine', while hundreds of choristers in white gospel robes emerge from both sides of the dome humming a wordless tune.

* * *

Close-up on the sun-splashed face of Stella Magnifica, beneath a gorgeous bun that is also speckled with stars; she flutters her fake eyelashes, as she sings the first two lines of the song softly.

'I dream of a world of peaceful days,
I dream of a world of starry nights . . .'

Reverse shot on Jimmy Giant, who looks up towards the dome, squinting slightly to filter out the blinding light, and sings in turn:

'I dream of you in blissful eternity,
I dream of us together with humanity . . .'

The choir stops humming, to launch into the fraternal message of the chorus with one sole voice, whose potent echoes spread across Death Valley.

'We are all
Star gazers,
Star lovers,
Staaar dreeeeamers!'

60. Shot

Month 12 / sol 332 / 15:05 Mars time
[451st sol since landing]

'Please stop insisting. There's no way I'm going to get back into five more months of speed-dating!'

I've been very clear with everybody since the start: I categorically refuse to go through all that again. But despite my protestations, the last I heard, the male side of the new team will still contain seven contestants. If the organisers think I'm going to change my mind at the last minute, they don't know me at all!

Kris, meanwhile, knows me better than anyone, and she knows how stubborn the Determinator can be. So why has she kept renewing this assault again and again since New Year's Eve, and why's she doing it yet again today during her weekly medical check-up?

'But why, Léo?' she asks for the thousandth time, gazing at me with her big imploring eyes. 'What have you got to lose?'

'My time – simple as that,' I say, returning my stethoscope irritably to the infirmary shelf.

A smile appears on Kris's lips.

'Your time, darling Léo? You have more of that than anyone. I often wonder what you do in the evenings, when you go back to your habitat alone.'

'I draw – just imagine! Not everybody's got to marry some guy just to give their life meaning.'

I immediately feel bad for the scathing tone of my reply.

Kris just wants me to be happy, I know that. She didn't deserve my sarcasm.

'I'm sorry,' I say. 'I'm just a bit on edge.'

'I can see that,' she murmurs, looking down at Günter, who is silently waiting for his 'mother' at the back of the infirmary.

'I don't mean to criticise what you have, you and Alexei. It's a very precious thing.' I glance nervously at the infirmary camera – even after a year I'm still not completely used to the idea of being permanently watched. 'Your happiness has amazing screen presence. I'm sure it inspires millions of people on Earth.'

'But what about you, Léo?,' asks Kris, looking up suddenly. 'Don't you want to taste it for yourself, this happiness? Samantha's right: your widowhood has lasted long enough. You have the right to be happy here on Mars. Do you know where that red chiffon dress has got to, your most beautiful one, the one that got torn the night before we landed? You could wear that one again if you decide to take part in the speed-dating.'

Yet again, I don't know how to take what Kris is saying. These moments of uncertainty, which become more and more common as the months go by, make me terribly uneasy. When she refers to my widowhood, she seems to have forgotten that Marcus is still alive somewhere deep inside the base. When she talks about the happiness I could find on Mars if I started trying to pick up some total stranger, she doesn't seem to remember that we've all decided to leave this planet as soon as the self-energising elevator shows up. She has such an enormous desire to be happy, at any cost, a mental strength that makes her idealise Alexei, and humanise Günter, and act as though all was for the best in the best of all possible worlds.

'I honestly don't know where that dress has got to, Kris,' I say, to bring this troubling conversation to an end. 'As for the speed-dating, I'll think about it some other time.'

'Is it because of Mozart?' she suddenly asks, out of the blue.

'What?'

'Is Mozart the reason you don't want to take part?'

My brain malfunctions.

Mozart?

Is that really the name that popped out of her mouth?

'You ought to tell the organisers,' she continues, spinning totally out of control now.

'What are you talking about?'

'There's something going on between the two of you, it's obvious.' Kris's eyes are sparkling with excitement, as if she's just unravelled the secrets of the universe. 'The more I think about it, the surer I am that's why you don't want to get into the Heart Lists business again: because your own heart is already spoken for, of course!'

'No, oh no, not at all!' I cry, feeling myself overtaken by an inexplicable panic. 'There's nothing between me and him!'

'Go on – admit it! We found the two of you curled up together on New Year's morning! Apparently back on Earth

365

the photo has hit the headlines in *Watcher* and *Heart to Heart* magazines!'

'*Curled up together?*' I choke. 'What crap! We were dead drunk on Kelly's booze. We must have just bumped into each other and fallen flat on the ground side by side, before passing out like everybody else! *Watcher* and *Heart to Heart* are barking up a whole forest of wrong trees!'

'I bet if the programme would agree to show us the footage of that night, I'm sure there'd be a lot to see.'

'You're just tripping, Kris!' I say, looking up at the camera that's still filming, and through it at the millions of viewers watching us. 'First of all, let me remind you, Mozart's married to Liz!'

'Right, so you should let Liz take your place in the speed-dating link-up with the new team of boys, as it's clear Mozart is having nothing to do with her, and wants everything to do with you!' declares Kris with a self-assurance that leaves me speechless.

I start to babble something, trying to find the words that will make her shut up, but at that moment the alarm sounds.

I jump to my feet, my heart about to burst through my chest.

My first thought is *They're depressurising the base!*

But the reflexes I developed during our training at Death Valley regain control: that isn't the sound indicating technical problems, it's a medical emergency.

Grabbing my first-aid kit, I race out of the panic room and into the Garden.

Through the glass dome I can see the building site for the base extension. Three of the six new Nests have already been assembled over these past months – in every respect they look just like the original habitats, with only one exception: their greyish colour, due to the material used by the 3D printer to make their component parts.

'What's happened?' I ask Samson, his sickle suspended over the oat field that he was in the process of harvesting.

'I'm not sure. I-I think one of the pioneers fell in a foundation pit,' he stammers.

And it's true – through the glass panels I can indeed see frantic-looking silhouettes gathered around a hole where a future habitat is going to be positioned. The maxi-rover is parked next to it, its digger down in the two-metre-deep pit.

Two pioneers are using ropes to pull out a third. One of the rescuers is Alexei – I recognise him immediately by the armband with the colours of the Russian flag on it, which he asked Kris to make him in order to exhibit his patriotism whenever he went out on a Martian sortie. The second rescuer has got to be Mozart. As for the suit that's emerging from the hole, it's slimmer than any of the boys and definitely belongs to a girl – but which one?

I hardly have a moment to wonder: the rescuers are already carrying the body to the airlock leading into the base. From the Garden side, the red light that shows the progress of the compression system comes on.

EQUALISATION 80%.
EQUALISATION 90%.
EQUALISATION 100%.

The airlock door opens with a hiss.

The rescuers were indeed Alexei and Marcus; I can see the names sewn on their suits now – and I can read the name of the injured girl too: Kelly.

Alexei lifts the visor of his helmet and shouts: 'There's been some damage to her suit!'

With his still-gloved hand, he points at a gash along Kelly's arm.

I hurry to the rescue, a syringe of adrenaline in my hand. It's the emergency antidote in the case of collapse – a severe state of shock. If necessary I can inject the adrenaline directly into the little self-sealing silicon patch that each suit has built into its right thigh.

But before resorting to this extreme solution, I have to follow the first-aid protocol for an accident occurring outside the base, which I swot up on my tablet every week.

1 – Check if the injured person is conscious.

I remove Kelly's helmet. Underneath she's pale as a sheet, but clearly conscious, as I can tell from the 'Shit, that hurts!' that she spits in my face. No collapse: so no adrenaline shot for her today.

2 – Locate and stop possible haemorrhaging.

I use the emergency release key from my kit to take Kelly's suit apart; in a few moments, the heavy sleeve has been detached from her shoulder and I just have to pull on it to free her arm. The black undersuit also has a tear in it, about five centimetres long. I don't need a release key here: I grab a pair of scissors and set about cutting the high-tech fabric until the skin is freed.

It bleeds a bit, but not too much. It looks like it's only a superficial wound, with no haemorrhage.

Alexei, who's pulled off his gloves now, automatically takes over dealing with the scratch, and applies a compress of disinfectant taken from my kit while I move on to the third stage of the protocol.

3 – Check whether there are any symptoms relating to the direct exposure to the Martian atmosphere.

Here I need to apply the Rule of T.H.R.E.E. (just a mnemonic technique I use to remember any possible effects, though there are actually four parts to it).

T for *Temperature*: Frostbite is the first worry, so I measure the temperature of the wound under the compress with the optical thermometer, to check whether the freezing atmosphere of Mars had time to burn the skin . . . No: her internal temperature is 37 °C. All fine.

H for *Hypoxia*: I put an oximeter on Kelly's finger to measure the oxygen saturation of her blood, and detect whether there's any hypoxia. Result: ninety per cent. That's at the low end of the scale, but it's still healthy. The tear in the suit must have been too tiny to have stopped Kelly getting access to breathable air.

R.E. for *Radiation Exposure*: I'm not especially worried about this either, as there's not much chance Kelly caught a blaze of Martian sun through such a narrow breach in her suit. And I'm right – the skin on her arm shows no signs of irradiation.

E for *Ebullism*: this is definitely the goriest of the lot, a possible result of the violent depressurisation of the liquid parts of the body. On Mars, in the absence of artificial pressure, the blood, lymph fluid and saliva can start to boil in a matter of moments . . . But fortunately Kelly doesn't seem to be exhibiting the most typical symptom of this, the generalised swelling of the body caused by bubbles forming inside it.

'Do you feel any internal pain?' I ask her, just to reassure myself that her organs haven't been affected.

'Does my arm count as internal?' she replies with a grimace. But I suspect there's nothing too terrible wrong with her, and the painkiller in the compress is taking effect.

'No prickling sensation? You don't feel any bubbling on your tongue?'

'No – it's a shame though; I'd love to feel some bubbles on my tongue – champagne bubbles, obviously, to cheer me up!' She calls out to Kenji, who has just run over to us, having taking off his suit too. 'Hey, Tiger, do me a favour, go get me a bottle of bubbly from our room?'

OK, I see, looks like she's totally fine!

While I put my instruments back in the case, the rest of the pioneers rush over to the poor wounded girl, who actually seems delighted to be the centre of attention.

'What happened, Kelly? Tell us everything!'

'Oh, it's just the digger jammed while I was digging a foundation pit, listening to Jimmy Giant in the maxi-rover cabin. I turned it off and came down to take a closer look. But at the edge of the pit, the sand slipped under my boots and I got a bit bashed up.' She pauses a moment to receive the bottle from Kenji's hands and take a big swig of the home-made drink. 'At the bottom of the hole I felt something sharp tear my suit – must have been a rock lodged in the sand, the same one that made the digger stop. I didn't really get the chance to have a proper look.'

Kelly is about to take another slug of alcohol, when Liz appears next to the group.

'I went down into the hole with my flashlight, after they pulled you out. I hoped I might find something that'd help with a diagnosis. But I couldn't see anything. There was no rock, there was nothing sharp there at all. There was only sand.'

She says the last words again, a dream-like echo. 'Only sand . . .'

61. Off-screen

Alphabet City, New York
Wednesday 20 March, 10:02pm

'Today, an ultimatum for the race to the stars has been issued,' *announces the TV newscaster, sounding worried.*

Projected on the wall behind him is an image made up of American and Russian flags flying in the breeze against the backdrop of a night sky, like two Titans ready to face one another in combat.

'We're less than a month from the launch of the Cupido, *with the audience numbers for the Genesis programme already smashing their own previous record, and Moscow has decided to stop waiting for a hypothetical U.N. resolution. The Russian president has ordered his American counterpart to recognise Russian sovereignty over the area of the base inhabited by Alexei, and without further delay to open up a direct line of communication between the young pioneer and the Kremlin. It would appear that the video filmed by Star Dreamers, the official band of Season Two, was what ignited the powder . . .'*

The picture of the presenter disappears and is replaced by the famous clip in question, shown here with no sound.

While we're seeing the shots of Jimmy Giant in his Stetson and Stella Magnifica wearing her star-spangled dress, the presenter's voice continues speaking. 'The whole of the Russian press – as well as some others in the international press – have roundly criticised a production that they considered too "American" for a project that is supposed to belong to all humanity. In the eyes of those accusing America of going it alone, the cowboy outfit worn by Mr Giant looks a bit like an admission of this. More seriously still, Ms Magnifica's dress has been interpreted by many as a version of the star-spangled banner, an American flag planted at the top of the training dome as if the U.S.A. were trying to claim it. Even the gospel choir's robes have been seen by some as a further attempt to Americanise the programme. In response to these criticisms, the Secretary of State has set up a press conference for this afternoon in Washington . . .'

The pictures from the music video disappear, to be replaced by the world-famous sight of the White House press room, with its blue background and the American flags flanking the podium.

Milton Sunfield is standing there, facing a whole horde of journalists. With his hair pushed back and his hands gripping the podium, he looks like a sailor alone at the helm facing a storm. 'The U.S. government officially denies these accusations,' he says. 'The Genesis programme was, and always will be, a private, international initiative. Because this initiative rests upon infrastructure that is in American territory, we have a duty to protect it, but this is absolutely not to annex it. By way of reasserting this in the strongest possible terms, President Green is this evening issuing – through me – a formal invitation to heads of state from around the world: Come to America, dear friends! You are all invited to Cape Canaveral for the launch ceremony on the seventeenth of April!'

The TV newsreader reappears on the screen. 'Will this invitation be enough to calm tempers? There's certainly no guarantee. The

373

Russian president has already said he will not be showing up at Cape Canaveral if his country's claims are not satisfied between now and then. Twenty-eight days – that's all the time we have left till lift-off.'

'The world's going nuts,' says Andrew, appalled, remote control in his hand.

He's sitting on the bashed-up old sofa, his metal leg resting on a stool to help with his circulation. His TV screen at the back of the dark cellar, opposite the sofa, is showing pictures of popular demonstrations organised in response to the events the presenter has just been describing.

On the streets of Moscow, protesters are carrying effigies of President Green dressed like a cowboy, like Jimmy Giant, with dollar signs for eyes, a gun in his right hand and the planet Mars tucked under his left arm. Most of the placards have one of two slogans: 'Space is not the Wild West!' and 'Yankees go home!'

On one side of the Atlantic, there are condemnations of imperialist ambition; on the other, a claim that they are trying to protect a universal dream. The two sides in juxtaposition look like a terrible misunderstanding.

'It's going nuts *now?*' asks Harmony, sitting on the old sofa next to Andrew. 'I thought it always was. I can't tell. Maybe I've never had enough hindsight. After all, you've known it – the world – ever since you were born, but I only discovered it a couple of years ago, when Mozart came to talk to me for the first time.'

The picture on the screen disappears.

Harmony is surprised and turns towards Andrew, her dyed brown hair whipping around her face. She's about to ask him if there's a faulty connection – after all, their equipment all comes from the dump, so things break down often. But she sees that he has turned it off himself – his finger is still on the button of the remote.

'I can't believe you're still in love with that guy,' he mutters icily. 'I swear I've totally tried, ever since we met, but I can't do it. How can you feel anything for him but hatred and contempt, after what he put you through . . . ?'

Harmony is silent for a moment, somewhat put out by these reproaches that she didn't see coming, since Andrew has kept them to himself for all these months.

'He didn't put me through anything,' she says at last. 'It was his gang, the Aranha, that got me addicted, not him. He had no choice. He was just a go-between, a fuse in a death machine, who could have blown at the slightest mistake. Mozart is a victim, a sacrifice, just like me. You can accuse me of being romantic if you want, but I knew from the moment we met that he and I were alike. We have so much in common.'

'But you only met him *once*!' cries Andrew.

'That's not what matters, what matters is the intensity. Look, it only took Cindy one day to fall in love with her soldier, it took an hour of speed-dating for the boys and girls to form their couples for Mars.'

'Mozart is married to Liz. He's spending *every hour of his life* with her!'

'Things aren't working between them – you only have to turn on the Genesis channel to see it.'

'Well, you can also see on that same channel that he has a crush on Léonor!'

'But she doesn't feel the same way. Just look how cold and distant she is with him.'

Andrew is running out of arguments, and sighs in despair and frustration.

But Harmony immediately puts a comforting hand on the young man's shoulder.

'I know I'm worthless in the eyes of a mother who wanted to kill me, and I've lost all hope of ever finding a father who's never deigned to give any sign of life – but I don't care too much about any of that because of you, Andrew. I consider you my big brother,' she says, her voice gentle, sincere. Mistaking her friend's feelings terribly, she believes she's giving him a compliment while she's actually skinning him alive. 'You've always tried to protect me, I know. You don't trust Mozart, that's normal, because you're scared he's going to hurt me. But I'm no longer the fragile little prisoner you freed from her cell a year ago. I've matured. I've grown up. I'm ready to live a life that up till now I've only ever lived in books.'

Harmony gives Andrew a smile, overflowing with friendship and confidence, not realising how pale he's turned, without hearing anything in his silence but the concerns of a worried brother. From Jane Austen to the Brontë sisters, William Shakespeare to Thomas Hardy, the beloved books in which she spent her childhood and adolescence taught her all the theory of human emotions in all their subtle complexities – but in practical terms, she's still a novice. This gap has never seemed as dramatic as it does at this moment.

'Go on – give me a smile – I promise I'll be careful when I see Mozart!' she says cheerfully.

That's the final blow.

Andrew literally collapses, the stool slipping from under his leg, his back slumping into the sofa with its distended springs.

Harmony is quick to react.

'Andrew, aren't you well? Are you ill? Is it your leg?' She straightens up the stool, then repositions the leg and the prosthesis on top of it. 'Do you want me to give you another anti-inflammatory injection? We've hardly got any left – I'm going to have to find some other way to get more.'

But Andrew gestures that there's no need.

Before she can protest, a beep announces the arrival of a new email.

Both of them propelled by a reflex they've developed from months in hiding, the two fugitives abandon their discussion and pounce on the workbench where Andrew has left the cellphone.

'Is it the professor?' asks Harmony, anxiously. 'Though he's written to us this week already, and he's usually asleep at this time.'

'No, it's not him,' says Andrew, scanning his inbox. 'It's Cecilia Rodriguez.' Behind the lenses of his glasses his pupils are darting back and forth, deciphering the message. 'Her cousin Miguel is the skipper on the Cuban presidential yacht. He'll be travelling to Cape Canaveral for the launch ceremony all the presidents are invited to. Cecilia is suggesting we take advantage of the excitement to have my mother and my sister Lucy go on board and extract them from American territory when the boat returns to Havana!'

62. Shot

Month 12 / sol 341 / 09:05 Mars time
[460th sol since landing]

'I don't know if it's something I ate yesterday or what . . .'

Kelly is sitting on the edge of the exam table of the infirmary, looking kind of off-colour. She asked to see me this morning for a consultation, because of a probable migraine (though to be totally accurate she didn't use this word, she said she felt like her 'brain was fried').

'We all ate the same things yesterday,' I answer, trying to think like a doctor. 'And the day before yesterday too, and every day since we arrived at New Eden. Food poisoning seems very unlikely. Unless . . . you didn't overdo it on the Martian champagne when you got back home?'

An outraged expression passes across the Canadian girl's face, which looks particularly ruddy this morning, as if she'd caught some sun inside her helmet . . . which is impossible as the visors are all one hundred per cent anti-UV. She tucks her blonde hair behind her ear, revealing small red veins on her forehead. *Circulation issue?* – I make a mental note. *That might be associated with a suspected drinking problem . . .*

'What are you saying?' says Kelly. 'Are you saying my champagne is poisonous?'

'Let's just say it hits kind of hard.'

'And you're also accusing me of drinking on the sly like an alkie?'

'The distillery is in your home. I'm sure you need to taste it even if it's just to perfect your recipe.'

'Not true!' replies Kelly, getting on her high horse. 'My recipe is already awesome, I don't see why I'd want to try and improve on perfection. And unfortunately the distillery isn't so productive that I could let myself have a little glass every night. I've got to save that divine nectar for very special occasions.'

At this point in the conversation I can see it wouldn't be a good time to ask Kelly to blow into one of the breathalysers I've got in the pharmacy cupboard. Besides, her breath is coolly scented like mint chewing-gum: I think she's sober.

'Let's check your blood pressure,' I say, putting the cuff around her arm, where she's already rolled up the sleeve of her undersuit.

The digital numbers scroll up the screen and stop at 145/95.

'Slightly above normal, which is nothing to worry about, though it's strange for somebody in amazing shape like you,' I say. I risk it one more time. 'It could be connected to stress from the work you're doing . . . or slight dehydration . . .'

'No way,' Kelly interrupts me. 'You're not going to start that again. I'm telling you I only drink water.'

I don't insist any more, and remove the cuff.

Then I notice the tiny scar from when Kelly fell two weeks ago. It's completely healed and to be honest it's almost invisible now, just a very slightly pink area.

'Your arm isn't hurting?' I ask, just on the off chance.

Kelly looks down, surprised – she'd clearly forgotten all about the injury.

'Hurting, this tiny little nothing? You think I'm a total wimp? It's ancient history!'

I can't argue with that: all the exams I carried out in the hours after Kelly's accident produced normal results, and she's definitely up to date with all her vaccinations, including tetanus.

'I'm sure you just need a bit of rest,' I say, not having any more specific diagnosis to suggest. 'You should stay in your habitat and take care of yourself.'

'But today's schedule is packed!' Kelly protests. 'We're supposed to start putting up the eleventh habitat, and it's my day driving the maxi-rover! When I came to see you, I thought you might just give me a little vitamin pill, something like that, not sign me off work completely!'

'Mozart can take your place,' I say with all the authority at my disposal. 'Just to be cautious. And we'll check in on your health again tomorrow morning.'

Kelly gets up grumbling and leaves the panic room – I can tell that if she could, she'd stomp her feet to express her mood, but her movements are slow, her body apparently weak. I can't help thinking I was right to make her stop, even if it's only for a few hours.

The day goes on, just like the four hundred and fifty-eight that have come before it since our arrival on Mars. First I spend two hours cramming my medical knowledge on my revision tablet, as protocol requires. Today's lesson: *pathologies of the thyroid*. A complex subject – like all subjects relating to endocrinology – but a vital one: cosmic rays can have a damaging effect on hormones, and I need to be able to recognise the symptoms if they arise.

Hyperthyroidism . . . thyrotoxicosis . . . myxedema . . . At around 11:30, when my head is so crammed full of polysyllabic words that not another thing is going to fit inside, I close the revision programme to devote some time to going over the medical files that are my responsibility. Even though we're both able to deal with any emergencies, Alexei and I each have five regular patients, as well as being each other's. For the last year, Alexei's list has been made up of Fangtao, Samsafia, and of course Kris; mine includes Kenkelly, Mozabeth and . . . and that's it, since Marcus's 'death'.

The thought gives me a pang in my stomach, a physical sensation of guilt that over the months has become chronic – my own symptom, which, as the Medical Officer, nobody will ever diagnose because I've forbidden myself from talking about it and I try hard to ignore it whenever it appears.

Why should I feel guilty for not visiting Marcus?

Why should a killer have the right to regular medical check-ups?

It was never discussed when we set up the terms of his detention. There's nothing we can do to cure the D66 mutation, which will carry Marcus off one day, and the other precautions seem unnecessary for somebody who never leaves the base. Anyway, if someone asked Alexei to administer them to him, he'd totally refuse to do it – and he'd be right. And as for me . . .

381

I don't know how I'd react, if I had to face Marcus after all this time. Honestly I'd rather not think about it.

'Léo?'

I jump, torn from my thoughts, and turn quickly away from the nutritional graphs on my screen, to stare at the doorway of the panic room.

'Yes?' I croak. 'Someone need a consultation?'

At once I recognise the shape that appears through the doorway, a silhouette against the bright Garden daylight, its head crowned with curls.

'Sorry to disturb you,' says Mozart. 'I should have made an appointment.'

'I'm always available for my patients, as protocol demands,' I say matter-of-factly, trying to adopt my most professional tone.

But Mozart just stands there in the doorway. Not surprising, given the distance I've insisted on keeping between us for months – considering that I'm the closest thing this planet has to a doctor, my bedside manner has left a lot to be desired.

'It's not really urgent,' says Mozart, visibly embarrassed. 'I just . . . needed to talk.'

There's something so vulnerable about his voice this morning that I'm touched in ways that are as sudden as they are unexpected.

'It's fine to talk even when it's not an emergency,' I say, slightly softened. 'Come in, Mozart. I'm listening.'

Finally he takes a few cautious steps into the panic room, and sits down dutifully on the chair facing mine. There's no bravado today, no charming smile or air of seen-it-all superiority; there's just a slight tremble to his big brown eyes, a hesitation that's totally unlike him and which seems to be as much – if not more – a part of him as all the rest of it. It's so surprising: it turns out that shyness suits the Don Juan of the favelas perfectly.

'Last night I had a really hard time getting to sleep,' he begins.

And in the harsh infirmary lights I can in fact see how drawn his features are, and the bags under his eyes.

'I'm sure it's fatigue,' I say. 'The work on extending the base is demanding, specially for you two Navigation Officers. You've been working flat out.'

'No, I don't think it's that. On the contrary – when I'm outside all day, when I'm busy at the wheel of my rover, I don't even notice time passing and that keeps my mind busy. It's the nights when it gets bad. When I find myself alone in the habitat and those thoughts start going round in my head.'

'You aren't alone, Mozart,' I say, trying to give a reassuring answer, like a real doctor would. 'Even if things aren't going very well between you and Liz, and you still aren't sharing a bedroom, I'm sure stuff will be able to sort itself out if you both want it to. You should just try to communicate with her more, in the evenings, when you have some private time together.'

But Mozart shakes his head.

'It's gone past just not sharing a bedroom. When night comes and everybody goes to sleep, she gets up and goes to spend the night in the seventh Nest.'

'What?!' I shout, astonished. 'You're saying she spends her nights with . . .'

But I stop at the very last second, catching myself mid-question with an awareness of the infirmary cameras that are still filming, the microphones still listening.

But even if my lips don't say the forbidden name, the taboo name of the guy who's supposed to be dead in the eyes of the world, there's a voice inside me screaming:

(Marcus!)

(Liz spends her nights with Marcus!)

'. . . with Tao,' says Mozart, completing my phrase.

'With Tao,' I repeat, mechanically, while the Determinator tries to process the information, with a mixture of relief and surprise.

Now I think about it, it makes sense; it's clear as day.

Every morning for the last year, the English girl and the Chinese boy have been together in the seventh nest to take care of Marcus – her bringing the food, him guarding the door with his wheelchair and his huge body to stop any attempt by the prisoner to rebel. This task, repeated day after day, and which nobody else on the team wants anything to do with, must have allowed them to bond. Besides, they have a lot in common: Liz has never really felt Mozart loved her; Fangfang's feelings for Tao faded the day she learned that he'd been in love with another girl before her. And so there, unseen and unheard in the seventh habitat, the two neglected spouses found their sanctuary. They've been sleeping together for weeks . . . and I had no idea!

'You know, in a year of marriage, I've never once seen Liz dance,' says Mozart. 'But if you listen carefully when you walk past the access tube to the Rest House when she's there with Tao, you can hear music. That 'New World' symphony, I think.'

'I'm really sorry to hear that,' I say quietly, realising that

Mozart, Fangfang and I are all now widowed before our time. 'I can see how Liz leaving would upset you. If you want, I can prescribe you some sleeping pills, a weak dose, to help you get over the worst and find your sleep again.'

'It's not Liz leaving that upsets me. If Tao can make her happier than I can, then she's right to spend the nights away from home. What bothers me is how ridiculous this whole thing is.' He looks around, taking in the infirmary – but I sense that his 'this whole thing' refers to the whole base, the whole planet Mars, maybe even the universe. 'They told us we'd form these legendary couples, models for the whole world to aspire to. They promised our Heart Lists would be carved into the marble of the centuries. But what's left of those promises today?'

The feelings Mozart's expressing aren't at all what you would expect from a newlywed, I know, and they don't respect the instructions about optimism and positivity that the Genesis channel requires of us. But I don't try to stop him. After all, he's just honestly describing the situation the viewers are watching daily on their screens – there's no earth-shattering revelation, no conspiracy unmasked, just the ravages of time on human feelings.

'On Earth, apparently, the self-energising elevator is ready,' Mozart goes on. 'Soon they'll be sending it into space with a super-launcher to secure it to the *Cupido*. And in three weeks, a new team will be lifting off. Guys and girls like we used to be a year and a half ago. Full of hope. Full of illusions.'

I only just catch the double meaning hidden in Mozart's words, those *hopes* and *illusions* which could also be referring to

385

the viability of the base; the viewers watching at this moment will only understand another meaning, which is enough: the need for love that comes from excessive hope, from painful illusions.

'When I think about those new pioneers I haven't even met yet, I think about us, the very first colonisers of Mars. Yes, we were making history: that was the second Genesis promise, along with Love. What we've written in the history books can never be erased. Not what we've built, either. Or how we've failed. It's too late to take the opportunities we missed. That's the idea that torments me during the night. I've got a sense . . . How would Marcus have put it? He had such a way with words, with big words for talking about things . . . I've got a sense of *inevitability*, which is keeping me awake.'

Mozart smiles, a sad smile I've never seen on him before.

For the first time, he's laying down his arms at my feet. By using Marcus's words, he seems to be acknowledging his defeat and admitting that he'll never feel he can measure up to the guy who came before him. I imagine the admission ought to bring me some peace, the promise of days to come with less tension between us, with fewer unsatisfied expectations.

But what happens is the exact opposite, as if Mozart's shyness was waking a new confidence in me.

Thanks to some strange chemical reaction, my heart starts beating a bit harder, sending slightly hotter blood pumping through my belly.

My throat tightens gently, as if held in an invisible silk knot.

My eyes start to prickle.

My lips tremble, but the words that come out of them flow

naturally, effortlessly, and they are no longer the words of a doctor.

'If there's one thing I've learned since signing up for this programme, Mozart, it's that nothing is inevitable. It's *never* too late.'

He squints – he's stopped being able to understand.

'For example, we thought we'd signed up for a one-way trip,' I say. 'But in a few months, we'll have the option of a return.'

He glances at the camera, afraid I might have revealed too much, but he needn't worry – I'm not talking about the Noah Report.

'We thought we'd find the love of a lifetime; but what does a phrase like that even mean, "the love of a lifetime", when in reality we each of us live several lives?'

'Several lives . . . ?' he repeats, staring at me.

'The person I was before I met Marcus was a different girl. She was an utter fury, who felt nothing but contempt for love. She was a fighter determined to draw a better number in the lottery of life. She was obsessed with a scar – the source of all her anxieties and all her strengths – and ready to do anything to prove to the world and to herself that she could make it.

'And then, then I met Marcus, that girl died and another was born. A second life began in his arms. The obsession with succeeding, the thirst for revenge, the desire to shine: all that was extinguished. What had mattered so much was suddenly not important any more. The only thing that mattered in my new life – as intense as it was fleeting – was to live for the moment as though nothing else in the world existed, nothing but Marcus. But Marcus left us. And with his going, my second life came to an end.

'Today, after three months of this routine, after having been through limbo like this, I think it's time for me to make a start on my third life. Oh, it's not going to be as drastic as my first, or as passionate as my second! A life that's more lucid, gentler. A bit of the path that we can try and walk together, without trying to race ahead, at the same pace as Liz and Tao. You remember the day you offered to teach me to drive a rover? Well, I'm ready to start my lessons.'

Mozart's eyes open wide, and his sad smile transforms into a delighted laugh.

Its warm, sunny vibration surrounds me completely, and suddenly I notice the loneliness and cold that I've been locked inside for the past year. Kris's clairvoyant words – those words I fought so hard to deny – chime in Mozart's laugh like the bells heralding a celebration. *There's something going on between the two of you, it's obvious!*

And so I start laughing in turn, and as my voice and Mozart's mix they seem to create a harmonious melody, an undeniable fact.

His face moves towards mine; his eyes fill my whole field of vision; his gentle lips come to rest on mine, sending waves right through my body: even in this kiss, we're still laughing.

It takes me several long seconds to recognise the vibration of the alarm going off beyond the sound of our laughter.

Mozart notices it first, pulling his lips away.

In his eyes, I can read the same irrational fear I'm feeling myself, as if we've just done something forbidden, as if we were the reason the alarm had been set off.

But at that moment, Kris races into the infirmary, shouting: 'Léo, come to the Garden, quick, we need you!'

'What? What's happened?'

'It's Kelly! She's ill, she passed out at the wheel of the maxi-rover.'

I glance over at Mozart, unable to understand.

'The maxi-rover . . . ? But I told her she couldn't use it today, she was supposed to let you take her place. I thought you were just on your lunch break when you came to see me here in the infirmary.'

'Kelly d-didn't tell me she wasn't supposed to be using it . . .' stammers Mozart. 'It's been her at the wheel since this morning . . .'

Ignoring our conversation, just as she's ignorant of what happened between us a few moments ago, Kris grabs my sleeve.

'Quick, Léo! Kelly's turned completely red – she's stopped breathing!'

63. Off-screen

'Are you sure, Andrew?' asks Harmony.

'Yes, it's our only chance to do this. It might never happen again. We should take it.'

There's a real determination in Andrew's voice. A real coldness too, which has been there since Harmony rejected him without even realising it, two weeks earlier.

'My mom and my sister will be safer in Cuba, far from the clutches of the Genesis programme. You might believe that the government is putting them up in Cape Canaveral just to protect them, and that we'll never see Serena McBee again, but I won't sleep easy till I know they're somewhere she can't get to them.'

'Cuba . . .' murmurs Harmony, as if trying to get used to the idea.

There's a long whistling in the cellar, like an alarm. The girl gets up off the bashed-up old sofa and walks over to the electric kettle with the melted lid, which is sitting on a corner of the old gas stove: temperatures are still glacial, even in early April, and hot drinks are essential for fighting against cold and immobility.

'I understand,' she says, pouring the hot water slowly into the teapot. 'And I know how much you worry about Vivian and Lucy. But the idea of you and me also getting on the Cuban president's yacht . . .'

'It's the only way we'll convince them to get on board: I've got to be there,' says Andrew. 'I've got to be there, for them. It's a thing we call *family*, get it?'

Harmony receives the comment like a blow, a snub that silences her momentarily.

'Cecilia and her cousin Miguel will come to pick us up in a Zodiac on Cocoa Beach,' says Andrew. 'April the seventeenth, at six thirty in the morning, when the yacht will already be in American waters but not yet within the secure perimeter around Cape Canaveral. We'll hide down in the hold, in the storeroom where they keep provisions, somewhere the security forces will never find us – Miguel has arranged everything. That's where my mother and sister will join us – Professor Mirwood, who I've brought into the loop already, will bring them as soon as the new team has been launched, then he'll get straight back to the base so his absence doesn't arouse too many suspicions. We'll leave Florida in secret, all four of us, and make it to Cuba, where we'll finally be safe.'

'It's just that last bit I'm not sure about,' says Harmony doubtfully. 'Is it really essential that we go to Cuba too? Couldn't we return to America once we've got your family out, and come back here, to New York? Do we really have to abandon our country?'

Andrew's eyes turn cold behind his black-framed glasses.

'It's not like I *want* to abandon my country!' he cries. 'On the contrary – I want to save it! I love America! I love these people who are so crazy about freedom, their values, their ideals, I love them with all my heart! But sometimes the people you love stray down impossible paths.' He backs his words up with a long stare at Harmony, a stare that is heavy with the love he can't bring himself to confess to her and which she is unable to guess. 'The diplomatic crisis America's getting itself tangled up in, the deadly TV show which fascinates it without anyone realising what it's really like, the shadow of Serena still hovering over its future: these things are all torturing me. All the uncertainty is making me ill. Who knows what's really going to happen in five months, when the self-energising elevator is deployed over Mars? What'll be the repercussions here on Earth when the Martians return and the Noah Report is revealed? How will the Genesis programme, Atlas Capital, the government, even *the general public* respond to the truth? I'd rather be somewhere where I have enough room for manoeuvre that I can come to the pioneers' aid, even if it's at a distance. I'd rather be in a country where C.I.A. drones don't have the right to patrol, so I can try to combat Genesis propaganda effectively, when the time comes.'

Harmony puts the lid back on the full teapot, with infinitely delicate care as if it were crystal rather than old chipped earthenware.

'I totally didn't mean to accuse you of being a deserter,' she says cautiously. 'You're the bravest man I know, whether in life – where I haven't met many men – or in novels – where I've known hundreds.' She picks up the teapot by the handle and carries it over to the sofa. 'But when you talk about *fighting*, isn't that a bit premature? At this point wouldn't it be wiser just to *wait*?'

'Wait for the pioneers to come back – one of them in particular, right?' says Andrew with a bitter grin. 'You really want to jump on Mozart the moment he comes out of the capsule? I'm warning you: with the shock of re-entry into the Earth's atmosphere and having to readapt to gravity three times stronger than on Mars, he'll be a human wreck. It'll be weeks before he's able to get out of bed and stand on his own two feet. Yeah, hard as it may be for you to believe, your Apollo's going to be even more crippled than me!'

Harmony puts the teapot down hard on the low table beside the sofa – really a basic upturned crate – and a bit of scalding tea slops out of the spout.

'I-I don't know what Mozart has to do with this conversation, Andrew,' she stammers. 'You know I have no intention of *jumping on him*, as you put it. And anyway, things have changed. It does look like he's been getting closer to Léonor recently. Maybe I was wrong when I thought there was nothing between them.'

Her gaze falls on the latest issues of *Watcher* and *Heart to Heart* on the crate next to the teapot. The photo of the kiss shared between the Brazilian boy and the French girl in the infirmary on the Martian base is splashed across the cover of both magazines. Only the headlines are different. LOVE STRIKES IN NEW EDEN, says the first; IT'S NEVER TOO LATE! says the second, quoting Léonor's own words.

'I have no problem at all going to Cuba with you, Andrew, if you think that's for the best.' Everything in the tone of Harmony's voice suggests the opposite, that it's a wrench: neither she nor Andrew are fooled, and yet she says it again, though too loudly to be convincing: 'No problem at all!'

64. Shot

Month 13 / sol 361 / 21:05 Mars time
[480th sol since landing]

'How's she doing this evening?' I ask, as I walk into Kenkelly's habitat, medical bag in my hand.

As he does on each of my twice-daily visits, Kenji answers me with a silent glare filled with reproach, beneath the white headband he's tied around his forehead – the kind of accessory Japanese warriors wear in martial arts movies and which he never takes off nowadays.

He doesn't need to say anything for me to know he holds me partly responsible for the state his companion's been in for the last three weeks, because I failed to stop her taking the wheel after examining her on the very morning of her illness.

'Well then, let's take a look at the poor invalid!' I say with forced jollity, to try to fill the Japanese boy's overpowering silence.

I pass the door to the second room, where I can see the equipment that served as Kenkelly's home distillery, and head for the master bedroom.

Kelly is lying there, stretched out on the king-size bed. I might have been kidding when I referred to her as the 'poor invalid', but the phrase suits her very well – the Canadian girl is just a shadow of her former self. A few days ago, she still had the strength to walk around the Garden, but this time she hasn't moved from the position I left her in when I visited this morning. Her body lies motionless on the white sheet. Her peroxide-bleached hair, whose dark roots she hasn't the strength to dye any more, are spread across the pillow in stiff rays that seem to have lost all their suppleness. But the most striking thing of all is her skin: once fresh and rosy, she now has bright red patches under her eyes, on her forehead, around her cheeks. Her arms, flat on the bed, are swollen and throbbing, with veins bulging from the joints as if they were carrying too much blood . . .

Too much blood . . . that's the diagnosis I ended up reaching, with the help of the infirmary's electronic microscope. Samples taken from Kelly show a concentration of red blood cells that gets higher every day, far beyond normal levels. The Genesis doctors gave this bizarre syndrome a name: *polycythemia*. There's a whole heap of different symptoms behind that barbaric word, which are exactly the ones Kelly was suffering from the morning she came to see me: headaches, tinnitus . . . and of course erythrosis, the reddening of the skin owing to blood-flow that is excessive, and too thick, too red. But deep down, these complicated words only give a superficial explanation, and they leave the deeper question unanswered: what set off this strange reaction in Kelly's body? On Earth, the Genesis doctors have consulted their manuals: polycythemia is either a genetic illness present from birth, which sometimes only manifests in adulthood; or a reaction by the organism to a

395

chronic lack of oxygen, with the production of red blood cells increasing to hold onto more O_2 molecules. So the doctors have carried out a genetic screening on Kelly's gametes kept in the programme's deposit (when we signed the Genesis contract, we girls all agreed to the removal of a few ova, half of which came with us to Mars to help out with fertility just in case, while the other half stayed behind on Earth). The result: negative; Kelly's genes aren't carriers of primary polycythemia. As for the hypothesis of a secondary polycythemia . . . Kelly isn't a smoker, she hasn't presented with any chronic respiratory problems and she hasn't spent the last few weeks at the top of a mountain, like those climbers who end up short of oxygen. In other words, there's no reason her spinal cord should have started playing the obsessive workaholic by tripling red blood cell production.

'Here she is, it's Vampirella again!' jokes Kelly in a hoarse voice when she sees me coming towards the bed – it took till I was less than two metres away before she recognised me. 'You're going to stick your fangs into an innocent victim again? *Vade retro!*'

I force a smile as I lay my medical gear out on the low bedside table – a syringe, compresses and the biggest sampling tube I could find. Without knowing the cause of Kelly's illness, all I can do is treat the symptoms, with the oldest treatment in the world: bloodletting, like in that old Molière play I studied in my last year of high school, before I closed all my books for good and headed off to work in the factory.

'Since we don't grow garlic in New Eden, Vampirella has nothing to fear!' I say, sticking the needle into Kelly's arm.

'And who told you I haven't got a wooden stake stashed away under the sheets to stick in your heart?'

I roll my eyes, pretending to be scared, to distract her from her illness, while the sampling tube fills gradually. Every evening, this is how I relieve her blood that's heavy with an excess of corpuscles – but for how much longer? Kelly's body seems to react by producing even more, and if this goes on I'm soon going to have to start taking samples by the litre to avoid the liquid in her veins becoming molasses.

'The Genesis docs still don't know why I've turned into a walking blood bank?' she asks, suddenly serious again.

She looks up at me with her blue eyes, their colour standing out strangely against the red of her skin.

'They're still working on it,' I say, pulling out the needle and applying a pad with a band-aid where it went in. 'They receive an analysis of your samples every day – the microlab in the infirmary is all synced with Earth.'

'Nice of them to keep on racking their brains, but mine's going to end up exploding,' says Kelly, with a sigh. 'I've had it up to here with being stuck in my bed, red as a cooked crayfish, with my brains boiling like they're in a pressure cooker.' She seems to be struggling to keep her eyes open. 'They haven't told you where they've got to? Have they got some clue at least?'

'Last I heard, it could be an unexpected delayed reaction by your body to the reduced gravity on Mars,' I say. 'At least, that's the hypothesis they're leaning towards at the moment. I'll give you a dose of aspirin to help you sleep tonight and to thin your blood. Tomorrow morning, if you're on form, we'll do an hour in the hyperbaric chamber to see if it makes the symptoms any better.'

'The hyperbaric chamber won't do any good,' says a voice behind me.

I jump. Kenji has been so silent since I arrived that I'd forgotten he was in the habitat.

'Sorry?' I say, turning towards him.

'Kelly's illness has nothing to do with the reduced gravity.'

I try to meet Kenji's gaze, trying to understand what he means. But it's no use – as usual, his eyes evade mine, unreachable under that white headband and his long pointy black hair.

From down on her bed, Kelly sighs again.

'Tiger's convinced my condition is connected to my scratch a month ago, when I fell into the hole of the foundations,' she says. 'It's ridiculous – I felt fine in the days after that, and there's zero trace of that teeny little cut today.'

As proof, she raises her arm, and it's true, there's no scar left. But Kenji doesn't give up.

'Something from Mars got into Kelly's body,' he murmurs.

Like an echo, Günter's synthetic voice sounds in my memory, as clearly as when he dropped his bombshell fifteen months ago. '*The seventh habitat is not secure. It was damaged during the Great Storm of sol 511, month eighteen. At 22:46, an unidentified body perforated its shell, from the outside.*'

An unidentified body: that vague term, as imprecise as the threat it's describing. What *unidentified body* could hide in the dark storms of Mars, under the dead ground of Mars? None – surely. Didn't Liz go down and check in person on the day of the accident? There wasn't anything in the hole Kelly fell into! We've been here more than a year, and we've never seen anything but sand and dust. The samples we've collected from the ground and which our Biology Officers Kris and Samson analysed never showed up even the tiniest trace of organic life – which is totally normal. What else would you expect in the hellish conditions on Mars?

But in spite of this certainty, despite everything my reason is telling me, I hear myself asking Kenji reluctantly, 'What thing? *What* thing got into Kelly's body?'

Kenji squints, his eyes still glued to the floor. A little wrinkle has formed on his smooth forehead, a contraction, as if it pains him to answer me. His words come out haltingly.

'A penalty . . . a revenge . . . a punishment sent by . . .'

He stops mid-phrase, suspended between the words.

I feel a feverishness overcome me, a mix of impatience and concern.

'A punishment sent by *who*?' I ask.

This time Kenji says nothing.

Does he know something we don't, or is he just making up ghosts?

Is his phobic imagination playing tricks on him, or is he the one toying with me?

'A punishment sent by *who*?!' I say again, aggressively, my voice betraying how uncomfortable I'm feeling now – not the calm, controlled voice you'd expect from a doctor.

'No one,' Kelly answers in her husband's place. 'I don't know what trip you two are on, but I can tell you the only punishment I'm feeling is like a hangover. Like the morning after getting wasted – even though I've been sober as a judge! It's so unfair!

Hey, I wonder if it might be treated the same way? I've heard people say the best way to recover from being drunk is just to open another bottle right afterwards.' The smile is back on Kelly's face, her expression begging. 'So what do you say, doc, am I allowed a little sip of Martian champagne?'

'It's not advisable in your condition,' I reply, distracted, still bothered by Kenji's mysterious suggestions.

'Will I at least be allowed to raise a glass with everyone else tomorrow, when we're celebrating the launch of the second season?'

That brutal reminder of where we are in the calendar tears me away from my speculations, back to the here and now.

The launch of the *Cupido*!

And it's tomorrow!

It's waiting somewhere out there, in the sky above the Earth, equipped with the self-energising space elevator that an unmanned super-launcher sent into orbit last week.

A wave of emotions sweeps through my chest, mixed with memories of our own launch and nerves about the meeting with the new pioneers. *I* may know that they won't be coming down to Mars, that we aren't going to let them, but they don't know that yet. They think they're setting off on a great romantic quest, just like we thought at the time. By letting them lift off from Earth, we're lying to them, even if it's our only way to save ourselves.

Precisely. You're lying to them by omission, just like Marcus lied to you! – I hear the voice of my bad conscience.

No! I tell myself, gritting my teeth.

It's totally different, we all discussed this for ages, all of us privately in the seventh habitat!

When Marcus lied, it was about a one-way trip, but this time a return ticket is guaranteed! The *Cupido* will have enough food, oxygen and water to bring us all back to Earth safe and sound.

'Some bug in the system, Léo?' asks Kelly. 'Did you hear my question?'

'Yeah,' I murmur, recovering my wits.

'*Yeah*, I can raise a glass with the others?'

'Yeah, I heard your question. I'll talk to the programme's doctors about it. I promise I'll do what I can. For now, try to get some rest – I'll see you tomorrow morning.'

I put away my instruments and walk out of the habitat, leaving Kelly in the care of the most attentive nurse possible. Even if Kenji does sometimes behave like a weirdo, I know he'd do anything for his wife.

I make a detour via the infirmary, where I put the sample tube in the machine that I set to carry out the blood analysis during the night. Then I leave the panic room, turning out the lights behind me, and cross the darkened dome towards my own habitat – OK, let's see, I should have a bit of tofu still in the fridge, and maybe an old piece of . . .

There's a delicious smell waiting for me in the access tube.

'Surprise!'

Mozart is standing at the stove of the kitchenette, and he's cooking. He's even put an apron over his sleeveless T-shirt: macho man transformed into chef. It's his hidden talent – which he learned from the girls in the favela and which he only ever uses in private. The domestic-man outfit makes him even sexier, as well as totally reassuring.

'What are you doing here?' I ask, looking at the cameras in the ceiling. 'We should wait till midnight and meet here in private, when at least they stop filming inside the Nests. The viewers . . .'

'They saw us kissing the other day,' Mozart reminds me, beaming. 'We've made the covers of the magazines on Earth, I know Kris told you that.'

'The other pioneers . . .'

'They're all in their habitats by now – and anyway, why should we hide any longer?'

I can't think of any answer to this question. To tell the truth, I don't even know why we ever decided to keep our relationship secret, limiting it to the off-camera hours between midnight and eight, as Liz and Tao have been doing in the seventh habitat. Just another of my stubborn ideas, probably. To protect the base's fragile social equilibrium, seeming to respect the couples that came out of the Heart Lists? To protect myself, slowing things down artificially? No matter. Tonight, with Kelly's illness that I'm unable to cure, and Kenji's mysteries I'm unable to understand, with the imminent launch of the new pioneers filling me with doubt, I don't want any more secrets.

'No reason at all,' I say, finally. 'There's no point hiding. As of tomorrow, we'll announce to the others that we're together.'

Mozart gives a cry of delight, which is sunny and expressive and warms my heart.

'*Meu amor*! The girl from Ipanema has earned her *acarajés* today!'

He steps away from the worktop, revealing a dish filled with golden fritters, far more appetising than the tofu fermented from our base-grown soya.

'I did the best I could, but they aren't as good as Samson's. There's some magic trick in his recipe, but what is it? I'd love to ask him his secret, but I don't dare, not after the crappy way I behaved towards him.'

'That's all water under the bridge. It's time for new beginnings. Anything's possible now,' I say, allowing myself to get totally swept away by the smell of the food, by Mozart's smile, by this serene domestic atmosphere, which is so unlike the strange thrill I felt with Marcus, and which is so sweet – so very sweet!

65. Off-screen

The sea breeze lifts Harmony's dyed hair, flapping her T-shirt, her scarf, all the old worn clothes rescued from the trash cans of New York – but which, on her long-limbed body, have taken on a new elegance.

Her eyes – darkened by her coloured contacts – gaze at the black expanse of the ocean, over which the day has not yet risen. All around her stretches Cocoa Beach, miles and miles of sand washed clean by the most recent tide. In a few hours, when the sun is shining, holidaymakers in their thousands will invade this virgin territory, one of the most beautiful beaches in Florida, and the last before the secure zone of Cape Canaveral; but for now, Cocoa Beach is as deserted as it was at the start of the world.

'I can't see anything,' the girl murmurs, worried.

'Have a bit of patience,' replies Andrew. 'It's not six thirty yet.'

Standing there with his hood pulled over his head, he is looking at his cellphone. The light from the screen is reflected in the lenses of his glasses, on his face made hollow-looking by the shadow of a three-day beard. His metallic prosthesis, whose end is buried a few centimetres in the sand to find some stability, makes him look like a pirate, a buccaneer.

'Cecilia has written to say they're running on time,' he says before he in turn looks up towards the Atlantic.

The two young people are silent for a few minutes, gazing out at the ocean mirror reflecting the moon and the constellations.

'I wonder sometimes what happened to Cindy, after she ran away,' says the girl, suddenly. 'I wonder if she found her soldier again, and if they're together right now.'

At that moment, a shooting star appears near the horizon.

A shooting star – no, that light isn't coming from the sky: it's appeared suddenly from between the waves, and it's getting bigger every second. Soon the shape of a Zodiac comes into view, at the prow of which stands a figure sweeping the sea with the beam of a flashlight.

Harmony closes her hand over Andrew's.

He closes his over his cellphone.

The humming of a motor is getting louder and louder.

'What if it's a trap?' Harmony asks suddenly. 'What if it's not Cecilia in the boat?'

'My email's still ready to send, as a last resort,' replies Andrew, his voice tense. 'Just one click and I can reveal the Noah Report.'

The noise of the motor cuts out abruptly, to be replaced by a woman's voice, calling out, 'Andrew . . . ?'

The shape turns the torch on itself, revealing a pretty blonde woman in a life vest.

'Over here, Cecilia!' the young man calls back.

The expression on Cecilia Rodriguez's face shows how delighted she is.

'Oh, Andrew! At last!'

With the motor off now, the Zodiac continues to slide silently over the last few metres to the beach. A second passenger comes into view in the darkness, sitting at the back: a dark-skinned man, aged about thirty, in a white uniform and matching cap.

'Let me introduce my cousin Miguel!' Cecilia says, quickly. 'And that person with you . . . I'm guessing that's Miss McBee?'

The girl shivers in the pre-dawn breeze.

'Harmony, Mrs Rodriguez,' she says. 'Just call me Harmony.'

'OK – if you call me Cecilia.'

Harmony nods.

Then she lends Andrew her arm, and walks down the shore with him towards the water.

With his skipper's trousers rolled up to his knees, Miguel briefly gets off the Zodiac to help the two fugitives up onto the craft.

'*Bienvenidos a bordo*,' he says simply. And then, in halting English, 'Welcome on board.'

'Thank you for agreeing to take this risk . . .' begins Andrew.

'You helped Cecilia, now is my turn to help you. Is like you are part of the family. But we have to hurry to get back to the yacht before it docks at Cape Canaveral.'

Miguel pulls the starter of the on-board motor, which bursts into life.

The Zodiac melts into the darkness, and soon even its humming has disappeared beneath the gentle lapping of the waves.

66. Shot

'Mozart and I have an important announcement to make . . .'

All eyes are on the two of us.

Not just the eyes of the pioneers in their Sunday best (even Kelly is present, sitting in Tao's spare wheelchair, her face spread with Rosier foundation to disguise the redness of her skin), but also Samantha's eyes, since her enormous image is being projected onto the inside of the dome (her sophisticated jewellery and white designer suit are not unlike Serena's usual look, as if she were aping her absent mentor), as well as – beyond the cameras – the eyes of all those Earth viewers who've tuned in to the Genesis channel on this exceptional day that marks the launch of Season Two (I imagine them in their T-shirts, their caps, their pennants, all in the programme's colours).

'We're moving in together, into my habitat.'

My words need thirteen minutes to get to Earth, but Kris doesn't wait that long – she responds right off the bat.

'I knew it!' she cries, clapping her hands.

She's about to throw herself into my arms, then immediately remembers Liz is standing next to her, and freezes.

'Um . . .' she stammers, flushing with shame. 'That wasn't what I meant.'

I'm about to explain to her that there's no reason for her to feel awkward, that this very morning Mozart and I have agreed with Liz and Tao to coordinate our announcement. But Alexei doesn't give me the chance.

'What do you mean, you're moving in together?' he growls. 'You might be single, Léo, but unless there's any evidence to the contrary, Mozart is still married. There's a name for this thing you're talking about: *adultery*. A fine example to be setting, on the day when thirteen new contestants are about to take off in search of eternal commitment!'

Standing ramrod straight in his white outfit, the same one he was wearing more than an Earth year ago during the speed-dating sessions, now with his luxuriant blond hair falling onto its shoulders, Alexei looks like an angel – the inflexible kind, an angel of divine justice, ready to strike down the sinner I am in his eyes.

'Hey, Stalin, any chance you could keep your nose out of something that's none of your business?'

'It is my business. You said your vows, the same ones I did. If you betray them, it's like you're betraying mine. Rules are made to be respected, that's the only thing protecting us from chaos.'

Rules, laws, discipline . . . Alexei hasn't changed his tune since Marcus's trial, when he tried unsuccessfully to get us to enforce the *Lex talionis*. To listen to him, you'd think we were at constant risk of anarchy, and he was the only person fighting against it.

'It's so nuts!' cries Mozart. 'This guy has already colonised his individual habitat, and now he wants to police the whole base!'

I sense my hot-headed Carioca is ready for battle, but I hold him back by the sleeve – the unity of the group matters more than anything.

'A marriage can be cancelled,' I say, forcing myself to stay calm as I answer Alexei. 'That's also in the law you're so keen on.' I take a deep breath, my eyes fixed on his. 'And there's also a name for that: *divorce.*'

The Russian guy gives an ironic laugh.

He turns to the other pioneers, and beyond them to the cameras.

'Just look at Léonor, trying to teach us about the law while destroying the couples!' He glares at me. 'It's not up to you, a woman having an affair, to claim a divorce. Only people who're actually married can do it. Mozart might be a piece of trash, but he might have more scruples than you do where his wife Liz is concerned.'

He's about to call on the English girl to testify, but she's already ahead of him.

'Léo and Mozart aren't the only people who want a divorce,' she says, her chest swelling with emotion. 'Tao and I . . . want one too.' She puts her hand on the shoulder of her new partner, sitting in his chair beside her. 'If my ex-husband wants to live in Léo's habitat, I'll invite Tao to move into mine.'

Astonishment on all the other pioneers' faces.

'Seriously, it's like *The Dating Game* this morning!' says Kelly from her wheelchair.

Liz and Tao have been together for much longer than Mozart and me, but they've been so discreet that most of the pioneers knew nothing about it. But Fangfang doesn't seem surprised. She knew, of course. And she's been getting ready, for weeks, maybe months, to appear on screen as a deserted wife. She looks up, bravely, and meets everybody's stare.

'I accept Tao's request for a divorce,' she says clearly – the voice of a woman who has been thinking about this for a long time and whose decision is final. 'And I would like to ask a favour.'

She turns to me, her eyes behind their square-framed glasses pleading.

'Léo, since you're in a couple again, would you let me take your place in the speed-dating with the new crew? Please . . .'

'Yes,' I say quietly. 'Of course.'

That's the moment Alexei blows his top.

'What the hell is everyone playing at – musical chairs?' he shouts. 'Because you clearly think this is all a game, don't you, all of you? The word *marriage* doesn't mean a thing to you?'

'Calm down, Alexei,' says Safia, who's in the saffron-coloured sari she wears for special occasions. 'Here on Mars, people are free.'

'Free to screw everything up?' he spits angrily – and I suddenly notice that he looks desperate too.

He spins around and sweeps his arm to gesture at the whole dome.

'Free to undermine the very foundations of Martian civilisation?' he says furiously, forgetting in his raving that this civilisation was stillborn to begin with. 'Free to break

410

all vows, to make a mockery of all oaths and trample on all traditions?'

His eyes narrow, becoming two slits, like the eyes of an animal.

'But what's the point of my talking about it to you, a girl who's always said she thought tradition was shit anyway? Sweet little Safia, who's always ready to come to the defence of other people in the name of human rights or some such crap, who's even more virtuous than Léonor herself. Always fair, always right, isn't that so? Or so it seems, at least. But if you're so progressive, why don't you admit what your own "marriage" is really like?' I can hear the quote marks in his voice, and all the contempt they suggest. 'Why don't you tell the viewers what kind of "husband" Samson really is?'

This time I'm not quick enough to stop Mozart before he launches himself at Alexei.

'You're going to shut your fucking mouth!' he shouts, grabbing hold of the back of his jacket.

'You have a problem with that?'

'Live and let live, OK? Give them a break! And most of all, you keep Samson out of this!'

'So you're going to start defending him now? You're the one who looked like you were going to smash his face in the day you found out he was really . . .'

'You're the one whose face I'm going to smash in if you say another word!'

Alexei pushes Mozart roughly away.

'Hey, viewers, listen up!' he shouts at the top of his lungs. 'Samson is . . .'

'. . . gay,' the Nigerian finishes his sentence in a booming voice.

Cut off mid-flow, Alexei abruptly stops shouting.

After me, after Liz, after Fangfang, it's now Samson who has all eyes and cameras on him, hungry for more revelations.

'I'm gay,' he says again, more quietly, slowly, as if trying out the taste of the words on his tongue. 'I always have been. I always will be. In the country I come from, it was easier to deny that part of myself. When I boarded the *Cupido*, I allowed myself to be convinced it was just a passing phase, that I was going to change. But today I know these things don't change. Today I'm not afraid any more, because I'm not ashamed any more.'

He takes Safia's hand.

His eyes have got that surreal glow they take on sometimes, which makes me shiver.

'Alexei's right,' he says. '*Marriage* isn't the right word to describe Safia and me. But he's wrong when he thinks that word's too good for us. What we have, her and me, is worth just as much as him and Kris.'

'One day we'll both fall in love,' says Safia, 'each of us with a different guy. Maybe it'll happen here on Mars, or there on Earth. But whoever they are, those guys whose faces we don't yet know won't separate us. While we're with them, we'll still be together, me and Samson. If Alexei can't understand that, that's a shame – we'll be happy whatever he thinks.'

There are a few moments of silence punctuating Safia's serious, beautiful words.

Even Alexei is speechless, as I imagine are all the spectators who, at some time lag, will be listening to this declaration of a love that's so different, that's unique.

412

Finally, it's Samantha who breaks into the solemnity of the moment, reacting belatedly to this flood of revelations.

'Léonor and Mozart together! I can see that there are some Martians who weren't expecting this. And same for Liz and Tao!' she says with a complicit smile. 'Here on Earth, those of us who've been tuning in faithfully to the Genesis channel have known about this for days. Whereas Samson . . . Whoa! What a scoop! Even I never suspected! This kind of surprise is just the thing to spice up the Genesis programme, as our brilliant Ms McBee devised it.'

Samantha pauses a moment in tribute to Serena, without realising that her idol – the programme's selector! the amazing psychologist! – demonstrated how totally manipulative she was when she pressed Samson to join a marriage game that didn't match his sexual orientation, risking his being unhappy for the rest of his life.

'If we'd known all this in time, we could have made arrangements,' the young interim producer continues, benignly. 'We could have supplied three extra guys for the next journey: one for Fangfang, one for Safia and one for Samson! We're all very open-minded at Genesis! But at the point we selected the new crew, only Léonor was unattached. Anyway, we have seven male candidates in the running. Seven straight guys, as far as I'm aware – though after the amazing revelations we've just heard, I wouldn't bet on anything. I don't want start a fight, but which of you is going to be taking Léo's place in the speed-dating?'

While Samantha tries to increase the suspense, the way her mentor would have done, there is a small voice at the back of the Garden.

It's Fangfang.

'Samson, Safia . . .' she says, 'now that Léo's given up on the speed-dating, are you . . . do you want to take part? Now that, um . . . now that the whole planet knows, about you?'

'No,' replies the Indian girl, 'don't worry. For now, I'm in no hurry to get someone between Samson and me.'

'Likewise,' says the Nigerian. 'Specially since I've sworn to myself I'm never falling in love with another straight guy.' Mozart, who Samson was referring to though without saying his name, is still ashamed at the way he responded to Samson's outing a year ago, and he lowers his eyes and presses himself against me. 'And anyway, if one day we've had enough of being single, we can always go back to Earth, like Safia said, in the self-energising elevator promised us by *our brilliant Ms McBee* – isn't that right, Samantha?'

67. Genesis Channel

Wednesday 17 April, 2:00pm

Wide shot of the launch platform at Cape Canaveral.

Just like twenty-one months earlier, the enormous aluminium rostrum is divided in two by tall curtains covered in hundreds of logos.

Standing there alone at the podium at the front of stage, Samantha looks too small and fragile to fulfil a role that's too huge for her. Everything in this gigantic setting conspires to crush her: the giant screens, four metres by three; the dizzyingly high girders bristling with cameras; the tiers of the VIP section with rows of more than a hundred heads of state who have come from all over the world, at the centre of which are proudly seated Edmond Green and his wife, the First Lady.

But the real crushing weight comes from somebody who is not here, the person Samantha is supposed to be representing, whose shadow hovers over the launch ceremony, over the entire programme.

The young deputy whispers shyly into her microphone. 'Thank you all for coming, ladies and gentlemen . . .'

The speakers, better suited to huge rock concerts, transform her murmuring into a roar that makes her jump.

On the huge screens, her overly made-up face grimaces, betraying a stress that's in sharp contrast with her boss's absolutely constant self-control.

'Thank you, on behalf of the Genesis programme,' she carries on as bravely as she can. 'Thank you on behalf of the new contestants, whose faces you will see for the first time in just a moment. But most of all, thank you on behalf of the woman who taught me everything, without whom this amazing adventure could never have happened: I mean, of course, Serena McBee!'

The screens stop showing Samantha's face, and instead are filled by a slide show with the old executive producer in her various incarnations: Serena as the muse of space, standing at the podium for the first launch ceremony; Serena as Mother Christmas, surrounded by smiling orphans and presents wrapped in Genesis paper; Serena as a dazzling stateswoman, on the morning of her nomination to the vice-presidency of the United States of America.

Samantha continues to supply a voiceover, while the images roll on. 'It's been over a year since I've seen Ms McBee,' she says. 'Time in which I've had to learn to get by without her. Like the rest of our viewers, I don't know where on Earth she has found refuge. But not a day goes by when I don't apply the lessons she so generously taught me. Wherever she is, I hope she's watching us now, I hope she will soon be back to full health, that she'll come back, because I miss her terribly. And I know you share my hope, my dear friends, dear viewers. The world has become duller since Serena McBee has been out of it . . .'

Overcome by emotion, Samantha is forced to pause for a moment.

Spontaneous clapping rises out of the presidential enclosure, and then more; within a few moments the hundred heads of state are all applauding like crazy, soon to be joined by the thousands of journalists squashed together at the foot of the launch platform.

The orchestra plays the first notes of 'Star Dreamers', flooding everything in sound.

68. Off-screen

Cape Canaveral Base, secure port
Wednesday 17 April, 2:20pm

'*We are all*
  Star gazers,
  Star lovers,
  Staaar dreeeeamers!'

The chorus, bringing Jimmy Giant and Stella Magnifica together in unison, makes the hold of the yacht shake like a sound box.

'You hear that?' asks Harmony. 'They've got to be crazy playing the music that loud!'

Sitting on the floor down in the storeroom, between the crates of provisions, drinks and cigars for the Cuban president and his hosts, Andrew shrugs.

'Maybe they think if they shout very loud, they'll manage to wake Serena up?' he says. 'I can't wait for it to be over. I can't take any more of this musical crap, we've been hearing it constantly for weeks.'

'You know, Andrew, they play "Star Dreamers" everywhere in Cuba too,' says Cecilia, sitting on a case of wine, at the foot of which she has put the torch that is lighting up the room. 'At train stations, gas stations, on every street corner . . .'

Andrew sighs.

'You're almost going to make us nostalgic for the days when your island was cut off from the rest of the world, before relations thawed with the U.S. At least they're not playing "Star Dreamers" in Moscow right now, I'll bet.'

'I wouldn't be so sure. The Russian and Chinese presidents may be skipping the launch ceremony, but their populations aren't necessarily behind them. Despite the arguments over territory that are keeping the war leaders busy, the Genesis programme is still an ideal that brings the whole of humanity together. Just look at it: despite Marcus's death, despite Kelly's illness, people on Earth still want to believe in this dream that's greater than them, that transcends them! Serena McBee might be the most self-centred person of our age, but she's managed to make this miracle happen . . . this kind of communion . . . it's so strange . . .'

'It's dangerous, more than anything else. This "communion", as you call it, is based on a lie. I can't wait for the programme to end. I can't wait for humanity to wake up. This dream has gone on too long.'

Beyond the metal walls of the hold, the tune of 'Star Dreamers' fades gradually, then disappears altogether. The moment to introduce the Season Two team has arrived.

69. Shot

Month 13 / sol 362 / 10:05 Mars time
[481st sol since landing]

'To the left of this curtain are our new female contestants. To the right, our new male contestants. Newly arrived from Death Valley, they will now take their oaths, live . . .'

While Samantha is saying her lines, the image shown on the inside of the dome flips around to show a reverse shot: the platform and its curtain, with six tiny shapes on one side and seven on the other; and behind them, the huge shadow of the launcher, crowned by the twin capsules in which the teams will take their places in a few moments.

Mozart's arms close gently around my waist.

I can feel his heart beating, like I did on that morning of January first when I woke up resting on his chest, right here on the floor of the Garden.

I can feel my own heart racing, like that July day when I was on that damn platform myself, millions of kilometres from Mars.

I close my eyes for a moment.

70. Genesis Channel

Wednesday 17 April, 2:40pm

'*Oskar, nineteen, from the republic of Poland, sponsored by Nektar beverages, Navigation Officer: do you agree to represent humanity on Mars from this day forth until the last day of your life?*'

Close-up on a young man with brown hair showing beneath the visor of his helmet bearing the slogan *Keep Calm and Go to Mars* – an ironic, casual touch, in contrast with his astronaut suit and the solemnity of the moment. A steel piercing on the arch of his eyebrow, a questioning look in his eyes. 'I accept!' he says with a big smile.

Cut.

Reverse shot onto a stunning girl, with tanned skin, her black hair crowned with roses that are as striking as the red on her painted lips.

'*Meritxell, eighteen, from the kingdom of Spain, sponsored by Sirena Cruises, Biology Officer: do you agree to represent humanity on Mars from this day forth until the last day of your life?*'

'I accept,' she answers, with a deep and velvety voice that could belong to one of the great soul singers.

Cut.

71. Off-screen

'*Nikki, eighteen, from the kingdom of the Netherlands, sponsored by Desiderius electronics company, Planetology Officer: do you agree to represent humanity on Mars from this day forth until the last day of your life?*'

Samantha's words, coming out of the loudspeakers on the launch platform nearby, are muffled as they reach the hold of the Cuban presidential yacht where Cecilia Rodriguez, Andrew Fisher and Harmony McBee are hiding.

'I accept.'

Harmony finishes the count on her fingers.

'That was the last one,' she says. 'That's the whole lot.' She starts counting out the countries selected for Season Two of the programme. 'Poland, Spain, Indonesia, Korea, Italy, Israel, U.S.A., Turkey, Mexico, Denmark, Switzerland, Sweden ... and the Netherlands. Thirteen countries – thirteen contestants.'

She and Andrew exchange a glance that is wordless, but heavy with questions.

Were they really doing the right thing when they decided

422

to delay the revelation of the Noah Report, letting this second team set off with the Genesis programme?

Will the self-energising elevator, which is waiting up there in orbit, work when the time comes?

As for these new contestants, how many will come back to Earth alive?

Is it fair to risk thirteen lives to save eleven more?

Cecilia – who can sense the tension, even though she can't know its cause – tries to reassure them.

'The launch is going to happen – nothing can stop it now.' She forces a smile. 'As soon as the rocket has gone, while the Genesis staff and officials are busy taking questions from the press, Barry Mirwood will bring Vivian and Lucy here. It's only a matter of minutes now.'

As if echoing her words, the programme's jingle – that is, the chorus to 'Star Dreamers' – sounds once again, marking the end of the solemn vows. The astronauts will soon be leaving the platform to go up into the launcher.

'I don't feel very well,' murmurs Harmony, looking pale, suffering from the doubts that are churning around in her belly. 'I need . . . to get to the bathroom.'

Cecilia looks at her, hesitates a moment, then finally gets up with the flashlight to unlock the storeroom door.

'Maybe it's because we're on the water. You're not used to it,' she says. 'There are bathrooms at the other end of the corridor. You can go there – Miguel made sure nobody's coming down to the hold today. But hurry.'

Harmony gets up and rushes down the long dark corridor, marked only by small lights at ground level. She runs past the

423

metal stairs that lead to the boat's upper levels, and doesn't stop till she gets to the toilets. Once there, she falls to her knees, not even bothering to turn on the lights, grips the toilet bowl with both hands and vomits painfully.

Once her stomach is empty, she remains on the floor in the dark for a moment, hunched against the teak toilet seat. Outside, beyond the yacht's windowless walls, the programme jingle has ended, to be replaced by one final speech, from President Green.

'. . . am proud and happy . . . new generation of astronauts . . . rising up from American soil . . .'

The words reach the little bathroom in scraps.

'. . . deeply regret the absence of my Russian and Chinese counterparts . . . wish to send them my cordial greetings anyway . . . mark of friendship between nations . . .'

Harmony listens hard. There's something else, isn't there? A repeated clanking that can be heard behind the president's words, a noise that isn't part of the speech, as if . . . as if there were footsteps treading on the metal staircase.

Could it be Vivian and Lucy already?

Harmony gets to her feet silently, and opens the bathroom door just a crack.

It's not Andrew's mother and sister who are making the stairs echo beneath their heavy boots, but half a dozen soldiers whose black fatigues are soon invisible in the darkness of the corridor: they are making for the other end of the hold . . . heading towards the storeroom!

Harmony stops herself from crying out when she hears a burst of machine-gun fire, which blows out the bolt to the room where Andrew and Cecilia are hiding.

'C.I.A.!' shouts a voice. 'Up against the wall, all three of you!'

All three?

Whoever these men are, they knew who they'd come looking for.

They're expecting to find Andrew, Cecilia and Harmony.

They haven't yet realised that the third of these isn't there to answer them.

At this moment, with her destiny – and perhaps the destiny of the whole world – up for grabs, this girl who was brought up among her books, far from any kind of action, doesn't hesitate for a moment: she races for the staircase that leads up to the surface.

The daylight explodes onto her face.

The speakers transmitting President Green's words crash against her eardrums. '. . . *a day that will for ever go down in the history books . . .*'

The enormous launcher looms up above the deck like a colossus rising from the waters.

'Who you are, señorita?' asks one of the officers on board in broken English, having almost to shout to be heard over the president's words. 'It is you those gringos appear from nowhere to look for? Why has Miguel bring them?'

Harmony races past him without answering.

'. . . *all your viewers, whatever your nationalities, will be able to say: I was there . . . !*'

She throws herself onto the gangway that leads to terra firma, close to the journalists' enclosure.

'. . . because before any of us are American, Russian or Chinese, we are all citizens of the wor—'

But at the very moment Harmony disappears into the crowd, there is an impressive explosion, blowing the sound system and bringing Edmond Green's speech to a premature end.

72. Shot

'. . . *because before any of us are American, Russian or Chinese,*
we are all citizens of the wor—'

BOOOOM! A wall of fire wipes President Green's face
from the inside of the dome.

The base is being depressurised! shouts a little voice inside
me, as I instinctively press myself against Mozart.

But when the flames disappear from the inside of the plates
of glass, what's left behind is not a shattered dome – no, it's
still intact over our heads, and the launch ceremony is still
being screened on it.

But with only one difference: in the middle of the presidential
area, in the place where Edmond Green had been standing
just a moment earlier, there's nothing but a blazing hole in
the stage, with lifeless bodies lying all around it.

73. Off-screen

First comes the yelling, then the sirens.

Panic seizes the crowd of journalists, while above them on the platform, the survivors of the explosion are standing back up with dazed expressions.

'It's an attack! *Attentat! Atentado! Terroranschlag!*' voices all around Harmony are shouting in every language.

The press and TV crews scatter in total chaos, like people struck down by the collapse of the Tower of Babel.

Harmony lets herself be carried away by this enormous wave, this human tide that quickly overwhelms the security forces that are supposed to be controlling the event.

To avoid people being crushed, the guards are compelled to unlock the gates to the rest of the peninsula. Trying to get to safety, the crowd pours out through the heather, getting back to the vans, campers and trailers in which they arrived.

'Miss, you're looking lost – have you gotten separated from your crew?' shouts a woman in a suit, a press badge around her neck.

428

'I . . . I . . .' stammers Harmony, distraught.

'Best not to stay outside! There could be terrorists on the loose – Jesus, President Green just disintegrated before our very eyes! Quick, get into our van!'

The woman in the suit grabs Harmony's arm and pulls the girl after her into the van with the logo of a major TV channel on its side.

74. Shot

'What just happened . . . ?' asks Kris very quietly, like a child waking up from a bad dream, hoping to be reassured.

But it wasn't a dream.

It's harsh reality, the stream of pictures that keeps flowing across the inside of the dome – no framing, no commentary, no direction – just the unfiltered output from the rolling cameras.

'Something terrible,' murmurs Kelly from her wheelchair, the foundation on her cheeks starting to melt from her sweat. 'That's what just happened.'

I feel my guts tighten with every second that passes, a grim premonition deep inside me.

'Look!' cries Safia. 'Samantha's back!'

It's true, the young woman is back on the screen – her elegant hairdo is devastated, her suit is torn, there's a trickle of blood down her forehead.

'An-an awful tragedy . . .' she stammers. 'An unspeakable act of barbarism . . . President Green and his wife are among the victims of the explosion . . .'

A horrified murmur runs through the Garden.

I feel Mozart's taut breathing against my neck, ruffling my hair.

The knot in my belly tightens a little more.

My premonition suddenly takes on a name and a face.

It's her!

Serena McBee is behind this crime!

I can't explain why or how I know, but all my instincts are screaming out to me. I'm sure it's true!

'We . . . we don't currently know whether the launch is going to go ahead,' continues Samantha, her voice trembling. 'The new team is up there, waiting, at the top of the launcher, in their capsules . . . The interim vice-president, Milton Sunfield, has not yet made his decision . . . And nor have I . . . like him, I'm just standing in for somebody else . . .'

You can see Samantha's distress and powerlessness written clearly on her face, as she looks more and more like the junior assistant she used to be.

'I so wish Serena McBee was back with us!' she moans, her words piercing my soul.

But the worst is that Kris is the first of us to answer, wringing her hands: 'Oh, you're so right, Samantha! Serena would know what to do!' And Kelly adds, 'She'd make that dumb rocket leave double-quick, with that dumb space elevator we've all earned!' And it's Fangfang who agrees: 'Say what you like about Serena, at least she had the guts to take decisions!'

I feel like I'm in a terrible trap, closing in from all sides.

Am I the only person who senses that everything has been orchestrated in such a way as to bring *her* back?

431

But what have we actually done this last year to *stop* her from coming back?

Nothing! Nothing at all. We've fallen asleep over the Noah Report! We've allowed ourselves to be lulled by the routine on the base! We've let the promise of the elevator allow us to dream!

If *she* comes back for another season, I know deep down, I know deep in my bones, nothing will stop her . . . but now, before the launcher has taken off, yes, maybe there's still a chance to stop her now!

'They can't let the rocket take off!' I say, my voice hoarse, crazy-sounding.

Everyone's eyes turn on me, incredulous.

'What the hell are you saying, Léo?' asks Kelly. 'What about our elevator?'

The elevator no longer counts.

Those billions of dollars swallowed up to recover eleven lives are no longer worth anything.

There are more important things than our survival – there's the salvation of the whole world, onto which an unprecedented threat is just about to launch itself.

The words are still pouring out of my trembling lips.

'We can't let the programme continue!'

Alexei is the first to realise what's about to come out of my mouth – because he's the one who distrusts me the most, and also, paradoxically, the one who understands me best.

He throws himself onto me at the very moment I say, live, in front of millions of viewers: 'The . . . Noah Report . . .'

His huge body crashes into me like a bull charging a toreador.

His powerful arms grip my shoulders, his hand presses against my mouth like a gag. This time nobody tries to stop him – not Kris, who just groans my name; not Mozart, who is looking at me with alarm in his eyes.

'She's turning hysterical! She's in shock, it's some psychological trauma from the attack!' says Alexei, offering his diagnosis to the viewers.

I struggle, I strike out and kick but he's too strong for me, and my efforts just make the diagnosis of my hysteria look even more believable.

'Mozart, Samson, Kenji – help me get her into the Rest House!' he shouts. 'She needs to unwind far from the cameras. In the dark, where there's no light and no noise, till she's herself again.'

Alexei's hand is obstructing my breathing. The hands of the three other boys close on my arms and legs, lifting me from the floor.

The vault of the dome rushes past my rolling eyes, while I'm carried across the Garden to the access tube leading to the seventh habitat, to the unseen living room in which my most traumatic experiences took place.

. . . the collapse of my first love . . .

. . . the trial at which we all lost our souls . . .

. . . and now my own damnation.

The boys drop me onto the sofa, the lights are turned off and the door slams shut.

ACT V

75. Off-screen

'So who are you then – a new intern? Bring us a pot of coffee to the editorial room . . . No, wait, make that two pots: no one's going to be sleeping any time soon!'

The man – in shirtsleeves, a cellphone in each hand – has disappeared before Harmony gets the chance to reply, vanishing into a room that's been set up at the back of the truck.

'Don't hang around in the corridor,' calls another reporter who also looks hassled. He turns around and yells: 'Hey, control room! Tell the photographers to upload their best pictures of the attack to the central share, so we can make our choices for the evening edition! And let us know when we're off this fucking peninsula so we can finally get a network to send the gear up to the Miami bureau!'

Harmony presses herself up against the wall of the corridor, alarmed at these men and women crashing into her, running in all directions like ants in a disembowelled anthill.

The floor of the truck, racing full-speed towards the mainland, sends shuddering vibrations up her legs, through her whole body.

437

Suddenly the various flat screens fixed to the sides of the corridor burst out of the silence imposed by the electromagnetic jamming and come on all at once: the vehicle has just left the secured perimeter.

Each screen is showing a competing channel, but the same pictures appear on all of them: President Green's speech, the devastating explosion, the lifeless bodies of the victims.

The voiceovers, however, are all different. There's a cacophony coming out of all the various speakers, an avalanche of superlatives, as if each of the reporters is trying to talk louder than their neighbours on the other channels.

'. . . the most powerful explosion we've ever seen . . . !'; '. . . a slaughter of heads of state . . . !'; '. . . the deadliest attack in recent years, despite the drastic measures taken following the attack on Serena McBee . . . !'; '. . . the same question on everybody's lips: what link is there between this bomb and the ultimatum set by Russia . . . ?'

Paralysed, unable to move a muscle, Harmony allows the images to fill her eyes and the shouts to flood her ears.

All of a sudden, the Gregorian chant of non-stop information halts; all screens cut to the Oval Office, in the White House.

All the members of the cabinet are there, dazed – and in the middle stands the palest of them all, Milton Sunfield.

A caption appears: Swearing-in of the new President of the United States of America.

A serious-faced man, the Chief Justice of the United States, approaches Milton Sunfield as is customary and says, pompously: 'Please raise your right hand and repeat after me: I, Milton Jeremy Sunfield, do solemnly swear . . .'

The man who, thanks to the presidential order of succession, is about to become the most important person in the United States, looks totally out of his depth, as helpless as Samantha was on the screens of the Genesis channel.

But he raises his hand uncertainly and drones in a halting voice: 'I, Milton Jeremy Sunfield, do solemnly swear . . .'

The Chief Justice of the Supreme Court continues: '. . . that I shall faithfully execute . . .'

'. . . that I shall faithfully execute . . .'

'. . . the office of president of the United States . . .'

'. . . the office of . . . No, I can't do it!'

The interim vice-president lowers his right hand, then wipes the sweat from his drenched hair with his left.

'I can't do it!' he says again. 'I . . . I'm not worthy of this.' A terrible expression of guilt distorts his face. 'I wasn't able to protect President Green. All along I've underestimated the risks, I've refused to see the dangers, I was so desperate to protect international relations that I was blinded!'

He gestures towards the presidential desk, behind which sits the empty chair, the vacant throne: 'I don't deserve to sit in that chair. I'm just a stand-in – and a pathetic one! The position belongs to one person only: the one who warned us all, who was the first to pay for her ideals with her own flesh and blood.' He turns towards the camera, eyes shining with hope – yes, an almost religious hope. 'Serena McBee, wherever you are just now, if you can hear me, answer my prayer. Answer the call of History. You alone can save the American people. You must be the new president of the United States of America.'

439

76. Reverse Shot

McBee Castle, the Scottish Highlands
Wednesday 17 April, 9:01pm

We are in a vast stone hall, its walls pierced by inaccessible ogive windows through which filters the pale moonlight.

Here and there, candles are stuck on the candlesticks, but their flickering flames create more darkness than light: on the paving slabs, between the teardrops of white wax, the shadows cast by the wrought-iron legs look like dancing skeletons.

Despite the thick tapestries with their bleached-out images, which are hanging down more than twelve metres from the shadowy ceiling, the storm can still be heard roaring outside.

But isn't there also a human voice, somewhere in the middle of the raging elements, among the roars of all the demons of the ocean?

Yes, there's a very tiny voice, even more fragile than the flames of the candles, which is begging: '*Serena McBee, wherever you are just now, if you can hear me, answer my prayer . . .*'

That minuscule voice is not coming from outside.

It's coming timidly from the back of the cyclopean hall, where there is a stone fireplace built on a scale to suit the giants who in some legendary time used to rule over northern Scotland.

'. . . *answer the call of History* . . .'

There is a luminous shape set above the hearth where a reddish fire is fading.

A screen!

An unlikely intrusion of modernity into this time-forgotten place!

How vulnerable Milton Sunfield looks, above the vast fireplace that bears engravings of bees the size of birds, in a castle worthy of a fairy-tale ogre!

Because those must surely be ogres, the figures seated in the high-backed carved wooden armchairs, turned towards the fire, their over-sized shadows cast across the floor . . . Those must surely be ogres, who have placed a pair of crystal goblets filled with blood-red wine onto the low table in front of the hearth . . .

'. . . *you alone can save the American people,*' concludes the Lilliputian speaker imprisoned in the screen. '*You must be the new president of the United States of America.*'

There is a tinkling sound in the hall, louder than the storm beating down on the castle's distant roofs, clearer than a shower of coins on the age-old paving stones.

A laugh.

A silvery laugh.

A hand emerges from one of the velvet-padded armrests. It's perfectly smooth and white, and on its ring finger sparkles a solitaire diamond set into the shape of an eye. The long fingers encircle one of the goblets and hold it out towards the other armchair.

One of the most famous voices in the world, which used to be broadcast daily into millions of homes, rises into the room – younger, it seems, more bursting with life than ever before.

'My fiancé did an excellent job, did he not? It's such a good feeling finally having a man worthy of the name – men have disappointed me so badly, before. But I don't need to explain that to you, my dear. Come now – a new age is opening up for the McBee clan, and a new phase of youth begins for me: time for a toast!'

Now from the second armchair a second hand appears, which could not look less like the first: it's bony and yellowish, stained with liver spots. With some difficulty, it takes the goblet and raises it, trembling so severely that several drops of wine are spilled on the floor.

There is a terrible croaking – rough and wretched – from behind this second armchair.

'That was the last time I do an operation like that, Serena, you understand? The last time.'

The silvery laugh sweeps away this warning.

'You always say it's the last time, Gladys, but you always end up agreeing to start over, again and again. What do you expect? You know you can't refuse me anything. So, to us, my dear sister!'

The white hand stretches out abruptly towards the yellow hand, making the two goblets clink.

77. Genesis Channel

Wednesday 17 April, 4:15pm

Long shot of the launch platform at Cape Canaveral.

Large white tents have been set up over the demolished presidential enclosure, to allow the first-aid workers to do their job without the vulture stares of the cameras.

Down below, the pit assigned to the press has somewhat emptied out, but there are still hundreds of reporters there on the alert, mics and lenses poised, waiting for the next bit of news. For now, there's not so much as the crackle of a flash. A silence that is tense, sticky, reigns over the base. Stock still behind her podium, paralysed by doubt, Samantha looks like she's been transformed into a pillar of salt. Behind her is towering the overwhelmingly huge launcher, at the top of which the thirteen new contestants have by this point already been awaiting the producers' decision for an hour: will they lift off as planned, or cancel the whole thing?

A shape appears in this otherwise unmoving tableau.

It's a technician from the Genesis team, with the programme's logo on his jacket and cap.

He takes the stairs up to the stage four at a time, and hurries over to the podium.

The camera is curious and zooms in on him: 'Miss,' he shouts, breathless, his voice quavering with excitement. 'A message for you!'

Samantha snaps out of her torpor. She looks in wonder at the small object that the technician is holding out to her.

'It looks like . . . my earpiece!' she cries.

She grabs the device she hasn't worn in a year, and screws it into her ear.

An amazed expression appears on her face, then the amazement quickly turns to delight.

'You . . . you . . .' she babbles, her lips trembling, eyes moist with tears of joy. 'You're back!'

Reverse shot on the press pit.

The journalists liven up, asking one another: 'What did she say? Did anybody hear? Have they made a decision about launching the rocket?'

The photographers' cameras flicker back to life; the sound booms are held out in every possible direction, with nobody knowing where the scoop is going to come from, but everyone ready to catch it when it happens.

All of a sudden, every one of the giant screens goes black.

A worried murmur runs through the crowd: is this another attack on the Genesis programme?

But before panic is able to resume its hold, the screens all come back on at once, to show the same image.

The groans of despair are transformed into shouts of amazement.

Several boom operators drop their gear.

The photographers forget to click their shutter releases.

For there on the screens is the face of the woman they thought was dead, or so infirm that they had despaired of ever seeing her again.

An echo – first disbelieving, then marvelling – flies back and forth: 'Serena . . . ! It's Serena McBee . . . ! It's a miracle . . . !'

They had remembered her creased, dried-up skin, deeply lined with wrinkles – but she has become lither and smoother than ever before.

Their recollection was of a mummy only barely alive – but here she is before them, radiating youth and health in a virginal white dress illuminated by tall candles.

'My fellow citizens, and all the friends of the Genesis programme,' she says in a deep, melodious voice, quite unlike the tremulous instrument of her last public broadcast. 'Your appeal has reached me in the depths of the retreat where I have been tending my wounds. I heard your howls of pain; your cries of despair tore at my heart. My soul was ripped in half when I heard about the deaths of my friend Edmond Green and the other six heads of state. My ears bled when I heard the crashing down of the dream that, once again, our enemies have sought to shatter: the dream of the American people. But our great nation never gives up on its dreams. I will never give up on them. You have persuaded me that my period of convalescence has come to an end; in truth, I feel it lasted too long. I have missed you too much. Remember what I promised you – I will remain your guard bee for ever. The *Cupido* will fly again, returning to the fray just as I have done. America will get back on her feet just as I have gotten back onto mine. And she will crush her enemies – without and within, wherever they may be. That is what I have come to tell you today.'

She raises her right hand, in a Christ-like gesture that looks like an oath and also a blessing. 'The office of the presidency falls to me, following the death of the much-lamented President Green. Milton Sunfield has reminded me of my duty. I cannot remain deaf to his appeal and to the appeal of the American people. I have come to offer myself to you: *one for all*, as the Mars pioneers swore on the day they left. And I hope you will be there for me too: *all for one*.'

A passing breeze gently lifts the fabric of her dress, creating the impression of a pair of angel wings rising at her back.

Thus transformed, she speaks the words that make her the most powerful woman on the planet without any hesitation, as if she has always known them by heart, as if she has lived her whole life for this moment. 'I do solemnly swear that I will faithfully execute the Office of President of the United States, and will to the best of my ability, preserve, protect and defend the Constitution of the United States.'

78. Shot

It's nuts how quickly you lose sense of how much time has passed when you no longer have the movement of the stars or the small rituals of your daily life to remind you.

How many hours have gone by since I got thrown into the dark of the seventh habitat? Ten? Twenty? Thirty? I can't say.

Even with the complete lack of light, I was quickly able to get to grips with this space, finding my way by touch to the kitchen, the dining table, the sofa, all the marker points – even the light switch, which I tried with no luck, as it seems to have been electronically disabled.

But time is beyond me. Impossible to figure that out by touch. It slips between my fingers like sand – and anyway, what's the point in trying to hold it back? At the moment when I was finally ready to reveal the Noah Report live on the air, just as I was about to do it, it was too late.

Too late.

And there you have it, the recurring theme of my life, the

447

two words to be carved into my gravestone, if everybody ever puts one up to me.

On that distant summer's day on Earth, when all my instincts rebelled against boarding the rocket, it was already too late: the insistent pressures from the cameras, the overwhelming excitement of the reporters, and above all the begging look in Kris's eyes made it totally impossible for me to turn around.

And this evening on Mars, when I finally found the courage to reveal Serena's true face to the world, no one wanted to listen. It's been a year since the pioneers started clinging to the hope of the elevator, and I've done everything to encourage them. I saw it as the best way of keeping our community bonded. I kept repeating it over and over, for months on end: 'We've got to stand firm!' I can't take that hope away from them now. The need to survive is more deeply rooted in them than any desire to see the truth come out one day.

I'm not going to kid myself.

The *Cupido* will set off back to Mars.

Serena will reappear on Earth.

Stronger, more powerful than she's ever been.

And us, well, we're weaker than ever before.

We might not die here, but we'll be returning to a world where our worst enemy is in the most powerful position of all; a world where individuals are manipulated, made to believe they're free, too stunned by images and screens even to bother *thinking*.

What's the point of that?

What's the use in fighting?

I know how Mozart would answer those questions. I know

he'd talk about happiness, love, the incalculable value of life –
this life we'll be able to spend together, once we're back on
Earth, getting old beside our children.

He wouldn't understand if I told him I don't want to have a
child on Earth if they're going to be subject to the total power
of Serena McBee.

There's only one person on the base – there's only one
person in the world – I could open up to about these doubts –
these doubts which really don't suit the Determinator, this
disillusionment that's so unlike Léo the fighter. That person
is just a few metres away from me now, and yet light years
away too.

A hundred times I've lifted my hand to knock on the closed
door to the second bedroom.

A hundred times I've pulled back at the last moment.

Marcus's name began to form on my lips, but my chest
refused to expel enough air to allow me to speak it.

And anyway, the door is soundproof.

Does he even know I'm here?

Does he sense my presence the way I sense his?

Is he thinking about me the way I'm thinking about him?

79. Reverse Shot

The White House, Washington DC
Thursday 18 April, 2:15pm

'Ms McBee, you're looking . . . stunning,' stammers Dolores Ortega, bowing her head as Serena passes. Serena has just entered the Oval Office, where the whole cabinet has assembled.

'*Madam President*,' she says. 'From now on, you address me as *Madam President*.'

'Of course, yes, what was I thinking?' babbles the image consultant, her eyes glued to her polished court shoes.

Serena walks elegantly round the office, making her black lace skirt twirl around her endless, perfectly shapely legs. The ministers look on, dumbfounded, at this apparition that's come out of nowhere – she looks so young, so fresh, so . . .

'You look well, Madam President,' says Milton Sunfield, his words quite ridiculous given how far they fall short of the miracle everybody can see with their own eyes, in a woman who, according to the doctors, was expected to be disabled for the rest of her life.

'The delightful tropical air!' replies Serena, all smiles, sitting down with great pleasure in the presidential chair. 'But you, my dear old Milton, you look a little out of sorts. The events of these past few hours must have shaken you. You should have a bit of a break. I've got a gorgeous place in the Virgin Islands – how does that sound?'

The man who has gone back to being Secretary of State does indeed look rather grey, with heavy bags under his eyes. Even his hair, of which he is usually so proud, looks dull and limp.

'The way things are at present, with diplomatic tensions at their very highest, I don't think I can take a break,' he sighs. 'I'm dreading the thought that the inquiry might discover some link between this terrible attack and the Russians. It would be war.'

'It's already war in reality,' says Serena, her smile replaced by a look of great severity. 'That deadly bomb that exploded at the exact moment the Russian ultimatum expired, you think that's a coincidence? Are you going to open your eyes or will you stay safely in your delusions? Honestly, you've got a world-view like one of the Care Bears! It's not harmony that naturally governs human relations, but conflict, the law of the strongest, and only the firmest political hand is able to impose order and ensure justice. Have you asked yourself how responsible you are, you and all the other stubborn pacifists, for the death of President Green and six other heads of state?'

This volley of accusations pours over the unfortunate Milton Sunfield like salt on an open wound. He gives a moan of guilt.

'I had no idea . . .' he sobs. 'I didn't see . . . I only hope posterity will forgive me . . .'

Satisfied by this *mea culpa*, which looks rather more like an exercise in public humiliation, Serena is smiling again.

'I don't know about posterity, as you've certainly made a grave error of judgement – but I, at least, forgive you. And I am going to replace you, because our country needs something other than a wounded man at this difficult time.' A somewhat grotesque expression of surprise grips the disgraced man's face while the new president continues: 'I'm naming Orion Seamus, senior C.I.A. officer, to the post of Secretary of State, in order to handle America's enemies with the firmness that is called for.'

Agent Seamus, who has been standing at the back of the office, takes a few steps forward, under the astonished gaze of the ministers.

'In theory, you will have to get confirmation from the Senate if you want a ministerial reshuffle,' says one quiet voice.

'In theory, in theory!' thunders Serena, leaping to her feet. 'Wake up, ladies and gentlemen, it's time to move into the realm of practice! Our national security is under threat! The barbarians are at the gates of Rome! The flame of civilisation is about to sink into an ocean of shadows!'

Floored by these apocalyptic predictions, those present seem to deflate, giving up any attempt at resistance.

'I shall be asking Congress to declare martial law, which will give me plenary powers,' says Serena, sitting back down slowly. 'Exceptional times call for exceptional measures: that shall be the first decision taken by President McBee. A historic decision!'

80. Off-screen

Ocean Drive, Miami
Friday 19 April, 10:00am

'Hey, miss, you can't sit there! That bench is for customers only!'

Harmony lifts her head from the armrest she's been slumped on, to look at the man speaking to her: tanned, thirtyish, wearing an apron and a cap branded with the logo of *Mario's Pizza*. The establishment of that name, a vintage van against which the bench is leaning, has just opened its service hatch through which a delicious smell of cooked dough is wafting.

'I guess you had a bit too much last night, miss, didn't you?' says the eponymous Mario. 'I get that. But there are hotels where you can sleep it off, you know. Or the beach, as a last resort. You're going to have to get moving. Unless you want to buy yourself a slice of pizza for your breakfast, of course.'

Harmony drags herself out of the mists of sleep at last. Pushing aside the brown hair hanging over her forehead, she reveals her strange-looking face, her cheekbones marked by sunburn. It's been nearly thirty-six hours since she got out of the TV truck on which she hitched a lift off the Cape Canaveral base; since then she's been wandering the streets of southern Miami, left to her own devices. Her too-pale skin, used first to the seclusion of the Villa McBee and then to the cellar in Alphabet City, has quickly burned in the baking Florida sun.

'I haven't got any money,' she murmurs, her voice so weak, so distant, that the pizza-maker shudders at it.

'You look exhausted. And starving.' He hesitates a moment. 'I guess I could give you a bit of pizza, yeah. After all, we Americans got to stick together right now – who knows what tomorrow will bring, what with those damn Russkis . . .'

He goes back into his van, turns on the radio and sets to work, while a journalist runs through the latest headlines.

'. . . *in the day's latest surprise: Congress has agreed almost unanimously to enact martial law. The parties have agreed to form a sacred alliance around President McBee following the Cape Canaveral explosion, the latest in the deadly sequence of events including the Caribbean Sea murders two years ago and the National Mall attack last year. The suspicion of Russo-Chinese involvement becomes stronger with every hour, as the C.I.A.'s inquiry proceeds. And in fact, it's a C.I.A. staffer, Orion Seamus, who has just been named Secretary of State, replacing Milton Sunfield. Although Mr Seamus is still not well known to the general public, he has President McBee's total confidence, having been in charge of her security detail up to now. Analysts consider him a hawk, and believe his redeployment indicates a likely hardening of U.S. foreign policy . . .'*

'Hey, miss?' the pizza man shouts over the radio. 'You prefer a Margherita, a Siciliana or a Leonora?'

'A Leonora?' says Harmony.

'My own creation!' says Mario proudly. 'In tribute to Léonor, my favourite of the pioneers on the Genesis programme! Tomatoes, peppers, chillies, hot salami – only red ingredients to match her hair, and spicy like her personality! Though actually I could also have called it the Kelly, since that poor girl's turned totally scarlet. Must be allergic to the Martian atmosphere – seeing her stuck in bed like that, it's a terrible sight.' His expression darkens. 'I so wish I could deliver a few pizzas up there, for both of them, to cheer them up. Léonor hasn't eaten in two days, since she went into the Rest House after that hysterical fit.'

'She had a hysterical fit?'

Mario looks at Harmony as though she were an alien.

'Are you seriously the only person on Earth who hasn't been watching the Genesis channel the last forty-eight hours?' he asks, incredulous. 'The murder of President Green, the return of Serena McBee, the *Cupido* lift-off – you skipped the whole thing? Then Léonor couldn't handle watching the attack, she went real hysterical straight after. She looked totally nuts – seriously – and said she was going to stop the rocket from taking off, stopping the whole programme. She started raving about Noey . . . ? Nua . . . ?'

Harmony's eyes widen – she's definitely awake now.

'Noah?' she says quietly. 'She said something about the Noah Report?'

'Yeah, that's it – Noah! You see, you have been watching the Genesis channel too, I knew it! You remember, Léonor just said those two words – "Noah Report" – before getting escorted to the Rest House to give her a chance to relax far away from the cameras. What did she mean? I'm guessing she just lost it, poor kid.'

Harmony doesn't answer.

Up in the sky, a squadron of drones splits the air, buzzing.

'The sneaks are on patrol,' says Mario, looking up. 'We've almost gotten used to them, with the state of emergency lasting a whole year now, but now we're living under martial law I bet they're going to follow us even when we go take a dump.' He sighs. 'I guess it's the price we pay to stay safe. Serena knows what she's doing, so we've got to trust her. Actually, I think I might name my next creation after her: the *Serena* will be my most up-market pizza: truffle oil, mushrooms, smoked salmon from Scotland as a reminder of her origins. And definitely a drop of honey, in tribute to the guard bee of the U.S.A.! So, can I give you a slice of the Leonora, kid?'

81. Shot

It's only the thinnest ray of light, but after countless hours in total darkness it feels as blinding as a laser.

'Léo . . . ?' murmurs a voice through the crack. 'Léo, it's me, Mozart.'

The door of the seventh habitat opens a little further, and two shapes are silhouetted against the light of the access tube.

The first is the Brazilian; the crown of blonde locks on the second can only belong to Kris.

'Don't shout, Léo – please,' says Mozart, coming into the living room, accompanied by a delicious smell I'd recognise anywhere: Kris's mince.

I suddenly realise I'm ravenous – I haven't eaten anything in what feels like several days.

There's a slight click. It's the light coming on. The halogen spotlights get slowly brighter, illuminating the faces of the two people I thought were the most devoted to me but who didn't lift a finger to stop my strong-armed imprisonment.

'Léo! I swear I've been doing everything I could to come

see you as soon as possible!' says Mozart, rushing towards me.

'I can vouch for that,' says Kris. 'He pleaded for you. And so did I! But Alex didn't want to hear it. He said you were too dangerous, out of control, that we had to let you have some time to calm down. He gave a formal order forbidding anyone from coming into the seventh habitat until right now. The others . . . the others all fell into line behind him.'

From the way Kris said those last words, lowering her voice as if it were a shameful secret, I can guess that she also 'fell into line behind him' herself, at least to begin with. As for Mozart, there's something resigned in the way he suddenly looks down. This guy who always used to be the first person to stand up to Alexei's fits of authority, why doesn't he say anything? Why has he waited all this time before coming to open my cell door?

'We were all so scared, Léo,' Kris tries to explain. 'Scared you'd blurt everything out, in a moment of madness. Scared we'd lose everything. Everything Serena promised us.'

'She's back, isn't she?' I ask, my tone so sharp I barely recognise it, as if all these hours in silence have made me forget even the sound of my own voice.

Kris shudders.

'Yes,' she says. 'Serena's back. In full health, and at the very top of the tree – she's the new president of the United States. Congress has just granted her plenary powers.'

I can't contain a groan of despair.

Kris cries out. 'Don't be sad, Léo! Serena's coming back is the best thing that could have happened to us! Now she's at the head of the U.S. government, she has access to all the levers to keep the programme going despite the terrorists who want to stop it! She was the person who gave the go-ahead for the launch of Season Two! It's thanks to her, our saviour, that the self-energising elevator will be able to reach us!'

Kris's naivety is a blow to my heart.

Serena, our saviour!

My ears are bleeding!

'Kris is right,' Mozart says, gently. 'You've got to trust Serena. She's never broken her side of the contract, so far. She'll respect it all the way to the end. Nobody and nothing will stop us getting back to Earth, I promise you!'

I know his words are supposed to reassure me, but he doesn't realise that they don't – on the contrary, they fill me with anguish.

I feel like I'm living in a waking nightmare, with no way to escape.

My intuition tells me that the 'contract' binding us to Serena won't end when we arrive on Earth, that she'll find some other way of blackmailing us to keep the Noah Report hidden. By waiting, we've already let her become president, obtain plenary powers . . . How far will she go now?

'You should eat a little, Léo,' says Kris, pushing the dish shyly towards me.

'How long have I been locked in here?' I ask, not looking at the mince, even if I'm dying to pounce on it.

'Forty-eight hours!' says Mozart. 'You must be starving!'

'That means that for the last two days Marcus hasn't had anything to eat or drink, just because Alexei decided nobody was allowed in to the Rest House?'

The expression on Mozart's face is one of pained surprise.

'*Marcus?*' he says, as if it were a word from some unknown language, a word he couldn't understand.

'Yes, Marcus. The guy who's been locked in there for a year.' I point at the locked door to the second bedroom. 'Have you already forgotten him as quickly as you forgot about me for the last forty-eight hours?'

I know the accusation's unfair, that Mozart must have fought to be allowed this visit by the guy who seems to have become the new master of this place.

He splutters with indignation.

'I promise I didn't forget about you, not for a single second!' he cries. 'Liz and Tao didn't have access to the Rest House either, but things will go back to normal from now on! They'll be allowed to look after the prisoner again!'

'The prison*er*? Because there's only one, all of a sudden? And what about me? I'm here of my own free will, I suppose.'

'I've negotiated your freedom, conditionally,' murmurs Mozart. 'In exchange for two things. First, Ruben Rodriguez's cellphone, which Alexei has confiscated.'

It hardly surprises me: given what it contains, that phone's a bomb waiting to go off, and you don't let a crazy person get her hands on a weapon like that.

'And the second thing?' I ask, bitterly.

'Your word of honour never to mention the Noah Report on the air.'

I frown.

'My word of honour? That's it?'

Mozart exhales slowly.

His brown eyes meet mine, wrapping me in a wave of warmth, kindness and – yes – love.

'I agreed that the others would lock our habitat from the outside between midnight and 8 a.m., when the cameras in the Nests are off, so you won't be tempted to go out into the Garden. And the rest of the time, I'll be with you every minute of the day to react instantly if you have another fit.' He takes my hands, which have suddenly turned as soft as a ragdoll's. 'I swore to protect the pioneers from any harm you could cause them. But most of all, I swore to myself that I would protect you. From yourself. So are you going to promise that you'll be reasonable now?'

Under supervision . . .

Like a woman in olden times passing from her father's absolute authority to her husband's . . .

It's a very hard pill to swallow – it stays lodged in my throat.

But I force myself to gulp it down along with my injured pride.

'OK,' I say. 'I'll be reasonable. I won't say anything. I'll just keep smiling at the cameras like Alexei, Serena and the rest of the world expect of me. But on one condition: when the Great Storm starts, when the time comes to leave the base and board the elevator, I don't want us to leave Marcus to die in his little three-by-two cell. I want us to release him when the dust clouds cut off visual contact with the Earth, and let him leave secretly to discover Mars, to head towards the Noctis Labyrinthus, like he asked to.'

82. Reverse Shot

*Cellar of the Villa McBee, Long Island, New York State
Saturday 20 April, 9:25am*

'Good morning, good morning!' trills Serena McBee, entering the cell, a windowless room with concrete walls lit by a white neon bulb.

The door slams shut behind her.

'Sorry to have kept you waiting, my dear boy, but you know, I've been very occupied these past few hours.'

Sitting on the ground, Andrew opens his eyes wide behind his black-framed glasses. His lips part in an expression of astonishment.

'*Serena McBee* . . . ?' he murmurs, his voice hoarse, rasping from dehydration. 'Your skin . . . your face . . . how's it possible?'

'Ah yes, I know, nature does spoil me,' she simpers, pulling her sable coat over her shoulders – there's a biting cold in here.

Collecting his thoughts after his initial surprise, Andrew tries to get up but his iron foot skids on the damp floor and he falls back down with a loud clanking of chains – the chains that constrain his wrists and connect them to the wall.

'Yes, the floor is obviously a little slippery,' says Serena, looking the prisoner up and down. 'At the same time, the damp's quite normal, since we're in a basement. The basement of my villa, to be exact. I prefer living here, in Long Island. It's cosier than Washington – more discreet too.'

'You have no right to keep me prisoner in some private place of yours,' says Andrew. 'Even if you are the vice-president of the U.S.A.'

'*President* –' Serena corrects him – 'since the death of poor Edmond Green. And actually, *president with plenary powers*, to be precise.'

The young man can't help shuddering violently.

'You're lying!' he yells.

The shout never gets beyond the thick walls of the cell.

'Well, lying has always been my little weakness – I'm not going to pretend otherwise to you. But this is even more enjoyable – telling the truth, when the truth is so delightful.'

'*Habeas corpus*,' says Andrew quietly. 'The fundamental right not to be imprisoned without trial, it's written into the Constitution.'

'How quick you are – yes, that is indeed the next thing on my to-do list: update the Constitution. Between you and me, that dusty old text dating back to the Founding Fathers, those foolish old greybeards, really isn't very well suited to our day and age. A dangerous time, that's what I keep telling my staff, where threats could come from anywhere . . . My dear fellow citizens will understand that it's necessary to curtail those freedoms – which are quite wrongly described as *fundamental* – to ensure our national security. Better still: I'm counting on them to ensure a whole culture of self-policing that would make the most authoritarian regimes go pale, thanks to our citizens' smartphones, their domestic drones, this wonderful image-obsessed society in which we live.'

Crushed by his jailer's self-confidence, Andrew goes all in.

'The Noah Report!' he says. 'When that's revealed, you'll lose everything!'

But Serena doesn't bat an eyelid.

'I have no doubt that even here, held by chains, you do have some way of making that damn report public. An accomplice, some technological set-up, an invocation of spirits, I couldn't possibly guess – you're crafty as a fox. But I don't think you're going to use whatever you have. For the good and simple reason that your mother and little sister are still at my mercy, tucked up nice and warm at the Cape Canaveral base.' A cruel smile appears on Serena's smooth features. 'Come now, don't pull that face, it makes you look quite stupid. Of course, they never suspected that you managed to get to within just a few dozen metres of them, in the hold of that yacht. Barry Mirwood never told them. In fact, he's never even spoken to them.'

Serena slips her hand into her snakeskin bag and pulls out a cellphone.

She taps a few keys, then starts reading out loud. *'We arrive at Cape Canaveral from Cocoa Beach, on board the Cuban presidential yacht, on the seventeenth of April, in the early hours of the morning. We'll be counting on you, professor: bring Vivian and Lucy to the landing stage immediately after the launch.'* She sighs. 'After a while, you stopped even bothering to send your messages in code. You were so sure your connection with the kind professor was secure, and that wicked old Serena

464

had definitely kicked the bucket. And yet here we are: ever since clumsy Professor Mirwood dropped his cellphone on the floor of my hospital room a year ago, I'm the one who's been answering your messages in his place, I'm the one with whom you've been sharing your secrets, and you were completely in the dark! Getting you captured was even easier than having a bomb planted under the presidential enclosure. As for that, I needed to rely on a trustworthy man acting alone – dear Orion Seamus, whom you know well – even though I'll admit, when it finally came to bringing you in, well-trained, obedient soldiers did the job perfectly adequately.'

Andrew's body seems to go limp, to hunch down in the corner of his cell.

'You killed Edmond Green, and Barry Mirwood,' he murmurs.

'Oh no,' Serena corrects him. 'The cowardly assassination of the president was definitely the work of the Russian secret services, as the investigation led by Orion Seamus will shortly prove. As for the professor, he's not dead – or at least, not yet. I still need him to finalise the self-energising elevator, and his help will be invaluable to me until the device has been deployed. For the last year, he's been working here, in the basement of the Villa McBee – a cell next to yours and the cell of the Rodriguez cousins. His teams have never thought to wonder why he's chosen to isolate himself in a secure location to complete his work, communicating all his instructions to them remotely. I suppose they just figured you never know what to expect from an old eccentric like him, not least one who seems to have become so paranoid lately – and how can you blame him, in this world where a terrorist threat could strike at any moment?'

Serena is quiet for short time, silently savouring her absolute, crushing victory over the creature lying on the ground before her.

But suddenly a light comes on behind the lenses of Andrew's glasses, a flash of intelligence that is stronger than despair.

'You say you've won on all counts,' he says. 'You've made me your prisoner, you're keeping my family hostage, you have the controls of the Genesis programme in your hands, and the levers of power for the whole country. But you've just spent fifteen minutes with me bragging like a kid. And you aren't the sort of woman who likes to waste her time: so what do you stand to gain from confiding your little schemes to me? This demonstration of force, it's intended to impress me, I'm guessing, and if you've come to see me it's because you want to squeeze something out of me.' Andrew narrows his eyes. 'There's some piece of information you haven't got . . . A clue . . . You haven't mentioned Harmony once. She wasn't with us when the soldiers turned up in the hold of the yacht. You have no idea where she is right now.'

Serena pulls the collar of her coat up around her neck.

'Touché,' she says. 'The disappearance of my only daughter does grieve my maternal instinct.'

'You ordered your butler to kill her!'

'Oh, that? Ancient history. Back then I was occupying a much less comfortable position than I am today. I felt betrayed by that invasion of my study, and I reacted a touch too harshly. But now I'm ready to forgive.' Serena's voice turns sugary. 'So tell me, do you know where my little darling is, then?'

It's Andrew's turn to smile – a smile as sharp as a whip-crack.
His words are cutting.

'Even if I did know, I wouldn't say.'

Serena takes a step back.

'Hmph! If I were you, I wouldn't commit too quickly to what you would or wouldn't tell me. I know some pretty persuasive techniques, including some rather creative ones, for loosening even the stubbornest tongues. And I have all the time in the world. As for Harmony . . . my daughter is a fragile, vulnerable creature, unable to survive on her own. I imagine she'll end up coming back to the Villa McBee of her own accord eventually, like a little puppy who thought it was a wolf ends up coming back to the kennel.'

With these words, Serena turns on her heel, closing the cell door behind her.

She walks along a concrete corridor flanked by identical, reinforced, silent doors, so many cells that have been set up over the years deep beneath the building, hidden from public view.

At the end of the corridor, she puts her eye to a retinal scanner similar to the one that monitored access to the bunker from where, two years earlier, she controlled the launch of Season One of the Genesis programme.

A chrome-plated door slides silently open onto an elevator.

While the cabin carries her up to the surface, Serena gives herself a moment to take three deep breaths, part of the relaxation technique she has always advocated. Harmony's disappearance seems to be troubling her more than she is admitting.

467

The elevator stops at the ground floor. The door opens – it's embedded in the bookcases of the enormous study. The transmission gantry connected to the Genesis channel is here, having been returned from the vice-presidential residence. The various screens are showing pictures from the Martian base, which is now twice as big, its six new habitats almost finalised.

But for now, Serena doesn't waste any time on the pictures. She leaves the study via the large French windows that open directly into the gardens – the glass that Andrew and Harmony had to smash, in their escape a year and a half earlier, long repaired now.

Serena is met by a warm breeze, which lifts her hair. In the springtime sun, it seems less silvery than before her long eclipse, more golden – a very pale white gold, a reminder of the blonde she once was, when she was Harmony's age. The garden air has a slightly powdery glimmer to it: tiny spores and pollen float weightlessly amid the exhalations of newly opened flowers.

Serena walks on through the peonies and crocuses, the forget-me-nots and the hibiscuses, as far as the part of the garden where her hives stand: dozens of little wooden houses with pointed roofs. There's a quiet buzzing from the swarms that are waking up from their winter sleep. Here and there, nectar gatherers are going off on their exploratory missions, in greater and greater numbers as the morning warms up. It's impossible to imagine that directly beneath this idyllic natural scene, scented and sparkling with sunlight, there are malicious roots stretching out, the secret entrails of the Villa McBee.

Serena stops at a small wrought-iron bench, positioned in

the middle of the hives, facing east. She takes off her sable coat, revealing a sleeveless blouse whose silk caresses her shoulders, her skin that is so pearly, so smooth, as if newly regenerated.

Then she sits down on the bench, closes her eyes and allows herself to be cradled by the growing buzzing of the bees.

'Serena?'

'Huh?'

The sun, at its full height now, is blinding.

The air is so rich in scents awakened by the heat that it feels denser, heavier.

The sounds from the hives are at their deafening peak.

'It's me, Serena. It's Orion.'

The new president sits up to look at the man standing on the gravel path along the edge of the lawn.

'Come over here,' she says. 'Don't be scared of the bees. So long as you don't disturb them while they work, they aren't going to sting you. That's the beauty of the species. Cleaners, nourishers, architects, fanning bees, foragers and guards: they're all utterly devoted to their tasks, and in their submission to their queen. Such a model of order and discipline for a human race that's mired in its pathetic little squabbles, ready to tear each other apart to own a scrap of Martian land.'

Orion Seamus leaves the path and walks over to the wrought-iron bench.

His steps are stoical, not panicking about the bees that come to rest on the shoulders of his suit jacket, on his gleaming black hair. His single eye is focused on one target: Serena.

'You look amazing,' he murmurs.

'You mean even more amazing than I did on my hospital bed, where you swore your undying love?'

Orion Seamus stops next to the bench; his eye blinks, like a camera shutter.

'Every time I see you, ever since you got back, I've been amazed,' he confesses. 'When I left you secretly in the hall of McBee Castle, as you asked me to when you came out of your coma, you were so frail, so ill . . . I've spent a year and a half dropping fake clues to send journalists hunting for you in the tropics. While they were tracing you to the wrong latitudes, I scrupulously carried out all the orders you sent me. The kidnapping of Professor Mirwood, the surveillance of the Genesis teams, preparing the attack on President Green . . . And the whole time I was anxiously waiting for you to come back, hoping your convalescence would have done you good. But I never could have hoped for a resurrection like this.'

A mysterious smile appears on Serena's lips.

She gets up, unfurling a body that has regained the suppleness of a young girl's.

'I guess there are still some secrets in the world that even the C.I.A. hasn't managed to unearth. And you know, my dear, back in the days of my talk show, that was one of the pieces of advice I shared most willingly: women who want to be seduced need to know how to surround themselves with an air of mystery. Always.'

She puts her long-fingered hand onto the agent's clean-shaven cheek, just beneath the eyepatch.

'But you've been keeping something in the dark yourself,

Orion, haven't you? What have you got behind this little patch of black fabric?'

The agent stays perfectly still under Serena's fingers. He gives no indication that he is going to stop her, when she runs her polished nail under the elastic of the patch. Never taking his other eye off her, he just says a few words.

'Wouldn't it be more exciting to carry on not knowing?'

Serena's smile widens.

'Oh, we really do understand one another perfectly,' she says, toying with the elastic. 'Men are often so predictable, especially when they know how handsome they are – and you are, undoubtedly. They're in such a hurry to undress, in the belief that revealing their anatomy will necessarily overturn the heart and reason of the woman they desire. Poor innocent little things, they don't understand that erotic power is found in the brain, not in the pecs! But you're different. When you come to me in our marriage bedroom, on that night – very soon now – when we will be together for the first time, you shall wear this question mark over your birthday suit, this little scrap of night-time, this possibility . . . Oh, certainly – it will be more exciting!'

Serena pulls her hand back quickly, without having lifted the eyepatch.

'But all in good time,' she says. 'Duty before trifles. I'm a woman of principle: we won't be consummating our union until we are married. In the months to come, you'll go to Washington to keep an eye on my government – if I can put it like that – while I'm organising major operations from here, in the privacy of the Villa McBee. We aren't adolescents any more, only governed by our hormones, unlike those unfortunate pioneers who've had a year of enforced abstinence – at their age, it must be absolute torture – and the funniest part of it is they've got to keep pretending that they're trying to make babies!'

'You think they're really abstaining, at night in their habitats?'

'Well, they must be using some very strict family planning technique or other – how else to explain the lack of any pregnancies, fourteen months after they were married? The poor sweethearts presumably want to wait till they're back on Earth, safe and sound, before giving birth.'

Agent Seamus nods.

'I'm sure you're right, Serena, as always. But . . . how exactly are you going to handle their return? The moment they've left the base, there's no longer anything stopping them revealing that Noah Report you told me about.'

Serena lazily pushes a windblown lock of hair back behind her ear.

'Indeed, there will no longer be anything stopping them,' she agrees. 'But nobody will be listening to them. Look, several days ago, Léonor named the Noah Report live on air and nobody on Earth is bothered, or trying to find out any more about it. The truth is, here on Earth people have other fish to fry: there's a major conflict brewing, everyone can sense it. The legendary Russo-American antagonism is starting up again just like during the Cold War – a delicious tried-and-tested recipe! But the war won't just be cold this time – it'll be glacial. International relations won't cool, they'll freeze over entirely. And consciences too. You see, Orion, I'm not dreaming of an atomic bomb or a blitzkrieg – on the contrary, what I want is a war that is never declared, a slow, entrenched war, with no missiles and no fighting – a permanent threat, which never explodes and which lasts for ever. My aim is to get America frozen into suspicion before the fall of this year, when the self-energising elevator arrives in Martian orbit. Then the pioneers can reveal whatever they want, it won't do them any good; you can accuse a president, but not the commander-in-chief when the security of the nation is under threat!'

Agent Seamus smiles.

'Brilliant,' he murmurs. 'You can count on me to stir things up. The C.I.A.'s investigatory commission, which I've been taking good care of, is about to reach the conclusion we anticipated: a bomb fabricated by the Russians. All we'll need then will be for the investigators to locate the detonator, which I've concealed in the rooms of the Kazakh delegation at Cape Canaveral. Minds will quickly be made up, with everyone seeing the hand of Moscow behind a country that's traditionally been allied with Russia.'

'Perfect! That will set off a chain reaction, fed by the destructive energy of individual and national egos, all of it sprinkled with a healthy dose of paranoia. In the society I'm envisaging, social networks will replace the police: citizens will become their own guards, conducting permanent surveillance of their neighbours and revealing themselves with an unquenchable appetite for exhibitionism. Starting with the U.S.A., we will establish a new world order – the one I've always

473

dreamed of.' With a broad wave of her arm, Serena gestures towards the busy hives. 'A new age is about to begin, Orion. A new phase in the evolution of the human species. After *Homo erectus*, the standing man, came *Homo sapiens*, the wise man. He must now give way to his successor: *Homo apicius*, the bee man. These human beings, each one connected to every other, in a tightly packed swarm behind their queen, will conquer the stars, and the universe, and achieve immortality!'

83. Off-screen

Ocean Drive, Miami
Friday 26 April, 10:05am

'It's official: following the conclusions of the Cape Canaveral investigatory commission, the U.S.A. is breaking off all diplomatic relations with Russia! The American ambassador to Moscow has been recalled, a complete embargo has been placed on the flow of commerce, and reservists have been put on stand-by for mobilising in the event of any military escalation. President McBee has announced the creation of "Citizens Swarms", open to any members of civilian society who wish to become "Guardians" and contribute in some way to the defence of the mother-hive against enemies from without and within.'

Mario sighs deeply through the hatch of his pizza van, from which the sound of the radio can just be heard.

'This time, war really is right around the corner. It's going to be terrible for business. But Serena's right – we've got to defend the country when we're attacked.'

He's just attaching an American flag to the tailgate, next to the slate listing the range of pizzas available – including his latest creation, the *Serena*. Behind the van, all the big art deco

475

hotels that flank Ocean Drive are also covered in star-spangled banners, and pennants in the national colours are clinging to the windows of all the cars: the whole country is mobilising against the aggressor that has been assigned to them.

'I don't think it's the Russians.'

'What?' asks Mario, turning down his radio so as better to hear his first customer of the day, who is sitting with the first pizza to come out of the oven.

'I have a hunch it isn't the Russians,' says Harmony again. A week on from her arrival in Miami, her sunburn has faded a bit to give way to a light tan. Her hair, which has been exposed to the sea air, is tangled; her sun-beaten clothes have started to fade. For seven days, she's been surviving by painstakingly gathering up coins lost by tourists on the sand of the beaches alongside Ocean Drive; every morning and evening she brings her hoard to Mario, who gives her a discount when the money doesn't quite add up.

'Of course it's the Russkis!' the pizza man exclaims. 'Because of Mars! The investigation proved it!'

'The investigation was ordered by Serena McBee,' says Harmony evenly, without taking her eyes off her slice of pizza.

'And what of it? That's completely normal, she's the president!' Mario is suddenly struck by a chilling idea. He goes on quietly: 'You aren't suggesting Serena interfered in the investigation, are you? First of all, the whole idea's nuts. And second, it's totally treason to say something like that! Stop talking crap, Jane – you're playing into the hands of America's enemies!'

Jane . . . the first name that came into Harmony's head

when she needed to invent a new one for herself – that of her favourite author. But nowadays opening up a novel isn't enough to escape from reality, as she used to back in the day at the Villa McBee. Forced to keep a low profile, to hide her face behind her curtain of hair, she only ventures onto the beach at dawn and dusk so as to avoid police drones and their ID checks. As for the nights, she spends those under bridges or on benches in isolated places, hoping that the hurricane season that regularly devastates Florida will be kinder this year. Maybe she should run away, but where could she go, this girl who doesn't know anything or anyone, who's lost her only friend in the world?

Giving up on the idea of convincing Mario of something he cannot accept, she bites into her pizza with the wordless rage of a prisoner biting into her gag.

84. Shot

Month 13 / sol 373 / 10:02 Mars time
[492nd sol since landing]

'When I woke up, he'd gone,' says Kelly, her voice tense.

Back in her bed now, she is weaker and redder than ever.

For the first time, when I came into her habitat to take her blood, I found her alone.

'He just left a note.'

Her hand is resting on the sheets, its fingers curled around her tablet.

Taking it from her gently, I decipher the message. It was written with a stylus, in a handwriting that's nervous and full of crossings-out – and I can feel Mozart reading it over my shoulder. He's stuck to me like glue ever since I came out of the seventh habitat.

KELLY,

At first, I hoped you'd get better naturally.
But now I don't believe that any more.

478

And I can't bear seeing you paying because of me, because of my cowardice, because I haven't got the courage to go meet THEM.

As I don't ever leave the base, THEY have punished me through you. But you're not the one THEY're after. You aren't the one being called when THEY knock on the walls during a storm.
It's me, and only me.

There's something I haven't told you, not you or the organisers or anybody. When I came to Mars, I came with a ~~secret~~ sacred mission. To establish our species' first contact with THEM. I've trained my whole life to carry out this mission. Everything was planned in advance. All except one thing: you. The moment I met you, something changed – in ~~my stupidity~~ my naivety, I thought I could escape my destiny if I just stayed by your side.

But you can never escape your destiny.
That's one of the basic lessons of the Temple of Cosmic Unification.
Destiny always catches up with us, because of the Karmic law that rules over everything in this world, from incarnation to incarnation. The Yoshiki Lama was reincarnated into me to go and find THEM; I must offer myself to THEM if I'm to have any chance to save you. Before I left, I injected some of your blood into my veins, so I'd have the same illness as you, because I'm the one who deserves the punishment. I won't come back till I've found the cure.

Forgive me for not having had ~~the time~~ the courage to tell you the truth face to face.

At least now, I'm no longer scared of fulfilling my destiny.
To tell the truth, I'm not scared of anything any more.
You have cured me of all my phobias.
~~I'm so grateful to you~~ I love you.

KENJI - けんじ

'Well, well,' whistles Mozart. 'I guess someone must have overdone it on the Martian champagne. I suppose we'll find him somewhere in the base, sleeping it off.'

'Not Tiger, it's just not like him!' Kelly objects weakly. 'He never drinks much. He always keeps himself so under control. I find him more reassuring than anyone else I've ever met.'

'Well, if this letter is supposed to be reassuring, it's definitely a fail.'

'Look, that guy is the best thing that's ever happened to me in my whole shitty life!'

'And you've clearly got under his skin too,' says Mozart. 'Literally, actually! Injecting your blood into his veins, that's pretty romantic – a real junkie for love!'

Kelly tenses up in her bed.

'How dare you use words like that, a fucking drug dealer like you?'

I hurry to the sick girl's rescue, lifting the pillow under her head to make her more comfortable.

'Calm down – please –' I say, trying not to think about the blood sample I took last night, which was missing from the

480

infirmary this morning – clearly the one the Japanese boy spirited away without my knowing. 'I'm sure we'll find Kenji. He'll explain what he meant by this note. There's absolutely no reason to think your polycythaemia's contagious. In the meantime, you need to look after yourself.'

I'm getting ready to take out my syringes to draw her blood, when the habitat door bursts open.

'Léo, Mozart, come quick!' calls Safia. 'I've just had a message from Earth saying Serena's going to be speaking to us in a few moments. Kenji didn't tell you?'

The Indian girl doesn't yet know that the other Comms Officer has vanished. I know it'll be another tough blow for the team, but there's no point putting it off.

'Kenji hasn't been seen since last night,' I say. 'I'm guessing he's not in the Garden?'

Safia shakes her head.

'Not as far as I know. He's disappeared? Where?' Her big kohl-ringed eyes widen. 'But he hasn't left the base, has he? Oh God, maybe that's why Serena wants to talk to us! Come, quick, quick!'

I drop my medical gear, touch Kelly's hand gently and murmur a few words to her – 'It's best you stay in bed, I promise I'll give you a proper debrief as soon as I can' – then I race out of the room after Safia and Mozart.

The team is already gathered in the Garden, looking up at the dome, which is still transparent.

Like every other time I've been with the group since leaving the seventh habitat, I can see suspicion in all the eyes that are on me – and fear too. It's like I can hear them all murmuring. '*Is she still planning to lose it, that lunatic girl? Has she got another one of her home-made missiles ready to launch?*'

When I see those looks in their eyes, I imagine the miracle of diplomacy Mozart must have performed to get me free. It's only thanks to him that I'm able to move about in the base today. And it's also thanks to him that Alexei agreed we'll let Marcus go free when we leave New Eden.

'Anybody seen Kenji?' Safia asks no one in particular, temporarily lifting the weight of all that attention off me.

The only answer she receives is a crackle that starts on the inside of the dome.

For a moment, it's covered in vertical stripes, then the Martian landscape disappears behind the face of Serena McBee.

Once again, I'm struck by the vitality that she's radiated since she's been back among the human race. The colour of her skin, her rosy pink lips, the light in her eyes: everything about her gives off a healthiness that is wild, exuberant, almost supernatural . . . specially when you know what she's gone through, the punctured lung that seems totally cured today.

'My dear children,' she begins, with that worried look I seem to be the last person to still mistrust, 'you're waking up this morning to the discovery that one of you is missing at roll-call. Even we on Earth didn't notice his absence until very recently. Last night, Kenji left the base so discreetly that we didn't realise right away. He found a way of getting through the decompression airlock without setting off the sensors – he must have figured out some way of hacking the system thanks to his technological know-how. It was only this morning, looking back at the footage, that we realised what he's done.'

An anxious murmur runs through the Garden.

So Kenji isn't sleeping off his champagne somewhere in the base after all: as he said in his note, he really has left us. Where is he expecting to find the cure for whatever's wrong with Kelly? Who are the 'THEY' he kept writing about in capital letters in his note?

'Did he take one of the vehicles?' asks Mozart, standing beside me. 'With the GPS linked to the base, we should be able to track him down.'

In a strange echo of his question – which she can't have heard yet with the communications latency – Serena says: 'He's gone on one of the mini-rovers, having disconnected its GPS signal. He's also turned off the radio relay in his helmet, so we're unable to communicate with him. But we're still able to track his movements from above thanks to our supplementary satellites connected to the main antenna on Phobos.'

Serena's face fades away, giving way to a sequence of satellite images that fit into one another, zoomed further and further in.

'*Kenji has already put twelve miles between himself and the base,*' Serena continues, in voiceover. '*Navigating according to the landscape, he seems to be heading west, towards the geological formation that brings the Valles Marineris to an end – a real maze of canyons bearing the name Noctis Labyrinthus – the Labyrinth of Night.*'

A shiver runs down my spine at the mention of the Noctis Labyrinthus. The first time I heard those words was from

Marcus's mouth, when he was asking to be given a rover to go and lose himself there.

But now, it's more than just a dreamy poetic name: it's a reality. The perspective view of Noctis Labyrinthus appears on the screen, with its crevasses, its cracks, its narrow chasms that never see the daylight. If the long gash of the Valles Marineris has always reminded me of a scar, I think of cancer when I see the Noctis Labyrinthus. Something deadly, but still alive . . . A curse that multiplies deep inside an organism, just the way THEY are proliferating in the guts of the planet Mars.

Stop it!

I shake my head to get rid of this morbid, irrational thought. There's nothing to prove that Kenji is really going all the way to Noctis Labyrinthus. And even if he does, it's ridiculous to think he's going to find something alive there. Mars is a sterile planet! Every robotic mission has presupposed that, every test carried out by our Biology officers for a whole month has confirmed it! Kenji is disturbed, quite clearly – after all, he was diagnosed with severe phobias. I shouldn't let myself get taken in by his crazy ideas.

'The forecast is saying there'll be clouds over Ius Chasma for the next few hours,' Serena continues, back on screen, 'so there's a risk we'll lose sight of Kenji. Our psychological experts are currently dissecting the note he left. Detailed analysis might be able to teach us a bit more about his intentions, assuming there is any sense to them. In the meantime, if you find any clues, if you remember even the tiniest fact that might help to explain his behaviour, don't hesitate to let me know, at any time of the day or night.'

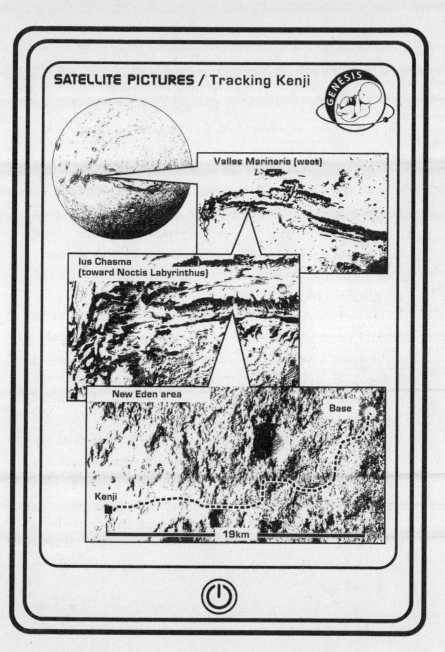

Alexei takes a step forward towards the wall of the dome, but seeing the look of fierce determination on his face I doubt it's to make a contribution to the Kenji investigation.

'President McBee!' he says in a stentorian, weirdly formal voice. 'We know you're very busy with your new responsibilities, but we have a request we'd like to make.'

There's something royal, autocratic in the way Alexei refers to 'we'. It's not a democratic 'we'. It's an autocratic 'we'. I imagine King Louis XIV or Ivan the Terrible would have said it the same way, with that same certainty that they alone represented a whole population. And actually, the pioneers standing obediently behind Alexei do suddenly remind me of a well-tamed court.

'We're delighted that you've made it to the highest position in the United States,' he says. 'You deserve it. That country really needs a woman like you, a visionary, not a pernickety little politician. Now that you're in power, we hope you're going to resolve the ridiculous situation that was put in place under President Green, that American seizure of the programme which infantilises all of us. We're grown-ups, not children. We have the right to communicate with our respective countries, I'm sure you will be in agreement, beginning with Russia which I'm representing here on Mars.'

Having completed this little rant, which has clearly been brewing inside him for some time, Alexei stands firm, his arms folded over his chest, with his armband in the Russian colours clearly visible.

While he waits for an answer from Earth, I'm struck by how silently all the others wait with him, as if there was nothing to add to their master's words. Even Louve and Warden are lying at his feet, their canine instincts suggesting he's now the head of the pack.

'Grievance noted loud and clear, my dear Alexei!' says Serena after a long silence. 'Your claim does make perfect sense. Unfortunately, for geopolitical reasons, I'm not able to give you a favourable answer. You don't know this yet, but the investigatory commission into the attack has just come to a terrible conclusion: Russia, motivated by its obsession with taking over a part of Mars, was definitely behind the attack on my predecessor.'

A thunderbolt runs through the dome.

Serena has just said 'no' to Alexei.

She's just undermined the newly acquired authority of our little Martian tsar.

When I see the look of amazement then rage on the Russian boy's face, my heart starts racing: Serena isn't as great a psychologist as she thought after all! Alexei's going to totally lose it! He's going to pull out Ruben Rodriguez's cellphone and spit the Noah Report right in her face! His fury is going to override his will to survive – we're all going to die from depressurisation, right now, within minutes!

'I'm not able to give you a favourable answer to your question,' Serena says again, calmly. 'But I can offer you more than you asked for. I was planning to do just that, this very day.'

My adrenaline drops as fast as it rose, giving way not to a relief that we'll survive a bit longer, but to a silent anguish about the words that will come next.

'You're so right, Alexei: you're all adults, you aren't kids. And adults are free to determine their own paths in life, without any supervision. Why would you want to demonstrate allegiance to your countries of origin? Countries which – I should remind you – you left without the slightest regret. And you more than anyone, Alexei – what has Russia ever given you but blows, and tears, and blood? Why would you want to reconnect yourselves to those old Earth nations, when you can create your own nation on Mars?'

A smile starts to form on Alexei's face, like a mirror image of Serena's gigantic smile on the inside of the dome. This icy symmetry is petrifying.

'I've always been in favour of people's right to self-determination,' Serena continues, her voice becoming more emphatic. 'That's the doctrine of the United States of America, and it's my own personal belief. And so today, in agreement with Atlas Capital, I declare your independence! The New Eden base, the equipment, the rovers, the entire planet: it all belongs to you, to you and to those others who make the journey to Mars! Don't let any foreign power colonise you, my friends! Take what's yours by right! And if you need a leader, they should be somebody who's risen through your own ranks. Someone like you, for example, Alexei . . .'

What appears on the Russian boy's face is no longer just a smile now, it's an expression of bliss, of pure gratitude. All loyalty towards the motherland swept away. All national claims out the window. Serena has just offered him the one thing he's always wanted, on a scale greater than he's ever imagined: *power*.

'Thank you, President McBee,' he murmurs, slipping with terrifying naturalness into the skin of a head of state addressing his counterpart. 'I'll be worthy of my office just as you are worthy of yours. You will be my example . . .' His blue eyes sparkle. '. . . my role model.'

85. Genesis Channel

Monday 29 April, 4:17pm

DEAR VIEWERS
OWING TO THE METEOROLOGICAL CONDITIONS
ABOVE IUS CHASMA,
WE HAVE LOST VISUAL CONTACT WITH KENJI.

WHILE WE WAIT FOR THIS TO BE RESTORED,
WE ARE PLEASED TO BE ABLE TO INVITE YOU
TO WATCH THE FIFTH OF OUR 'ORIGINS' REPORTS,
DEVOTED TO OUR JAPANESE PIONEER.

*(PROGRAM ENCRYPTED — ACCESS TO
PREMIUM SUBSCRIBERS ONLY.)*

Close-up on a face hidden in shadow.

It's impossible to make out any more than the tip of the nose and chin sticking out into the beams of the spotlights.

The title of the report appears in white letters over this black void, providing a name for the character in the absence of a face.

KENJI
JAPAN

A man's voice, off: '*Welcome to the audition for the Genesis programme, . . . uh . . . Kenji. That's you, right?*'

A voice replies, nervous, from somewhere in the darkness. 'Yes.'

'*Well, then. You're going to have to take your hood off, you know.*'

'I'd rather not.'

A few seconds of confused silence go by, heavy as drops of lead.

Embarrassed now, the camera pans back. The clothing that continues down from the hood is gradually revealed. It looks like a cross between the kimono of a medieval ninja – a cope over the shoulders, complicated lacing around the waist – and a high-tech biker outfit – protectors on the joints, knee-high boots.

Having understood that the candidate isn't going to volunteer to say any more, the man doing the casting resorts to speaking himself. '*What do you mean, you'd rather not?*'

'You said this was an audition.'

'*Right. I don't see what that's got to do with it.*'

'Audition is to do with the perception of sound. It's the

transformation of sound waves into a bioelectrical current transmitted to the brain. It's not the same as vision.'

An angel passes, again. In the bare studio, simply furnished in the Japanese style, the tension is palpable. Against a backdrop of rice-paper sliding panels, the candidate's dark silhouette looks like a meteorite that has crash-landed out of nowhere.

The casting man clears his throat. '*Ahem . . . Well, in the context that's brought us all here, the word "audition" does not only refer to hearing. It's rather – how should I put it – a* presentation. *McBee Studios need to see the candidates, not just hear them. The Genesis programme is a TV broadcast, not a radio show. Do you understZZZZZZZZZZZZZZZZZZZZZZZZZZZZZZZZZZZZZZZZZ ZZZZZZZZZZZZZZZZZZZZZZZZZZZZZZZZZZZZZZZZZZZZZ ZZZZZZZZZZZZZZZZZZZZZZZZZZZZZZZZZZZZZZZZZZZZ ZZZZZZZZZZZZZZZZZZZZZZZZZZZZZZZZZZZZZZZZZZZZZ ZZZZZZZZZZZZZZZZZZZZZZZ . . .*

86. Reverse Shot

The Villa McBee, Long Island, New York State
Wednesday 15 May, 4:05pm

'Come on, come on, children, strike a pose!' shouts the photographer.

Opposite him, in the middle of the flowering garden, against a background of sun-splashed hives, stand dozens of children. You don't immediately recognise them as the kids from the New Jersey orphanage, partly because they've grown up, but mostly because they're no longer wearing their badly fitting, threadbare outfits. Instead, they're all in brand-new uniforms, made to measure: shorts and shirt for the boys, skirt and blouse for the girls, made of white cotton and decorated with three red velvet bands at the end of their sleeves and above their hems. The two-colour stripes remind you of those on the American flag. The blue scarf tied around each neck, held by a metal ring decorated with a honeycomb, completes the tribute to the famous banner – except for one detail: instead of stars, the fabric is dotted with small white bees.

In the midst of this human swarm is Serena McBee, seated on her wrought-iron bench in an ivory-coloured dress.

'Everyone in position?' asks the photographer, checking in the viewfinder one last time. 'One . . . two . . . three . . . *One for all . . .*'

'*. . . All for one!*' reply all the children in unison.

After a good twenty shots, the young models are allowed to relax from their poses and go have an afternoon tea made by Balthazar and the rest of the Villa McBee staff at the end of the garden: gingerbread made with honey from the estate and lemonade with propolis extract.

Serena watches them entertaining themselves, while Orion Seamus appears beside her in the shade of a lime tree.

'All done then; the photos of the first Junior Citizens Swarm and all its delightful little Guardians are in the can, ready for flooding social media!' says the president.

'The first in a long line of them, I'm sure, going by the popularity of the adult version – and only a month after the scheme was created,' says Orion Seamus.

'Yes, people do feel a need to come together in reassuring structures when they feel threatened,' answers Serena distractedly, watching her protégés. 'What do you think of those uniforms? Not a bit too boy scout, maybe? I really would have liked to add a few military badges, some armbands, some medals, but spiteful tongues would have found some reason to criticise them. America isn't ready to march in step just yet. But it's not serious: they will be soon, the way things are going. For now, I did still manage to get a camera fitted inside each scarf ring: you see those honeycombs? Those devices film everything my little guard bees see, and transmit it in real time to our central database!' She turns towards her interlocutor with a satisfied smile. 'But you wanted to see me, Mr Secretary of State? Some news from our Russian friends?'

'Their anger is growing daily,' replies Orion Seamus, smiling in turn. 'They're not at all happy about the independence you unilaterally granted to the Martians, which pulls the rug out from under their feet and demolishes their ambition to extend their influence to the red planet. Up till now, they've been accusing the United States of imperialism, but now they're the ones who look like imperialists in the eyes of the whole world, by contesting that independence. According to our intelligence services, they've just increased their arms budget even more than ours. Tempers are heating up. The U.N. is totally paralysed, torn between those representatives who want to recognise the Martian state officially and those contesting it. You've really played a masterstroke!'

'Thank you,' says Serena modestly. 'But tell me, did you really make the journey here from Washington today just to congratulate me?'

'I would do it every day, gladly, you deserve so much praise.'

Serena waves away the flattery with a yawn.

'Spare me your cooing – you're starting to sound like Montgomery and you're better than that.'

'Well, you can be reassured, I actually didn't just come here to give you my congratulations. But to receive yours.'

Serena raises an eyebrow, intrigued.

'Mine? What do you mean?'

'For the last several weeks I've been working on a sensitive file, at the C.I.A. – where I still have my contacts. I didn't want to tell you till I was sure. But I am now.' His single eye gleams in the shade of the lime tree. 'As you know, the Agency has always maintained links with the underworld – in the intelligence business, you can't turn down any possible source. That's how the Aranha gang came to contact us in mid-April, through their American wing. They claimed to have captured a man on the small island of Guanaja, in the Caribbean Sea, off the coast of Honduras, which is still within their zone of influence – an American national of some importance, in exchange for whom they're asking for a ransom.'

Orion has Serena's full attention now.

'An American national, in the Caribbean Sea? I imagine if you're telling me about him, we're not just talking about some tourist out having fun who's lost his passport.'

'Indeed not. The man in question, known to the local fishing population as *El Gigante* – the Giant – arrived in Guanaja a year and a half earlier. Swimming, with an airplane life jacket around his neck and his suit pockets full of American dollars. Since then, he's lived in a prefab hut on a beach. He's kept a low profile, living an isolated life, apparently hoping to be forgotten by the world. It was only when a local hoodlum connected to the Aranha broke into his shack to burgle it, that he discovered the man's papers. And his identity – an identity known the world over.'

Orion Seamus slips his hand into his jacket pocket and pulls out a photograph, which he holds out to Serena.

It's the picture of a man of impressive build, his arms cuffed behind him, sitting on a chair in a neon-lit shed. Despite the faded T-shirt that's replaced his suit, despite the tan that's darkened his face and his bald head, there's no possible doubt: the Aranha's hostage really is . . .

'. . . Gordon Lock!' gasps Serena, recognising the Genesis programme's old technical director. 'He survived the plane crash!'

'Yes, it seems he was the only one to escape from the disaster. But he's done everything to stop us finding out. Up to his neck in the Genesis conspiracy, suspected by the media of being responsible for the plane hijacking, with no political allies, and you in the vice-presidency . . . he preferred to play dead rather than face his country's justice system and the judgement of his family. Until the Aranha captured him and tried to sell him to the C.I.A., thinking they'd caught a highly ranked American citizen – and therefore a highly lucrative one.'

Serena creases the photo in her manicured fingers.

'And . . . where is he now?' she asks.

The agent looks down at the ground.

'Oh, he's right here, my love. Beneath your feet. I've had him brought here, to the dungeons of the Villa McBee, by soldiers sworn to secrecy. Consider it my engagement present. If we're very persuasive, we could get him to admit publicly that he's responsible for the crash that wiped out the Genesis staff . . . and that he's acting for the Russians. Making the situation even more explosive.'

Serena throws her arms around her fiancé.

'Come here and let me kiss you!' she says. 'I'm so lucky to have met you! But tell me, how much did you have to pay to get that piece of trash back?'

'Not a cent.'

'What do you mean? I thought you said the Aranha expected him to be very lucrative.'

'At first, yes. But when they learned they were dealing directly with the American president, the negotiation moved up to their top guy in Rio, the one they just call the Boss. And it wasn't money that the Boss asked for in exchange for Gordon Lock, but the promise to free another hostage. You see, even among the biggest crooks, there's still something more precious than gold: honour. And revenge. If the Season One team ever returns to Earth, the Boss has asked that we hand over the Brazilian pioneer, Mozart, to him. I took the liberty of agreeing on your behalf. I have done well, haven't I?'

By way of reply, Serena plants a kiss on Orion's lips.

87. Off-screen

South Beach, Miami
Thursday 16 May, 7:05pm

'Don't you just want to be one with the cosmos, sister?'

Harmony looks up from the sand she was combing through with her fingers, hunting for coins.

There's a young man standing in front of her, his tall gangly silhouette cut out sharply against the setting sun. He's wearing a white tunic a bit like a kimono and there's a white headband knotted around his forehead. But the young man isn't Japanese; he's a local, with his tan verging on sunburn, his faded dreadlocks and the vague look in his eyes that seems to be floating in a haze of marijuana.

'Well, the cosmos wants to be one with you!' he says, his voice bright with exhilaration.

He turns around and points over to a group of young people sitting in a circle not far away on the beach. Some of them are doing a kind of slow-motion gymnastics that looks like tai-chi, while the others are nonchalantly hitting tambourines while intoning chants mixing English with some more guttural language – could that be Japanese?

'Don't just sit here on your own! Come join us!' says the young man encouragingly. 'In these dark times, with the world tearing itself apart, solidarity is the only thing that can triumph over chaos. We humans have to learn to unite with one another, if we expect to be able to unite with extra-terrestrials one day, right? My name's Hiroto-Sammy, by the way. Sammy's my name from before, when I was just a sales assistant at a surfing store; Hiroto's the name they gave me along with my hachimaki when I joined the Temple of Cosmic Unification, the moment they started talking about it on TV. I immediately connected with the temple's message: Love, Peace, Unity.'

Harmony gets up, on the defensive. Worry has become her default setting ever since she first started wandering alone around the beaches of Florida.

'The Temple of Cosmic Unification?' she says, wiping her sandy hands on her torn jeans. 'Isn't that the obscure organisation Genesis pioneer Kenji talked about in his letter, before he left the Mars base?'

A blissful smile appears on Hiroto-Sammy's face at the mention of the Japanese pioneer.

'Glory to the Heavenly Jewel!' he says, excitedly. 'As we speak, our beloved guide is walking gloriously towards his destiny!'

'He's gone off the radar, from what they were saying on the radio,' says Harmony darkly.

'That's because where he's gone, no other human being and no satellites can follow him!'

'His spacesuit can only stay self-sufficient for thirty-six hours, and there's been no news for twenty days . . .'

'Our divine guide's body is not like that of simple mortals!'

When she sees that nothing will be able to shake Hiroto-Sammy's fervent faith, Harmony decides to try another tactic.

'This temple of Cosmic Unification, I guess that does sound kind of interesting,' she lies. 'Could you tell me a bit more about it?'

'Of course! It's the best possible religion! It's so nuts – only a month ago, nobody knew about the temple, and ever since it was named on the Genesis channel it's been wild! My beloved tutors explained the whole thing to me in an express-training course, like the ones they've been organising all over the world since requests to join have exploded. It all started with a Japanese guy, the Yoshiki Lama, who had visions in the 1980s. Like, aliens talked to him in his dreams – friendly aliens though, not the horrible monsters you see in movies! Later on, Yoshiki's trip was confirmed by loads of scientific data, a history of space probes and photos from the surface of Mars . . . To be honest I didn't follow that part of the lecture completely, the tutors had organised an awesome cosmic party the night before to celebrate the arrival of the recruits and my head was a bit messed up.

'Anyway, what matters is that the E.T.s have been waiting ages for us to lift off from our little planet to go meet them. They – that's all we call them in the temple, just *They*, till we learn their real names – They could have contacted us earlier if They'd wanted to, because They're super-intelligent and much more advanced than we are. But They wanted us to take the first step – to be sure we were ready for the age of peace and prosperity They were keeping for us. Since Yoshiki died before the technology was able to get us to Mars, it's his reincarnation who's making the journey in his place: *Kenji himself!*'

Stunned by this avalanche of mysticism – poorly digested and regurgitated any old how – Harmony pauses, just enough to catch her breath.

'I see,' she manages to say, finally.

The truth is, all she sees is a bit more absurdity in a world that seems to her to have stopped making any sense.

But in spite of everything . . . she hears the gentle tapping of the tambourines through the falling dusk, and the friendly shouts of the faithful calling to her . . . the scent of miso soup floating in the air, more convincing to a hungry belly than any profession of faith . . .

'Could I join you?' she asks quietly.

'Course you can, I'm telling you!'

That evening, for the first time in ages, Harmony feels a little better, a little less alone.

The lull of the chanting, the warmth of the soup and the beer numb her spirits a bit, anaesthetising the silent anxiety of knowing that the worst is yet to come, and the powerless guilt of not having been able to save Andrew.

In the mild tropical night, among these dreamers who are totally unaware of the world that is about to take shape, she allows herself to dream too.

'Isn't the universe magnificent?' asks a tall blonde Californian girl, looking up at the Milky Way.

'Totally.'

'And They are also magnificent . . . Big, beautiful and noble, according to the visions of our revered founder who saw their faces on the hills of Mars, in the Cydonia region. Like us, they have two eyes to see, a mouth to taste, ears to hear. But do they have a heart to love? Sometimes I imagine that after the great Unification, when our two species finally meet, I'll fall in love with one of Them. I tell myself that He's thinking about me now, someplace up there . . . But what am I saying, you must think I'm being ridiculous, imagining I have a lover waiting for me up there in the sky!'

'No,' replies Harmony sadly, her eyes lost in the stars and her hand clutching the small golden locket she wears around her neck. 'On the contrary, I totally get it.'

The tall blonde girl turns towards Harmony with a kind smile, her blue eyes gleaming beneath the white headband that she wears around her forehead.

'I'm Sakura-Shirley, by the way,' she says. '*Sakura* means *flowering cherry tree* in Japanese. I chose it because I love flowers. And what about you, Jane? You'll have to take a new name too, now that you're one of the faithful. Maybe something to do with those amazing dark eyes of yours. Hang on, let me look in the dictionary.' She turns on her tablet and consults a list of Japanese words with their English translations, drawn up specially by the Temple of Cosmic Unification for the Western faithful who are pouring in in huge numbers. 'Here you are, I've found it: Kuro! It means *black*! Welcome among us, Kuro-Jane!'

She rummages around in her backpack and pulls out a new headband, which has been carefully ironed.

'Here's your hachimaki. It's a headdress in absorbent cotton, which the Japanese traditionally wear as a sign of courage and determination, to soak up the sweat of their labour. But for those of us in the Temple of Cosmic Unification, it's mostly the white flag that tells Them that we will meet Them in peace. May I . . . ?'

Harmony lets her new friend tie the headband around her forehead, while the faithful intone another chant.

'I see the roots of your hair are as blonde as mine, maybe even more.'

Harmony tenses suddenly, as if those roots were betraying her.

'I really like the colouring; that brown really works for you.'

'Thank you.'

'There, the hachimaki suits you beautifully – now you're really one of us! But tell me, you don't seem like you're from around here. Where's your family?'

'I haven't got one.' Realising that her answer is too terse and requires some explaining, Harmony adds immediately, 'Or, that is, I don't any more. I've burned those bridges.'

Sakura-Shirley nods, understandingly.

'I totally know what you mean. Those parents who just get it into their heads that they aren't going to understand . . . Those relatives who accuse the temple of being a cult, calling our fellow believers cranks . . . A lot of us have been there. America's too busy arming itself to see that we're at the dawn of a new age. There's so much bad energy around here, so much paranoia, so much aggression, so many police drone patrols. President McBee's an awesome girl – after all, she's the woman behind Genesis, bringing people together, all those beautiful

504

ideas – even in "Cosmic Love" you have that word *cosmic*; it's a kind of promise of the universal love that's waiting for us after Unification! – but she lost her way, getting into this arms race with the Russians. Only tonight they announced the public confession of one of the top people on the Genesis channel, and it just encourages this climate of informers that's seriously anti-cosmic, totally against the spirit of Unification.' Sakura-Shirley hesitates suddenly, before continuing: 'Or maybe it's necessary for Unification? The Yoshiki Lama prophesied in his sermons that the radiant meeting with Them, in space, would be preceded by a dark and troubled time, here on our planet. And the Yoshiki Lama, in his great wisdom, was always right – glory to the Earthly Jewel!'

Moved by some conditioned reflex, the faithful who are within earshot of the girl repeat as if in an echo: 'Glory to the Earthly Jewel!'

Sakura-Shirley gives them an encouraging look.

'The rest of us have decided to get to Europe, a neutral place where we'll survive while we wait for Unification,' she says. 'There's a freighter heading for Britain in a month, and we've bought tickets that weren't too expensive. It's not going to be super-comfortable, but it's the most discreet way to get out of America. Want to come with us? Don't worry if you need fake papers: we've got the contacts for that.'

Harmony blinks.

'Britain?' she asks, disbelieving, as if it was an imaginary country that only existed in those old novels where she'd spent her childhood.

'Yes, Britain. You haven't been, have you?'

'Yes . . . Well, actually, no . . . I mean, only through books.' Harmony's pupils dilate suddenly behind their brown lenses, as if she's just seen a secret light, a hidden fire. 'That's mostly where my family's from.'

'Your family?'

'My ancestors. They lived in Scotland. My mom told me I still had an aunt there, but I've never visited her.'

'Well, this is your chance! With a bit of luck, she'll be cooler and more cosmic than your parents. What do you say?'

Harmony is pensive for a moment, suddenly sobering up when faced with these young people who are ultimately just as cut off from the world as she is. But what they're offering her isn't just mantras and nice words – it's also a ticket back to her past, and possibly to her future.

She looks east, towards the unknown, where the black of the ocean blurs into the blue of the sky.

'Deal,' she says.

88. Genesis Channel

Thursday 16 May, 8:00pm

Open onto an entirely white room, at the centre of which is a chair, facing the camera.

On this chair sits a man.

The last time he appeared on the Genesis channel, he was standing proudly up on the stage at Cape Canaveral, in an expensive suit tailored to his tank-like body. But now, with his skin tanned by open-air living and his bald head peeled by the sun, he has to make do with the orange jumpsuit that is the uniform for those detained in the American penitentiary system.

A caption appears at the bottom of the screen: PUBLIC CONFESSION OF GORDON LOCK.

Deep in his sagging eye sockets, the prisoner's irises are moving about, sweeping across the area that's out of frame, as if waiting for a signal from the people filming him.

Suddenly he stares straight into the camera and begins: 'I, Gordon Lock, the former technical director of the Genesis programme, am speaking today to the American people and to all the channel's viewers around the world. I have betrayed both, in the vilest, most cowardly way possible. By repeating live on TV the confession I have already given to the C.I.A., I am not trying to awaken your pity, or to beg for your clemency, as I'm well aware I deserve neither. But I can at least hope to relieve my conscience.'

He swallows uncomfortably, as if trying to get rid of the bitter taste of his words, before continuing: 'Some years ago, the Russian secret services contacted me, wanting me to spy for them from inside the Genesis programme. In exchange for a promise of substantial recompense, I agreed to send Moscow confidential information about the base, the spacecraft, the rocket, the whole protocol. From the very beginning, the Russians wanted to launch their own Martian space-conquest programme, its technical components copied from ours. My spying mission was supposed to be completed in a blaze of glory, with a flight to Russia of a hijacked plane carrying the programme's senior staff, who would be forced to work under orders from Moscow. But those colleagues fought back bravely against my attempted hijack, even though they were unarmed; they preferred to plunge the plane into the Caribbean Sea rather than serve the enemy.'

The camera zooms gradually in on the prisoner, as if trying to drag more out of him than just a confession.

And the closer it gets, the tenser the voice emerging from those dry lips becomes, trembling as if an invisible hand were slowly strangling the throat it was coming from. 'Most unfairly of all, I was the only person to survive the plane crash. But the Russians are cruel masters, and I knew that if I handed myself over to them I wouldn't get any payment or help, just a gulag, as I had failed in the final part of my mission. And so I wasted away on a small island, being gnawed at by guilt as badly as Judas himself, until the C.I.A. found me and transferred me to a secret prison used for terrorists.'

Gordon Lock's eyes, in very tight close-up now, start to shine.

Could it be that this man – such a force of nature – is about to cry?

Such is the power of a genuine *mea culpa*! Or at least, that's what the billions of viewers watching this on their screens must think, convinced they see repentance in what are really tears of terror.

The voice of the man who, in a different life, was the Genesis programme's number two, is barely audible now, as he concludes: 'In the depths of my sleepless nights, when the ghosts of my victims return to haunt me, I have only one thing to comfort me: the fact that Serena McBee was not on that damned jet. I thank Providence, which protected her from my cynical manoeuvrings and the murderous intentions of her adversaries. She alone can purge America of the parasites infesting it – the stateless, the traitors, the profiteers – of which I'm just one among thousands.'

Fade to black.

Cut.

89. Shot

'OK, Kelly . . . I'm not hurting you?' I ask, pushing the needle into my Canadian friend's skinny arm as delicately as I can.

'Meh, I can't feel anything any more.'

'Polyneuritis,' I say, thinking aloud, mentally consulting my lessons.

'Bless you!' croaks Kelly.

'Sorry. It's a word for the inflammation of the nerves, which sometimes leads to a loss of nervous feeling. But polyneuritis isn't normally one of the typical symptoms of polycythaemia.'

Kelly gives a dry cough.

'Poly my ass! My nerves are fine, for your information. Actually, better than fine, given how bad the aching can get at night. It's my heart that can't feel anything any more.'

And there it is, we're onto the subject I dread more than any other, which makes me feel totally powerless, totally useless: Kenji. However much I may try to reassure Kelly about her mysterious illness, and show her that a lot of her indicators haven't changed, and allow her to glimpse the possibility of some future treatment, I still can't lie to her and claim that Kenji will come back and that there's any hope he's still alive. Three weeks after he disappeared, without provisions or any oxygen reserves, he has to be dead . . . whether he also developed polycythaemia from injecting Kelly's blood or not.

'Don't think about him too much – you need to focus on yourself, on getting better.'

Hollow words, I know even as I say them, but they're the only ones I can think of.

'Getting better for what?' Kelly asks me at once, touching a nerve.

How can I answer her?

Getting better only to die in the next Great Storm, which is racing towards us?

Getting better only to return to Earth and give Serena a big, grateful kiss?

'*Getting better for what?!*' Kelly asks again, her voice hoarse, half sitting up in her bed, red and furious like a creature possessed, like something straight out of *The Exorcist*.

'Take it easy!' says Mozart from behind me, ready to intervene at the slightest outburst.

The invalid is shaken by a hoarse giggling.

'Good old Mozzie, always there to keep an eye on things!' she says sarcastically. 'So interesting to see how easily the rebel of the favelas has transformed into a KGB collaborator!'

'Alexei has nothing to do with the KGB, and nor do I,' answers Mozart, defending his erstwhile enemy – because he has to? Because he really believes it? I've stopped asking myself those questions too.

'Alexei isn't Russian any more. I'm not Brazilian. And you've stopped being Canadian, Kelly. We're all Martians now, since the declaration of independence.'

Kelly rolls her eyes.

'Léo, pass me my music player, please. I'd rather relax to the sweet voice of Jimmy Giant than have to listen to more of this crap.'

I can see how exhausted Kelly is. She can't even reach over to her bedside table any more.

'We're going to go,' I say gently, handing her the music player and putting the sample tube away filled with very red blood. 'We'll be back this evening.'

But she's already stuck her earphones in, and her eyelids are closed. I don't know if she's really fallen asleep or if she just prefers to close her eyes to what New Eden has become.

Kris meets us with a big smile as we come out of the habitat. She's dazzling in her unbleached silk tunic, which she chooses to wear inside the base, looking like she's blossoming so healthily it pains me.

'I was waiting for you, Mozonor!' she says. 'I've finished making your armbands!'

She proudly holds out two pieces of Martian silk, onto which she's embroidered numbers: 3 on one and 4 on the other. It's Alexei's latest brainwave for the administration of the base: assign each person a number, according to their importance in the social structure – a practice that seems to date back to his Moscow past, that worrying iceberg that was once submerged but more of which is revealed every day. He's assigned himself number 1, replacing the Russian flag on his arm, and Kris has inherited number 2 as Mars's First Lady. The assigning of 3 and 4 to Mozart and me is an honour that must be largely thanks to my friend's intercession.

'Thank you very much,' says Mozart, genuinely touched.

He puts on armband number 3 and gives me number 4 with a tender smile.

'For you, my love.'

I might often get exasperated at the way he seems to bow to Alexei's will, I might sometimes feel stifled by his constant presence at my side, but his luminous smile, filled with optimism, makes me melt every time.

So now it's my turn, and I pull on the armband, watched benignly by the two people in New Eden who love me the most – actually, the two people in the universe, I'm sure of it. If it'll make them happy, I'll wear this number without flinching.

'Now the armbands are finished, there's another bit of embroidery I want to get started on . . .' says Kris. 'An incredibly important job. I've talked to Alexei about it: he agreed that I should do it with you.'

'You know embroidery and me don't exactly get along,' I warn her. 'The only needles I know how to handle more or less right are the ones on my hypodermic syringes . . . and even there I'm not totally sure, given the way I've been butchering poor old Kelly.'

'Don't worry, I'll deal with the actual embroidery part. What I want you to do is come up with the design – for the Martian flag!'

Kris's request leaves me speechless.

'A new country needs a new flag!' she explains, thinking perhaps that I haven't understood.

But I have understood, I've understood perfectly: she's so far gone in her delusion that we really are creating a country, something that's going to last, with its institutions, its flag and – well, why not – eventually, like, folk festivals and everything! We might be at month fourteen, just four Martian months from the next perihelion, but everybody in New Eden is acting like we're here to stay! Am I seriously the only person in this shitty little base who remembers those two words I'm not allowed to say – *Noah Report* – and what they mean? At the time of the penultimate Great Storm, all the Martian guinea pigs disappeared without a trace, for fuck's sake! There's no future for us, or for any living thing, on the red planet!

Cutting this ridiculous conversation short, Fangfang bursts out of her access tube and rushes over to us, shouting: 'Kris! Help! I can't get my hair plaited the way you taught me the other day – can you help me out, please? It's my turn inviting today, and the speed-dating starts in ten minutes!'

I can't blame the Singaporean girl for her excitement. Since the *Cupido* set off a month ago, she's already been invited by two boys – the Mexican and the Indonesian, I think – and today's her turn to choose one of the candidates. But she seems to be forgetting one crucial fact too: these speed-dates are not going to end in Martian marriages. Watching her strutting around in the dark green bandage-dress that she wore two whole years ago now, when she was trying to seduce Tao on board the *Cupido*, I feel dizzy, like I've just fallen through a time warp.

'Quick, quick!' she says, pulling Kris by the sleeve of her tunic. 'I've decided to invite Valentin, the Swiss boy, who I'm sure I have a lot in common with. After all, don't people say Singapore is the Switzerland of Asia? Two fine countries, where every last detail counts: I've got to be as perfect as a piece of high-quality Swiss timekeeping!'

'Don't worry, I'll transform you into a Rolex of seduction!'

The two of them disappear giggling into Fangfang's habitat, which when the time comes will be linked up to the vessel carrying thirteen new heroes towards Mars – thirteen new dupes.

'Right, I've got to go analyse Kelly's sample,' I say, very weary all of a sudden.

'I'll go with you!' says Mozart enthusiastically.

The words rush out of my mouth, sharply.

'You don't exactly need to tell me that. You go everywhere with me, whether I like it or not.'

Mozart's smile vanishes instantly.

'Léo . . .' he says, 'I'm only escorting you for your own protection . . . In case you have . . . you know . . . *another attack.*'

That's the official version, which is supposed to justify our co-dependency to the viewers, from his accompanying my visits to Kelly's room to the excursions in the rover on which I follow him religiously.

Léo the hysteric.

The crazy girl who could fall apart at any moment.

That's the character the rest of the team have created for me – and the ironic thing is, the unfairness of it all really does make me want to lose my shit completely!

515

But not today.

I don't want to get too excited.

I just want to see Mozart beaming again, lighting me up again.

I need it.

'I know you're doing it for my own good,' I say gently. 'Shall we go?'

I take his hand in mine, a simple gesture that's enough to make his face light up again.

But I don't get the chance to savour this moment of tenderness that belongs only to us: the giant screen on the dome is suddenly illuminated brightly against the star-speckled, inky sky.

The first notes of 'Star Dreamers' fill the space.

The credits of the Genesis programme have just begun – I guess we must have special permission to see it, because it's Fangfang who's inviting: Team Mars is playing at home today.

'Six girls on one side . . .' announces the voiceover, as the Cupido *appears on the screen.*

The camera passes through the hull of the craft to reveal the girls' quarters, with the 2D cut-outs of the six new contestants, with their respective roles. They scroll past in close-up, these girls I couldn't stop from leaving . . .

Caption: MERITXELL, SPAIN (BIOLOGY) – *the bearing of a flamenco dancer; the glamour of a movie star; and the look in her eyes of a killer prepared to do anything to win.*

Caption: YOUNG, KOREA (ENGINEERING) – *purple hair gathered into bunches with fluorescent-coloured elastic bands; eyes that look too big to be natural, with coloured contact lenses that make* their irises violet too; the disturbing sense that you're looking at a character in a computer-generated image, someone who's escaped from an anime.

Caption: LUCREZIA, ITALY (MEDICINE) – long snakelike black hair; almond-shaped eyes gleaming with mystery; the head of a Medusa or Pythia, enigmatic, that immediately makes me want to draw her to try and get inside her secret.

Caption: MERYEM, TURKEY (NAVIGATION) – an intelligent gaze from beneath a headscarf of dark blue fabric, matching the turquoises decorating her ears and neck; a mixture of modesty and sophistication, a totally confident smile.

Caption: SAGA, SWEDEN (COMMUNICATIONS) – an extraordinary physique; a gigantic frame, that must be over a metre ninety tall; a shaven head, perfectly oval; no hair or jewellery to detract attention from the two light blue eyes in this Viking warrior face.

Caption: NIKKI, NETHERLANDS (PLANETOLOGY) – the first shock: the red hair framing her face, lush and flamboyant; second shock: the freckles covering her skin, countless as a scattering of wheat bran.

'Hey, Léo, did you see that?' says Mozart. 'The Dutch girl looks a lot like you!' Then he quickly adds: 'But of course you'll always be unique to me, my darling Léo.'

I nod, unable to take my eyes off the dome, which suddenly seems to have been transformed into a giant mirror.

'A second carrot-top?' I say. 'That'll be good, I was getting fed up with being the only redhead around here. We're going to stick together, me and Nikki.'

I don't get a chance to say any more: the credits have already moved on.

517

'Six boys on the other . . .' *continues the voiceover, while the camera swoops into the boys' quarters, revealing their outlines and their faces.*

Caption: OSKAR, POLAND (NAVIGATION) *– a kind of rockabilly quiff, way too stylish; a pierced eyebrow over two blue eyes that are sparkling with mischief; an aura of cool attitude that's almost palpable is coming off this guy, which makes you immediately want to be his friend.*

Caption: FARUKH, INDONESIA (MEDICINE) *– smooth dark hair combed to one side; a white shirt and black tie; a moody, aristocratic style.*

Caption: URI, ISRAEL (ENGINEERING) *– three-day stubble; dark, piercing eyes; a square jaw; masculine charm in the raw, as intense as a very strong coffee.*

Caption: MARTI, MEXICO (COMMUNICATIONS) *– tousled blond hair; a slightly dreamy look in his eyes; this arty, airy side of him has something seductive about it.*

Caption: LOGAN, USA/HAWAII (BIOLOGY) *– the reverse of the stereotyped image of the Hawaiian surfer, with no tan, skin as white as an aspirin; instead of long hair discoloured by the sun, his is dark and cut very short; as for the colour of his eyes . . . it's impossible to make it out behind his trifocal lenses.*

Caption: VALENTIN, SWITZERLAND (PLANETOLOGY) *– again, nothing like the Alpine or Tyrolean stereotypes darkish skin, hazelnut-coloured eyes; a smile to die for . . . like a bar of Swiss chocolate?*

Caption: INÚNGUAK, DENMARK (PLANETOLOGY) *– a second Planetology Officer, of course, to replace Marcus. High cheekbones,* *almond-shaped eyes; long plaited black hair, like a Native American or an Inuit.*

'Looks like he might be from Greenland, that one,' says Mozart. 'It's a territory that's a part of Denmark, apparently.'

The face of this final contestant disappears in turn.

The credits continue, showing the Visiting Room, the planet Mars and finally the Genesis logo, while the voices of Jimmy Giant and Stella Magnifica sing the chorus of 'Star Dreamers'.

And then, all of a sudden, everything stops.

The pictures disappear and the dome is transparent again, revealing the eternally unchanging landscape of Mars – the rest will only be shown in Fangfang's room, and on millions of screens on Earth.

90. Reverse Shot

The Villa McBee, Long Island, New York State
Sunday 20 May, 3:55pm

'*I've been asking for a meeting with you for weeks, Ms McBee . . .*'

Serena McBee's face is reflected in the shining orb that serves as a face for the android Oraculon. The android is sitting there, unmoving in his dark suit, on a chair facing the president's desk. Through the large French windows that open onto the gardens, it's possible to see the helicopter on which Atlas Capital's representative arrived a few moments earlier.

'*Your office has kept postponing this audience,*' he says in his affectless synthetic voice, in which it's impossible to detect any annoyance or bitterness.

'Well, you're having your audience now,' replies Serena, making no attempt to hide her own irritation. 'But I can only give you ten minutes. You and your employers will understand that a president's schedule is kept regular as clockwork.'

Two red dots light up at the back of the android's translucent head, to carry out the security scan that is conducted before every contact with the Atlas Capital board.

But Serena tuts impatiently. 'There's really no need to hunt for hidden microphones! We're at my own house, the Villa McBee, and the place is perfectly secure.'

The scan stops.

The red eyes go out. And they are replaced by the blank, anonymous mask through which the mysterious administrators of Atlas Capital express themselves.

The tone immediately becomes accusatory.

'You've gone too far this time! You had no right to offer the New Eden base to the pioneers: it doesn't belong to you – not to you and not to the American government! It belongs to our organisation, like every part of the Genesis programme equipment. Mars's declaration of independence is considered illegal under international law; it makes a mockery of the law of the market and constitutes a flagrant violation of property rights. Not to mention this ludicrous imminent war with Russia, which is going to destabilise the global economy and harm our interests. If you don't reconsider Martian independence right away, we intend to hasten your fall.'

Serena stifles a slight yawn behind her manicured hand.

'Come now, come now, let's not have any pettiness. The emancipation of the people of Mars will go the same way these things have always gone in history. You'd do better to accept their independence with good grace, as I have, rather than trying to cling onto your dollars.'

On the surface of the helmet, the digital lines drawing the synthetic face begin to tremble with rage.

'That's enough! We won't allow ourselves to be fooled any longer by these big speeches that do nothing but serve your own personal ambitions! If you don't comply, you'll be hearing about the Noah Report again!'

'I don't know what report you're talking about.'

'*Don't play the innocent! Even though we haven't kept a copy for security reasons, we would still be able to reconstruct all the components. And we could have it sent to the Russians without needing to reveal ourselves in the process. As soon as they have the information in their possession, they'll make it public!*'

Serena receives the android's threat with a burst of wild laughter.

'The Americans are now aware that the Russians are behind the attacks that have punctuated the history of Genesis for the last two years – any statements from them will be assumed to be lies, with good reason! We're practically at war, you said it yourself! And in times of war, people unite behind their leaders, and they're suspicious of stateless organisations that seek to advance their own interests before society's.' She wipes away the tears of mirth that have formed in the corners of her eyes. 'Let me be quite clear: if Atlas Capital attempts to destabilise the presidency, putting the nation's safety in danger, all its assets on American soil will immediately be seized – its property right across the country, its headquarters in New York, the Cape Canaveral base: *all of them*. I'm sure you understand me, and that you are now going to cooperate in putting the country right. And as a sign of our renewed trust, I am inviting the android Oraculon to take advantage of the hospitality of the Villa McBee until the time of our next meeting. While he waits, he can have a little rest.'

With these words, she takes a Taser out of her desk and fires at the robot.

The projectile hits him in the middle of his chest, making him short-circuit. The synthetic face disappears like a ghost being exorcised, while the mechanical body collapses onto the floor with a crash.

'And so – entirely gracelessly – falls the dumb capitalism I've always despised,' murmurs Serena McBee by way of an epitaph. 'Here lies the ultra-libertarian ideology. A new age will soon begin.'

She replaces the Taser beneath her desk, gets up and walks calmly over to open the door.

Orion Seamus is waiting right behind it, digital tablet in hand. 'Well?' she asks.

'It was perfect. The android was in contact with the Atlas board for long enough to allow us to geolocate the origins of the satellite emission.'

He holds the tablet out to Serena: there's a map on the screen, zooming gradually in on an area in the north Atlantic.

'The Bermuda archipelago,' says Orion Seamus. 'That's where the board sent their signal from.'

Serena gives a small contemptuous sigh.

'A fiscal paradise, naturally! What else would you expect from those greedy rats? Well, if they thought they were safe on their little island . . .'

'Not on their island. On their boat. A crafty method for being always in motion, elusive.'

The image zooms in to the max, focusing on a gigantic yacht moving through the waters of the archipelago.

'But don't worry; at the slightest sign of rebellion, we'll take them. The boat will never be off our radar.' A fierce smile appears on the lips of the new Secretary of State. 'And the day we do, those rats won't get a chance to leave their sinking ship, I can promise you that!'

SATELLITE SIGNAL LOCALISATION /

**Transmission from andriod Oraculon
19 May, from 3:50pm to 3:59pm**

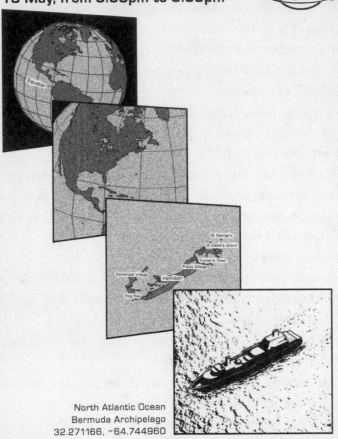

North Atlantic Ocean
Bermuda Archipelago
32.271166, -64.744960

91. Off-screen

The Thames Estuary
Monday 24 June, 3:35pm

'Are you sure you don't want to go on a bit further with us? Apparently the temple here in London is one of the biggest in Europe – they've already got tens of thousands of followers. The number of conversions keeps going up, specially since America and Russia have got into this arm-wrestle and taken the whole world hostage along the way! And after England, we'll go further east, to Japan – that's my dream.'

Sakura-Shirley is leaning on the guardrail of the upper deck, the ends of her hachimaki flapping in the wind. She and Harmony are looking out at the banks of the Thames where the freighter has entered, making its way slowly up from the North Sea towards the industrial port of London.

'I'll definitely visit the London temple when I get back,' Harmony promises her. 'But for now, I can't wait to go up to Scotland, to try and find my aunt.'

The Californian girl nods.

'I understand. It's your last chance to reconnect with your biological family, before . . . the apocalypse?' Her eyes drift out of focus, and she starts to recite the precepts of the Temple of Cosmic Unification, so regularly repeated that they're part of her now. 'The Yoshiki Lama predicted it . . . and chaos will reign, before the cosmos . . . It will be the struggle of each against each, before the union of all with Them . . . It will be an age of great turbulence, before the great Unification . . . Glory to the Earthly Jewel!'

Calmed by this profession of faith that promises a happy outcome to troubled times, she turns to her friend.

'If you don't manage to find your aunt, or if the person you find isn't what you were hoping for, never forget there's another family always waiting for you, sister. Within the temple, the Yoshiki Lama is our father, all of ours, and Kenji is our beloved big brother! We'll always be there for you.'

She gestures towards the deck behind her. All the faithful, their foreheads wrapped in their white hachimakis, are carrying out their afternoon ritual movements, which are supposed to encourage the circulation of cosmic energy, in front of three large portraits in frames set with glass beads to look like diamonds. The first picture shows an old Japanese man with a long white beard and bushy eyebrows – the Yoshiki Lama, the Earthly Jewel; the second is of his apparent reincarnation, a young Asian man whose eyes, part-hidden behind his brown hair, look lost – Kenji, the Heavenly Jewel; and as for the third portrait . . . it's really a print of the surface of Mars, depicting a hill in the Cydonia region, the relief of which looks troublingly like a humanoid face, long and enigmatic.

Ignoring the prayers and dances, the freighter's crew are busying themselves with preparations for the ship's imminent docking. It's a strange sight, these two worlds which for the six days of crossing have lived side by side without ever really meeting. One group believes history is moving in a single direction, speeding towards a prophesied destination; the other group has been tirelessly repeating the same gestures, round and round, for generations, according to the seasons and the tides that never stop.

'Thanks, Saku,' replies Harmony at last. 'I promise you I won't forget what you've said.'

'Better for you if you don't. I'll wait for you to come back to us. But tell me, do you at least have a clue for finding this aunt of yours? A phone number? Maybe an address?'

'No, I haven't got any of that,' admits Harmony, staring out at the cranes of the port standing on the horizon, like gigantic gallows. 'But I do have a name.'

'Just a name? That's not very much.'

'It's not a common name, though, not at all,' says Harmony, just a bit more quietly. 'If my mother was telling me the truth, there's only one person left in Scotland with that name today.'

'Don't say any more. We Cosmicists don't believe in surnames inherited from the past – they're just dead skin in the long process of reincarnation that led to our current encasings; they're just cinders on the noble path of Unification. To me, you'll always be Kuro-Jane, and every day I'll pray to the cosmos to watch over you.'

Harmony smiles sweetly at the girl who has taken her under her wing, then turns back towards the port.

It's thirty hours later.

With her forehead glued to the window of the coach,

Harmony watches the passing landscape, broken up by hedges with impossibly stretched-out shadows. She's been sitting in the same seat since leaving Inverness, the biggest city in the Highlands, where she arrived that afternoon after a long train journey – now it's evening, the kind of endless dusk you get during northern European summers. Over the hours, the coach has been gradually emptying of its passengers, especially after it passed the bridge connecting mainland Scotland to the Isle of Skye, in the Inner Hebrides. The towns were replaced by villages, then the villages by hamlets, and now there's nothing but heather. This whole time, Harmony hasn't taken her eyes off the landscape, lulled by the sound of the coach radio that's broadcasting the latest world news.

'. . . *one month since the breaking-off of diplomatic relations between the U.S. and Russia, the American government has decided not to backtrack on the independence of Mars, and the Russian government continues to deny any involvement with the attacks. Moscow is still refuting outright all Gordon Lock's claims, in which the Genesis programme's former number two confessed to being an agent in the Russians' pay charged with organising the former NASA heads' escape to Russia. The phrase that has become current in the press and on the streets to describe this cross-purposes conversation between the two superpowers is "the Frozen War".*

'*In the first weeks of the conflict, observers were predicting a return to the geopolitical configuration of the Cold War, when the U.S.A. and the U.S.S.R. forced every country in the world to choose allegiance to one of the two blocs. But this twentieth-century vision no longer seems suited to describe the current situation. Instead of setting off an extensive game of shifting alliances,*

President McBee's America has seemed instead to focus on itself –
to close in on itself, some say. A termination of international
trade deals, the closure of borders, the government omnipresent
on social media: for weeks now, the McBee administration has
maintained policies that are inward-looking. Matthew Conrad,
our programme's political editor, joins us down the line to talk
about it. Hello, Matthew.'

'Good evening, Edward.'

'This autarkic movement from the leading global superpower,
a traditional defender of free trade and political interventionism,
is surely very surprising?'

'There are precedents in American history, notably the famous
Monroe Doctrine that was in force right through the nineteenth
century.'

'But we're in the twenty-first century now, a time when the
planet is more connected than ever before! And the new president,
Serena McBee, played a not insignificant role in that globalisation
herself, when she was producing the Genesis programme!'

'And she still is, Edward, and that's the paradox – but that's
also why she's such a strong figure. It's hard to accuse President
McBee of being reactionary, when she's been elected on an
ultra-libertarian ticket, when she's contributed to implementing
one of the most innovative, progressive projects of all time – the
conquest of Mars via a global TV show. No one but her could
have persuaded the American people to accept the curtailing of
their beloved individual freedoms, which they agreed to in the
name of the nation's greater freedom.'

'It does seem like voices are beginning to be raised though, in
the United States itself, against the authoritarian turn the regime

is taking. Voices that are also condemning the accumulation of powers you're referring to: political power and media power being concentrated in the same hands . . .'

' . . . which is precisely the argument being used by the Russians – who know a thing or two about propaganda themselves – which is why it's so hard to make the American public listen in the current context. Those who use it risk being accused at best of being politically naive, at worst of being traitors to the nation. The McBee administration seems set to last.'

Each time one of the speakers says her mother's name, Harmony shudders. And she tightens her fists squeezed in the pockets of her sweatshirt – a hooded one like the kind Andrew often wore, bearing a tourist slogan: 'I Heart London'.

In her right hand, she's gripping a wad of banknotes – the fruits of her selling her locket, bought by the ounce and paid in cash by a goldsmith near King's Cross station in London.

In her left hand, she's holding the lock of hair Mozart gave her, which no longer has its own precious case, and the little gold nugget from Andrew, which nothing in the world would persuade her to sell.

'Last stop!' calls the driver, yanking his one remaining passenger out of her silent reverie.

'Thank you, sir,' she murmurs, hoarse and slurring, the first words she's spoken in hours.

She grabs the last bag from the luggage rack, a shoulder bag she bought at the station and filled with items of clothing at the first shop she found before leaving the capital.

Then she steps out of the coach, the door closing behind her with a mechanical hiss.

The vehicle pulls away, leaving Harmony alone in a tiny village square flanked by a little church, a grocer's with its shutters closed and half a dozen dark stone houses. In front of one of these, there hangs a rusty metal sign, its paintwork flaking off. It's still just possible to read it.

ANN AND ANGUS MURPHY

BED & BREAKFAST

BOAT TRIPS IN FAIR WEATHER

The sea breeze coming off the nearby coast gives the sign a persistent swaying movement, which makes it creak painfully.

From up above, on the moss-covered slate roof, a gull watches the intruder with a round yellow eye.

Harmony shivers in her tracksuit: it's after 9 p.m., and up here, in the east, night has finally decided to emerge from its den and swallow up the land.

The girl pulls the hood of her top over her jet-black hair – she topped up the dye job at a small hairdresser's in Inverness. Then she puts the strap of the bag over her shoulder and walks over to the Murphys' door, where she knocks lightly. A long minute later, the door opens on an old lady, face craggy from the elements, wrapped in a tweed shawl.

'Yes?' the woman asks, staring at the visitor from behind her glasses.

'I'd like a room, please.'

The owner of the house doesn't seem to understand her meaning right away.

'A room?' she asks.

The sign gives a louder creak, attracting her attention.

'Oh, a room! I'm sorry, dear, but I shut up shop such a long time ago!'

Harmony's face sets in an expression of distress.

She rummages in her bag and pulls out the second-hand guidebook she bought in London.

'But there's still that sign in front of your house. And they refer to your Bed & Breakfast in this guidebook . . .' She opens it at a dog-eared page, and reads out loud. *'We can't emphasise enough how worthwhile it is for the adventurous traveller to push up as far as the northernmost extremes of the Isle of Skye. Their perseverance will be rewarded with splendid, almost deserted landscapes, and the delicious haggis – the stuffed sheep's belly – made by Ann Murphy in one of the most isolated guesthouses in the area. When weather conditions allow, Ann's husband Angus offers trips out to sea, around neighbouring islets, between the Isle of Skye and the Outer Hebrides, deserted archipelagos which are the nesting places of countless species of seabirds: Garbh Eilean, Fladaigh Chùain, Gearran Island, Bee Island . . .'*

The owner shakes her head sadly.

'My husband died two years ago,' she says quietly. 'I stopped taking in tourists soon after that – they were coming less and less often anyway. Your guidebook doesn't make me feel any younger, my girl.'

She pulls the shawl tighter around her neck, shivering in the evening breeze – unless it's just her memories that are making her shiver.

'But don't just stand there, you'll catch your death,' she says finally. 'You'd best come in. I've still got clean sheets in the cupboard, and I haven't forgotten how to make my haggis – I'll do it for your breakfast!'

'Well?' asks Ann Murphy, looking at her guest with some concern.

After a good night's sleep, Harmony is sitting at the table in front of a plate steaming with the famous haggis praised by the guidebook, accompanied by some mashed potatoes and swede.

'Oh . . . it's delicious!'

Her hostess smiles.

She puts her hands on her hips proudly, either side of her red apron bearing the Genesis logo and a fake recruitment stamp: *Selected for Mars mission as Cooking Officer*.

'Good to know I haven't lost the knack, and I still deserve this apron!' she says. 'It was my granddaughter Fiona who gave it to me for my sixty-fifth birthday. Young people love this show – and I'm sure you do too, right?' Then she adds, 'Not just the young ones either, mind. I'll admit I'm just as crazy about it myself. My days have been so lonely since Angus left me. Fiona and her parents live in Glasgow, and only come to visit in the holidays. The rest of the time . . . well, it sort of feels like the Mars pioneers are a bit my family too.'

And indeed the framed portraits of several of the pioneers are arranged on a lace doily positioned on the TV set among those of the Murphys: we can recognise Liz, Tao, Léonor, Marcus, Kris . . . and Mozart.

'So tell me, which is your favourite Martian?' Harmony's hostess asks, pouring her another cup of tea.

'I don't know,' answers the girl, toying with her haggis with her fork, trying not to look at the photo of the Brazilian boy. 'I like all of them.'

'Did you know Serena McBee's ancestors came from around here?' Ann Murphy continues, pointing at the photo of the executive producer and president of the United States, who sits in pride of place among the others like a mother hen surrounded by her brood. 'Not many people know it, but it's true. There's even still a ruined castle, on Bee Island, the ancestral home of the clan her forebears come from. Quite a journey, from this lost little place to the American presidency!'

Harmony looks up quickly.

'Did you know her?' she asks, out of the blue. 'Serena McBee, I mean?'

'Know her? Oh no! She never set foot in this place, not even in this whole area as far as I know. I think she was born in America, wasn't she? I'm not sure. What I do know for sure is the last McBees left Scotland before she came along. Bee Island has been uninhabited for such a long time now. It belongs to some ornithological society down in Edinburgh, a very private society that sometimes arranges exclusive tours for its members – and it's true, the island is a sanctuary for arctic terns, puffins, and other seabirds that nest in its high cliffs and the ruins of the castle. Access is forbidden to the general public, though back in the day my Angus used to bring his little boat close enough for our guests to see all the birds.'

Ann Murphy falls silent, carried away by her memories once again.

But Harmony doesn't allow any time for melancholy to set in.

'That boat – have you still got it?'

'Oh yes, but –'

'Would you know how to sail it yourself?'

The old woman puts her gnarly hands down on the dining table, as if the ground were pitching and tossing under her feet.

'I'm the daughter and granddaughter of sailors, I've got the sea swell in my blood and I was always the one who went out on the water when Angus didn't feel up to it. But like I told you already, I've stopped doing tourist trips now.'

'You also told me you'd stopped offering food and board, but I've just slept like a baby and I'm eating the best haggis on Skye!' Harmony's eyes are sparkling. 'Please, Mrs Murphy – I so want to see Bee Island from close up. The truth is, that's why I've come.'

At that exact moment, something changes in the way Ann Murphy is looking at the girl. It's as though she's seeing her for the first time; she turns to look at the portrait of Serena on top of the television, then back to the girl.

'Your – your face . . .' she stammers. 'It's like . . . like you're . . .'

'The resemblance is striking, isn't it? A lot of people have said that. But it's not real. I'm not a McBee. And I'm not a member of any ornithological society or any private organisation, I'm just a simple backpacker who loves birds. And I'd so love to visit Bee Island. Will you help me?'

92. Shot

Month 16 / sol 430 / 09:43 Mars time
[549th sol since landing]

For the hundredth time, I hold my stylus over a new page on my sketching tablet.

For the hundredth time, I wait for inspiration to come to me for a design for the Martian flag.

This commission I've been given seems ridiculous to me, but I know it would make Kris so happy . . . and Alexei too. I need to rub him up the right way, flatter his pride as our little leader, if I want him to free Marcus when the Great Storm hits Ius Chasma, like he promised.

From our bedroom, I can hear Mozart in the kitchenette humming a samba while he makes breakfast. Finally able to benefit from Samson's advice, now they've been reconciled, he's perfected his recipe for *acarajés* – much better than a bowl of oats in soya milk to start the day! I can hear the music of the fritters browning gently, but I can't smell their aroma: like every morning, I'm staying in bed for a bit after waking up, my head buried under a sheet still warm from Mozart's

536

body. It's here, in this little enclosure lit up only by the screen of my tablet, that I try to draw. I prefer to be hidden from the view of the cameras, given the attempts I've come up with so far: every attempt to create a flag ends up with a caricature of Serena McBee. They're the only things that come to me: Serena as a vampire, Serena as an ogress, Serena as bogeyman. My tablet is full to bursting with these pictures, like so many silent screams. It's my only outlet, in this base where nobody wants to listen to me. Pathetic, right?

'Ready!' calls Mozart, before I've managed to produce a thing this morning; not a flag nor even a caricature.

I turn off my tablet, pull back the sheet and allow the delicious smell to lead me to the living room.

Mozart is standing there, smiling like a sun, a chef's apron over his bare chest: sexy as hell.

'Good morning, my goddess!' he says. 'Good night's sleep? I hope you're well this morning, as this is the morning we're doing your rover lesson. Come have some food, get your strength up, I don't want you to pass out with exhaustion at the wheel.'

'Are we allowed to take a bite out of the driving-school instructor himself?' I say, taking him in my arms, pretending I'm about to eat him up.

His laughter does me a world of good; it clears my head, driving away the quiet anxiety that's been bothering me for months.

He runs his hand through my thick red hair, and I put mine in his silky brown curls. I've learned to avoid touching the death's egg implanted in his neck by the Aranha, while his caresses usually skirt the edge of the Salamander on my

537

shoulder. In this way, over the past days, our imperfect bodies have been tamed, with gentleness and respect.

But right now, as if she can't stay out of my mind for a single moment, Serena McBee appears on the living-room screen.

'Attention, all pioneers,' she says. 'Gather in the Garden in half an hour. The programme has an important announcement to make: storm season has officially begun.'

Thirty minutes later.

All nine of us are gathered beneath the dome, in our undersuits, except Kris who prefers wearing her Martian silk tunic. The dogs and robots are there too. Only Kelly wasn't able to move, being too weak to leave her bed.

Opposite us on the giant screen, Serena McBee's face looks down lovingly at us with its vast water-green eyes.

'My dear pioneers, the perihelion is approaching,' she announces gravely. 'The moment when the planet Mars – your planet, remember, which now belongs to you – will be at its closest to the Sun. Martian temperatures are already starting to rise. Our satellite images are showing us huge dust devils forming on the great southern plains, stirred up by the heat that rises every sol.' Serena pauses briefly, staring into our eyes, and into the eyes of all the Genesis programme's viewers. 'The thing is, it seems this phenomenon is more advanced and intense this year than ever. Based on our preliminary observations, our meteorological experts have extrapolated a picture of what the Great Storm will look like, in two Martian months' time.'

Serena's face is replaced by a satellite view of the planet, with well-delineated reliefs and the long gash of the Valles Marineris right in the middle.

'Here on the screen you have the surface of Mars as it is today,' Serena continues in voiceover. 'As you can see, the atmosphere is still clear. But over the coming weeks, the temperature will climb so high and so much dust will rise that the entire Martian atmosphere will be saturated with particles. My friends: we can now see a planetary storm as modelled for you by our experts . . .'

With these words, a second view of the planet is superimposed on the first. Now it's just a smooth round sphere, with no relief or texture, totally covered in an opaque screed.

'This year, the Great Storm will last a whole month. For twenty-eight days, visual contact and maybe even radio contact will be lost with the surface. The New Eden base will be completely cut off from Earth.'

A murmur of distress runs through the Garden.

Mozart squeezes my hand in his, Kris shivers in her tunic and presses herself against Alexei's undersuit.

The modelling of Mars subjected to a planetary storm hangs over us like a mysterious crystal ball in which it's impossible to read the future.

Suddenly Serena is back on screen, a big smile on her face.

'I know – isn't it really something! Even though the New Eden base was developed to withstand the most extreme meteorological disturbances, I imagine some of you will be apprehensive at the thought of being cut off from the Earth for a month – especially with one of you being ill, as Kelly is, and having to monitor her condition every day. But don't worry:

METEOROLOGICAL REPORT /
Forecast for the next Great Storm

Today:
Month 16 / Sol 430

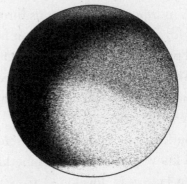

In two months:
Month 18 / Sol 486

we have a solution! The *Cupido* and its elevator will arrive in Martian orbit on the morning of sol 483 – that's August twentieth, by the Earth calendar. Once it's been deployed, the self-energised satellite will have to do four cycles around Mars's orbit, lasting seven hours each, in order to build up enough charge from solar energy. The transit capsule will then be sent down. It will land on Martian soil on sol 484, which is to say, four days before the storm has spread across the entire planet, according to our predictions: just in time for you to come safely up to the craft. You will then spend a month in orbit with your counterparts from Season Two – this time we've supplied enough provisions to withstand a siege, and we've increased the recycling capacity tenfold as well as the reserves of water and oxygen! When the storm calms, you'll be able to return to the surface, all of you, to take possession of New Eden once again. What do you say?'

Kris is first to respond, clapping her hands. 'Thank you, Serena!' she cries.

'The Martian nation is very grateful to you,' announces Alexei in that unbearable formal tone he's started using whenever he speaks to her.

As for the others . . .

Nobody says a word.

Nobody says that, no, once they're in orbit, they won't be coming back down.

Seriously? After we've left New Eden, where we're constantly under threat from brutal depressurisation, they'll be prepared to come straight back?

'And what if we don't want to come back down?' I say

541

suddenly, staring defiantly at the giant who's looking me up and down.

Mozart's powerful hand is crushing my fingers.

His terrified eyes bore into mine.

All around me, I can feel everybody ready to leap over and gag me.

But I've said all I have to say. I won't be making any shocking revelations about the Noah Report, nothing – my one question is already travelling across the void to Serena's ears.

'There's no reason not to come back down once the danger's past,' says Alexei, threateningly. 'Mars is our country now. Our world. Our home.'

'Alex is right,' says Kris. 'We've built something up here. Something that belongs only to us.'

'The Earth is at war, or nearly, while here we can try and build a civilisation of peace,' says Liz, with a friendly squeeze of my arm. 'Remember when I said I was going to be the first star dancer on Mars? Well, there are in fact going to be two of us. Me and Tao have been working for weeks on a piece of choreography to the "New World" symphony.' She places a hand tenderly on the shoulder of her new partner, who is an artist like she is. 'We'll be ready to perform it right after the Great Storm, when we come back to retake possession of the base.'

As a coup de grâce, Mozart murmurs a few gentle words. 'They're right, Léo – there's nothing waiting for us on Earth. Or rather, yes, the Aranha is waiting for me, waiting to take me out. But up here we're happy, aren't we?'

Suddenly I really want to cry – a feeling that catches me by surprise, and yet which I know is also feeding on all the tension that's been building up for weeks, for months.

(Serena's won!) hums the Salamander, putting this admission of failure into words. *(Whatever you do, whatever you say, she's won. Here on Mars, or there on Earth, she's no longer afraid of you. She's no longer afraid of the Noah Report. Wherever you go now, you'll always be her prisoner.)*

Serena speaks again – echoing my thoughts – with an answer to the question I asked fifteen minutes earlier.

'And if you don't want to go back down, Léonor?' she asks, revealing her perfectly straight white carnivorous teeth. 'Well, in that case there'll be nothing to stop you remaining on board the *Cupido* when it returns to Earth. And I'll be here to welcome you with open arms, my dear.'

93. Off-screen

Sea of the Hebrides, off the coast of the Isle of Skye
Wednesday 26 June, 1:32pm

You can hear Bee Island before you see it: the cries of the seabirds pierce the impenetrable fog, shriller than the purr of the motor.

Behind the helm of the little fishing boat, with an oilskin on her shoulders and a woollen hat pulled down to her eyes, Ann Murphy is holding their course. She still trusts her instincts more than the on-board equipment.

Harmony is sitting at the bow. Bundled up in her tracksuit, her hat pulled low on her head, she's looking out over a nothingness filled with echoes, cries, flapping.

And then, all of a sudden, without warning, the island's sharp silhouette bursts through the mist.

A rocky spur breaking out of the foamy sea, its shape is like a monstrous tooth – a fang torn from the jaw of a giant. Flocks of black-and-white wings swirl squawking around vertiginous cliffs, from the stormy tides all the way up to the tip of this gigantic canine: it's the shadow of the castle, all the way up there, and its dilapidated keep.

Ann Murphy slows the motor and turns the wheel; the boat changes tack, rounding the sheer cliff to a small inlet hidden behind an outcrop of rock. There's a very low sea wall in greenish stone, covered in algae, in bird droppings and shells. The hull of the boat moves closer, wedges in, comes to a complete stop. Here, protected within the inlet, all sounds seem muffled. When the motor cuts out, even the cries of the birds and the crash of the waves seem to disappear: total silence.

'Well, here we are,' says the boatwoman as she ties the painter around a rusty post attached to the tip of the sea wall.

A worm-eaten wooden sign is rotting here, on which it's still just possible to read:

BEE ISLAND
PROTECTED BIRD RESERVE
PRIVATE PROPERTY OF THE FRIENDS OF THE BIRDS
ORNITHOLOGICAL SOCIETY

'Private property? You're having a laugh! Those Edinburgh twits have got some nerve!' Ann Murphy gives a sniff that expresses her contempt for the city dwellers. 'Before it belonged to some obscure ornithological society, even before it belonged to the McBee clan, this bit of Earth was everybody's, like everything God's made hereabouts. Off you go, Jane. Just remember to be back by six o'clock: we need to be back on Skye before dusk, as the forecast's warning of serious weather for tonight. Anyway, it won't take you long to get around it. For a few hours, you'll be the sole mistress of Bee Island – as if you were a real McBee yourself!'

Is Harmony's hostess implying more than she's saying?

Does she suspect that the resemblance between this girl and the most famous woman on the planet is more than mere coincidence?

Has she sensed the secret relationship that unites them?

Harmony hasn't time to ask herself these kinds of questions: she's gone too far in her search for her origins to turn around now. There's only one possible direction, one possible choice: forward.

She steps over the edge of the boat.

She puts the soles of her old Rangers that she picked up in a New York second-hand clothes store down onto the wall. The stone surface drenched by the sea spray is slippery, but Harmony doesn't lose heart and runs straight down the few metres to the small grey sand beach, barely wider than the room she used to occupy in the Villa McBee. A badly maintained path, eaten away by wild grasses, climbs steeply up towards the heights.

Harmony turns around just once before reaching the end of the path; all the way down, the beach is no more than a comma, the boat a dot half erased by the mist, like a possibility that's already fading.

Harmony turns around sharply and hops nimbly over the last piles of scree to the summit.

The cries of the birds, previously muffled, now explode into her ears.

Then she sees the castle, still some distance away but much more imposing than she could have guessed from the bottom – and much better preserved, too. Approaching it from this angle, unseen from the sea, its façade isn't a crumbling wall exposed to the heather and the broods of birds. On the contrary, the stones are well sealed, there are no crenellations missing from the ramparts, and the various roofs still have all their slate tiles.

But the most unexpected, most fascinating thing about this concealed side: the valley that's nestled in front of the building, also invisible from the sea, protected from the wind by the crater that envelops it. There, at the heart of this dry, rocky, black island, are at least two hectares of *lawn*, covered in *flowers* of every colour!

'It looks like . . . like Mom's garden,' stammers Harmony.

The exact moment she says these words, a ray of sunlight pierces the clouds, illuminating the mysterious valley, awakening the yellow of the buttercups, the violet of the primroses, the red of the wild roses – because surely these flowers must all be wild, mustn't they? Because who could be growing them in a place like this?

That's when Harmony sees them.

The bees.

Their little downy bodies float in powdery blankets over the blossoming corollas, gathering pollen here and there, between the scents that rise up in the sudden gust of heat. Behind them at the end of the valley, gleam the roofs of several rows of hives.

Hives!

Here, on this uninhabited piece of land!

And next to them, that white shape flapping about in the wind, does it belong to a scarecrow?

No, there's no wind blowing in the valley.

It's impossible – a scarecrow couldn't pull itself up from

the ground where it was planted, to race away at full speed in the direction of the castle.

'Wait!' yells Harmony, as loud as she can manage to make herself heard at the end of the valley. 'I want to talk to you!'

Now it's her turn to throw herself among the bees, not worrying about getting stung, not thinking about the thorns on the roses that tear at her tracksuit trousers.

But when she finally reaches the castle, out of breath, she stops dead at a closed door: a thick oak panel, freshly waxed, the nails recently coated with anti-rust paint. It's clearly not the door of a ruin, but of an inhabited place. Harmony puts her hand on the heavy bronze knocker in the shape of a bee – the same image she knows from the gold signet ring on her mother's little finger.

She knocks once.

No answer.

Twice.

Still nothing.

She takes a step back, to get a better view of the whole building that crushes her with all the bulk of its black stone, all doubtless quarried from the belly of this same island by generations of builders. The dark windows, narrow as arrow-slits, all have glass panes, preventing the birds from getting inside.

'Open up!' yells Harmony.

The valley echoes back:

'*Open up!*'

'*Open up!*'

'*Open up!*'

'I saw you going in!' yells the girl. 'Are you Gladys McBee? Or are you a ghost, just another of the ghosts my life is filled with? Open up! Open up!'

Harmony lifts the knocker again and again, but soon that isn't enough, and she starts bashing the wood with her bare fists and all her desperation – with the rage she's contained until now, the rage of a whole life spent keeping quiet.

'I have the right to come in!' she calls, breathless. 'I have the right to come into this castle! I'm also a McBee . . . ! I'm Harmony McBee . . . !'

She's just about to say her name again, when the window positioned immediately above the door opens. Harmony falls silent at once, as a quavering, ageless voice comes out of the dark gap.

'Harmony McBee? You're lying. It's impossible. The girl you're claiming to be is in America.'

'Well, I'm not there any more, not now,' replies Harmony, coming back to her senses.

'The girl you're talking about never could have made the journey on her own . . . She's too weak, too dependent.'

'When I was little, my mother used to threaten to send me far away to my aunt in her mysterious castle, if I didn't behave. I had nightmares about it. But I grew up, and today I've made my own way here. To see you. You: Gladys McBee.' Harmony's voice sags slightly. 'It was Mother who exiled you here, wasn't it? It was her who put you in this prison, wasn't it? Since when? Why? Is she also hiding my father somewhere in this castle? My whole life I've been surrounded with questions. But today I've come to find some answers.'

549

Harmony's request is followed by a few seconds of silence. Then she hears the mysterious voice again, and a clap.

'Let her in.'

The girl holds her breath and steps away from the door, behind which she hears muffled footsteps.

There's the sound of a heavy bolt, then the wood moves on its hinges with a slight creak.

'Aunt Gladys, I'm so pleased to . . .' Harmony's words lodge in her throat.

Her hands grab hold of the wall to stop herself falling, and her face freezes in an expression of horrified surprise.

'Mom . . . !' she manages to say.

And Serena McBee really is standing there, just inside the door, wearing the long white blouse she was wearing when Harmony surprised her collecting the honey from the bees.

'How in God's name . . . ?' stammers the girl, staring at those water-green eyes, the bob of silvery hair, the perfect oval of the chin.

Perfect?

In fact, the skin on her neck is a bit wrinkled, not as tight as that of the woman who appears daily on the world's TV screens. The hair is duller, the eyebrows less well shaped, and there are crows' feet at the corners of her eyes. As for that look . . . it's the same colour as Serena McBee's, but not the same sharpness. It's lost, vulnerable: the look of prey, not of a predator.

'You're not Mom,' says Harmony.

The woman doesn't answer.

It's as if the question just slid right off her, like a wave on the shingle.

'Aunt Gladys?'

In response to that name, a faint light comes on in the woman's dull eyes.

'Gla-dys?' says Harmony again, louder now, articulating each syllable – maybe the woman is hard of hearing. 'Are you Gla-dys?'

Seeming to understand now that Harmony is talking about her, the strange apparition shakes her head.

Then she puts her hand on her own chest, and with a voice that's more like the cry of one of the island's birds than a human voice, she wails: 'Ah-Mo-Ni-Wun.'

'What?' asks the girl, paralysed.

The woman in the doorway moves back humbly, like a servant or a dog, to let the visitor inside. Half a dozen quivering shadows are waiting obediently behind her, in a dark corridor with tall panelled walls. They're all wearing the same white blouse, which on closer inspection looks more like a hospital smock than a bee-keeping outfit. Their features are startlingly similar, though with some subtle differences: the second woman in the row looks slightly younger; the third ten years younger than the first, and so on down, like the kaleidoscopic projection of a single person across the phases of her life, all the way along to the last who looks barely older than Harmony herself.

They all have the same empty look in their eyes, strangers to themselves.

'Who are you?' screams the visitor, somewhere between anger and horror.

551

Faced with the silence of these creatures in front of her, Harmony is overcome by a panic that makes her legs turn to jelly and her knees tremble. She's about to turn on her heel to run as far away as possible from this nightmare, while she still has her strength, while she still has her sanity.

But at that moment there's a voice from the shadows of the corridor – the same quavering intonation that addressed her from the castle window.

'They're your sisters.' Harmony freezes. 'The ones who were born before you, between these same walls where you yourself began nineteen years ago.'

A silhouette emerges slowly from the shadows, a body shrivelled under the weight of age, bending over its walking stick. The severe black dress holding in the thin chest seems to come from another age, the time of those old novels in which Harmony used to try to lose herself. The nodding head atop the thin lace collar is so wrinkled that the eyes are barely visible. The hair might once have been silvery in colour, but now it's so sparse that the scalp shows through in a number of places. The only jewel worn by this strange apparition is a key around her neck, over her hollow chest.

'*Gladys?*' asks Harmony reluctantly, this human fossil who looks old enough to be her great-great-aunt.

'I am. Your aunt. And also your midwife. Come in then: this is your home.'

The next part unfolds like a dream. Barely conscious of what's happening to her, Harmony allows herself to be escorted to a hall deep in the bowels of the castle, to an armchair positioned in front of a vast stone fireplace engraved with bees. Her 'sisters' get her to sit down, while Gladys takes a second armchair. Then, fluttering around like hurried, mute servants, the women perk up the fire and bring her some hot tea in a porcelain cup.

Reaching out towards the low table to put down a pot of honey, the youngest inadvertently lets the sleeve of her blouse ride up a little, revealing the milky skin up to her elbow – the crook of her arm is marked with bluish puncture wounds, like bruises left by the repeated use of a syringe in the flesh of a junkie.

'You may withdraw now,' says the old woman.

The shadows disappear through the doorway of the hall and the door closes quietly.

Only now, wedged in the thick velvet-padded armchair, feet firmly on the paving stones, does Harmony find the strength to speak again.

'Those women you called my *sisters* . . . Who . . . who are they? One of them claimed to be called Harmony, but I'm not sure, she seemed to have trouble saying her name. I thought she'd said a number at the end – number one.'

Gladys nods slightly.

'They are indeed called Harmony, all of them, with only the number to differentiate between them. Your number is ten. Your genes are identical to theirs.'

'So . . . twins?'

'Clones. Produced at regular intervals over forty-five years, from my laboratory in the keep.' With her trembling index finger, she points at a reinforced door beside the fireplace. 'Here in this place, far away from men and their morals and their laws, I've been developing the Harmony Project for the past half-century.'

Gladys McBee's eyes, reflecting the hearth, are glowing between the folds of flesh formed by her eyelids.

'You have no father. No more than any of the others do. You only have a mother, just like the way the bumblebees in a hive are the product of the unfertilised ova of the queen.'

Harmony is gripping the arms of her chair with both hands.

All the scenarios she's constructed in her mind over the years, all the reflections of that unknown father she went looking for in the pages she read, they've all been shattered in an instant.

'Wh-why?' she stammers.

'To keep my word.' Gladys's face is too deeply marked, her skin too wrinkled for her expression to be read easily; but her voice, though damaged, betrays an intense emotion. 'Because I swore it. Because a long time ago, I promised Serena I would give her eternal life.'

As these memories come back to her, the lady of the house shudders like an old mare that's too weakened to brush away the flies that are pestering it except by shivering.

'I have no father,' Harmony repeats the words, as if to convince herself, to digest the terrible truth. 'I've never had one. I never will. I'm just a genetic photocopy: an attempt at survival by a woman who thinks she can live for ever through me.'

But Gladys shakes her head.

'Not through you, not through any of your sisters. Serena doesn't simply want to perpetuate herself through her descendants, the way other humans have done since the world was new. She doesn't consider the clones her children. She considers them . . .'

The old woman swallows, unable to complete her sentence.

It's as though the vice-like grip of a guilt nourished in reclusiveness and silence over dozens of years were stopping her throat.

'She doesn't consider us her children?' Harmony presses her. 'What, then . . . ?'

But Gladys doesn't have the strength to answer that question, not right away.

'In my heart of hearts, I've always known that one day my conscience would come and confront me,' she murmurs. 'But of all the faces it might take, I never imagined it would be yours! The other clones are completely unable to hold me to account; they've never known anything but Bee Island, they know nothing of the outside world, and nobody's ever bothered to teach them human language.'

With these words, she drags her exhausted body out of the armchair without having touched her tea, making all her bones crack.

'Follow me,' she says hoarsely, heading for the laboratory door, leaning on her walking stick.

With the help of the key hanging on the little chain around her neck, she unlocks the door, which opens soundlessly onto the narrow lift shaft up to the keep.

Harmony hesitates a moment, turning towards the narrow vaulted windows; but the need to learn the truth is stronger than anything else, and she follows her hostess in.

* * *

There is an elevator platform attached to the wall, lit up by LEDs whose modernity contrasts with the ancient candelabra of the hall. The lady of the house and her guest take their places on the platform's seat. Like a flying carpet controlled by a djinn, the platform moves up the wall as far as a steel trapdoor that lifts automatically for them to pass through and closes straight behind them.

There, on the first landing, the age-old stone of the walls is replaced by a surface that is metallic, surgical: that of a biological lab furnished with microscopes and all kinds of sophisticated equipment. There are also large screens linked up to central processing units, whose internal fans are giving off a gentle hum.

'The only thing we produce on this island is honey,' says Gladys, as the seat continues to rise. 'Serena wanted to keep up the clan's ancestral tradition, and the clones have learned to take care of the bees – that and a bit of gardening and housework are the only things they know how to do. Anything else we need here – provisions or medical equipment – is brought by aerial drone from Scotland. "Friends of the Birds" is a smokescreen organisation that allows me to receive these deliveries quite discreetly, on the pretext of supplying ornithological materials.'

'A nice way to cover up the delivery of illegal goods!' says Harmony, trying hard to sound confident. 'I saw the arms of one of your poor captives just now, and I'm guessing they're all the same. That's how you force them to stay here. I know better than anyone how drugs can transform people into zombies!'

'You're wrong. They stay on Bee Island of their own volition.

How could they have a desire to leave, if they've never known anything else?' The elevator passes through a second steel trapdoor, which opens and closes again as silently as the first.

An operating table stands in pride of place at the centre of the second landing, lit by powerful spotlights. Mechanical arms ending in pincers are suspended all around it, frozen in the air like the legs of a dead insect.

'Long ago, I was a very brilliant surgeon,' Gladys continues. 'I was as skilled in reconstructive medicine as my sister Serena is today in psychiatry. But that was a distant time, and the world has long forgotten me. I could never operate again on my own, at my age, with my Parkinson's. These arms are good stand-ins for me – they never tremble.'

The elevator passes through a new trapdoor and stops at the third landing.

Here there's no technical equipment, no medical gear: the room is just surrounded by tall chrome-plated cabinets, on the sides of which are small digital screens indicating refrigerated temperatures and a humidity level close to zero. You would think it was a high-tech frozen-food store . . . or a morgue.

This time Gladys says nothing.

And Harmony doesn't ask any questions.

She just gets up off the seat and moves slowly towards the first cabinet . . . until its contents become visible through the thick glass doors.

Pouches of blood.

Harmony takes a step back, her eyes wide with horror.

'The marks I saw on that girl's arm,' she says. 'The syringes aren't to inject them with anything, but to draw their blood!'

557

Gladys does not move or speak, leaning her full weight on her cane, while Harmony is already running over to the second cabinet.

Dozens of opaque medical containers are lined up on shelves, with handwritten labels: PLASMA, STEM CELLS, GROWTH FACTOR.

'It's like . . . a bank . . .' stammers Harmony. 'A bank of biological material.' She turns sharply towards Gladys. 'What exactly are they to my mother, those clones? Why am I Harmony 10, when I only saw six other clones in the hall? Where are the three missing ones? Answer me, right now!'

She grabs the old woman's frail shoulders and shakes them, repeating again and again: 'Answer me! Answer me! Answer me!'

Gladys allows herself to be manhandled without reacting. Her cane falls to the metal floor with a clunk.

Her tiny eyes are shining even more brightly in the depths of their sockets, and this time it's not fire that gives them their intensity, it's tears.

'My heart is going to break,' she sobs in her tremulous voice, which suddenly sounds much more like a young child's than an old woman's. 'Oh, if only it could just stop beating now, after all these years! You've come to free me from my cursed promise, from my hellish oath, at long last!'

'No, I haven't come to free you at all! I'm the one I've come to free! And the clones! And Andrew Fisher and his family! And Mozart and the pioneers! And all my mom's victims! If you claim that I'm your conscience, then you should at least have the guts to tell me what's going on here!'

Harmony lets go of her aunt roughly, and without the support

558

of her walking stick the old woman is forced to grab hold of the girl's shoulder so as not to fall.

Their faces are only a few centimetres apart; and Gladys only needs to whisper, to make the confession she's been keeping in for so long.

'The clones are like cattle for my sister. A herd of livestock! There's no need to furnish them with even the basics of human culture, since their only function is to produce flesh and vital fluids. For decades I've been taking fresh blood from your sisters, and extracting the plasma and other essential elements to send to your mother. Her staff at the Villa McBee inject her with this rejuvenation treatment, knowing nothing about its origins – and it's totally biocompatible because it comes from her own DNA.' A painful grimace twists her thin lips. 'Sometimes Serena needs major operations to keep her body functioning perfectly . . . to keep it all in perfect *harmony*, to use the name of the project that gave you life. That's when she comes here in secret and I transplant an organ taken from one of her certified true likenesses. In some cases, the donor survives, like Harmony 3, who gave her a kidney. In other cases, it's impossible, like poor Harmony 7, who gave her lungs for Serena to be able to breathe again properly after the attack.'

Harmony's face freezes in an expression of horror.

'That means three clones are dead, if there are seven of us and I'm number ten!'

Gladys's mouth twists a little more.

'The project has involved fourteen numbers to date,' she admits. 'The four Harmony numbers who came after you had to be . . . sacrificed . . . As time goes by, my sister's youth gets harder to maintain.' The old woman shrivels up a bit more, crushed by the guilt for a never-ending crime, by the weariness of a task that was never completed. 'You're the only one from whom I haven't taken anything, because the moment you were born Serena got it into her head to bring you up in America, not as an animal but a real child. But she loses interest quickly – and she lost interest in playing mother, like she does in everything that distracts her from her boundless ambition. To tell the truth, I'm amazed you survived to the age of nineteen. I wouldn't have given you that long, when I saw her carrying you off with her like a doll. Isn't that what we all are now, in her hands, you and me, and those poor devils she sent off to Mars, and all the millions of people who depend on her now that she's president? We're all nothing but dolls, marionettes . . .'

The more Gladys sags, becoming like a disarticulated marionette, the taller Harmony seems to stand.

Her eyes narrow.

Even her features seem to harden with a new determination.

'You asked me to free you from your oath,' she says. 'Fine, I free you. The time has come for the marionettes to cut their strings.'

'But I can't do it,' begs Gladys. 'I swore to Serena I'd do what she asked . . . The oath I took – I can't cut loose.'

'Well, I can!'

Harmony snatches the chain holding the key around Gladys's neck, and snaps it.

'I don't know what kind of satanic pact binds you to your sister,' she says, breathless. 'I don't know what kind of devil is making you stick to a promise that's tormenting you. But I do know that while you're locked in this tower, you can't obey anybody's orders.'

Harmony pushes her aunt against the wall, and rushes over to the elevator, activating the controls the way she saw Gladys do a few minutes earlier.

The seat begins its descent, carrying the girl down; the steel trapdoor closes behind her without a sound.

94. Reverse Shot

The National Mall, Washington DC
Thursday 4 July, 11:00pm

'A lost bee returning to her hive. That's what I feel like as I speak to you today, my dear citizens, from the stage where a year and a half ago my enemies tried to silence me for ever.'

Serena McBee is seated beneath the giant obelisk on the National Mall, wearing a dress in the colours of the American flag, not unlike the one worn by Stella Magnifica during the 'Star Dreamers' video but even more sumptuous: a red damask velvet corset, pinned with the black remembrance ribbon; a belt encrusted with rubies and sapphires; a blue train speckled with stars, arranged around her artistically like the robes of a monarch in a historical portrait.

Behind the president, all the members of the McBee administration are sitting in rows. Secretaries and advisers in concentric lines, their suits and outfits in neutral colours so as not to steal the limelight from the president, while she is addressing an audience of hundreds of thousands of Americans on this national holiday, the fourth of July.

A bank of cameras as extensive as those that assembled for the *Cupido* launch is arranged all around the stage. They run back and forth on rails to capture every aspect of the spectacle, which is also being streamed onto enormous screens erected on both sides of the obelisk.

'It is your fervour as a people that has guided me back,' Serena says. 'It's your commitment that will allow this country to become great again! On this sacred day, I would like to thank *all* Americans, with a special mention for the millions of Guardians who have already signed up to the Citizens Swarm, devoted to the defence of our great nation. Let's have a big cheer for them!'

At these words, there is thunderous applause from the first rows of the audience, where the new president's most ardent supporters are gathered. The young people from the Junior Citizens Swarm, who are supposed to represent the nation's life-blood, have been put in prominent positions by the ceremony's organisers. The cameras pan across the ecstatic faces of these people who, only months ago, were among the Genesis channel's most loyal fans – the generation who grew up by the light of their screens, who were suckled on a desire for glory, who are themselves the peers of the pioneers sent to Mars. But now their fervour goes far beyond what you would expect from the viewers of a reality TV show. Now they are actors eager to perform in a new world that's just coming into being. And like all actors, they're performing a script written for them in advance by someone else – most of them are wearing an earpiece attached to their temple, the latest addition to the Citizens Swarm outfit.

'*One for all* . . .' begins Serena from the stage.

'*All for one!*' answer the thousands of boys and girls dressed in the Swarms' regulation uniform, demonstrating their total devotion to the woman who, if she is not yet queen by title, does already have most of the attire for that role.

At first glance, one might mistake the large banners they're waving for the famous American Stars and Stripes; but here the fifty stars representing the fifty states have in fact been replaced by fifty bees. The same motif appears on the scarves they've got knotted around their necks, with the ring-cameras that surveil their territory day and night, in the name of national security.

With a graceful gesture, Serena calls for silence.

As disciplined as an army, her troops immediately go quiet to drink in her next words.

'For nearly three centuries, the fourth of July has been the day we Americans celebrate our independence from Great Britain, just as the Martians have recently gained their independence from Earth.' Serena emphasises her words with a look deep into the camera, as if in challenge to all those who would contest this established fact. 'Today, it's time for us to make a new declaration of independence. *A triple declaration.*'

She raises her thumb.

'First, I declare our geopolitical independence. Since my mandate began, as you know, I have been working to liberate America from the network of alliances, of agreements, of concessions that are stifling it. Just as a hive needs nothing but itself to function harmoniously, a state should likewise be self-sufficient. I've started eliminating one by one all those commitments that were restricting our national sovereignty and opening our borders to those who wanted to harm us. Abroad, the lines of defence put in place by our army are stronger than ever, to protect us from any foreign attack. At home, thanks to the vigilance of the Citizens Swarm and of all the little guard bees that are part of it, civil society is capable of tracking down anti-American speech whether on the streets or on the internet. The attacks that were possible in President Green's America will not be possible in President McBee's!'

Another ovation, while a squadron of fighter planes fly gigantic red, white and blue furrows above the obelisk.

Serena uncurls her index finger.

'Second, I declare our economic independence. It's time to turn the page on the Ultra-libertarian party, who have failed to restart our economy and who, instead of strengthening the nation's prestige, have merely increased the power of anonymous money. Liquidating public institutions, offering America's most valuable jewels for sale to the highest bidder, was more than a mistake; it was a failing and even, I dare say, a crime. Well, nobody is compelled to take on the responsibilities for a crime they have not committed; as your new president, I declare the renationalisation of all the institutions wrongfully given up by the Green administration, starting with NASA!'

A veritable flood of cheering overwhelms the National Mall.

But the greatest enthusiasm comes from those on the stage – the ministers who have survived from the previous ultra-libertarian government, ready to renounce their former political convictions if that will allow them to keep their place in the sun.

Once again, Serena re-imposes silence with a simple wave of her hand.

'Even so, there's no question of slipping into bolshevism or of injuring anybody. Atlas Capital will be repaid in Treasury bonds – and I'd like to thank the company's board via their representative, the android Oraculon, for having agreed to grant us all the aerospace facilities at a tenth of the price for which Atlas bought them a few years ago.'

Serena bows slightly towards the robot that is standing to her right, rigid in its dark suit, beside Orion Seamus. The translucent globe that serves as its head is slightly chipped since the Taser shot that sent it crashing to the ground at the Villa McBee – but the wildly applauding audience knows nothing of this episode, of course, nor do any of the viewers watching the ceremony being broadcast. Nobody suspects that Atlas Capital's 'generosity' was extracted via blackmail, by threatening to freeze all the group's assets in the event they did not comply. Inside that glass helmet, the synthetic face is somewhere between a fixed smile and a bitter grimace.

'The advertisers who have invested in the programme will also continue to get plenty of bang for their buck,' the president goes on. 'We will continue to show their commercials on the Genesis channel, as long as the cameras keep rolling, in partnership with our generous sponsors . . .'

She gestures to the side tiers, whose seats hold the representatives of all the programme's platinum sponsors, from the two seasons combined, dispatched by their respective companies. Most are battle-hardened senior executives, communications directors or CEOs, but the central spot is taken by a girl who looks young enough to be an intern: Phoebe Delville, now freed from her pregnancy, is sitting there in an exquisite black silk dress that matches her raven-black bob. On this patriotic day, she is doubly deserving of this honour. Firstly, because she is an American; secondly, because she represents Eden Food International, the only company to have sponsored two consecutive pioneers: Marcus in Season One and Logan in Season Two.

At last the president raises a third finger.

'Finally, I declare our *moral independence*. After having spent a good part of the twentieth century fighting against the ideology of communism, in the twenty-first we are about to free ourselves from the ideology of ultra-libertarianism. Each is as bad as the other. It falls to our great country to invent a new model for enlightening the world. It falls to the American people to work for a fairer society, a higher-performing society, where every person will be able to find his place and express his full potential. A society united not by the yoke of Marxism or an enslavement to capital, but by the power of images, by the emotions that we all share and which connect us to one another. A society in which we will no longer lose ourselves in lies or omission. Every desire, every fear will be shared with one another, so we might live a life together that is more intense and more true.' The president's water-green eyes open wide, like two frozen mirrors reflecting the young faces trembling with hope, the raised flags, and circling cameras. 'Total transparency!' she shouts. 'That is the magic key! The constant gaze of other people upon us will ward off any temptation towards selfishness or hypocrisy, committing us to be always virtuous and exemplary. Since the beginning of the century, the extraordinary development of social networks has opened up the way – the Citizens Swarm and their on-board cameras are just the most accomplished manifestation of this today. But we will go further still. Because the Genesis programme has allowed us to see the tremendous potential of a humanity connected to itself twenty-four / seven, like a hive where full employment and social harmony reign, where information is constantly circulating via pheromones, where nobody has any secrets from each other and everyone is working for the common good!'

The giant screens around the obelisk show the faces of the twenty-five Mars pioneers, from Seasons One and Two combined. They are Serena's moral backing, their twenty-five silent smiles seeming to validate her speech and tell the world: *'You can trust this woman who's given everything to us, to people like us who had nothing at all: glory, love, independence!'*

With a triumphant gesture, Serena raises her arms to her audience.

'Together we can achieve anything. Together we can touch the stars!'

This time it really is the climax: from the base of the obelisk to the end of the National Mall, the crowd seems bewitched into a patriotic trance. Everybody is shouting Serena's name at the top of their lungs.

Everybody?

No: down there on the white steps of the Lincoln Memorial, a small group is not waving flags or streamers. These men, women and teenagers are wearing expressions that are serious, determined.

One of them starts to speak through a microphone connected to a powerful speaker, making himself heard over the cheers.

'Lincoln, awake!' he shouts, gesturing towards the giant statue of Abraham Lincoln, sitting behind him in his monumental marble chair. 'Serena McBee is betraying your inheritance and plunging the democracy you saved into dictatorship!'

A deathly silence falls over the mall, while hundreds of thousands of faces turn towards the effigy of the sixteenth president of the United States, the winner of the American Civil War.

'Americans, awake!' continues the speaker. 'Open your eyes! This woman you're cheering for is taking away the thing you hold most dear: your freedom!'

The crowd gathered on the enormous lawn shifts around, growling like an animal disturbed in its sleep: whistles, insults, projectiles begin to be hurled in the direction of the protesters.

On the stage at the foot of the obelisk, the ministers exchange dumbfounded expressions, unsure how to react. The soldiers on duty cluster around the president to protect her with their bodies encased in bulletproof vests.

'What on Earth . . .' hisses Serena McBee, her eyes electric with fury.

Clouds of police drones are already flying towards the Lincoln Memorial, tearing the air with their shrill sirens and their metallic voices.

'*Public order disturbance – you are under arrest! Put your hands above your heads! I repeat: put your hands above your heads!*'

But the man at the microphone keeps bellowing himself hoarse.

'Even if you manage to silence us today, others will rise up to speak tomorrow, right across the territory that Serena thinks she can keep under lock and key, on the internet she thinks she can control! Fellow citizens, you should know that not all bees are fated to remain trapped inside hives, serving under the yoke of a queen! There are species in nature that live alone or in freely consenting communities. We call them *wild bees*, and they – like us – will never submit to tyranny!'

The drones descend onto the steps, their insect-like trunks

spraying out powerful smoke bombs, which soon flood the whole memorial with a thick white fog.

One last cry sounds from the hidden amplifier – 'Long live the Wild Bees! Long live America! Long live freedom!' – then nothing more is heard but the muffled echoes of an invisible struggle, as riot squads in gas masks plunge into the mists.

After a few minutes, the fog dissipates, revealing the steps now deserted: the demonstrators have all been removed from the sight of the public and the cameras.

Bounding up to the front of the stage, at the foot of the obelisk, Orion Seamus takes the microphone.

'Ladies and gentlemen, there's no cause for alarm! The situation is under control. These agitators, clearly in the pay of foreign powers, have been neutralised. They will receive the justice they deserve.'

He doesn't get a chance to say any more: the murmurings of the troubled crowd cover the rest of his words.

'Where's Serena? Where's Serena?' cry the members of the Citizens Swarm, looking everywhere for her, petrified with worry at the thought of losing her a second time.

The front rows are already storming the stage, a human tide ready to submerge the alarmed ministers.

But just at this moment, the president emerges from the wings where her security service had whisked her off, raising her hand in a V for Victory.

There is a great sigh of relief across the National Mall, which seems to sweep away the last wisps of smoke and, it would appear, every last memory of the rebels' desperate appeal.

95. Shot

Month 17 / sol 473 / 19:00 Mars time
[592nd sol since landing]

'I declare the work on extending the base officially complete!'

Alexei raises his glass towards the top of the dome, towards space, towards the Earth that is somewhere out in the depths of the night sky.

This evening we made do with apple juice for a toast, since the stocks of Martian champagne have run out, and it's been a long time since Kelly has been up to the task of working her home-made distillery.

Behind the honeycomb panes of the Garden, in the light of the projectors, it's possible to make out six new grey Love Nests alongside the seven original habitats: the fruit of twenty months of labour. The last few weeks we did get slowed down a bit by the disturbances that marked the beginning of storm season, but they were only passing dust devils, and it was possible to get the building site finished in time.

'New Eden is ready to receive its new citizens!' announces Alexei.

To him, there's no doubt that the thirteen Season Two

pioneers are going to be joining the base after the Great Storm, which will arrive in fifteen sols now; he has no doubt that most of the Season One pioneers will come back down too.

The truth is, I'm the only person who's said they want to turn around (Samson and Safia have just made vague reference to the possibility). But now that Serena has said she'll welcome with open arms anyone who wants to do it . . . I'm not sure of anything any more.

And so I raise my glass with the others, mechanically holding up my arm with its armband on, not knowing what tomorrow will bring, just because it's easier to follow a leader when you can't make a decision for yourself. And imagine, it was only weeks ago I was criticising the others for following Alexei's guidance too thoughtlessly!

'We meet in the Garden in one hour to commemorate the end of the job and have dinner together,' proclaims the lord of New Eden, turning on his heel.

The various couples head back towards their respective habitats.

But just as I'm about to follow Mozart, I feel a hand on my arm.

I turn, and it's Kris, in her silk tunic.

'Léo, could you . . . could you please come and help me collect some extra apples? I don't have enough to finish my tart.'

I can tell at once she's speaking in code. Going up to the orchard means going out of sight of the cameras, a strategy Kris and I have used many times before. She needs to talk to me in private.

'Of course,' I say, gesturing to Mozart that I'll join him later.

573

Within a few moments, I'm at the top of the plantations, among the narrow boughs covered in thick leaves.

'We haven't been talking much lately,' says Kris, half-buried among the branches. 'It's a shame. And there's something you don't know. Something I haven't told you.'

I feel a chill that makes me shiver.

Something she hasn't told me – those are the words Marcus used, the day he told me he was a carrier of the D66 mutation.

'What's going on, Kris?' I ask. 'Are you ill? Do you . . . you have the same thing Kelly has?'

I lean forward, suddenly noticing the slight marks darkening her face – that's how the Canadian girl's polycythaemia started up, with what looked like sunburn before it spread over her whole body. Besides, Kris's cheeks do look slightly puffy, as if they're inflamed – could it be some kind of auto-immune reaction?

'Ill?' she says. 'No, though I've been having acid reflux and nausea, but you wouldn't call it an illness.'

But I don't give up.

'Is Alexei looking after you properly? Has he given you a blood test to check your red blood count? Has he . . . ?'

Cutting my questions off mid-flow, Kris takes my hand and places it on her belly.

I'm surprised at the roundness of the flesh under the loose silk fabric that hides it from our sight – I'd noticed Kris had filled out lately, but I hadn't expected this.

'Can you feel it?' my friend asks, her big eyes still visible between the leaves.

Can I feel it?

I can!

A quivering – very faint, shy, but definitely there, beneath my fingers.

'You're . . .'

'Yes – I'm pregnant.'

I pull back my hand as if I'd been singed.

Kris's 'sunburn' is nothing of the sort: it's a pregnancy mask, a hormonal discolouration of the skin I learned about in my medical training.

And those tunics she's always wearing, they're to hide the changing shape of her body!

I feel dizzy, and the leaves and apples seem to dance around me – those enormous Martian apples, deformed by the weak gravity, the very ones that made me worry about the development of any future babies in these unknown conditions.

'Here, in this orchard, one Martian year ago,' I babble. 'Me and Alexei, we swore to do anything to prevent a pregnancy on Martian soil.'

'Because at the time, you didn't yet know whether this planet was right for us,' replies Kris, with a gentle smile. 'But we know it now.'

'Right for us? Are you kidding?' I say. 'With Kelly who hasn't been able to leave her bed in months, and Kenji who's gone off to die in the desert? With a storm about to overwhelm the planet in a flood of toxic dust? *With that thing that bumped off all the animals in the seventh habitat?*'

But Kris never loses her smile.

It's as if her pregnancy has plunged her into a state of serenity that trumps everything else.

'You worry too much, darling Léo,' she says, with a calm that staggers me. 'Mars isn't as inhospitable as you make out. This is our world now. And this is the world where I'm going to give birth to . . . my daughter! Because it's a daughter, Léo – Alex has done an ultrasound, and everything's going beautifully!'

She takes my hand again and holds it in hers.

'He wants to be the father of the first child of Mars. It's understandable – it's normal for a leader to want to guarantee his legacy. You know, he's never really considered Günter his child.'

I have no idea whether this reference to the robot butler is a joke or something serious.

I don't know if I should laugh or cry.

I feel as though I've lost Kris, lost her for ever.

'Alex and I will be announcing this happy news at dinner. But I wanted you to know before the others. And also to ask you to stay with us on Mars, to not go back to Earth on the *Cupido*. You're my best friend – my darling leopard – and I want you to be godmother to my daughter.'

96. Off-screen

Bee Island, the Sea of the Hebrides
Tuesday 13 August, 8:07pm

'My-Nem-Is-Ah-Mo-Ni-Nine.'

The creature's mouth trembles as it moves, with muscular spasms.

Each syllable is a terrible effort, both for the tongue that has never been used to articulate whole sentences, and for the brain behind those helpless eyes which has never before learned language.

'I-Yam-A-Klo-Nuh.'

These words are no more than sounds, a phonetic sequence followed mechanically in front of the lens of the cellphone that is filming it.

Harmony McBee is holding the phone out and miming the words silently, like a speech therapist – while opposite her, the clone who shares her genetic code but not her upbringing, repeats the words docilely without understanding what they mean.

'De-Klo-Nuh-Ov-Suh-Ree-Nuh-Muhk-Bii.'

Harmony turns the phone off with a sigh.

'Very good, my dear sister,' she says to the creature.

For the six weeks since she arrived here on Bee Island, she's persisted in addressing the clones like this, as *her sisters*. None of them, of course, understands the meaning of that word – or of any other.

Clone number nine looks at her, with the troubled expression of a pet that doesn't know if it's done its trick correctly. Harmony puts her hand tenderly on her shoulder – a universal sign of kindness.

A happy smile lights up clone number nine's face.

'My sister . . .' Harmony says again, her voice choking.

She places a kiss on the forehead of this creature who looks like her twin, then gestures for her to join the other older clones waiting obediently beside the fireplace.

They've all taken off their identical white blouses and put on a variety of clothes chosen by Harmony from the old castle wardrobes – dresses, suits, blouses worn by Gladys McBee in her youth. But it's no use – despite these outfits that are supposed to differentiate them, the clones all still have the same characterless expression on their faces.

'I so wish you could learn to be yourselves, fully individuals,' mutters Harmony to herself, knowing that no one else will understand her words. But what can that possibly mean, being yourself, when you've spent your whole life being treated like a thing?

She forces herself to smile in spite of her sadness, then adds in a louder voice that echoes through the ancient hall: 'You've all done great work today! I'm very proud of you. You can go and have your dinner now.'

She mimes the act of bringing food to her mouth to signify eating, then she points at the clones so they know they are to have their dinner, not prepare hers.

One by one, the creatures leave the room, a fearsome parade of pale-haired spectres wearing the attire of bygone times.

Harmony finds herself alone in the vast dark hall, which is lit only by the Gothic ogive windows beyond which a summer dusk is festering, the colour of blood. As every evening, the cries of the seabirds nesting on the cliffs redouble in intensity, sounding more and more like human wails.

Harmony brings her hand to her neck where she's wearing the key that makes her the new lady of the house; with her other hand she takes a sharpened knife out of her pocket. Then she heads for the entrance to the keep beside the fireplace.

The reinforced door opens in silence.

The elevator carries her up, the steel trapdoors opening and closing in turn as she passes up to the third landing.

A quavering voice greets her – the only voice able to make intelligible phrases in this forgotten place.

'You still haven't decided to leave this cursed island?'

Harmony gets up from the seat, knife in hand.

She arms herself more out of principle than necessity whenever she goes up to visit her prisoner each evening. In truth, Gladys McBee is far too old and drained to be a real threat, and not once in six weeks has she displayed the slightest aggression in her behaviour. She spends her days prostrate on the chair that was brought up for her – along with a mattress, a pitcher of water, biscuits and a chamber-pot – mulling over her memories of a life spent in her sister's service, and cursing herself.

'You just need to call the woman who brought you here to come back and fetch you,' says Gladys McBee.

'Ann Murphy thinks I left Bee Island a long time ago, on board another fishing boat. That's what I wrote to her.'

'Why are you so determined to stay? What's the use of spending your days surrounded by the clones?'

'So I can try and give them a bit of what they've been deprived of their whole lives.'

'It's too late for them. Their brains have developed without any recourse to language – it's always going to be beyond them now.' The old woman sighs deeply, her bronchi whistling like a December wind. 'To be honest, it's too late for everything. Too late to correct the past. Too late to undo what I've done. Too late to control the all-powerful monster Serena has become.'

But Harmony won't admit defeat.

'No, it's not too late!' she says. 'Apparently in America the rebel group calling themselves the *Wild Bees* is growing all the time.'

'She'll neutralise them like she has all the others.'

'In one week's time, the Mars pioneers will board the self-energising elevator, and from then on they won't be at risk of the base being depressurised, and then I can reveal what happened in the Noah experiment.'

'She'll deny it just like she's denied everything else.'

'When the American people learn of the existence of the clones, this disgusting secret hiding behind their president's eternal youth, they'll take up arms!'

'She's already armed those people who'd rather see her as their saviour.'

Enraged by this total defeatism, Harmony stamps her foot. 'You're wrong to think that everything's so totally bleak!' she shouts. 'When I came here, to McBee Castle, I was guided by my instinct, I didn't know what I'd find here. It was fate that led me to the clones. And maybe to you too, so that you can redeem yourself. We should be teaming up! Mom is not invincible! Not everybody is a victim of her spells!'

But Gladys shakes her head.

'You persist in calling her *Mom*,' she says, with a bitterly ironic smile. 'In spite of everything she's done to you, in spite of everything you've learned about her . . . My poor child, you're spellbound too: *you yourself were the very first victim of her enchantments!*'

Harmony freezes, struck hard by this cruel fact.

'I've come to see if there's anything you need to make you comfortable,' she says icily. 'Do you need any fresh water, any food?'

'I thought that confessing my crimes would relieve my conscience,' says the old woman, not answering the question. 'But it hasn't helped at all – on the contrary. Even if I'm no longer in day-to-day contact with the clones, the memory of them never stops haunting me, day or night. My memories of the ones who died get jumbled up with the ones that are still alive, I muddle up all the numbers, I've lost count . . . and sometimes in the middle of all these accusing faces I see hers: the woman who inspired them all, who bred them all – Serena, accusing me of not having properly guarded McBee Castle and promising to wreak terrible revenge on me!' Gladys holds her nearly bald skull in her hands. 'Oh God, I'm going mad. My head's going to explode!'

Harmony shivers at the pathetic sight of Gladys McBee in a state of collapse; this person who is too deeply buried in her own foul actions to experience the grace of genuine repentance, to be able to see any redemption. If she stays in this room a moment longer, Harmony too might surrender to despair.

'I see you don't need anything,' she says decisively, breathless. 'I'll come back tomorrow evening. Goodnight.'

She turns on her heel and hurries to sit back down on the elevator platform, which starts moving at once. It's not until the steel trapdoor closes that Harmony is able to breathe again.

The moving platform carries her down to the first landing, the one where the machines and computers are stored.

The biggest screen is on a table where an empty cafetière is heaped with a cup, at the bottom of which are coffee grounds, and the traces of a meal of bread and fruit. Harmony puts the crockery into the tub – she'll wash it tomorrow – then she positions herself in the place where she's spent most of her time since her arrival.

The surface of the switched-off screen reflects her torso, like an obsidian mirror. Her black-dyed hair has grown a good centimetre since her arrival at the castle, its blonde roots reappearing. She's no longer wearing her coloured contact lenses. Her skin has lost its Florida tan, and recovered its translucent, porcelain whiteness.

'Andrew, wherever you are, I'm thinking about you,' she murmurs quietly. 'It was you who got me out of the Villa McBee, you who opened my eyes to the world, you who taught me everything I know about technology . . . and most of all, it was you who taught me what bravery is. I know you

582

would have done the same thing I'm planning to do in one week's time, I know you would have taken this opportunity to reveal the truth, when my mom is no longer able to harm the pioneers.' The girl swallows, her eyes starting to shine. 'What makes me hesitate is the thought of the revenge she could take on you. You're still in her claws. Will I have the strength to press *Send* when the moment comes? Oh, Andrew, I miss you so much! If you can hear me, send me a sign!'

As if in answer to her prayer, the cry of an unknown bird, sharper and louder than the rest, pierces the thick castle ramparts.

Harmony pulls herself together.

She connects her cellphone to the main unit, presses the power button: the light of the computer screen erases the reflection of her face and, for now at least, all her hesitations.

In a few clicks she uploads all the videos she has made – one for each clone – and she gets to work editing the film that, in one week, will reveal the hidden face of Serena McBee to the whole world.

97. Shot

Month 18 / sol 483 / 08:00 Mars time
[602nd sol since landing]

'My dear pioneers, it's the big day!' says Serena McBee, who has appeared on the inside of the dome.

I hear her velvety voice, calm and poised, through the speakers in my helmet.

Today she's wearing an elegant cream-coloured suit, its collar revealing the frills of a pale pink lace blouse on which the black remembrance ribbon is visible. Her make-up is in the same reassuring pastel tones – I imagine there's nothing insignificant about this choice, at the dawn of this day that awaits us, the longest and most worrying of all.

Just like twenty-one Martian months ago, when we were facing the final disturbance of the preceding storm season, we've all put on our undersuits – Louve and Warden too. Even Kelly has had to leave her bed and strap herself in like the rest of us, putting her helmet over her red face and pulling on her numbered armband. She's currently sitting in Tao's spare wheelchair; when the time comes to leave the base to board the elevator's capsule, she won't have the strength to push herself of course – Samson has offered to take charge of that.

'*I can see you've prepared the base perfectly to handle the weather,*' Serena continues, referring to the tarp-covered plantations, all the materials stored, the rovers parked. '*All you need to do now is go – turn out the lights and leave . . . all the better to return, of course! You'll see, this brief month in orbit on board the* Cupido *will be like a vacation. And when you come back down, you'll be full of energy to continue building your great nation, despite all those people who want to annex you, to colonise you, to strip you of your liberty. You will, at last, give birth to the first baby of Mars, and of all those that will follow!*'

The reference to Kris's pregnancy, whose revelation to the public a few days ago was supported by many commercials and TV celebrations, makes me shudder. I know Serena doesn't give a shit about the baby or her health – or rather, she does, but only because she's benefiting from the burst of enthusiasm that accompanied the announcement, because it suits her propaganda. All the freedom she's been promising us in her lofty speeches is no more than a lure, a decoy designed to hide the freedoms she's flouting in America a bit more every day. A fake liberator on Mars, but a true tyrant on Earth!

I'm aware that we are her stooges.

I'm aware of our immense responsibility for what's happening on our home planet.

Yes, I'm aware of all that, but I don't know what to do. I'm paralysed like a fly trapped in a spider's web!

(Speak at last, or continue to keep quiet?) chants a voice that isn't coming from my speakers. *(What will you choose, in a few hours, when you've left the base?)*

(Stay on Mars, or return to Earth?) the song continues. *(Which direction will you go, on the* Cupido, *once the Great Storm is over?)*

'*But all in good time,*' continues Serena, briefly tearing me away from the Salamander's obsessive refrain. '*The big event this morning is of course the announcement of the new Mars couples: those from Season Two of the Genesis programme! Tonight the* Cupido *has entered Mars's orbit, in the wake of the moon Phobos. Its journey is over. The time has come to reveal the final Heart Lists!*'

I hear a small anxious murmuring through the comms system that connects all the pioneers. I recognise Fangfang's voice. She alone among the Season One pioneers has been through the speed-dating a second time, and she's in the same state of anticipation we experienced almost two Earth years ago. How far away that seems!

'*The algorithm is busily working away,*' says Serena, always ready to build up the suspense. '*Just a few more moments . . . Here it is!*'

There's a pre-recorded drumroll, sending feedback through my earphones.

Serena's face disappears and is replaced by a chart showing the list of seven couples accompanied by their Dowries.

Couple	Him	Her	Combined Dowry	% of Total
1	Oskar (POL) $300,155,130	Meritxell (ESP) $299,126,783	$599,281,913	17%
2	Valentin (CHE) $162,569,321	Fangfang (SGP) $401,896,541	$564,465,862	16%
3	Inùnguak (DNK) $254,896,321	Nikki (NLD) $302,148,963	$557,045,284	16%
4	Logan (USA) $210,589,632	Meryem (TUR) $298,632,478	$509,222,110	15%
5	Uri (ISR) $199,568,326	Lucrezia (ITA) $225,968,333	$425,536,659	12%
6	Farukh (IDN) $198,632,221	Young (KOR) $201,201,123	$399,833,344	12%
7	Marti (MEX) $302,098,567	Saga (SWE) $79,589,631	$381,688,198	11%

'Yes!' Fangfang yells from deep inside my helmet, showing her delight. 'I'm with Valentin! And we've got enough for a king-size Love Nest!'

Echoing her words, Serena comments on the rankings of these people we don't yet know, who for now are only names to us – even Fangfang herself has only met the boys who invited her or who she invited, and the girls are all still totally unknown.

'A superb performance from our charming Singaporean, our Fangfang, who's managed to collect the best individual Dowry of the two seasons put together! Far from holding her divorce *against her, the viewers are saluting her courage and resilience with their donations! She's ended up with her heart's choice, the handsome Valentin!*

'A disappointing performance, meanwhile, from our fiery Swede, Saga, who even combining her winnings with Marti, the most popular of the boys, ends up last in the rankings. Regular viewers of the Genesis channel know why . . .'

The viewers might, but we don't.

From the very start, from the day we set foot on the launch platform, Serena has only allowed us to see what she's wanted us to see.

We're the extras in a film whose script is being kept from us.

But I sense I'm the only person who's aware of this, as the pioneers uncork our penultimate bottle of Merceaugnac 1969 vintage to celebrate Fangfang's ranking.

(Speak at last: release the Noah Report, bring down Serena on the air and hope that the people of Earth get rid of her before she finds a way to take her revenge? Or stay quiet: not take any risks, play the game a little longer, knowing that every passing day strengthens her grip?)

(Return to Earth: go down and confront Serena directly, in her own stronghold, surrounded by her supporters? Or stay on Mars: far away from her, but at the mercy of the red button she could press at any moment?)

'. . . to you!' says the woman who's been haunting my thoughts, back on the screen to raise a cup of tea to the pioneers who are passing around the champagne bottle.

588

'We'll celebrate all these lovely marriages on New Eden once the Great Storm has ended, when you return to the base – and you'll be doing it with a new consignment of the finest Merceaugnac wine: from 1961, the year of the first space flight! We'll use the opportunity to remarry the newly formed couples from Season One properly – Tao and Liz, and Mozart and Léonor . . . if she finally decides not to return to Earth, though of course it's up to her; I'm not going to force anybody.' Serena the Magnanimous gives a toothy smile, a smile of complete and utter victory that crushes me with its sparkling whiteness. *'But our indecisive beauty will have plenty of time to think about it while in orbit. Let's have a look now at the schedule for the coming hours . . .'*

Serena's face disappears again, this time to be replaced by one of those computer graphics that have become the trademark of the Genesis programme.

'Two hours ago, at oh-six-hundred Mars time, the self-energised satellite detached itself from the Cupido *and was deployed in space to charge itself with solar rays, on its own orbital path.*

'At ten hundred hours tomorrow, after four cycles around the planet, the necessary energy should have been stored, and the satellite will be properly aligned for the release of the transit capsule.

'At eleven hundred, that capsule will touch down in the valley of Ius Chasma, as close to the base as possible to avoid your having to travel too great a distance in those dusty, windy conditions.

'At seventeen hundred, the self-energised satellite will once again

be passing over Ius Chasma, during the course of its fifth circuit, and it will release a powerful burst of microwaves to draw the capsule back up into space, with all of you on board.'

The graphic fades away, and a countdown in lit-up digital numbers appears at the top of the dome.

TRANSIT CAPSULE LIFT-OFF – 32H 00M

But Serena is not done yet.

'Oh, one last thing!' she says, with a look that is both concerned and reassuring, just what people expect of a president in a time of crisis. *'Our weather service tells me that the Great Storm is currently ahead of predictions. It should strike Ius Chasma in less than two sols – and we can expect preliminary disturbances in the coming hours. Keep your helmets on properly, my dear pioneers – but don't worry! You can count on your Serena to get you out of there. As for you, my dear citizens, my dear viewers, buckle up: there's about to be quite a show on your favourite channel: the Genesis channel!'*

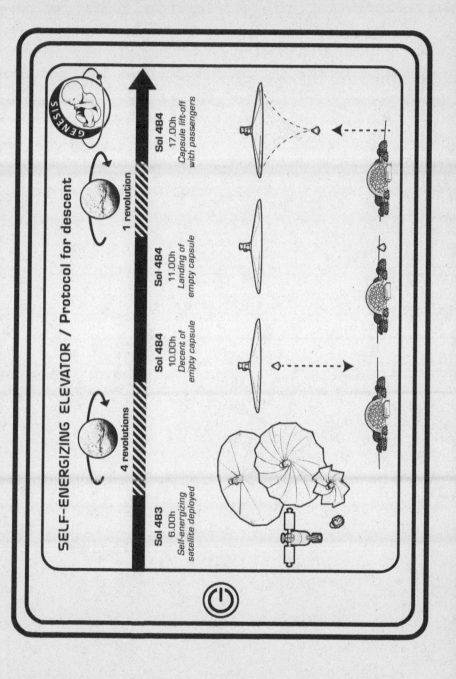

FINAL ACT

98. Reverse Shot

The Villa McBee, Long Island, New York State
Tuesday 20 August, 4:00pm
| *Transit capsule lift-off – 32h 00m* |

'There's going to be quite a show on your favourite channel: the
Genesis channel!'

Serena McBee smiles with all her teeth at the aluminium
gantry covered in its cameras and spotlights, from the desk
behind which she is seated for her commentary on the final
hours before the evacuation of the New Eden base.

Behind her, on either side of the French windows that open
onto the blossoming gardens, two large flags are hanging from
their poles. To the right, the old star-spangled banner of the
United States; to the left, the brand-new flag of the Citizens
Swarm, with its fifty bees arranged in their neat rows. For
several weeks, since the fourth of July celebrations, only the
first of these has been permitted at the presidential podium,
with the second being reserved exclusively for supporters. But
today, as if under the effect of a gradual shift, the two have
been placed on a level footing.

The great show-woman puts down her microphone and

pours herself a cup of tea sweetened with honey from her estate, while her words travel across space.

Sipping the hot, aromatic liquid, she watches the pioneers on the huge central screen. They look tiny and vulnerable in their off-white suits, like bee larvae removed from their alveoli. On one side of the gantry, a small screen representing the Earth records the global audience for the Genesis channel in real time, broken up by country and by type of connection. The world map is entirely lit up in red, which is the colour that corresponds to the maximum audience. From Iceland to Argentina, Tokyo to New York, there is not one nation, not one town – not one individual, it would seem – who isn't tuned in to the Genesis channel. Even Russia, which is officially boycotting anything coming out of the U.S., is sparkling with millions of pirate connections getting around the blockade set in place by Moscow: beyond any political rifts, beyond any borders, languages and cultures, people want to be a part of the Martians' destiny. They want to communicate with *their* candidates, *their* pioneers . . . *their* friends, whom they've never met and yet whom they feel they know very well, via the hypnotic enchantments of the Genesis programme.

Serena calmly finishes her cup of tea, and takes an enjoyable bite out of a little ginger shortbread. Then with a practised finger she manipulates the control panel set into the wood of the desk, zooming in to the visors of the different helmets at the moment her last words reach the Martians' earphones.

Astonishment.

Anxiety.

Panic.

The editing software doesn't miss a second, and sends the flow of raw emotion down the pipes of the Genesis channel, for it to be disseminated to the four corners of the globe.

Close-up on Fangfang, Planetology Officer, who's shivering in her spacesuit. 'The Great Storm is ahead of schedule? Oh God, that's what I was afraid was going to happen while I was studying the atmospheric movements in the last few days! Oh, Serena, let me meet my Valentin!'

Cross-fade to Kirsten, her gloved hands held together in prayer, as if she were addressing the Lord God in person. 'Dear Serena, watch over us! Our ten lives are in your kind hands . . . and also the eleventh, that of my and Alexei's child.'

The camera pans across to the Russian, standing ramrod straight beside his wife, his arms crossed over his chest to show his armband with its large number 1. He lifts his square jaw towards the dome. 'President McBee, in this moment of crisis, we know we can count on you, that you have always been the greatest ally of the new Martian nation. I'd like to take advantage of this historic moment to make a double announcement. First of all, from an official point of view, we have decided to make you an honorary citizen of Mars; second, and more personally, Kris and I have naturally agreed to name our daughter . . . Serena.'

Sitting comfortably in her study in the Villa McBee, millions of miles from the storm that's about to devastate an entire planet, Serena savours these images as if they were manna from heaven.

Manna from heaven – these souls who put themselves blindly in her hands.

Manna from heaven – these great declarations of loyalty broadcast to viewers right across the world.

Manna from heaven – the legitimacy being conferred on her by the most popular personalities of all time – the young people whose faces are on every screen, their stories in every magazine, their names on everybody's lips.

These people who yesterday were her worst nightmares have today become her most ardent champions.

'Thank you, my children, my dears . . .' she says, picking up the mic again. 'I will never abandon you. I will always be there for you. I will be there for little Serena Junior and for all your future children.' Her smile widens, and her eyes shine like a snake's while she says again, in a reptilian voice, 'Always.'

99. Off-screen

Bee Island, the Sea of the Hebrides
Tuesday 20 August, 9:21pm
$\boxed{\textit{Transit capsule lift-off – 31h 39m}}$

'*I will always be there for you. I will be there for little Serena Junior and for all your future children. Always.*'

In the dark laboratory of McBee Castle, in a time zone five hours ahead of New York, the only source of light is coming from the computer screen streaming the Genesis channel.

The executive producer's face in the broadcast is radiant, lit up by dazzling spotlights.

Opposite her, as if facing her in a mirror, is a similar face, with no lighting except for the glow of the screen.

Harmony McBee sits here, alone, in the silence.

But ultimately, aren't they *all* alone, every one of those Genesis viewers, those billions of human beings caught in a magnetic attraction to their TV screens, so convinced they're communing with the rest of Earth, that they're in symbiosis with the pioneers on Mars?

Harmony knows what she's looking at now is a lie, an illusion. She *knows* she is alone.

The objects arranged in front of her at the foot of the screen, like relics, are there to remind her: the lock of Mozart's hair; the little gold nugget from Andrew – the mementos of the two men in her life, who are lost now, perhaps for ever.

On the screen, next to the window on which the Genesis channel is being streamed, two tabs are open. The first is the email software, full of addresses of thousands of journalists; the second is a mirror site for *Genesis Piracy*, which is currently off-line but which once it goes live it will be consultable by millions of private individuals. It will take Harmony only a few clicks, when the time comes, to reveal the video of the clones to the world – to reveal *the truth*.

100. Shot

Month 18 / sol 483 / 11:32 Mars time
[602nd sol since landing]
Transit capsule lift-off – 29h 28m

'There it is, the storm front's on its way,' murmurs Fangfang,
gripping the Planetology tablet in her gloved hands.

The pioneers are gathered around her, trying to read over
her shoulder.

'*Meh, I think it's disappointing. They've really oversold this
Great Storm of theirs,*' says Kelly's feeble voice through the
relay linking the helmets.

Samson has pushed the Canadian girl's wheelchair up against
the covered plantation, at the foot of which Fangfang has been
sitting for the last three hours.

'*It really doesn't look much worse than the one that hit us
a Martian year ago . . .*' Kelly continues. '*Honestly, it's such a
lightweight!*'

The pictures on Fangfang's tablet do actually look strangely
like the images from the final storm of last season, which did
frighten us a lot, it's true, but which we actually got through
without a scratch.

'*Maybe the meteorological situation has improved?*' ventures Safia.

Fangfang gives an anxious sigh.

'*You don't understand! What you're looking at are last year's archived pictures, which I've pulled up for comparison. The most recent satellite images are down here!*'

With a finger made clumsy by the astronaut glove, she scrolls up on her tablet, making a very different picture appear: a gigantic whirling eye, opening across thousands of miles to the south of Ius Chasma.

'*What the hell is that monster?*' says Mozart.

'*A dust cyclone,*' replies Fangfang tonelessly. '*It's headed straight for us. The south-eastern part of the Valles Marineris has already been swallowed up.*' She looks up, eyes wide with fear behind the visor of her helmet, and points towards the valley behind the glass of the dome. '*Look, the air's already started filling with particles.*'

It's true: even though it's nearly noon, the brightness of the day has dimmed. It seems gloomier now, redder.

'*And that's just the finer dust that's being pushed ahead by the front of the cyclone,*' says Fangfang. '*When it gets this far, in two hours at the very most, we won't be able to see at all.*'

'*Will the self-energising elevator still work?*' asks Kris, concerned, her hand on the belly of her suit.

'*The microwaves have a wavelength long enough to get through clouds,*' answers Safia, drawing on what she's learned as Comms Officer. '*The self-energised satellite will be able to bring the capsule up, even if the atmosphere is full of dust, and visual contact between the surface and space has been completely cut off.*' She turns her

METEOROLOGICAL REPORT /
Live tracking of the Great Storm

Archive images
Regular storm, as on sol 578 (last year)

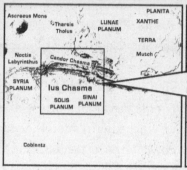

Ascraeus Mons

Tharsis
Tholus

LUNAE
PLANUM

PLANITA

XANTHE

TERRA

Mutch

Noctis
Labyrinthus

Candor Chasma

SYRIA
PLANUM

Ius Chasma

SOLIS
PLANUM

SINAI
PLANUM

Coblentz

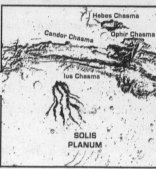

Hebes Chasma

Candor Chasma

Ophir Chasma

Ius Chasma

SOLIS
PLANUM

Satellite pictures, real time
Great Storm, sol 483
Captured 11:00h, Mars time

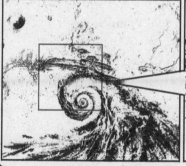

big kohl-ringed eyes towards the dome. They are shining with hope – this girl who yesterday was the most rational of any of us, is today reduced to sending prayers up to heaven. *'Isn't that right, Serena?'*

While she waits religiously for the apparition of the great goddess, I feel a huge excitement overtake me.

I turn to Liz.

Our eyes meet through our visors.

She heard what Fangfang said too: visual contact between space and the surface of Mars is going to be lost soon.

The moment for us to free Marcus is coming closer.

'Can we go have a quick look at the seventh habitat, Alexei?' Liz asks the new master of Mars, whose permission is needed for anyone to do anything just now. *'We know the Rest House is the most vulnerable part of the base, as it's been damaged in the past. Tao and I just want to check its status one last time before the Great Storm arrives.'*

That's the code we've agreed in advance to justify to the viewers and organisers why our two Engineering Officers want to go to the seventh habitat.

'OK,' replies Alexei, sticking to the promise he made me, in exchange for my promise to behave. *'You can go.'*

Liztao head off towards the other side of the Garden.

My heart starts to race. I know that from now on, everything has to run like clockwork – if anyone puts a single foot wrong, our secret plan to extract Marcus will descend into total chaos.

As I watch the English and Chinese pioneers disappear into the access tube, I run through the plans in my head for the hundredth time:

604

1) IDENTITY SWAP: Once they're in the seventh habitat, out of sight of the cameras, Tao will take off his suit and let Marcus put it on in his place. With the help of the 3D printer, I've created a mask that reproduces Tao's face. Marcus will have to wear that behind the visor of the helmet to complete the illusion.

2) EXITING THE SEVENTH HABITAT: Liz and Marcus leave the Rest House, her on foot and him in the wheelchair, leaving Tao behind them. But the viewers will have no idea: they'll think they're watching the two Engineering Officers returning to their screens having completed their checks on the habitat.

3) EXTRACTION FROM THE BASE: Liz will then ask permission to check that all the outdoor tarps are properly in place – a perfectly normal request coming from our engineer. She and the fake Tao will go outside and get onto one of the three mini-rovers we still have (after Kenji went off with the fourth). They will do their circuit of New Eden, pretending to inspect the installations – but in reality they'll just be waiting for the sky to be completely blocked out by the dust. Only then will they smash the mini-rover's camera and disable its GPS system, for which they can blame the storm. From then on, the vehicle will no longer be connected to the Earth by satellite, or video link, or GPS signal. Marcus will now be able to remove Tao's suit without any risk of being recognised, to put his own back on – which has previously been put into the rover, its own helmet having had its audio system broken, too.

4) REPATRIATION: Liz will leave the vehicle, pushing the wheelchair – occupied by Tao's suit, empty now but inflated with oxygen. The viewers will think they're watching two pioneers returning to the base, having seen two pioneers leave it. On the pretext of having spotted a possible breach in the outer shell of the seventh habitat, the English girl will ask to do one final check with her 'partner' – which in reality will allow her to reunite Tao with his wheelchair and his suit. During this time, Marcus will have left at the wheel of the mini-rover towards Noctis Labyrinthus, the Labyrinth of Night, under cloud cover. And in one month, when the storm dies down and it turns out we're missing a vehicle, we can all blame the cyclone for having buried it.

'Oh yes, Safia, you're absolutely right!' says Serena, pulling me out of my thoughts. *'The self-energising elevator will work whatever the weather conditions, if it's raining or snowing or windy. I actually think it will be a stunning sight from space as the capsule breaks out through the thick layer of clouds, tearing itself away from the dust cyclone with the ten of you on board!'*

Leaving Serena to get carried away with her latest idea for a TV spectacle, I focus all my attention on the access tube leading to the seventh habitat.

In there, in the secrecy of the Rest House, is everything going according to plan?

Has Marcus already put on Tao's suit?

(Why didn't you say you wanted to be part of this monitoring mission too, to see him one last time?)

There are so many rational ways I could answer this question: because there's no way to justify my presence in the Rest House to the viewers; because the extraction plan will be simpler with as few people involved as possible; because long ago I decided to draw a line under Marcus.

At this thought, an invisible grip clenches my guts.

(You're never going to see him again!) hisses the Salamander's horrible voice. *(Once he's out of his prison, it'll be too late, too late, too late!)*

'*Alexei!*' I shout, spurred on by regret.

The thoughts race through my head – maybe it's not too late for me to find some excuse to go into the Rest House! After all, I'm supposed to be the resident hysteric these days, and what with the stress of the approaching Great Storm I'm sure the viewers will understand if I need to get away from the cameras for a bit!

'*Yes?*' asks the Russian boy, the visor of his helmet turning towards me.

'*I want to . . .*'

But I don't get the chance to say any more: there, at the far end of the Garden, the inner airlock of the access tube leading to the seventh habitat has just reopened.

Liz comes out first, easily recognisable from the shape of her body, slim despite the suit, carrying her toolbox that actually contains provisions for the banished man. She's closely followed by Tao's wheelchair, in which we can see Tao's suit . . . but in accordance with our secret plan, that's not Tao who's pushing himself forward so clumsily, hampered by an outfit that's too big for the body it contains.

(It's him! It's Marcus!) The Salamander bursts out laughing.

(You're screwing up your last-ever meeting!)

'*What was it you wanted to say, Léo?*' asks Alexei, looking hard at me with his glacier blue eyes, as if to warn that anything out of order from me will bring the extraction operation to an end and Marcus will return to his cell to die there like a rat during the Great Storm.

'*I just . . . nothing.*'

As the two pioneers come closer, I look at their faces through the visors in their masks.

Liz's is incredibly stressed.

Tao's expresses nothing at all, for good reason: his face is only a mask, made out of the substrate from this cursed planet.

I'll never see Marcus's face again, and I'm the person who created the barrier keeping it from me.

I can't even hear his voice one last time – the mic and speakers in Tao's helmet have been disabled to prevent the guy wearing them from saying anything on air.

'*Nothing to report from the seventh habitat – everything's shipshape,*' says Liz, in a high-pitched voice. '*Everything inside the base is now all set for the Great Storm. Tao and I still want to do one last circuit of the outside, in the mini-rover, to check the tarps.*'

'*Fine, go do that,*' says Alexei, reciting his part of the script.

Before I can say or do anything, Liz and Marcus are crossing the Garden, in full view of the cameras and Serena's enormous grinning face, headed for the decompression airlock.

The wheelchair slows down as it passes me; the helmet of

the guy sitting in it turns slightly towards me, as if he wanted to say something.

'*Do it quickly!*' says Alexei. '*The storm is coming!*'

I feel Mozart's hand close over my arm to support me – or to hold me back.

Liz is already activating the airlock.

The reinforced door opens without a sound, letting the two pioneers into the narrow cylinder, and closing behind them.

(That's it.)

(It's over.)

(For ever.)

'*I've got to go outside!*' I shout.

Mozart's hand on my arm tightens.

All the helmets, connected to mine on the radio relay, turn sharply towards me.

'*What's she saying?* growls Alexei.

'*I need to go outside too!*' I say again, breathless, braving the lightning bolts coming at me from Alexei's eyes. '*It's not a good idea to let the engineers out on their own, when the Great Storm is about to reach us. What if something happens to them? There should be a Medical Officer with them. And you're our leader, Alexei, so you've got to stay in the base – so I'm the one who's got to go.*'

Alexei half-opens his mouth, and I can tell from the flaring of his nostrils that his reply is about to be scathing, but Mozart jumps in first.

'*I'll go with her. You can count on me.*'

Is that determination in my companion's voice? – but Alexei just nods and, miraculously, allows me to run over to the airlock.

By the time Mozart has joined me, the cylinder has opened up again.

I hurry inside.

The door closes behind us.

'*Ready? Can I initialise the equalisation procedure?*' I say, turning to Mozart, my hand on the button.

By way of response, he just takes me in his arms, suit against suit, helmet against helmet.

'*I love you, Léo,*' he murmurs, his big brown eyes shining behind his visor.

'*I . . . me too,*' I reply, touched, but suddenly realising what my insistence on seeing Marcus again could mean to Mozart.

'*I love you and I don't want to lose you.*'

I feel a sharp pain in my right thigh.

An icy chill runs through my veins.

'*What's . . . ?*'

My tongue turns to mush in my mouth.

My brain freezes.

Blackout.

101. Genesis Channel

Transit capsule lift-off – 29h 50m

The confined space of the decompression airlock, filmed by the camera attached to the ceiling of the unit.

Léonor and Mozart, in their suits, are pressed against each other in a marble embrace.

In his astronaut glove, the Brazilian boy is holding a hypodermic syringe.

The needle is stuck into the little silicon disc sewn into the right thigh of the French girl's suit. She isn't moving at all.

Mozart pulls the syringe out of the injection patch and takes a step back. Léonor slips through his arms, like a ragdoll which he catches just in time.

With his free hand, he activates the command to reopen the airlock's internal door.

Cut.

Long shot on the pioneers gathered in the Garden, all looking towards the airlock that's just opened.

Samson hurries over to help Mozart carry Léonor's lifeless body.

The Brazilian's voice comes through the inter-suit radio relay, which is also connected to the Genesis channel feed. *'She was about to get hysterical . . . You saw it as well as I did, and the viewers did too, she was about to throw herself into the storm . . . I had to use the syringe Alexei gave me yesterday . . .'*

The Russian's head nods in his helmet.

'You did well, Mozart. You acted just as we'd agreed you should in case Léonor lost it during the Great Storm, to protect her.' He turns to the camera, to address the Genesis viewers directly. *'We saw it coming – she's always been emotionally fragile, with that scar of hers, and Marcus dying, and everything . . . You remember how upset she got at the attack on President Green; we even had to isolate her that time. It's our duty as Martians to look after one another – especially the weakest among us.'*

Alexei turns back to Mozart and Samson, gesturing – with his arm marked *1* – at the far side of the dome. *'Take her into the Rest House; you can lie her down there until she recovers. Given the dose of sedative she got, she's bound to sleep for several hours.'*

Cut.

102. Shot

Month 18 / sol 483 / 15:05 Mars time
[602nd sol since landing]
Transit capsule lift-off – 25h 55m

I feel like I'm floating in an ocean, listening to a gentle melody.

The song is in a foreign language that sounds like blue skies, sandy beaches and warm seas.

Each word brushes over me like a delicate ripple, like a smooth breeze, like the tenderest caress.

I am well.

At peace.

I could stay on this wave that's carrying me away and be lulled by it for ever . . .

. . . and never . . .

. . . wake up.

Wake up?

With the sudden awareness that I'm asleep comes the wrench, the brutal awakening.

613

My eyes open instantly.

The harsh light from the halogen spots burns my retinas.

'Where am I?' I say, but there's no audio feed coming into my ears – someone's taken off my helmet.

'You're safe, my darling Léo . . .' replies Mozart, who's suddenly stopped singing his favourite Brazilian song, the one he once dedicated to me – 'The Girl from Ipanema'.

He's taken his helmet off too.

'. . . in the seventh habitat, with no cameras, without the others – just you and me.'

The memories all rush back: the removal of Marcus, my last-minute regrets, my abortive attempt to see him one last time . . . the feeling of the needle sinking into my thigh.

'You drugged me!' I shout, sitting up abruptly. 'What time is it?'

'It was for your own good, to stop you doing something stupid.'

'*What time?*' I ask again, louder this time.

I look around me and realise I'm on the bed of the small room in the seventh habitat – the room that's been Marcus's jail cell for the past Martian year. The walls are covered in marks. At first I think it's Marcus's tally of the days he's spent in prison. But as I look closer, I see they aren't little lines Marcus has carved in the white plastic using a fork, a knife or even his fingernails: they're stars. Hundreds, thousands of stars, recreating the constellations he knew so well, and which he was denied for the long night of his imprisonment.

'It's fifteen hundred hours. You should try to rest, sleep a bit more. The capsule of the self-energising elevator won't be here for several hours yet. I'll watch over you in the meantime.'

The numbers race through my brain – fifteen hundred? That means the extraction process started more than three hours ago!

'And what about the Great Storm?' I ask, forcing myself to lower my voice so as to hide my panic. 'Has it started?'

'Yes, just after noon. The visibility's been falling since then.'

He takes his digital tablet from the bedside table and shows me the meteorological bulletin: the pictures of a dust tsunami overflowing from the edges of the canyon into the valley of Ius Chasma, getting denser and denser, gradually blocking out the atmosphere.

'So that means the surface of Mars isn't visible from space any more,' I babble. 'That means – Marcus is gone.'

Mozart puts the tablet down again, and places his gloved hand gently on mine.

'He's gone, as you wanted him to,' he murmurs. 'You gave him a generous gift, one final journey towards that strange labyrinth of his. And now you've got to forget him. And think about yourself. About us.'

His eyes are overflowing with tenderness.

They are entirely focused on me.

He's forgotten the master key sitting on the bedside table, next to the tablet and our two helmets.

I try to make my tears of distress look like tears of love.

I order my lips to smile, in a kind of invitation.

Mozart leans gently towards me.

The second his lips meet mine, I hit him hard in the middle of the chest.

With all my strength, with all my rage, with all my despair.

He falls backwards onto the bedroom floor, his face twisted

in an expression of surprise and pain.

Quick as a flash, I grab my helmet and the master key, and hurl myself out of the room, double-locking the door behind me.

There, panting, my wits still numbed by the mists of the sedative, I recover my breath. The hoarse whistle of my breathing mixes with the noise of the wind roaring beyond the habitat walls. Marcus is somewhere out there, in that storm which is carrying him far away from me for ever!

The thought pierces me like a sting.

I frantically screw on my helmet – I'm not even thinking of it as an astronaut's helmet now but an American footballer's. My whole suit has become armour, filled out with imaginary shoulder and knee pads.

I take a final deep breath, then I hurtle down the access tube like a rocket, with only one obsession in mind: I mustn't stop till I've found Marcus again.

METEOROLOGICAL REPORT /
Live tracking of the Great Storm

Video images, real time
South-eastern view from external Garden cameras
Sol 483, midday Mars time

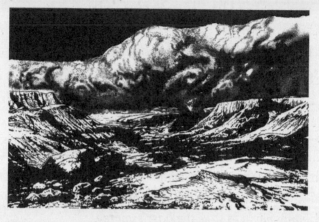

Luminosity gauge
Drop over the last few hours and over
the hours to come

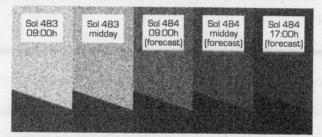

| Sol 483 09:00h | Sol 483 midday | Sol 484 09:00h (forecast) | Sol 484 midday (forecast) | Sol 484 17:00h (forecast) |

103. Reverse Shot

The Villa McBee, Long Island, New York State
Tuesday 20 August, 10:15pm
Transit capsule lift-off – 25h 45m

A human cannonball.

That's what it looks like, the shape that suddenly bursts out of the access tube from the seventh habitat. It splits the dome of the Garden, which is only halflit, the spotlights on the ceiling working in economy mode to save the base's energy.

The other pioneers, sitting all together at the foot of the plantations, waiting anxiously for the arrival of the self-energising elevator, are stunned to see it rush past.

Voices start to come through the radio relay:

'It's . . .'

'It looks like . . .'

'Léonor!'

Sitting at the desk opposite the editing screen, Serena McBee jumps.

She puts down the cup of tea she was sipping, so abruptly that it smashes against the porcelain saucer beneath it.

The burning liquid spreads across the desk and the president's fingers, making her cry out in pain.

Alexei's reflexes are the fastest, and he jumps to his feet to try to tackle the fugitive. But the momentum Léonor has gathered, combined with the weak gravity on Mars, sends him flying like a skittle on a bowling green. He falls onto his hands and knees as the French girl enters the decompression airlock.

Shaking her burnt right hand, Serena McBee brings her left down onto the control panel set into the desk. But with five of her fingers out of action, she seems to have lost all her dexterity – she fumbles around, trying to locate the buttons, but can't find them, and spits out swearwords instead.

On screen, the Russian is already getting back to his feet, ready to follow Léonor into the airlock to stop her pressing the equalisation button.

But she stops him with a scream. 'Let me go see Marcus one last time! That's all I ask for – to be able to mourn at his graveside . . . silently!'

Alexei freezes the moment she says the last word, like a promise, like an oath: 'silently'.

The airlock door closes.

The equalisation procedure has begun.

The picture cuts sharply to a close-up of Louve, snoozing at the foot of the plantations.

On the editing screen in the middle of the aluminium gantry, the crew's dog gives a long yawn. Behind her desk, the executive producer has regained control of the show. She had only lost it for a few seconds.

'Little bitch,' she hisses between her lips. 'Let her go die in the storm on the tomb of her beloved Marcus and nobody will ever mention her again. Good riddance!'

Suddenly there's a knock on the study door.

'Yes?' Serena calls out. 'Come in.'

Balthazar the butler, wearing his usual earpiece, comes into the room.

'Ms McBee, is everything all right? I heard you shouting . . .'

He looks down at the desk, covered in shards of porcelain swimming in a pool of tea.

'I dropped my cup of tea,' says Serena. 'Come wipe this up. And bring me a bowl of cold water to soak my fingers – I scalded myself.'

'Right away, Ms McBee.'

While the butler hurries off, Serena leans over her control panel again. She lowers her left hand, which has regained its confidence now, and returns the view to a long shot of the whole Garden – of the nine remaining pioneers, the ones over whom she's certain she still has one hundred per cent control.

104. Off-screen

Bee Island, the Sea of the Hebrides
Wednesday 21 August, 11:17am
Transit capsule lift-off – 17h 43m

'It's now been eight hours since we heard from Léonor. The moment she rushed out into the storm, at fifteen sixteen Mars time, all contact with her was lost. Has she been able to find Marcus's grave in the storm? Has she lost her way? It's impossible to locate her from space; what with the layer of clouds blanketing the planet, and there's no longer any signal coming from her helmet.'

The presenter puts on a sorrowful expression well suited to the announcement of a terrible tragedy. But we can also sense the weight of inevitability in his eyes and in his tone of voice – Léonor's disappearance, after all, is not all that surprising.

'For several months now – some would say, since the start of the Genesis programme – the French girl has been the most unstable member of the team, the weak link. This recent hysterical fit, which seems likely to have cost her her life, is just the latest in a long series . . .'

Archive footage starts to play on the screen behind the presenter.
Sequence no. 1: the launch ceremony at Cape Canaveral.

Close-up on Léonor, standing very straight in her suit, as the voice of Gordon Lock asks her: 'Do you agree to represent humanity on Mars from this day forth until the last day of your life?' Léonor hesitates. She opens her mouth. Closes it again. 'Well then, Léonor,' insists Director Lock, 'I'm waiting for your answer. The boys are waiting for your answer. The whole of Earth is hanging on your lips . . .' But Léonor's face is frozen in doubt. She murmurs something inaudible, pulls herself together, then finally gives a rasping yell: 'I accept, of course! I said I accept!'

Sequence no. 2: the first day of the mission, on board the Cupido. Flushed with shame, Léonor appears in the living room, where the girls are huddled around Kris, who's sporting a big bump on her forehead. 'Girl, are you totally nuts or what?' shouts Kelly. 'Have you seen what you did to Kris when you closed the hatch on her head? Have you? You've really got to be careful!'

Sequence no. 3: the end of the journey through space. Léonor, in a red chiffon dress, has just been surprised rummaging through her teammates' belongings. The girls are looking down at her through the trapdoor in the bedroom ceiling. 'She's having an attack of paranoia,' murmurs Safia. 'Totally crazy. I really think I have to talk to you about it, girls, for her own good.' Léonor throws herself at the ladder, grabs hold of the fabric hanging down from Safia's sari through the trapdoor; she pulls on it like a slipknot, until the Indian girl can't say another word. 'Let go of her! Let go of her! Let go of her!' the other girls scream in shock.

Sequence no. 4: the announcement of the attack on President Green. Léonor looks pale, standing outside the Garden dome, onto which the images of the devastated launch platform are being projected. She starts screaming. 'They can't let the rocket *take off!' Her voice trembles, about to crack. 'We can't let the programme continue!' The others are looking at her as if she's crazy. 'The Noah Report . . .' Alexei throws himself onto her, grabs her around the waist and declares to no one in particular: 'She's turning hysterical! She's in shock, it's some psychological trauma from the attack! Mozart, Samson, Kenji – help me get her into the Rest House! She needs to unwind far from the cameras.'*

Sequence no. 5: just eight hours ago. *'Let me go see Marcus one last time!' Léonor shouts from inside the decompression airlock. 'That's all I ask for – to be able to mourn at his graveside . . . silently!' Close-up on her overexcited face through the visor of her helmet, just before the airlock door shuts.*

Sitting at her computer in front of the streaming news, Harmony McBee is pale. She's been up all night, glued to the screen, alternating between the Genesis channel and news sites around the world.

Instinctively she closes her hand over her lucky charm, the lock of hair given to her two years ago by a boy she barely knew and who is now many millions of miles away.

'. . . the most highly qualified psychological experts have in recent hours commented on the French pioneer's behaviour,' continues the presenter on the screen. 'The general consensus is that Léonor's case is clear enough: the arrival of the Great Storm brought too much pressure to bear on her, reawakening the stress from the previous storm. Like Kenji some months ago, she "cracked up", in common parlance, once and for all. But by throwing herself into the tempest on her own to try to return to Marcus's grave,

following his death from a heart attack a year and a half ago, she must unfortunately have signed her own death warrant.'

At these words, a black-and-white photo portrait of Léonor appears behind the presenter; he observes a moment of silence, as though already marking a death.

'Make Léonor come back,' mutters Harmony as if in prayer, twisting the lock of hair between her fingers. 'Even if she was with Mozart, I never wished her dead, God's my witness! They built something together, something real. And what's Mozart to me, except a dream? I've never built anything with him, nor with anyone else in the world.'

Just as Harmony says these words, she catches sight of the small gold nugget glinting at the foot of her screen.

Her eyes widen, as though seeing it for the first time.

She drops the lock of hair, its strands scattering in the whistling draughts of McBee Castle.

105. Shot

Month 18 / sol 484 / 00:59 Mars time
[603rd sol since landing]
Transit capsule lift-off – 16h 01m

A dark ocean, with no beginning and no end.

This is the environment I've been travelling through for nearly ten hours now, judging by the little round clock set into the dashboard. Along with the compass, the radar and the digital map loaded with the exact coordinates of the threshold of Noctis Labyrinthus, it's the only piece of equipment still working. I cut off all the others as soon as I boarded the mini-rover when I left the base, starting with the GPS signal. I also took off my helmet, having disconnected the radio relay and turned off the integrated camera. Where I'm going, nobody can follow me. No viewers, no producers, not even the other pioneers – and besides, that's what I promised Alexei – even if not explicitly – when I claimed I wanted to go mourn at Marcus's grave: I was promising *my silence*.

All around me, through the windscreen of the pressurised cabin, there's no more up and down, there's no ground and no sky, no dunes, no stars. All points of reference have disappeared, drowned in the flood of dust that's hiding everything. It was

625

reddish at first, when it was still weakly lit by the distant Sun. But since night has fallen, it's no more than a black tar that the headlamps can't penetrate. There's only the compass to tell me that I'm still headed west, towards Noctis Labyrinthus. There's only the radar to allow me to avoid any obstacles lying in the way. I'm totally blind.

And to tell the truth, I have been for a long time.

I chose to put out my own eyes. I did it myself, for all these months when I forbade myself from visiting the prisoner in the seventh habitat.

It was so easy not to see him, to act as though he no longer existed, not hearing the insistent tick-tock of the D66 mutation reducing his chances of survival every day, every hour, every minute – and more than that, it was so cowardly.

I let somebody else open the door of his cell this morning, with the anguish in her belly of not knowing whether she'd find him dead or alive. It's Liz who's fed him, washed his clothes, taken care of him, who's carried the weight of this seclusion I begged for myself on the day of the trial – I was all words, no actions! And when I negotiated his freedom, if I'm totally honest with myself, I have to admit it was really so I myself would be freed, so my conscience would be clear, to convince myself that when I boarded the self-energising elevator I wouldn't be leaving anybody behind.

Except it doesn't work like that.

Except my conscience will never be clear, as long as I haven't looked Marcus in the eyes one last time and said: *Goodbye.*

And so I keep on going, straight ahead, ten hours on, knowing that every metre I travel takes me a little further from the base – and also a little further from any possibility of turning around and getting back to the capsule in time.

'*Obstacle detected fifty metres ahead*,' says the cybernetic voice of the on-board computer all of a sudden, though it's partly smothered by the wind that doesn't stop howling.

Torn from my thoughts, I disengage the clutch and slow down, my eyes glued to the navigation tablet. I'm surprised to notice that I've reached the threshold of the vast region of Noctis Labyrinthus, at least according to what the map is telling me based on the landscape perceived by the radar.

I touch the screen to switch to radar view, while still continuing ahead at walking speed.

'*Obstacle detected thirty metres ahead*,' says the machine soberly.

What has Mars got in store for me this time? A rock? A crater? A crevasse?

'*Obstacle detected twenty metres ahead.*'

It's not a rock, or a crater, or a crevasse that appears on the tablet.

It's a rover.

I feel my hands turn sweaty on the steering wheel.

A rover! Kenji's or Marcus's?

I hurriedly pull on my gloves, screw on my helmet, crawl onto the back section of the rover and press the equalisation button. An airtight partition closes behind me, protecting the driver's cabin from any dust getting in, while the rear section depressurises slowly.

After what feels like an eternity, the door finally rises.

There, outside, it's pitch black, an enormous nothingness beaten by the winds, a nothingness that roars.

The two little flashlights fitted to my helmet, on either side of my neck, are powerless to pierce any further than a few centimetres into the night. I can't totally trust the radar of my suit, which is much less effective than the one in the rover – the landscape shown in my visor, reconstructed by my on-board processor according to the data received from the radar, is vague and trembling. The outlines of the rocks seem to vibrate, undulating like a swell. The shape of the rover appears and vanishes again according to the whirlwinds of dust disturbing the radar, sometimes seeming to double up like an uncertain ghost.

I allow myself to slip to the floor, without a clear view of where I'm landing.

My legs sink up to the knees into a soft and viscous substance: the layer of the densest dust particles, which have settled on the Martian surface over recent hours.

Moving ahead through this treacle that threatens to swallow me up, I make my way slowly towards the motionless rover.

Who am I going to find in the driver's cabin?

Kenji, who's been dead for weeks?

Or Marcus, still very much alive – unless the D66 mutation's suddenly decided to get him, right here in the middle of the storm, stopping his rover's progress dead?

When I'm a few metres closer, I suddenly realise that what I thought was double vision caused by atmospheric disturbances is actually no illusion – what I'm looking at isn't a mini-rover, but *two* mini-rovers! Marcus and Kenji must both have used the same map and the same coordinates as me, leading them to the exact same place.

I switch back to the normal view setting and press the

visor of my helmet up against the windscreen of the first of the vehicles, as close as possible, so that no dust can obstruct the beams of the flashlights. The driver's cabin is empty.

I hurry over to the second rover, but in vain – it's also empty.

Marcus and Kenji both came here, four months apart, but they're not here any more.

Where have they got to?

It's impossible to see even the faintest footprint in the powdery foam that's covering the ground of Mars.

I turn right around, distraught, allowing the processor in my suit to reconstruct the howling landscape in my visor.

Rocks . . .

More rocks . . .

Nothing but rocks . . .

No! Over there, to the north-west, a few dozen metres from the abandoned rovers, there's something else! There's a hole the height of a man in the side of the cliff: the entrance to a cave!

I'm sure this is the only place Marcus could have taken refuge, so I head over towards the crevice, panting like an ox inside my helmet, unsettling cubic metres of dust with each step.

Once I've crossed the rocky threshold, my mobility improves slightly: the dust hasn't been able to get in here so easily. I head into the passageway. The roaring of the wind, heard through my helmet's audio sensors, lessens gradually, and bit by bit the flashlights manage to break further through the densely laden air. After about fifty yards down a gentle incline, I'm finally able to turn off the radar and switch back to normal vision.

Only now do I look at my surroundings.

The beam of my lamps sweeps across the rocky walls, which rise several metres above my head. The place is much vaster than I'd expected – the passageway actually gets wider, the deeper it goes.

I feel my stomach clench at the sudden thought of my insignificance in the heart of this mineral universe which can't have changed in millions of years, and which will be just the same for millions more after I've died. This cave might stretch on for miles, and anyway I have no proof that Marcus has ventured here, and my efforts to find him will be pathetic, and . . .

My racing thoughts stop dead the moment my torches light up the floor.

There are boot prints.

There, on the fine layer of sand carpeting the rock floor.

Any sense of apprehension vanishes instantly.

With my heartbeat amplified by the bubble of my helmet, I start running straight ahead – or rather, 'rouncing', that motion adapted to Martian gravity which has become natural to me after all these months on the red planet.

Under my boots, the downward gradient of the ground keeps increasing.

Around me, the walls keep widening.

It's no longer a passageway, or even a cave: it's a crypt opening up ahead of me, as vast and steep as a mountain slope, and over there . . . what look like trees!

Trees, on Mars?

As tall as sequoias?

I'm losing it. This can only be some kind of hallucination caused by oxygen deprivation.

I glance nervously at the vital indicators glowing in digital letters in the corner of my visor.

INTERNAL PRESSURE: 100%
OXYGEN RESERVES: 33H
THERMAL REGULATION: 25 °C
PHYSICAL STATUS: NOTHING TO REPORT
CLOCK: MONTH *18 / SOL 484 / 03:54*

Everything seems to be working, I've still got enough oxygen . . . And I've already been out of the rover for three hours – three hours moving deeper into the belly of Mars. I hadn't noticed the time passing.

I turn my attention back to the 'trees', only to realise this is not what they are.

What I took for sequoia trunks are really huge mineral formations. Stalagmites, with multiple perfectly smooth surfaces as wide as doors, rising up from the ground into the shadowy heights of the crypt. Giant crystals.

Gripped by amazement at these wonders of nature, I approach the first one. My torches light up the crystalline surface, awakening their colour – an orangey red that looks like amber, and transparent too.

It's stunning.

Taking another step further forward, I realise I am perfectly reflected in this strange standing-mirror: my dust-covered boots; my thick suit with its unit for extravehicular survival on its back; my helmet slightly obscured by the condensation from my breath.

It's me: Léonor.

Me, who sold my image for ever.

Me, who is still being reflected on a screen, even in the depths of Mars.

631

The moment I mentally formulate this thought, a glow catches my eye.

There, down in the crypt!

What looks like a will-o'-the-wisp passes across the forest of crystals, stealthily illuminating their sides!

My heart leaps in my chest.

'*Marcus!*' I shout, starting to rounce again.

I disappear in among the age-old crystals, sweating big drops inside my suit, ignoring the numbers of the thermal regulator going wild in the corner of my visor.

There really is a human being walking there ahead of me; an astronaut in a spacesuit.

'*Marcus . . .*' I murmur.

My gloved hand comes down on his shoulder.

He turns around, sharply.

It's him.

It's his grey eyes, wide with surprise.

It's his thick brown eyebrows, now frowning in disbelief.

It's his jaw, shaven clean for his final outing, thinner after months of seclusion.

His lips half open, trembling, but no sound comes out.

I remember now that the mic and speakers in his helmet were destroyed, to stop him communicating with Earth while in exile. I have the dizzying feeling that we're back on the day of our catastrophic landing on the surface of Mars, when the relay radios between the suits had stopped working and I was going over to meet him for the first time. He could not, and cannot, hear me or speak to me.

But – now, like then – he can see me.

I manage to decipher the name that forms on his stammering mouth, as if he was struggling to understand who is standing there in front of him: *Léonor.*

'*I've come for one last goodbye,*' I say, articulating each syllable carefully so that Marcus can read my lips too.

The sound of my own voice, coming back out of my earphones through the audio relay, seems strange to me.

Marcus's silent eyes, trembling in the light of my helmet torches, make me shiver.

'*I've come to say . . . goodbye,*' I manage to say again.

Marcus's face blurs before my eyes.

More mist in my helmet?

Or just my tears, which I no longer have the strength to hold back?

'*I've come to . . .*'

The words stick in my throat.

That's not why I've come.

I've come to stuff my ears full of Marcus's voice! I've come to inhale his woody ferny scent! I've come to run my fingers over the texture of his skin! I've come to hear him, to feel him, to touch him, to permeate all my senses with him, one last time – that's why I've really come!

But the thickness of our suits is still between us – the thickness of the whole universe! Angrily, unable to bear any more of the sound of my totally useless voice, the noise of my struggling, whistling breath, I cut off my own mic and the speakers in my helmet, shouting the command: '*Audio off!*'

Total quiet.

As if in a silent movie, Marcus's glove comes up towards

my cheek then stops, blocked by the helmet before it can touch my skin.

His broad forehead leans towards me then freezes, colliding with the glass barrier before it can come to rest on mine.

His face is just there, a few centimetres away, so close and yet unreachable – his eyes I've never been able to forget, despite all the hatred, all the disappointment, all the time that's passed, eyes like two stolen jewels, that I've never stopped loving in secret, deep down.

Suddenly he brings his hands to the rim of his helmet, as if he's about to take it off.

In a panic, my reflex is to push him back, as hard as I can.

His body, weighted down by its suit, crashes hard into one of the enormous crystals, and the shock gives off a strange mineral vibration, a kind of feedback sound that spreads through the translucent column . . .

. . . and which I can hear despite my earphones having been disabled.

It's a revelation. I'm so used to the cameras and the mics, to the whole technological jumble I've been living with for months, that I've forgotten I can do without them! The reality is, there's only the glass of my visor between me and the stalagmite. If I was able to hear the crystal vibrating without my earphones, then Marcus should be able to hear my voice resonating – so long as I'm shouting, not murmuring.

'**Don't do that! I forbid it!**' I shout as loud as I can, the moment he brings his hands back to his helmet.

He freezes.

He heard me!

Realising that he can speak to me too, he shouts back.

The volume of his rough voice is reduced by the two visors it has to pass through, but it reaches me.

'And I forbid you from staying! I came here to lose myself. I only stopped my rover when I ran into Kenji's. It's my turn to disappear after him. You've got to get out of here, go back to the living!'

My heart rises in my throat.

'That's how you thank me for having got you your freedom? That's how you thank me for coming to see you one last time?'

'You shouldn't have done it,' he roars, frowning angrily. 'Your place is with Mozart. In the elevator.'

'And what if I decide it's here, with you, for the rest of your life?' I say, spluttering with rage and distress against my visor.

'Then you leave me no choice. Once I've died for good, if that's what's keeping you here, there'll be nothing to stop you turning back.'

For a third time, he grabs the rim of his helmet, and this time I know I won't have the element of surprise to unbalance him and stop him from doing what can't be undone.

'Wait! I can't turn back now! In one hour I'm also going to die, I won't have any oxygen left in my suit!'

It's a lie, but Marcus has no way of knowing that.

His expression changes instantly, the cold determination to put an end to it all giving way to alarm.

'You won't have any oxygen left?' he asks, his voice so weak now I can barely hear it.

'No!' I say, my throat sore from the shouting. 'I left the base in a hurry, without recharging my survival unit! That's what's

635

written on the control screen of my visor, I can see it: I've only got fifty-nine minutes of O_2 left!'

Marcus's gloves let go of his helmet and drop slowly down.

A heartrending moan comes from his lips.

'Léonor! Oh, Léonor!'

His eyes are getting moist now.

'**I didn't manage to save you! My lies were no use after all!**'

I hurry towards him, taking his shoulders in my arms.

'**Stop going back over those lies again and again!**' I shout, the rising adrenaline making my heart beat even harder. '**You've confessed them already! You've atoned for them already! And I . . . I've already forgiven you!**'

I shout these words almost aggressively, as if I was breaking free of my chains, or taking my revenge.

The thoughts race through my overexcited mind: as soon as Marcus has calmed down, I'll tell him I actually do have enough oxygen. I'll take him back with me to the rover, and to the self-energising elevator! I'll come up with some story to tell the viewers to explain his resurrection! The other pioneers won't dare to put the Noah Report back on the table! I defy them to try to separate us again!

But Marcus doesn't seem about to calm down.

Maybe he didn't hear me?

'**I've forgiven you for your lies!**' I shout again, even louder now.

'**You don't understand . . .**' he gulps, tears streaming down his cheeks, marking furrows on his visor. '**My confessions *were* the lies! I . . . I didn't know about the Noah Report before we boarded the rocket.**'

106. Off-screen

Meanwhile, 45 million miles from Mars . . .

Transit capsule lift-off – 13h 00m

'Here in Times Square, in New York City, the atmosphere is scorching!' the journalist says into his microphone. The temperature at least does seem to be scorching, judging by the way he's sweating through his open-necked shirt.

He steps aside to allow the cameraman to take in the famous square currently flooded with sunshine, surrounded by buildings covered in screens – all of them showing pictures from the Genesis channel, of the Martian base where the pioneers are awaiting the arrival of their elevator.

As on each of Genesis's great occasions over the last two years, the place is thronged with a crowd so dense it's practically impossible to see even a centimetre of tarmac. From the launch to the marriage ceremony, the general public has always shown up, in ever greater numbers, to commune with the pioneers on their most momentous occasions. The imminent meeting of the Season One participants with their Season Two counterparts, up in the Cupido, is definitely one of those climaxes, and people are already here in huge crowds, well before the scheduled time.

Despite the state of emergency, there's a festive mood, some excitement on this hot Manhattan day. Children are holding red helium balloons shaped like the planet Mars; here and there, embracing couples are together biting into giant toffee apples, specially grown to resemble those on Mars. Everybody, young and old, is certain that President McBee is going to save the pioneers from the Great Storm, while also providing them with a sensational spectacle just as she promised.

However, this joyful atmosphere, like an open-air cinema – such an American experience on this stunning summer day – is strictly boxed in by the steel barriers dividing the whole square into segments, along with the streets and avenues around it. A reinforced security team is patrolling the walkways: soldiers in black combat gear, submachine-guns in their hands. But the surveillance isn't only coming from the soldiers, who are doing the job they were trained for; every few metres, amid the smiling civilians, are positioned men, women and teenagers wearing the Citizens Swarm uniform. They are not carrying guns. But alveoli cameras glint around their necks, and shining earpieces are fixed to their temples.

The camera focuses back on the journalist, as he repeats, like the host at a drive-in just before the session begins, 'That's right, a scorching atmosphere! In six hours' time, the self-energising space elevator will touch down on Mars. And seven hours later, it will take off again, carrying the Season One pioneers, who will spend a month in space – that's the time it will take for the Great Storm to come to an end. But how many of them will there be on board that elevator? After the loss of Marcus and Kenji, will they also have to leave without Léonor . . . ?'

Zap!

From her glass-and-steel desk, Phoebe Delville presses the remote control she's holding. Her eyes are focused, under her fringe of gleaming hair, the same deep black as her smoky eye make-up and her designer suit.

Opposite her, on the wall of a huge room furnished in a minimalist design, between the large windows looking out over the Los Angeles skyline, there's a flat screen showing news channels from all over the world with simultaneous translation. For the woman inheriting a group like Eden Food International, who is also responsible for the partnership with the Genesis programme, it's vital to be able to remain in close contact with current events.

The young woman's attention is suddenly caught by a French channel.

Long shot of the Champs-Élysées, in Paris, where people have gathered regularly over the last two years, alternately to cheer or to boo and hiss their strange and unpredictable representative.

It's late afternoon, but for this special occasion the city lighting has already come on all the way up the avenue, as well as on the Arc de Triomphe, below which there hangs a large screen showing the Genesis channel. While the heat is as stifling as in New York, the mood is less cheerful, tenser. Some members of the public have lit small candles to represent their hope that Léonor is still alive – or is it to come to terms with having lost her already?

A reporter appears on the screen, her forehead gleaming despite the anti-shine powder covering it. 'This evening, the whole of France

639

holds her breath,' she says seriously into her microphone. 'Where is Léonor? Where is the girl who for the last two years has worn our colours, and embodied our dreams? Even if she is officially a Martian, now that France has come into line with her American allies in recognising the pioneers' independence, she'll always be a French girl in the hearts of a lot of viewers.'

The reporter turns to an old woman with carefully set white hair, sitting with a glass of Perrier at one of the café terraces that have been overrun with visitors.

She sticks the microphone under the old woman's nose. 'I gather you are one of the people who've been here since this morning, madame?'

'We have both been here since this morning, Mirza and I,' the old lady corrects her, pointing to the dog lying on her lap. 'At our age, we're frankly better off here in the fresh air than in our building where there's still no air conditioning – and we've asked the condo for it enough times, I tell you . . . And besides, we came to support Léonor during the Great Storm. We had no idea she was going to throw herself right into the middle of it!'

The reporter nods despondently. Then she moves the microphone a little closer to her interviewee's mouth, hoping for some emotion. 'So tell me – what does Léonor mean to you, a pensioner who lives alone with her dog? Is she, perhaps, a bit like a granddaughter to you?'

The old lady is silent for a moment.

Distractedly she strokes Mirza's fur, thinking about the question instead of just trotting out some pre-formed, predictable answer, as her questioner is expecting, and as the pathos of the moment demands.

'A granddaughter?' she says finally. 'No. I'm very well aware *that despite all the hours I've spent in front of the Genesis channel, I hardly know Léonor. The truth is, who on Earth can really claim to know this orphan girl who grew up without a family? Whether we boo her or praise her to the skies . . . whether we stick up posters of her beauty in the Rosier campaigns or turn away from the sight of her scar . . . whether we compliment her calm as a doctor or call her a hysterical lunatic . . . none of us here knows who she really is, or what's going on in her head.'*

There's a mischievous twinkle in the old lady's eyes; she puts her hand on the arm of the reporter holding out the mic. 'You do know, young lady, a TV reality show is not really reality.'

'Huh? I, um, yeah, of course . . .' stammers the reporter, caught off guard.

She's about to pull back the mic and go in search of a more conventional eyewitness, but the old lady's hand is still weighing on her arm – she's not done yet. 'You asked what Léonor means to me? Well then, this is what she means. The unknown. The unpredictable. The little will-o'-the-wisp redhead who follows her own path, even in the best-planned show.' She thinks for another moment, searching for just the right words. 'Léonor is the flame of freedom!'

Zap!

Phoebe Delville changes the channel again.

She seems somewhat troubled by the description of the French pioneer.

Surfing distractedly around the global TV landscape, she stops more or less at random on a Russian channel.

* * *

A radical change of décor: after the human tides that have swept across Times Square and the Champs-Élysées, Moscow's Red Square is like a desert.

Here there are no giant screens broadcasting live pictures from Mars, no barriers set up to contain the crowds: there's not a soul to be seen.

The image gives way to a presenter seated at his desk, his face tense.

'Good evening, my fellow patriots. As you can see from these pictures, this is an evening just like any other here in Russia. No pointless gatherings, no useless excitement: there is calm on the streets of Moscow. You can sleep soundly in your beds tonight.'

After this introduction, which is intended to be reassuring, he coughs and then continues with the real message he's been asked to convey.

'The government has instructed us to remind you that the Genesis channel is now banned in Russia. Any attempt to access it, via the internet or any other means, will be punished. I repeat: any attempt to watch the Genesis channel will be punished.'

There's a ringing in Phoebe Delville's office, making her turn her attention temporarily away from the screen.

She presses a button on the phone on her glass desk.

'Yes?'

'Miss Delville, James has just woken from his nap, and he's calling for you. Shall I bring him to you, or are you too busy following the progress of Logan, the new Eden Food-sponsored candidate?'

'Bring James to me, Adelaide. There's nothing to watch

642

now anyway – there's nothing to do but wait for the elevator capsule.'

The heiress brings the conversation to an end and looks back at the screen, which is currently showing a Japanese channel.

Beyond New York and Paris, further east than Moscow, it's the middle of the night in Japan. And yet the square at Shinjuku Station is brightly lit, packed with people. Even though the Japanese pioneer died four months ago in the Martian desert, the Japanese people's passion for the programme hasn't cooled – on the contrary. The Tokyoites are getting ready to stay up all night to offer their joint support for the surviving pioneers, watching big screens that have been put up on the side of the station, with (for some, at least) a bit of hope remaining that Kenji might yet return from the dead. In the front rows, the now-famous outfits of the members of the temple of Cosmic Unification can be seen: their kimonos and the white hachimakis tied around their heads. They are there in their thousands. Some of them are holding up portraits of the two 'Jewels' and the mysterious Cydonia 'face'; others are carrying out their tai-chi ritual which is supposed to send positive cosmic rays to Mars; the whole thing is surrounded by a police cordon, to prevent a riot.

A very slight journalist enters the shot, microphone in hand. 'This evening in Shinjuku, the Cosmicists have gathered in large numbers, despite their sect still being illegal in Japan,' she says in a thin voice. 'Extortion, intimidation, kidnappings . . . The movement created in the late 1980s by the Yoshiki Lama has been condemned many times by the justice department, and its main leaders are today rotting away behind bars. As for the faces they

643

claim to see sculpted on the Martian surface by a hypothetical unknown civilisation, scientific analysis of the images has long since proven them to be no more than natural geological formations. But the movement's crimes and demystified beliefs don't seem to be dissuading an ever-growing number of people – a group getting younger by the day, and more and more international – from pledging themselves as Cosmicists.'

The journalist slips cautiously under the police cordon towards a group of young Western adherents to the faith.

She holds her mic out to a tall blonde girl, whose long straight hair is held back elegantly by her hachimaki.

'Hello, miss,' begins the journalist, in English.

'Call me Sakura-Shirley,' answers the girl. Her big smile is radiant with hope and confidence.

'Hello, Sakura-Shirley. Have you and your friends travelled a long way to be here tonight?'

'We've come from all over the United States. We've crossed the Atlantic, then Europe and Asia. It's kind of like a pilgrimage for us, you know? It's such a great honour to be here, in the country of Kenji's birth! Glory to the Celestial Jewel!'

'Glory to the Celestial Jewel!' echo her companions in a thunderous chorus.

The journalist – slightly concerned – glances over at the police, as if to reassure herself that they would be able to contain the fervour of these believers if it were to get out of hand.

'And do you really think you're going to be seeing Kenji on those screens again, four months after he disappeared, when all the experts are certain there's absolutely no chance at all that he's still alive?' she asks.

A light comes on in Sakura-Shirley's eyes, a mixture of faith and determination.

'Yeah, we know that Kenji might have returned to the Great Cosmic Body – but what we want to see now is Them*!'*

Phoebe turns off her TV when there is a knock at her office door.

'Come in!'

A nanny in a tracksuit bearing the Eden Food initials comes into the room, holding the hand of a little one-and-a-half-year-old boy, with long brown curls and a face entirely dominated by two huge grey eyes.

A smile lights up his cute little face.

'Ma-ma!' he says.

He lets go of Adelaide's hand and runs over to his young mother.

'He's so fearless for his age!' says the nanny, delighted. 'I'll bet his father was a real adventurer, a great explorer! Isn't that right, Miss Delville?'

'Now, listen, Adelaide – my family and the press have both tried to get me to talk, so don't you start now!' says Phoebe, her voice sharp and inflexible, the voice of someone used to being in charge. 'Once and for all, I don't owe anybody an explanation and I will never reveal his father's identity. He didn't want a child, and I did, so I did it all on my own without his knowledge. And that's that.'

She takes the toddler in her arms and her voice turns gentle right away.

'But you're right, yes, he was an adventurer . . . a shooting star.'

107. Shot

Month 18 / sol 484 / 04:05 Mars time
[603rd sol since landing]
Transit capsule lift-off – 12h 55m

'I didn't know about the Noah Report before we boarded the rocket. There was no computer in the Genesis animal store, only cages, nothing but cages!'

What?

What did Marcus just say?

I feel like I'm struggling to understand his words, suddenly, through the double barrier of our visors.

'**It's all because of the self-energising elevator,**' he pants behind his helmet, his cheeks streaked with tears. '**When they told us about the plans, I knew deep down that I couldn't go back to Earth to die of my illness there like a beggar, after so long dreaming about being extinguished in the sky like a star. But I also knew I could never be the ball and chain that would stop *you* from leaving, from going back towards life.**'

Slowly I let go of Marcus's shoulders.

'**I didn't want you to decide to stay on Mars to die with me, so I invented a repulsive crime to make you hate me!**' he shouts, his voice rasping, a thread of snot escaping from his nose.

646

The last two years race through my mind.

'I accused myself of a terrible betrayal so you'd reject me!' he yells, his mouth foaming with saliva.

All those empty days, all those sad evenings and lonely mornings . . . meant nothing at all?

'It's Mozart you should have married, right from the beginning!' Marcus turns around and hits the immense crystal column behind him furiously, so hard it looks like he might dislocate his shoulder. 'He was the guy who said you were precious like jarosite crystal! I was sure you'd be happy with him – that he'd look after you, like a treasure, that you'd have children with him, without having to be afraid of passing some genetic illness on to them, however small and manageable the risk. But he's not here now, and you're running out of oxygen. I'm coming close to the all-time record for surviving between D66 attacks, and I know I haven't got long left – but you had your whole life ahead of you! And now you're going to die too, when you should have lived, lived, LIVED!'

He slumps down at the foot of the impassive crystal, like an electronic toy astronaut that's been broken and tossed away into the trash, stuck on the same pre-recorded refrain – 'You should have lived . . . You should have lived . . .'

Marcus is innocent.

He always has been.

The confessions, the trial, the detention – the whole thing was no more than a smokescreen, a big illusion, the highlight of the show before the performer vanishes into thin air, melting into space.

(He chose the planet Mars over you . . .) a very familiar voice

starts hissing in my ear. *(He chose to die alone rather than spending his last few days by your side . . . He chose . . . cho . . . ch . . .)*

Strangely, I can hardly hear the Salamander, in these desolate depths where it should be shrieking like all the organs of hell.

Weirdly, I have no trouble suppressing it, even faced with this enormous waste that should be pitching me into an abyss of rage and despair.

On the contrary, I feel a wave of peacefulness wash over me, sweeping away even the feverish avenging restlessness that took me over at the thought of bringing Marcus back to the base, forcing him onto the other pioneers, the Genesis organisers, the viewers all over the Earth.

In my photographic memory, I look back on that other moment when he was on the verge of death, before the execution of his sentence, when the syringe was about to empty its poison into his flesh.

I see his arm with the prominent veins . . .

His skin blossoming with tattoos . . .

The mysterious shape of Schrödinger's cat . . .

The word CHOICE carved into the crook of his elbow . . .

. . . which spins around in my mind, appearing upside-down to show the word *DESTINY*.

Destiny

I crouch down next to Marcus, pressing my helmet against his. A slight vibration makes our visors tremble; it's the noise of his muffled sobs.

'**I will live, Marcus, I promise you,**' – pressed right up to him, in the middle of this silent crypt where no wind has ever blown, I realise I barely need to raise my voice to make myself heard.

He looks up, his eyes misted up, the colour of the sky after a tempest.

'**But . . . your oxygen . . .**'

'**I've got enough left to get back up to my rover, return to the base and catch the self-energising elevator in time.**'

An expression of pure joy appears on his face, chasing away the clouds in his eyes and any reproach for my having lied to him: there's nothing left but the gladness that I'm going to survive.

I engrave this picture of a dazzling sun into my memory, for ever.

'**I can't go with you, my love . . .**' he says, with a sudden shiver.

'I know.'

'Please try to understand . . .'

'I do understand, my beautiful Marcus.'

I try my best to smile.

I manage it effortlessly.

Because I really do understand Marcus – completely, totally – for the first time.

'*I can't change the direction of the wind, but I can adjust my sails to always reach my destination.* That's James Dean, right?'

Marcus nods.

His beautiful eyes widen like two whole universes expanding.

From them I draw the strength to experience this moment, the most intense moment I've ever known. In them I find the eloquence I thought only he possessed. As if, despite the non-negotiable barrier of our suits separating our bodies that have never truly made love, and which never will, we were at this moment and for ever, each of us a part of one another.

'**When you were fifteen, the doctors planted a fatal diagnosis on your forehead, and social services planned for you to end your days in a home. But you refused to accept this sad story, this epigraph written in advance by other people, choosing instead to create your own legend. You couldn't change the direction of your genetic wind blowing you towards the grave, but you adjusted your sails: you ran away from the hospitals to throw yourself into a life on the road, in space, all the way to Mars. You transformed lead into gold. You transformed your fate into your choice. You transformed a predetermined destiny into a destination you have chosen!**'

I'm not crying any more, because I know that despite all our doubts and our fears, beyond all the errors of judgment we've made and the misunderstandings that have kept us apart for so long, Marcus's is a story of conquest, the noblest thing a man can achieve in this world: the conquest of freedom.

'**I promise I'll live, Marcus,**' I say again, feeling myself suddenly filled with a new strength, which I know will never leave me again.

I no longer have any doubts about what comes next, for me.

There'll be no more lying, hesitating, allowing myself to be tossed about in the winds blown by Serena.

The time has come to adjust my sails. I'll go up in the elevator; once I'm up there, I'll reveal everything; I'll fight the president and I'll win; at the end of the journey, I will return to an Earth that won't be hers, but mine: my world, my own destination!

'**I promise I'll brave all the Serenas in the universe to make myself as free in my life as you've been in yours – you, my star, a dark star but such a radiant one!**'

'**My red giant . . .**' he murmurs, smiling sweetly, tenderly.

He slips his glove into the all-purpose pocket of his suit and pulls out a carefully folded piece of red fabric. It's my chiffon dress. The one I thought I'd lost.

'**Liz gave it to me,**' Marcus admits. '**I fell asleep with it under my cheek every night for two years, so I could be with you.**'

He unfolds the gossamer fabric and holds it above our heads, like a bridal canopy.

We stay like this for some time, in the chiffon cloud, arms around one another, bathed in one another's gaze, like two stars fusing together in the middle of a reddening nebula.

And then suddenly I feel Marcus's breathing falter. In a matter of seconds, his spacesuit stops its regular rise and fall beneath my gloves.

'Marcus . . . ?' I say.

'The D66 mutation . . . It's time . . . I recognise its scent . . . the sound of its footsteps . . . all those senses, like five years ago . . . But I'm not afraid any more.'

Horror jolts me awake, the nameless terror of nothingness, the colossal anguish of losing him for ever.

I open my mouth to scream, but Marcus stops me with a smile.

'I no longer need a chiffon pillow under my cheek . . .' he says, his voice weaker with every passing second but echoing more and more loudly within me. 'I no longer need a pen-knifed tattoo in my flesh . . . I'll be with you for ever . . .' With one final gesture, he places his hand on my heart, this man who once carved my name onto his. '. . . here.'

My fear evaporates instantly.

His eyes, speckled with stars, blink one last time.

His peaceful smile is engraved onto his handsome face, for all eternity.

108. Genesis Channel

Wednesday 21 August, 5:00pm
$\boxed{\textit{Transit capsule lift-off – 07h 00m}}$

Open onto Mars, as seen from space. The whole southern hemisphere is now no more than a gigantic blur: an entire half-planet covered in dust.

A caption appears at the bottom of the screen: SPACE VIEW FILMED FROM REAR *CUPIDO* CAMERA / MARS TIME 10:00 / RELEASE OF TRANSIT CAPSULE

The camera pivots silently on its axis, revealing the moon Phobos, in the wake of which the vessel is in orbit. From this angle, that celestial body looks more like a human skull than ever, and the main communications antenna relaying all the images from the base to Earth resembles a needle lodged in one of its eye sockets.

The camera pivots further. A second structure appears, between the spacecraft and the moon, also aligned in the same orbit – a giant umbrella, two hundred metres in diameter: the newly deployed self-energised satellite, crammed full of the rays of the sun that's shining behind it.

Suddenly a small ovoid shape detaches from the satellite.

It's the transit capsule. It hurtles towards the surface of Mars, with no detectable retrorockets at work: there's also no obvious sign of the powerful beam of microwaves guiding it from the satellite. Driven by this invisible, almost magical wind, the capsule disappears into the opaque atmosphere, directly above the Valles Marineris, just south of the storm front that's stretching out over the whole planet.

The great self-energised satellite, meanwhile, continues on its majestic, elliptical course.

When it next passes over the canyon, in exactly seven hours' time, it will be to bring the capsule back up with its passengers on board.

109. Off-screen

Cellar of the Villa McBee, Long Island, New York State
Wednesday 21 August, 8:52pm
$\boxed{\textit{Transit capsule lift-off – 03h 43m}}$

There is a metallic rolling sound from behind the cell door.

Andrew looks up, like a dog driven by a Pavlovian response: the lunch trolley, which comes past regularly to bring the meals and take away the dishes, has been his only chronological reference point since he's been locked up in the cellars of the Villa McBee.

Behind his cracked glasses, Andrew's face, which hasn't seen daylight in four months, is pale and gaunt. His body, which had already become thinner after the amputation of his foot, is now even scrawnier. The orange jumpsuit he's wearing over his hunched shoulders is heavy with damp, so that fungus is starting to grow on it. At his feet is a tray with the remains of a bland meal, waiting to be taken away on the next evening circuit.

The reinforced door squeals open on its hinges, to reveal the trolley being pushed by a woman in military fatigues, cap pulled down low over her eyes.

Andrew cowers a little further against the wall to which he's chained – a small remnant of dignity that comes over him whenever somebody else's eyes are on him: he refuses to let anybody see the human wreck he's become.

The soldier enters the room; she walks past the tray without even pausing and leans over the prisoner.

He flinches; expecting a blow, he draws in his head, closes his eyes . . .

. . . but instead of the dull sound of the Rangers boots on his sides, he hears the click of the padlock releasing his chains.

That's even worse than being kicked: they're going to drag him into the laboratory again to extract a confession!

'I've told you everything already!' he cries. His voice is a real animal wail. 'I haven't got anything else to confess!'

The soldier puts her hand on his shoulder.

'Andrew . . .' she says gently, in a voice that's . . . familiar.

The young man finally dares to look up.

In the shadow of the cap he can make out a face he knows, red hair tucked under the brim, eyes full of empathy, so unlike the soldiers who usually treat Andrew like the dangerous terrorist they've been led to believe he is.

'C-Cindy . . . ?' he stammers.

She brings a finger to her lips and helps him up, leaving his unlocked chains behind him.

Twelve minutes later.

Andrew is sitting on a bench in the rear compartment of a military truck into which he's been led, after leaving the villa by the service elevator. With a blanket over his shoulders and a thermos of coffee in his hands, he finds himself sitting opposite Barry Mirwood and Cecilia and Miguel Rodriguez, all of whom are as skinny as he is. A young African-American soldier, barely older than Andrew, is on guard duty at the back of the truck; he's sitting behind a bulky computer, which is connected to a camera that's pointing at the passengers like the mouth of a cannon. On the side wall of the vehicle, a large screen is tuned to the Genesis channel.

The two panels of the rear door open suddenly, making Andrew jump. He spills a bit of his coffee – part of him still believes that this is a trap, some kind of twisted new torture that's come out of Serena McBee's Machiavellian brain.

'Here's the final prisoner on today's guest list – we can go now,' murmurs Cindy.

She climbs into the truck, followed by a third soldier who's escorting a giant dressed in the same orange jumpsuit as the other prisoners – but this one hasn't had his handcuffs removed.

Andrew's eyes widen, and the thermos starts to tremble in his hands: he's immediately recognised Gordon Lock, the erstwhile technical director of the Genesis programme.

'Cindy, what does this all mean?' Andrew babbles hoarsely, in a voice that's lost the habit of speaking, while the vehicle pulls away into the dusk, guided by an invisible driver.

'You needn't worry, Andrew. You're safe.' She turns towards the other passengers who are staring at her, looking drawn and worried.

'You're all safe now.'

She takes off her hat, freeing her red-dyed hair, which she now wears short.

The soldier who boarded the truck with her does the same, revealing the square face of an athletic-looking forty-something.

'This is Captain Derek Jacobson,' she says quietly. 'Other members of our unit are driving the truck now. We're going through the checkpoints surrounding the Villa McBee, which explains why we'll be stopping frequently. But don't worry – on the route we're taking, all the soldiers are on our side, on the side of the Wild Bees.'

A flash of determination crosses the rebel's face – she seems so unlike the quiet little waitress Andrew used to know.

'I owe you an explanation,' she says to him. 'And an apology. I shouldn't have run away like I did, a year and a half ago. I should have believed you when you tried to persuade me how dangerous Serena McBee was. The things that have happened since then have proved you right a thousand times over . . . Specially since her rise to the presidency.' She breathes out slowly, and puts her hand on the captain's – he takes it tenderly. 'As soon as Serena declared martial law and was granted plenary powers, one section of the army started distrusting her – among them my Derek, who's my husband now. The president's increasingly authoritarian decisions, the setting-up of the Citizens Swarm, the increased numbers of surveillance drones in the public space . . . Well, anyway, the concerns of those officers who were worried about the Constitution just grew as the months went by. And I remembered everything you'd told me about that crazy woman, everything I'd refused to believe at the time.'

A bitter smile appears on Cindy's face, while the truck starts up again after another stop, this time to keep going without any further interruptions. Even though we can't see anything of the night-time landscape from this neon-lit, windowless compartment, we can guess that the vehicle has finally made it onto the federal highway.

'It's not too late,' she says, turning to the prisoners. 'Right across the nation, there are men and women ready to rise up against the president, in the real world and in the virtual world, on the streets and on the internet – there are soldiers refusing to follow unjust orders, but also civilians, because the Wild Bees have been forming their little nests of freedom in every stratum of society!'

A patriotic flame lights up in Cindy's eyes, reflecting the courage of those generations before her who fought to build and protect the American dream.

'We've been planning Operation Apocalypse for months,' she continues. 'We've chosen the name as the exact opposite of Genesis – that fake creation of a new world that's bewitched the people of Earth. The media apocalypse we're planning should mark an end to Serena McBee. Freeing all of you is the first phase – Andrew, Gordon, Cecilia and Barry, you're our four horsemen of the apocalypse, whose testimony will strike four great blows at the heart of the tyrant. We've chosen to get you out at the exact moment when all eyes in the Villa McBee are turned towards space, towards the Martian storm, towards the Genesis channel. The guards have ended their shifts, so nobody will notice your disappearance tonight.

'In three hours, when the pioneers board the self-energising elevator and are finally safe from the threat of depressurisation, we'll launch phase two: the release of damning testimonies on Genesis's own screens!' Cindy turns to Andrew. 'It was you who inspired that idea: hacking the channel the way you did a year and a half ago, when you revealed the plans for the self-energising space elevator to the world.'

'I don't understand,' says the young man. 'The Genesis transmission codes have changed . . .'

'We managed to get hold of the new codes, thanks to our informers at Cape Canaveral. The long process of infiltration was possible due to the presence of officers at the launch base who are supportive of the Wild Bees' cause. By transforming the place into a militarised fortress, Serena allowed us right into the heart of her sprawling network of lies!'

Cindy's eyes blaze a bit brighter in the neon light, while Captain Jacobson gets up and goes over to the screen attached to the wall of the truck.

'Officer cadet: the ops plan!' he commands the soldier who is sitting behind the computer.

'Right away, captain!'

The cadet touches a few keys on his computer keyboard; the Genesis channel disappears; the dumbfounded prisoners watch as a vast battlefield, comprising tens of millions of square kilometres, appears on the wall screen.

'This is the centre of operations,' says the captain in a martial tone, curt and entirely confident. 'We're going to beat the enemy at her own game, turning her own weapons against her. A quick briefing on the functioning of the Genesis interplanetary network – you'll forgive us for not showing the supplementary satellites or the converted laser or radio signals, in the interests of keeping things simple.

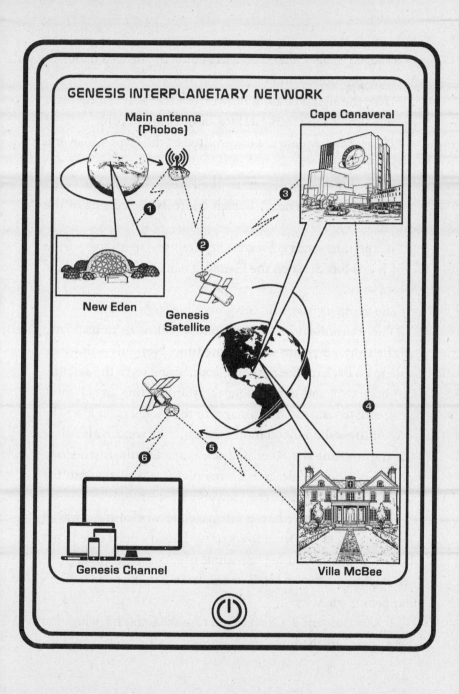

'One: all images filmed on Mars come up, first, to the main antenna positioned on Phobos;

'Two: the signal coming down from the Martian moon is received by the Genesis satellite, in the Earth's orbit;

'Three: the raw data are transmitted to the Cape Canaveral base in Florida;

'Four: the transmission is then sent on to the Villa McBee, where the enemy herself controls the editing of the broadcast . . .

'. . . then she sends it back to the satellite – that's five – from which it is broadcast on the Genesis channel across the whole world – six.'

The captain crosses his arms over his large chest.

'The transmission codes are going to allow us to hack into all the strategic points at the same time. Not only will we be able to go back up the network, connecting us to the satellite in phase two, and eliminating the transmitting signal going upstream to send our own images to the pioneers on Mars the way Andrew did nineteen months ago; but we can also clear the transmitting signal coming *down*, heading downstream to phase six, and broadcast the same pictures directly onto the Genesis channel where the viewers can see them.

'The only thing we haven't managed to work out is a way of receiving the signal from Mars, as we haven't been able to get hold of the codes: during the whole of Operation Apocalypse, we might have to act blind, without being able to see what's happening on Mars.

'In short: at time *T*, Officer Cadet Franklin, this I.T. whizz-kid here from our shadow army, will personally run the hacking

662

into the network right from this truck, which is fitted with a parabolic antenna.'

'Ready to defend my country, captain!' replies the officer cadet, clicking his heels behind the camera. He also adds a few gushing words about his admiration for Andrew's benefit: 'May I say, sir, it's an honour to meet the mastermind behind *Genesis Piracy*, a masterpiece of the hacker's art! You're seriously one of the greats!'

'We estimate having a maximum of one hour before the Genesis teams manage to identify the source of the piracy and resolve the problem,' Captain Jacobson concludes, unfolding a plan that has been developed down to its tiniest details. 'During this hour, the nation's destiny will be in play. While the prisoners broadcast their testimonies live from this truck, our commando squads posted at Cape Canaveral, at the Villa McBee and in Washington will spring into action on the ground, to convince our brothers in arms to join us and to reassure the people. They'll only open fire in cases of extreme necessity.'

'A coup d'état without any bloodshed – it's possible!' says Cindy enthusiastically. 'We want to defeat Serena McBee without doing even more harm than she's already done to this country we love so much. With one weapon alone: truth! Yes, the Wild Bees are only a minority, but we're convinced your testimonies *can* sway public opinion – the American people are a great people, who throughout history have always been ready to accept the truth, however hard it might be!'

She turns to the man who, in his time, was the Genesis programme's number two.

'You, Gordon Lock: we know you once had a hand in Serena's little schemes, and we also know that she extracted false confessions from you on the air, to make you accuse the Russians and justify her policy of autocratic isolation. It's time to redeem yourself, by revealing what you know – the transitional government that takes power after the tyrant is defeated will show you some clemency.'

The fallen man's eyes are wet with tears, and he's trembling with gratitude. He tips his bald head forward in a nod of agreement.

'You, Barry Mirwood: you thought you could trust a psychiatrist, a scientist like you are, but she turned you into her slave. The time has come to show the whole of the international scientific community the true face of Professor McBee.'

The scientist, who has been particularly changed by his detention, his face emaciated under a beard that's curly with damp, also agrees, clenching his fists.

'You, Cecilia Rodriguez: your husband incriminated himself when he came into contact with Serena, and his remorse sadly came too late – and he paid the ultimate price. You can redeem his memory and correct his failings by giving testimony beside us.'

The Cuban-American widow takes hold of her cousin Miguel's arm. 'Ruben will be avenged!' she swears.

'You, Andrew, who I insisted on liberating in person: your testimony will be the most valuable of all, because you've been tested more harshly than anyone. The Genesis programme cost you your leg, so you'll have a disability for the rest of your life. It took your father, who burned his wings when he tried to fly in the same skies as this demon. It's taken your mother and sister too, as they've been held hostage at Cape Canaveral for over a year, without their knowledge, thinking they were being protected by their government while really they were prisoners.' Cindy pauses. 'But the president made a mistake. When she thought you were finally past being able to harm her, locked away in her jail, she sent Vivian and Lucy back to California a few weeks ago – officially because they no longer constituted a priority target for the terrorists, but really because Serena no longer needed them to put pressure on you.'

With these words, Cindy slips her hand into one of the pockets of her fatigues and pulls out a cellphone.

'The house in Beverly Hills was sold to clear the debts your father left,' she says as she dials a number. 'Vivian and Lucy are now living in a small apartment in a suburb of L.A. That's where our men went to find them, less than an hour ago, to escort them to a secure location. Here . . .'

She holds out the cellphone to Andrew, who grabs it in his sweaty hand.

'Hello?' he says quietly into the phone.

'*Andrew . . . ?*' cries a voice he hasn't heard in nearly two years. '*Is that you, Andrew?*'

'Mom . . .'

Behind his cracked glasses, his eyes have started to shine.

'*You're alive, son! So the men who came to fetch us were telling the truth! Where . . . where are you?*'

Cindy shakes her head to signal to Andrew that he shouldn't say too much, it's still too early.

'I . . . I'm safe, Mom,' he stammers. 'I'll see you soon, you and Lucy. In the meantime, you've got to do what those men tell you, OK?'

A second voice bursts suddenly out of the phone.

'Drew! Come back . . . come back home!'

The young man's face is seized by an uncontrollable twitching – the last time he heard this voice, it was still high-pitched and childlike; it's resonant and feminine now, the voice of a young woman, not a kid. So much wasted time!

There's too much emotion.

Andrew cracks.

A sob shakes his skinny frame.

The phone slips from his fingers.

Cindy picks it up gently.

'He'll call you back later,' she says – and she's overwhelmed, too. 'Better than that, he'll be able to hug you in person. Just a few more hours to wait, I promise.'

She hangs up and puts the phone away, then leans over to Andrew to try to calm him.

'You're a national hero!' she says. 'The only person who stood up to Serena McBee, back in the day when the entire world was in thrall to her charms!'

'No, I wasn't the only one,' he says, taking off his glasses to wipe his cheeks of the tears that are embarrassing him. 'There was somebody else with me. Don't tell me you've forgotten her.'

A shadow passes across Cindy's face.

'I'll never forget Harmony,' she says. 'And when we've triumphed, we'll get justice for her, we'll make sure America never forgets her.'

'You mean . . . ?'

'We've got to expect the worst. She disappeared the day you were captured.'

Cindy takes Andrew's hands in hers.

'We mustn't lose heart, not now! Think about Vivian, about Lucy . . . about Harmony! If she's fallen, then you've got to get yourself back up all the stronger, stand firmer than ever. To honour her memory. To let the whole world see the Noah Report that the two of you safeguarded!'

A confident smile, already anticipating victory, appears on Cindy's face.

'So tell us everything, Andrew,' she says. 'In what little crannies of the global internet have you hidden your copies of the Noah Report? That dossier's going to be our fatal weapon, which will kill Serena when it strikes her!'

But Andrew doesn't share her enthusiasm.

'I don't have access to it any more,' he says with a grimace.

The smile freezes on Cindy's face.

'What?'

'The Noah Report. Serena forced me to reveal all the locations where I'd backed it up. She . . . she's wiped them all. I wasn't allowed to sleep or eat, and under hypnosis with truth serum in my veins, there was no way I could resist her.' The young man's voice cracks. 'But I did fight it. I swear I did fight . . . but those eyes of hers! Those horrible snake eyes!'

'It's not serious, Andrew, we'll manage without it,' murmurs Cindy. 'We've been planning this operation for such a long time, all the Wild Bees are in position to act. And we still have the testimony from the other prisoners.'

But she's finding it hard to hide her disappointment, even her distress.

'That does change our plans, though, my love,' mutters Captain Jacobson, dropping his military manner. 'That report was going to be the centrepiece of our attack, the tangible proof we could use to unite the army, Congress and the public to call for the president's impeachment. Everything else, as you say, is witness statements . . . and witness statements are always taken with some scepticism.'

For a few seconds, nobody says another word; the only sound is the engine going faster and faster, like a train on its tracks, which nobody can stop.

'There's something my old boss Mr Bill always used to say, when we were preparing breakfast for the guests at the motel,' Cindy says finally. '*Coffee boiled is coffee spoiled.*' She looks up, determined again. 'Our coffee is ready to be served. At seventeen hundred hours Mars time, when the pioneers are safe in their transit capsules, which is midnight Eastern. It'll be incredibly strong coffee too, a bit of shock therapy to wake America up, and the world, from the long hypnotic sleep Serena McBee's had them in. We can't postpone Operation Apocalypse at this point – with or without the Noah Report, we've got to go for it!'

110. Reverse Shot

The Villa McBee, Long Island, New York State
Wednesday 21 August, 11:15pm
Transit capsule lift-off – 45m

'My dear Martians, the time has come!' says Serena McBee from her desk, where she's sitting opposite the aluminium gantry. 'Up in the sky, above the dust clouds, the self-energised satellite is getting ready to fly back over Ius Chasma. In three quarters of an hour, it will be able to transmit microwaves from a point precisely perpendicular to the surface of the valley; the optimal conditions for bringing the transit capsule back up. The time has come for you to leave the base!'

She claps her hands, like a schoolteacher announcing the end of break-time.

'Don't worry, you won't be outside long enough for the dust to cause any abrasions to your suits. The capsule has landed just two hundred metres from New Eden – that elevator is such a wonder of technology and precision! You're being quite spoiled – but you deserve it! On you go then – everybody on your way, single file so nobody gets lost in the storm.'

Having rallied the troops, she presses the button that

temporarily cuts off filming, while her words travel up to be heard by the pioneers; then she holds her glass out to Orion Seamus, who is sitting out of frame, for him to pour her some more champagne.

'Oh, the 1961 vintage is even better than the 1969!' she says, once she's moistened her lips with the sparkling liquid. 'I was right to get you to replace the contents of the Season Two bottles with sparkling wine, like we did with the first lot, so we could keep this divine beverage for ourselves. I feel positively perky, I could stay awake all night. But there won't be any need to stay up too long – the business will be wrapped up soon enough. The elevator will be back in orbit, the pioneers nice and warm on board the *Cupido*; and the viewers will be thrilled with the whole thing and they can head off to bed. And so can we, darling,' Then she add with a teasing smile, 'In separate beds, but not for much longer.'

Orion Seamus's one eye widens.

'You mean . . . ?'

'Yes – we're going to get married. At the same time as the Season Two candidates, when they go down to their rotten planet in a month's time – that would be perfect timing, I think. We'll organise the ceremony by live link-up: them in the Martian desert, and us amid the splendours of the Earth. It'll be a stunning spectacle!'

She sighs with pleasure, clinks glasses with her fiancé and glances back at the editing screen.

The pioneers have come to the end of their long wait.

While Serena's giant face gives them instructions from the inside of the dome, which is shuddering in the Martian winds – 'On you go then – everybody on your way, single file so nobody gets lost in the storm' – they are doing a final check on the airtightness of their helmets, their oxygen reserves, the settings of their extravehicular survival units.

Even Kelly makes an effort to sit up in her wheelchair. Kris and Samson check on the dogs' suits, and everybody is good to go.

Except for one pioneer, who's just sitting there on the floor, helmet in hands.

'Looks like someone's had a terrible heartbreak,' murmurs Serena, amused.

She puts down her champagne flute, then quickly zooms in on the picture.

The name embroidered on the suit is still invisible at this angle, but it's possible to see armband number 3, which the Martian government has allocated to Mozart.

A second astronaut crouches down beside him, a number 1 on his arm. 'Up you get, man – we've got to go.'

Mozart looks up. Behind his visor, the look on his face is pure despair. 'But . . . but what about Léonor . . . ?' he stammers.

'She's gone. You know that. She won't be coming back. Wherever she went, in her madness, she doesn't need anybody any more. She doesn't need you.'

But the Russian's voice has no sarcasm in it at all.

He holds his hand out to the Brazilian, a genuine gesture of friendship, quite unlike the provocations and the swagger we've seen between these two enemies until now.

671

'She doesn't need you any more,' he says again. 'But I *do*. You're my number 3. You're already a legend of space navigation – tomorrow you'll be a founding father of Mars.'

The distress on Mozart's face eases a little.

An encouraging smile appears on Alexei's. 'Life goes on. Your name's going to be written into the history of Mars. Come on – let's go.'

He helps Mozart to his feet, then he puts his hand on Samson's shoulder – the other pioneer he's clashed with most often. 'You too, pal, we all need you,' he says, meeting the Nigerian's green eyes frankly. 'We could look pretty hard and we wouldn't find such a talented biologist . . . or such a courageous guy. Just by being yourself, you've given me a hell of a wake-up call, and taught me a lesson in bravery I won't forget in a hurry. I know I reacted like a total loser at the time. I'm guessing you might want to go back once we're up there, so you can live your life on Earth. But if you do decide to stay here . . . you should know there'll always be a place for you.'

'Such stunning scenes of camaraderie!' gushes Serena, coming back on the air. 'Such marvellous examples of solidarity!' Then she quickly adds, drawing a parallel with her own situation, 'A people who unite around their leader can weather all kinds of crises and get over any losses!'

The pioneers head over to the decompression airlock, under the benighted dome over which the storm is beginning to rage.

Everybody naturally reverts to a pack instinct.

Alexei goes first, supporting his pregnant wife with one arm,

*followed closely by their dog Louve and their robot butler Günter,
who Kirsten absolutely insisted on bringing with them – an
entourage fit for a king.*

Mozart isn't far behind them.

Then come Tao and Liz, wearing numbers 5 and 6.

*Then Safia, Samson pushing Kelly's wheelchair, Fangfang, and
finally Warden, bringing up the rear.*

*The only figure remaining at the foot of the tarp-covered
plantations is Lóng, the robot acquired by the Chinese boy and
the Singaporean girl back when they were a couple: it has been
agreed that he – now an orphan – should remain behind to guard
New Eden in the pioneers' absence.*

*'We're not saying goodbye for ever,' says Alexei, turning back to
the Garden one last time. 'We'll be back – this base is the cradle
of our civi—'*

*Before he's completed his sentence, the Garden-side red warning
light comes on beside the airlock, indicating the start of equalisation.*

'I-I don't understand . . .' stammers Alexei. 'I haven't pressed . . .'

*'Maybe it's some disturbance linked to the electrostatic charges?'
suggests Fangfang, looking up worriedly at the panes of glass that
are trembling more and more violently.*

*'Or . . . or it's that horrible thing that's hiding in the storm!' cries
Kris, terrified. 'I'm almost certain I heard a noise, like last time!'*

Quick as a flash, Serena's hands are on the control panel in her
desk, and she switches the Genesis channel onto the dome's
exterior camera, which is showing the dark night, caught up
in the tempest.

Hurriedly she taps a message onto the keyboard. It appears

instantly on the screen, superimposed over the fearful images of the storm.

NOTICE TO VIEWERS

THE PIONEERS HAVE JUST PASSED THROUGH
THE DECOMPRESSION AIRLOCK.
EXTERNAL VISIBILITY CONDITIONS
PREVENT US FROM FOLLOWING THEM.
WE WILL RE-ESTABLISH CONTACT
ONCE THEY ARE IN PLACE
IN THE TRANSIT CAPSULE.

Once she's sure the viewers can only see a black screen, Serena turns her attention back to editing: she and Orion Seamus are now the only people on Earth who can see what the airlock reveals as it opens.

111. Shot

Month 18 / sol 484 / 16:28 Mars time
[603rd sol since landing]
Transit capsule lift-off – 32m

The airlock door in front of me slides silently open. There they all are, in the Garden, under the dimly lit dome, in front of the tarp-covered plantations: the nine pioneers of Mars.

Behind their visors, their faces are distorted in astonishment, as if they're seeing a ghost. They never expected me to return, the crazy girl who rushed off into the storm more than twenty-four hours ago.

But here I am, standing right in front of them.

Alexei's the first to jolt himself out of his amazement.

'And – and Marcus . . . ?' he stammers, looking at the airlock behind me, terrified at the thought I might have brought him back with me, in sight of the dome's cameras.

'He's resting in peace.'

Words with a double meaning, once again – to the viewers, Marcus died nearly two years ago; to the pioneers, I've just announced his death now.

'I'm ready to go with you,' I say, refusing to let sadness get

675

its claws into my heart, focusing on the best that Marcus left behind with me.

No, I can't change the direction of the wind.

No, I can't turn back time.

But I can adjust my sails – and that makes all the difference, that means my freedom, which Serena will never be able to take from me, because my destiny has not been written in advance!

'I'm ready to board the elevator, and go back up to the Cupido.'

The pioneers just stand there, unmoving, unsure how to react. Mozart especially hardly dares to look at me.

Finally, Kris is the first to take a step towards me. My darling Kris, my friend for life, always the first to comfort me!

'There's no need to be sad, Kris,' I murmur as she puts her arm affectionately around my shoulder to give me support. *'Marcus will always be with me, here . . .'*

I gesture towards my heart, the place where Marcus put his hand for the last time, but a *click* makes me stop – the sound of my helmet being detached.

I look down – instead of an embrace, Kris has put her arm behind my neck to press the *unlock* button.

'W-what are you doing . . . ?' I stammer, looking back up to meet Kris's eyes behind her visor.

But there's nothing there: her pupils are two fixed points, staring blankly without seeing me.

She takes hold of my disconnected helmet, pulls it off and drops it onto the floor.

Before I'm able to react, her gloved hands are back on my body – on my bare neck.

112. Reverse Shot

The Villa McBee, Long Island, New York State
Wednesday 21 August, 11:39pm
Transit capsule lift-off – 21m

'*Serena to Kirsten.* I repeat: *Serena to Kirsten.* Squeeze harder. Harder! *That is my will!*'

Standing behind her desk, Serena McBee stares at the editing screen, which is focused on Léonor's face, turning purple above the gloved hands of her best friend – the Genesis channel, meanwhile, is still showing pictures of the fearsome storm roaring outside.

As soon as the French girl entered the base, the producer immediately connected her mic to the German girl's audio feed to give her orders in a hissing voice.

'What kind of witchcraft . . . ?' murmurs Orion Seamus.

'The witchcraft of my eyes and my voice!' answers Serena, never taking her attention off the editing screen. 'It was so easy for me to hypnotise the kind, sweet, impressionable Kirsten when she was living at the training camp in Death Valley.'

'So she's the kamikaze!'

'Kamikaze, or killer – in any case, a slave who's been

677

mentally conditioned to carry out my commands. She can't refuse what I've just slipped into the earphones of her helmet – kill her, once and for all, kill that . . . that . . . that insect! Now the machine's been set off, nothing can stop it: Kirsten won't be herself again until Léonor has drawn her last breath. My only regret is that it's not my hands doing it in place of hers!'

Serena sits back in her armchair, eyes still glued to the screen.

'It's the perfect moment to get rid of this uncontrollable little bitch, who's been playing havoc with my nerves for too long – and those of the other pioneers, who've come to hate her as much as I do! What was she planning this time? Another little comment about the Noah Report? Now we'll never know, and it's just as well. In a few moments, when we go back live to the Garden, we'll just have to attribute Kirsten's murderous insanity to a pregnant woman's paranoid frenzy. It's been demonstrated in the psychiatric literature, you know, it's even got a name: *puerperal psychosis* – normally it's something that happens right after childbirth, but after all, this is Mars where everyone will understand that things are a bit different.' She gives a little laugh, clenching her ring-bedecked fist. 'What with the communication latency, Léonor must be dead already. She'll never upstage me again!'

On the editing screen that's receiving the images from Mars – with some minutes' delay – Léonor's face is no more than a swollen mask. The cyanotic blood filling it is already turning a purplish blue. The girl's beautiful gold eyes are rolling up slowly to reveal her bloodshot corneas.

All around her, the other pioneers are shouting, gripping Kirsten's arms to get her to let go, but their thick suits hamper their movements, and no amount of strength seems enough to stop the death machine that Serena has set in motion.

113. Shot

Month 18 / sol 484 / 16:41 Mars time
[603rd sol since landing]
Transit capsule lift-off – 19m

First there was surprise – the astonishment of seeing my best friend launching herself at my throat, a stranger's mask on her face.

Then came the pain – the feeling of Kris's hands becoming harpy talons around my neck.

But now I feel neither of these.

I feel nothing at all.

The commotion made by the other pioneers is getting quieter in my ears.

The glass dome shuddering under the storm is fading away before my eyes.

My head spins, my body getting lighter and lighter, as if my flesh were evaporating.

I'm flying away.

'Léééooo . . .'

Far away.

'Léééeooo, can yoooou heeeeear me . . . ?'

Far away from everything.

'Answer meeeee, Léééooo . . . !'

Huh?

What hands are these pressing on my chest? They aren't Kris's now.

Whose mouth is this on mine, blowing the breath of life into my chest? It's not Mozart's.

I feel myself floating back down, returning to my physical body.

My body is subject to gravity again. It presses with all its weight against the hard floor of the base where I'm stretched out.

My eyes can see the countdown ticking away at the top of the dome, like a beating heart. *T –15 mins*. Right above me, Alexei is in close-up, looking down worriedly.

He's taken off his helmet . . . to give me mouth-to-mouth to revive me.

'Say something if you can hear me!' he says, using our good old first-aid protocol: *1 – Check if the injured person is conscious*.

'Yes . . .' I manage to croak through my painful throat.

'Praise the Lord! I don't know what came over Kris, it's incomprehensible . . . She went totally nuts! We couldn't get her to let go – her arms seemed to be locked around your neck, like they were made of iron. Fortunately, I still had a syringe of sedative on me, otherwise she'd have killed you.'

I raise myself up onto my elbow, to see Kris's unconscious body on the floor. The hypodermic syringe Alexei used is next to her, close to the injection patch in the thigh of her suit.

'You – you saved my life,' I stammer.

681

'I did my duty as a doctor. Now you do your duty as a Martian and follow us, without any more drama, like you said. There's still time to get that elevator!'

He doesn't manage to say any more: a white shape rises up behind him.

However bruised my vocal cords, I still scream the moment I recognise Kris.

Despite the drug that's running through her veins, she's gotten back up, like a zombie!

She's holding the syringe in her glove and aiming at my bare face!

'No!' cries Alexei, throwing himself in the way just as the needle is about to stick into my eye.

Instead it sinks into him, right in the carotid artery.

114. Off-screen

Somewhere on a highway on the east coast of America
Thursday 22 August, midnight
Transit capsule lift-off – 00m

'It's midnight on the east coast of America here on Earth, seventeen hundred hours on Mars – it's time. What are we doing, captain – are we launching the operation, or not?'

Hands suspended over his keyboard, Cadet Franklin is waiting for the go order to hack the Genesis channel's transmission signal.

But the big wall screen that's supposed to be showing the lift-off of the self-energising space elevator is in blackout. For the last half hour, the programme's official broadcaster has shown nothing but a fixed view of the Martian night, the only soundtrack the persistent whistling of the storm.

'No, Derek!' cries Cindy, turning to her husband. 'We don't know if the pioneers have got on board the elevator! That was the condition for us to launch the operation.'

The captain clenches his square jaw, a sign of stress in this man with nerves of steel.

For the tenth time, he glances at his watch, where the

minutes continue to tick by; for the tenth time, he asks Cadet Franklin, 'Still no communications from Genesis to explain the unchanging pictures of the storm?'

'Negative, captain. The whole world's media are on the alert.'

Suddenly Andrew jumps up from his seat, startling Cecilia who is sitting beside him.

'We've just got to do it!' he says, his voice clear as a bell. 'Now, right away – no more waiting!'

All eyes turn to him – Cindy's, anxious about the pioneers; Gordon Lock's, heavy with guilt, deep bags under them; Cecilia's, Miguel's, Barry Mirwood's, exhausted after their months in detention; Captain Jacobson's and Cadet Franklin's, feverish with indecision.

But Andrew's own eyes show no fear or tiredness, just fierce determination.

'Too often I put off confronting Serena,' he says quietly. 'Too often I decided to delay sharing what I knew. Because conditions weren't all perfectly aligned, because there was still a possible risk to the pioneers . . . because I wasn't brave enough to have their deaths on my conscience, if things turned out badly. But each time I chose to keep silent, Serena got stronger, and more dangerous.'

Shaky on his iron foot, thin with malnutrition and ill-treatment, he still holds himself as upright as he can.

'No, we haven't got all the guarantees that this is the perfect moment. We don't even have all the weapons we need, because we're missing the Noah Report. But even with all these doubts, one thing is certain: the longer we wait, the harder it'll be to wake the world up. You said it yourself, Cindy: "*Coffee boiled is coffee spoiled!*"'

'He's right!' says Gordon Lock, the first words he's spoken since the truck started moving. 'We all know he's right! I'm ready to testify!' He turns his large sweaty face towards the young man. 'Your dad . . . would be proud of you. He was the best of us . . . or the least bad. He admired you so much! But in the weeks before he died, he didn't have the courage to look you in the eye, or to tell you how much he loved you . . . except in the way he named those dogs: Louve and Warden. He confided in me before he was killed: they're a simple anagram. *Love U Andrew*: that's the legacy he left you.'

Andrew's eyes widen. Two years earlier, he'd suspected something like this; some instinct had made him want to discover some secret in the names his father had given the dogs. He'd rummaged around in the library at Berkeley to research every meaning of the English word *Warden*, every allusion to the French word *Louve*. But if his hunch about a hidden meaning was correct, the way he went about finding it wasn't, as he was looking with his head and not his heart. Back then this I.T. genius, so great at code-breaking, wasn't able to decipher the simplest, almost childish message! But he's received it now, a final gift from his father beyond the grave. It offers the possibility of grieving in peace, perhaps even of a reconciliation.

'Let's go!' cries Cindy now, all her doubts swept away. 'For Sherman Fisher! For Ruben Rodriguez! For the pioneers on Mars! For all the victims of Serena McBee! Long live the Wild Bees, long live America, and long live freedom!'

Captain Jacobson gives Cadet Franklin a very deliberate nod.

685

'Go for it, cadet! We're launching Operation Apocalypse! Frame up Lock!'

'Yessir, captain!'

He turns on the projectors attached to the ceiling of the truck, points the camera at the big man, then brings his hands down onto the computer keyboard and starts tapping away quickly.

A few moments later, the Genesis channel on the wall screen blurs . . .

. . . the unchanging image of the storm is covered in stripes . . .

. . . and gives way to the face of Gordon Lock, in close-up.

115. Reverse Shot

The Villa McBee, Long Island, New York State
A few minutes earlier
Transit capsule lift-off – 10m

'Serves him right!' says Serena McBee when the syringe sinks into Alexei's throat, which has been unprotected since he removed his helmet to help Léonor.

On the editing screen in the middle of the gantry, the executive producer is still following the pictures coming in from the base; the viewers of the Genesis channel, meanwhile, still only have access to the fixed view of the darkness of the Martian storm, with a caption assuring them that the pioneers are on their way to the transit capsule.

'No pathetic little tranquilliser injection is going to subdue a killing machine I've programmed myself!' Serena gloats. 'That idiot got himself in between the weapon and the target: that's too bad for him. And to think I believed he had the soul of a leader! All he needed to do was let his own wife eliminate his main political opponent on his behalf.' Serena turns to Orion Seamus and whispers seductively: 'Just as I rely on you for my dirty work, my dear.'

'This slight hitch has delayed the pioneers' boarding of the capsule,' she continues, 'but it's not serious; even though seventeen hundred hours did correspond to the perfect angle for the microwaves, the self-energised satellite will still be within range of Ius Chasma for an hour or so, before continuing its circuit of the planet. That leaves plenty of time for the survivors to get on board – and with four fewer passengers, they'll be travelling light!'

On the screen, the girl who used to be the most loving of wives has been transformed into an engine of death. She keeps striking mechanically, over and over, with a syringe that has become a dagger. The blood of her dazed 'ice prince' is spurting in all directions, streaming from his neck onto his white suit.

But soon the maniac's blows weaken.

Soon the other pioneers manage to restrain her.

With a delayed effect, the sedative seems finally to have got the better of the 'machine' that Serena programmed.

'No!' Serena shouts into her mic, the channel still connected to the German girl's audio feed. 'Defend yourself, Kirsten, I'm ordering you! Strike back! Get them! Kill! Alexei first but mainly Léonor!'

Stamping her feet like a bookie at the ringside, she's too caught up in the fight unfolding in the Garden to notice that the window devoted to the Genesis channel is suddenly striped over.

'Serena . . .' murmurs Orion Seamus.

The psychiatrist gestures in irritation to shut him up and make him understand that she needs to devote all her attention, and all her hypnotic powers, to her faltering champion.

But the man in the eyepatch insists: 'Serena, there's something strange happening on the Genesis channel.'

'Shut up! Can't you see I'm concentrating?'

'SERENA!!!'

Caught off guard by this unaccustomed commanding tone, the president finally looks away from the window showing the Garden and at the one tuned to the Genesis channel, as it's being broadcast right across the world.

The storm has disappeared.

The black screen is now brightly lit.

Filling the frame, Gordon Lock seems to be looking her straight in the eye.

Close up on a face well known to the viewers of the Genesis channel, the programme's erstwhile number two, his forehead dripping with sweat. 'This message, broadcast by the Wild Bees, is addressed to the American people, and to all the viewers of the Genesis channel. Some months ago, on this channel, I offered a confession. It was false, at least in part.

'Yes, the plane transporting the senior team of the programme was the victim of an attack. But it wasn't my fault – a drone controlled remotely from Cape Canaveral caused the crash, killing the pilot mid-flight.

'And yes, I did sell my soul to the devil. But demons aren't always to be found in the Kremlin: the one I had my dealings with lives in the White House.'

The former technical director wipes his forehead with the sleeve of his orange prison jumpsuit.

'The Martian base is not viable in the long term,' he continues hoarsely. 'A secret experiment demonstrated this, sending animals to New Eden before the Season One pioneers went up. All the guinea pigs died suddenly, during a storm like the one currently taking place on Mars. Atlas Capital, greedy for profit, preferred to keep this vital information quiet and launch the show anyway. They sent twelve young people to their deaths, in agreement with the executive producer . . .' A glow as cold as revenge flashes from Gordon Lock's eyes. '. . . Serena McBee!'

Behind her desk, the President of the United States is terribly pale.

She can tap away on her panel until she breaks her fingers, but to no avail; she's lost all control of the images being broadcast to the viewers. The Genesis channel is stubbornly tuned to Gordon Lock's sweating face, to his eyes stabbing straight into her.

'Disloyal heap of shit!' shouts the president, beside herself, abandoning her usual elegance. 'Overgrown lump of treacherous –'

'Could it be another hacking attack?'

Serena suddenly remembers the presence of Orion Seamus, sitting right beside her – the man to whom she promised a speedy marriage just a few moments earlier.

She turns towards him, her face twisted with hatred.

'You!' she screams. 'You were in charge of the prisoners!'

'I . . . well, yes, of course . . . it's just . . . I don't understand . . .' he stammers, losing his composure for the first time. 'I'll go right down to the cellars to see what's happened.'

He hurries out of the study, while Serena presses frantically on her bee-shaped mic-brooch.

'*Serena to Cape Canaveral base!*' she yells at the top of her lungs. 'Answer me! Answer me!'

A new window opens up in one corner of the screen, connected to the Cape Canaveral editing suite, in the middle of which stands Samantha, quivering.

'Return control of the editing to me *at once*!' barks Serena, so loudly that her assistant grimaces in pain, bringing her fingers to her earpiece. 'I'm the president! With plenary powers! I demand total control!'

691

'It's . . . it's not an editing problem, Ms McBee,' stammers Samantha. 'It's a broadcast problem. We no longer have any control over the transmission signal being sent by the Genesis satellite, either towards Mars or towards the Earth. There's no way to stop the hacked picture . . . Somebody's locked all the codes.'

Serena gives a roar.

'Incompetents! A bunch of incompetents, every single one of you! Heads will roll!' She swallows back her rage, using self-control techniques to regain her grip on the situation. 'This hacking is clearly just a cowardly attempt to destabilise me, my dear Samantha. My enemies are waging war on me: an image war. I need to counterattack . . . to reassure the viewers . . . and quickly.'

'The Citizens Swarm site?' suggests the young assistant, trembling. 'It has a lot of followers and many of the media keep an eye on it. Maybe they could help with your little speech, while we haven't got the Genesis channel?'

A light goes on in Serena McBee's eyes.

'Film me!' she commands. 'I'm ready!'

The assistant shouts some frantic orders around her, and engineers and I.T. technicians race for their computers.

As the connection is being set up, the president keeps her eyes closed while chanting a relaxation mantra – '*I'm in a large, tranquil ocean . . . I'm swimming with the dolphins . . .*'

Her breathing calms; her mouth unclenches; the muscles of her face relax.

'Three . . . Two . . . One . . . You're on, Ms McBee!'

She reopens her eyes abruptly, looking straight into the gantry camera, whose red light has just come on.

The face of Serena McBee appears, full screen. Majestic, resolved, completely confident: presidential to her very fingertips.

'This is a serious time,' she says, with no preamble. 'At this very moment, the Genesis channel is the victim of a hateful act of terrorist hacking, forcing me to speak on this site to reaffirm the truth. Tonight I am speaking not only to you, our Guardians, but also to all American citizens, and more widely to all the viewers across the whole world.

'I don't know how the traitor Gordon Lock was able to get onto the screen. But I must tell you, all of you, looking you straight in the eye, that what he has just said about me is a vile slander!' The speaker backs up her denials with an intense stare into the camera, as if through it she might bewitch the whole of Earth. 'How could you ever believe a single word from a man who is ready to tell any lie to save his skin? He's confessed it himself: he's currently in the hands of the people who call themselves the "Wild Bees", anarchists who have nothing in common with bees but their name! I have no doubt they've promised him his freedom in exchange for this shameful defamation of me.'

Serena McBee strikes her chest. 'Accusing *me* of having neglected the safety of the Mars pioneers, I who am like a mother to them! It's . . . it's just hateful! From the self-energising elevator to the declaration of their independence – hasn't everything about my presidential mandate been a resounding demonstration of how those young people are the apple of my eye?'

'. . . why, I'd give my life to protect my beloved pioneers!' Serena is saying as Orion Seamus rushes back into the room.

Seeing that the president is currently filming, he positions himself in her eye-line and opens his mouth to tell her something.

But with a gesture she prevents him.

While she continues with her speech, she fumbles around frantically for a sheet of paper on her desk, which is out of shot, and starts to write on it quickly.

'The society we are trying to build, all of us together, will not be threatened by little clusters of bees who are dissidents, and who have no future,' she says.

She pushes the paper over to Orion, who reads it nervously.

URGENT: launch operation capture Atlas board.

'I won't let them intimidate me!' Serena is still talking. 'And nor should you, my dear Guardians, dear citizens, dear viewers: don't allow yourselves to be intimidated either!'

Out of frame she is waving her hands in exasperation, to try to get her secretary of state to carry out his mission. But although he is usually so prompt to obey, he stands frozen in place. His lips are trembling, and he can't bring himself to leave the study without delivering the information he's come to tell her. Desperately, he turns over the sheet of paper Serena's just handed him, grabs the pen and starts to scribble.

'Together, we will be stronger than ever! Together we ca— oh!' Serena can't help a little exclamation when she reads the message.

Not only Lock escaped. Also Rodriguez, Fisher, Mirwood.

At that moment, in the Genesis channel window, Gordon Lock is replaced by a new speaker – a new witness.

694

The glare of the spotlights is reflected in the glasses of the young man who has just appeared on the screen. Unlike Gordon Lock, his face is totally unknown to the general public. His terribly pale skin, his sunken cheeks, the dark bags under his eyes, all give the impression that he's never been out in daylight, let alone exposed to the glare of camera flashes. He's a creature of the shadows, an outlaw, a stowaway, exposed for the first time to the world's curiosity.

'My name is Andrew Fisher,' he says, with the resonant voice of somebody who has been silent for a long time and who is speaking at last. 'I'm the son of Sherman Fisher, the Genesis programme's communications instructor. You were told my father was killed in a car accident. That's not true. He was murdered. Just like Ruben Rodriguez, the man who looked after the Genesis animal store, whose wife Cecilia is here next to me.'

The camera zooms out, revealing something of the setting – it looks like the inside of a truck. A young blonde woman is sitting next to Andrew Fisher, also wearing an orange jumpsuit. 'It was Serena McBee who killed them both!' she says. 'To shut them up! To stop them talking about the Noah Report, the document proving the deaths of the guinea pigs and the dangerousness of the base!'

The camera continues to pan out, taking in Gordon Lock and a fourth character, an old man with a thick beard and an alarmed expression. 'Professor Barry Mirwood, PhD,' he recites, slightly stiff, as if delivering a university lecture. 'I . . . I'm the inventor of the self-energising space elevator. My life's great work, which I thoughtlessly handed over to Serena McBee. That woman . . . is a disgrace to science!'

Alone once again in her study, now that Orion Seamus has rushed out to comply with her orders, Serena is growing paler by the minute. She is determined to stay on the air on the Citizens Swarm website, but her speech is becoming less confident, her tone less presidential.

'I'm just learning that other traitors are getting their fangs out to spit their poison at me . . . !'

She keeps glancing at the Genesis channel. There are now four accusers facing her, dressed in orange as though clothed in flames, their eyes burning like embers, like the judges of hell.

'. . . and I say again, these are slanders! The Fisher kid is a fugitive, a lunatic! That virago with the Latino accent, is she even really American? As for that senile old man who bears a vague resemblance to my special scientific advisor on space matters, he's just an impostor! A common lookalike!'

Suddenly the window connecting to Cape Canaveral opens again. The president's eyes light up as she recognises her assistant: *That's it, they've managed to regain access to the Genesis satellite, they're going to return all the controls to me!*

But Samantha's crestfallen face shows nothing but distress. She's holding up a tablet in front of her, which reads:

ANOTHER CYBER-ATTACK HAS APPEARED ON ANOTHER FRONT.
ALL THE MEDIA ARE CURRENTLY PICKING UP
THE GENESISPIRACY.COM WEBSITE!

Trembling, Serena McBee types genesispiracy.com into a new browser window. Her own reflection appears, like the enchanted mirror looking back at the evil fairy-tale queen.

696

The girl on the screen bears a striking resemblance to Serena McBee. Despite her dark hair, she has the same smooth, light skin, the same perfect oval chin, the same water-green irises.

'. . . and I repeat, speaking to you live from right here on Bee Island: everything the Wild Bees have just said on the Genesis channel is true,' she says, staring unblinking at the webcam that is filming her, a poorly lit laboratory her backdrop. 'The Noah Report, the sacrificing of the pioneers, the killings of members of the Genesis team one after another, the collusion with Atlas Capital: *it's all true.*

'The woman you've been inviting into your home every day for two years; the woman who seems so close it's almost like she's a member of your family; the woman who, having first declared herself a mother to the orphans on Mars, now claims to be a mother to the whole nation; the woman, in short, who I myself actually called *Mom* my whole life: that woman is a monster, who in reality has never given birth to anything but nightmares!'

The girl raises her chin. Her whole body seems to lengthen, stretching out like that of a butterfly finally tearing through its cocoon after its long metamorphosis . . . finally taking flight.

'My name is Harmony McBee, but I'm not Serena McBee's daughter. *I'm her clone.* The tenth in a long line of clones, mass produced and regularly sacrificed to serve as an organ bank for their model.

'*All for one* – that's the slogan of the president's supporters, isn't it? Those people who scream these words at the top of their lungs should know how literally she takes it. She really does demand everything from those who've submitted to her: their bodies, their blood, their souls – for her and her alone!'

'That . . . that's another lie,' stammers Serena, overtaken by a nervous trembling.

She's built her impressive rise on images, but now the images are rebelling against their mistress and surrounding her on all sides.

Above her: the cameras that are still filming her speech, to go out live on the Citizens Swarm site.

Below that: the window of the Genesis channel, populated by prisoners she thought she had silenced for ever.

To the right: the link to the Cape Canaveral base, from where Samantha is looking at her boss with growing shock.

And finally, to the left: the tab open on the Genesis Piracy site, and on the darkest secrets of this woman who not long ago was swearing she wanted to usher in a new age of total transparency.

'That website, Genesis Piracy, is a fraud,' she barks, forgetting that by mentioning it on the air, she's only helping to promote it. 'That girl is a fraud! Who'd be crazy enough as to believe a word of what she's just said! It's an utterly preposterous cock-and-bull story!'

At that moment, Harmony McBee's face disappears from the pirate site to be replaced by a woman who is their spitting image, hers and the president's, but much older.

'My-Nem-Is-Ah-Mo-Ni-Wun,' says the woman, staring vacantly into the camera.

While she drones through the next line – 'I-Yam-A-Klo-Nuh' – the screen splits in two, revealing a second woman who resembles the first, but with slightly fewer wrinkles.

'My-Nem-Is-Ah-Mo-Ni-Tu,' says the new apparition.

The screen splits again to reveal another spectre, who intones in turn: 'My-Nem-Is-Ah-Mo-Ni-Tri,'

And on it goes – four, five, six clones, getting younger and younger, share the screen, making up a hellish, demented choir, with the same phrase repeated again and again like a refrain:

'De-Klo-Nuh-Ov-Suh-Ree-Nuh-Muhk-Bii . . .'

'. . . Ov-Suh-Ree-Nuh-Muhk-Bii . . .'

'. . . Suh-Ree-Nuh-Muhk-Bii . . .'

'. . . Nuh-Muhk-Bii . . .'

'. . . Muhk-Bii . . .'

'. . . Bii . . .'

Behind her desk, Serena is petrified.

'It's just a ridiculous bit of editing,' she babbles, unable to take her eyes off the kaleidoscope that is returning her own image back to her six-fold. 'It's just special effects – maybe good enough to impress dumb teenagers, fans of horror movies . . . This attempt to present me as some kind of monster is grotesque, it's pathetic . . . I'm sure nobody on Earth would believe such a crude hoax . . . When the pioneers are back on the screen, they'll be able to testify in my favour and sweep all these disgraceful things away.'

While she's making these denials in a monotone voice, Serena can't help opening window after window in her web browser, clicking on the most-read news sites on the planet. Each new site she opens is like another eye staring at her, weighing her up . . . judging her.

699

LIVE FROM TIMES SQUARE, NEW YORK CITY

A muted anguish has fallen on the place that should be hosting the high mass of the self-energising elevator, a celebration dedicated as much to the glory of the regime as to the saving of the pioneers.

The atmosphere of jubilation has deflated like a soufflé. The couples in love have stopped biting into their toffee apples. A lot of the children are crying, and have let go of their planet-Mars-shaped balloons; the balloons now rise slowly up the buildings which show the face of Andrew Fisher, reproduced hundreds of times on hundreds of screens, as he says, 'Serena McBee claims that the pioneers will testify on her side. But for the last two years, she's always found some excuse to hide them from you whenever they've threatened to reveal the Noah Report.'

 LIVE FROM THE CHAMPS-ÉLYSÉES, PARIS

'And she's just done it again, a few minutes ago, serving pointless images up to the viewers to distract them!' says Andrew Fisher on the giant screen hanging from the Arc de Triomphe.

A murmur rumbles all the way down from the Place de l'Étoile to the Place de la Concorde, somewhere between astonishment, anger and disbelief.

A reporter appears in frame, mic in hand. 'Another scoop!' he shouts. 'The pioneers on Mars would seem to have known about this mysterious Noah Report already! That makes some sense of the words from our Léonor when she mentioned those two words – "Noah Report" – on the air, before she was forcibly escorted into the Rest House because of some alleged "hysterical fit"!'

'I can't see the pioneers at this moment,' continues Andrew on the big screens affixed to the side walls of Shinjuku Station. 'But they can see me and hear me! Or at least, they can so long as their protector, which Serena claims to be, hasn't pressed the button allowing her to depressurise the base remotely.'

Many of the Cosmicists stop their ritual movements to focus more closely on the feverish face of this young man. Reproduced dozens of times over, he's continuing to hammer home his message. 'Serena's remote control is the sword of Damocles she's been holding over New Eden since the start of the mission! It's her secret weapon, and this threat is how she's been able to guarantee the pioneers' silence, as well as Harmony's and mine, for two whole years!

'Pioneers!' Andrew calls out to them now. 'Alexei and Kirsten! Samson and Safia! Tao and Elizabeth! And you, Mozart, Fangfang and Kelly, who have already been widowed by this death programme! If you're already in the transit capsule, you no longer have any need to lie: the world knows now what kind of monster Serena is. If you're still in the base, you needn't be afraid: she wouldn't dare depressurise it, now that everybody's aware of her remote control.'

The young man's lips are trembling. 'And as for you, Harmony . . . I beg you, don't take any risks. The Wild Bees' sympathisers in Scotland are on their way to Bee Island. I . . . I can't wait to hold you in my arms.'

His voice falters – the words that modesty has held back for such a long time are so hard to say! 'I . . . I . . .'

'*I love you too, Andrew!*' cries Harmony. '*Thanks to you, life has given me a nugget of gold more precious than you could find in the pages of any novel!*'

They are at opposite sides of the big editing screen in the middle of the gantry, him in the official window of the Genesis channel, her on the Genesis Piracy site.

In the real world, they're separated by the many thousands of miles between the Wild Bees truck and McBee Castle; but they're united in the virtual world by the magic of images travelling at the speed of light down optical fibres stretched all around the planet.

As a powerless spectator of this conversation she has no way of stopping, of this union she has no way of breaking up, Serena McBee is trembling with rage . . . and also, so it would seem, with fear.

At this moment, there's the sound of a distant explosion out in the night, beyond the French windows that open onto the gardens.

Serena yanks herself back to the lenses of the cameras that are still trained on her, still filming her.

'This business with the remote control is just another fantasy . . .' she says weakly. 'I'll say it again: the pioneers will speak for me, and they'll confirm what the truth is . . .'

She looks at the corner of the editing screen where the pictures from the Garden are still running on: images of the base continue to arrive at the Villa McBee, where only she can see them, even if she cannot currently give any sign of this, upstream or down.

* * *

Alexei is lying in a pool of his own blood, motionless next to his sleeping wife. Léonor, leaning over him, is trying to stop the bleeding from his neck. The other pioneers are frozen in astonishment watching the giant face of Andrew Fisher on the inside of the dome.

They've all seen and all heard the successive testimonies from the president's prisoners, via the transmission that travelled up from the Wild Bees truck to the Genesis satellite, then to the antenna planted on Phobos, and finally to the New Eden base.

Another explosion of noise tears through the night, longer than the first – and closer too. There's no mistaking it – machine-gun fire.

Orion Seamus bursts into the study again, forgetting any notion of remaining discreet while the cameras are rolling.

'Armed rebels are attacking the villa!' he shouts, once again reacting with the reflexes of a security man. 'We've got to get you to a secure location, Madam President!'

'Just a moment!' she says, in a desperate plea. 'I can't go off the air, not now!'

'You haven't been on the air for half an hour,' he reminds her. 'All you have is an internet link. And you've got to say goodbye now, before it's too late.'

But it's as if Serena is glued to her chair, unable to turn away from the gantry with all its various images, which are hypnotising her – her, the great hypnotist herself.

'Just one minute!' she says hoarsely, bargaining now.

Pressing a button on her control panel, she pauses the cameras filming her, then grabs hold of her snakeskin bag, turns it upside down and shakes it violently to empty all its contents at her feet. Among the open lipsticks and broken powder compacts lie her cellphone, her small automatic pistol . . . and her remote control for Martian depressurisation. She snatches it up and puts it on her knees, under the desk. Somewhat reassured by the contact with this fetish object, she turns trembling towards the window linked to Cape Canaveral.

'Samantha!' she says. 'Have we recovered the transmission signal? Say yes, for pity's sake!'

'Yes.'

Dazed by this immediate answer that she's been wishing for with all her soul, Serena allows herself just a moment's pause.

'Our engineers have identified the fault and reprogrammed the satellite with new transmission codes,' explains Samantha.

'Hallelujah!' cries Serena, erupting like a volcano, her bob of hair flying in all directions, her normally impassive features distorted by a wild delight. 'Get control back to me immediately!'

But in the little window opposite her, Samantha's face is tight as a fist. After the shock and then the distress, what's furrowing her brow now – beneath her model assistant's ponytail – is horror.

'Ms McBee, you lied,' she says blankly.

'What?' Serena asks, distracted. All her attention is already back on the Genesis channel in the centre of the screen, ready to resume control. Andrew Fisher is no longer there, replaced by the Martian storm on which the executive producer left it before losing the signal.

'You were lying when you said the pioneers were on their way to the cabin,' Samantha continues. 'I've looked at the pictures from Mars – they're still in the base, and Léonor's come back, and Alexei's seriously injured.'

Serena freezes.

'How could you have dared to do such a thing?' she gasps. 'You had no right. The feed coming down is supposed to travel to the Villa McBee, for my eyes and mine only.' Quick as a snake, she presses on her brooch-mic and starts to whisper in her hissing, reptilian voice, her enchantress voice: '*Serena to Samantha. I repeat: Serena to Sa—*'

But before she's able to say the magic words, '*That is my will*', that transform all her staff into zombies carrying out all her orders totally blindly, the young assistant rips off her earpiece.

'I don't want to hear from you any more, Ms McBee!' she cries, pressing her hands over her ears. 'I don't want to hear from the Wild Bees any more! It's the pioneers I want to hear from now! Only they can tell us who's right, who we should believe, and what the truth is!' Quivering with emotion, she adds, 'We . . . we're taking control of the editing back . . . here, to Cape Canaveral . . .'

At these words, the Genesis channel window in the middle of the spiderlike gantry cuts sharply back from the storm to a wide view of the whole Garden.

116. Shot

Month 18 / sol 484 / 17:19 Mars time
[603rd sol since landing]
Transit capsule lift-off – 19m delay!

Suddenly Andrew Fisher disappears from the dome.

The permanent dusk of the Great Storm replaces his rebellion-lit face.

The insistent whistling of the wind sweeps away his insurgent words.

He's been cut off in mid-phrase, in mid-flow, and right now it's as if nothing had happened, as if it had all only been a dream: his astonishing testimony; the testimonies of Gordon Lock, Cecilia Rodriguez and Barry Mirwood; the uprising by the Wild Bees.

All around me the other pioneers are staring at one another, distraught behind the visors of their helmets, with no idea how to react.

Their leader is unable to show them the way. He's lying in my arms; I haven't been able to stem the bleeding from the stab wound in his neck.

'A-Alexei . . .' I stammer.

The only answer I receive is an inarticulate burble from his mouth, which is bubbling red.

At that moment, the dome is striped over again, white stripes all the way up, dazzling me like camera flashes.

I feel my whole body tense up, shrink, ready for the staggering blow of Serena's return to the screen.

But it's her assistant Samantha who appears – not wearing her earpiece, I notice that at once – and superimposed above her is the countdown for the elevator, its big flashing red numbers indicating a nineteen-minute delay on our original schedule.

'Hello, pioneers! The Wild Bees no longer have control of the Genesis channel,' she says, confirming my fears 'But Ms McBee has lost control of it too.'

What?

What did she say?

'We've taken control of the broadcast back here to Cape Canaveral,' she adds, trembling. 'All those appalling revelations about Ms McBee! All the president's denials! We . . . we didn't know what to think any more. We've heard stories from everybody – except the voice of Mars.'

Instinctively I look down at Alexei.

That's him: *he's* the voice of Mars.

But he's hardly moving any more, he's barely breathing.

Unable to speak a single word, he slips his hand into the all-purpose pocket of his suit, and pulls out Ruben Rodriguez's cellphone, which he confiscated from me; he holds his other hand out towards me, soaked in his own blood.

He places his index finger on my suit, in the middle of my

chest – and slowly, with some of the little strength he has left, he draws a big number 1.

Then his arm drops back, lifeless.

He's dead.

I wipe my bloody fingers on my suit; I put the precious telephone into my pocket; I pick up my helmet that's lying upside down on the floor, where Kris dropped it when she went nuts; I yank it firmly back onto my head.

The other pioneers' anxious breathing is back in my eardrums, through the radio relay. The way they look at me has changed since the dying leader chose me and anointed me with his blood, before passing away. The constantly surprising Alexei. For two years, he did nothing but humiliate me; he alternately had me locked up, spied on and sedated – then at the last moment he saved my life, giving up his own, offering me this final gift: the power to be heard at last.

'Tell us the truth now,' begs Samantha, *'before you board the elevator! Our engineers tell us the capsule can still wait for about another forty minutes. But the viewers can't! The whole Earth is waiting with bated breath! Does this Noah Report really exist? Did you know about it? Has Ms McBee been forcing you to lie for the last two years?'*

117. Genesis Channel

Thursday 22 August, 00:25am
Transit capsule lift-off – 25m delay!

Long shot on the Garden bathed in the glow of the spotlights.

The ultra-modern base seems to have been transformed into a theatre lit by candles, as in Shakespeare's day.

Everything is in position for the final scene, the one following the death of the doomed lovers, whose lifeless bodies the audience have just discovered on stage when the lights came up on a new scene – Alexei and Kirsten, like a new Romeo and Juliet, him the stabbed suitor, her the poisoned beauty.

The other actors in this tragedy stand unmoving in their suits – *their costumes* – their faces in shadow behind their visors – *their masks*. Even the dogs have been transformed into sphinx-like statues, positioned symmetrically on either side of the stage along with the robot butlers.

In the middle of this frozen tableau, only one figure is moving, stepping forward for the final monologue: it's the heroine, the lead.

The camera zooms in slowly, gradually focusing on her freckled face. On either side of her triangular chin, her luxuriant hair curls thickly against the visor, like an animal force that the glass is barely able to contain. Her big eyes, gold and catlike, reflect and amplify the yellowish light, transforming the trembling spots into flaming torches.

'People of Earth!' she calls out to the dome, to the unseeing tempest, to the cosmic void of a theatrical auditorium as vast as the universe. 'You want to know the truth? You want to hear the last word on this story? Well, here it is: Serena is innocent of all the crimes she's been accused of.'

118. Reverse Shot

Transit capsule lift-off – 31m delay!

Serena's finger hovers over the red button of the remote control
that's resting on her knees.

Opposite her, in the Genesis channel window, on the big
screen in the middle of the gantry, Léonor has just exonerated
her in a few simple words.

The girl turns around in the middle of the vast Garden setting,
showing herself to all the cameras, to all eyes.

She calls upon her audience and the whole universe to bear
witness: 'The rebels' accusations? A tissue of lies!'

Then, with a big theatrical gesture, she walks over to the
decompression airlock.

'Seriously, we've got to leave, Serena – now!' shouts Orion
Seamus, putting his hand on the president's arm. 'Your
helicopter's waiting for you by the hives!'

As if to highlight the urgency of the situation, two bursts

of machine-gun fire tear through the night, closer than ever.

But Serena snorts violently, her hand roughly brushing her bodyguard and fiancé away.

'Leave now, when I'm just about to win back the image war?' she gasps. 'Not on your life!'

On the Genesis channel screen, Léonor is still speaking.
'Alexei's death? An unfortunate accident!'
She presses the button opening the reinforced door.

'Serena, I'm ordering you to follow me!' growls Orion Seamus, gripping the president's shoulders firmly. 'Don't spoil what you can still save!'

'Let go of me, idiot! You're the one who's going to spoil everything! Two years of intense psychological pressure are finally paying off! The pioneers are now completely under my influence for ever – even Léonor! It'll only be a few minutes before that little fool Samantha lets me have the transmission controls back, and the people will flood out onto the streets to show their support for me, and the attempted coup will collapse pathetically!'

'The Noah Report?' Léonor chants at the screen. 'A total invention, made up by the president's enemies based on distorting, misinterpreting my words. I think I was just trying to say something like, "no, a report on President Green's assassination needs to be concluded properly before we can let the programme continue", but Alexei brought me down before I could finish what I was trying to say – so "No, a report . . ." was all I managed

to get out! Though now I think about it, yeah, I guess this place does have a bit in common with Noah's ark actually! Thanks to Serena, we've been able to benefit from this ark of peace far from the conflicts of Earth: yeah, that's what I meant!'

'Oh, my good little girl, how badly I misjudged you!' says Serena, smiling delightedly.

At that same moment, one of the panes of glass in the French windows shatters from the impact of a bullet from the far end of the gardens.

This time Orion Seamus doesn't bother to ask: he grabs Serena by the waist and drags her bodily out of her chair.

'No!' she whines, trying to cling onto her desk.

Her sharp nails stick into the wood of the table, but the former C.I.A. agent is too strong for her: she leaves behind her several long furrows scratched into the surface and several broken nails.

'Be reasonable, Serenaaaaa!'

The agent yells in pain the moment his betrothed's teeth sink into the flesh of his hand.

He lets her fall to the ground, amid the lipsticks and upturned powder compacts.

Panting like a wild beast, Serena grabs hold of her automatic pistol – the very one she threatened Orion with on the day he declared his love.

Today she doesn't give him the chance to say a word: she turns around and empties the magazine into his body.

Then she rushes back to the screen in the middle of the gantry, as addicted as the Genesis channel's most fanatical followers, prepared to kill just to be able to find out what happens next.

Léonor turns back towards the other pioneers who are watching her closely, so focused that they barely notice anything else, not even the roaring of the storm, which is getting more and more furious outside the dome: they know it's up to her now. She's in the lead role, it is she who will dictate how the scene is going to end, come what may.

'Hurry up!' she says. 'We've got to leave the base right now to return to the bosom of our protector Serena, up in orbit. It'll take some time to get the two wheelchairs through the storm, so come on, Martians – let's get going!' She slips her hand into the all-purpose pocket of her suit and pulls out a long piece of wispy red fabric. 'Follow this flag through the storm: the flag of Mars, our land for ever, thanks to the great Serena McBee!'

She disappears into the airlock – into the wings.

Fangfang and Safia follow her, leaving the stage in turn;

then Liz and Tao;

then Samson, pushing Kelly's chair, with Louve and Warden close on their heels;

then Mozart, carrying Kris's body, light as a feather despite her suit;

and finally Günter, who's the last to disappear into the airlock.

The reinforced door closes soundlessly, like a theatre curtain falling at the end of a performance.

'I won!' screams Serena, quite deaf to the gunshots that are still coming from the gates of her property. 'Samantha will return control to me any moment now!' She turns triumphantly to the man lying on the floor: 'You see, Orion? I wo—'

The words stick in her throat.

Orion Seamus's single eye is looking at her.

The bulletproof vest he was wearing under his suit protected all his vital organs, the bullets hitting only his shoulder and his thighs.

In his bloody hand, he's holding the remote control that Serena dropped when she fell.

A look of terror paralyses the executive producer's face, beneath her dishevelled bob.

'No! Nobody can know I have that remote control! If you pressed it, it'd be a terrible admission. We . . . we still have a future together!'

The cyclops-man presses down on the red button, with all his strength.

119. Genesis Channel

Transit capsule lift-off – 43m delay!

Long shot on the Garden of New Eden.

There's nobody on the large circular platform, with the exception of Lóng, the second robot butler, who seems to be watching over Alexei's lifeless body.

He stands like a funerary statue, perfectly still in front of the covered plantations.

Suddenly a seismic shuddering far more powerful than the trembling of the storm shakes the whole height of the dome. The glass panels, on which Samantha's face is still projected, start to vibrate furiously.

The camera pans upwards, in an instinctive movement: a fault has opened up at the very highest point of the dome.

The tarps attached to the plantations only hold out for a few more seconds: sucked by the powerful in-draught, they are torn upwards, spiralling towards the opening that grows bigger and bigger, and disappearing into the howling storm.

Countless invisible hands seem to be ripping the leaves and the fruit off the apple trees, then their very branches. Harvested by the swipe of a colossal scythe, the plants in the oat fields start to whirl around, immediately joined by the carrot plants, the strawberries, the potatoes, the soya, the lettuce and the mulberries. The dome is now no more than a vast vortex in the middle of which Alexei's body is being raised up as if some greater power were calling him towards the sky.

Unable to resist the effects of the turbulence any longer, the access tubes detach from the habitats; the panes of glass shatter one by one, under the artificial atmospheric pressure that is desperate to escape through every possible gap; under infinitely more pressure than it was expected to withstand, the whole structure of the base finally gives way in a deafening explosion.

The picture vanishes.

A black screen, with a caption across it: ALL CAMERAS DESTROYED. SIGNAL FROM NEW EDEN DEFINITIVELY LOST.

The Genesis channel cuts to a view of Mars from space.

A caption appears at the bottom of the screen: SPACE VIEW FILMED FROM REAR CUPIDO CAMERA / MARS TIME 17:44.

The planet is wrapped in a veil of reddening clouds.

Except at the intersection of the equator, where a vertical line demarcates day from night: the region of Ius Chasma.

The depressurisation of the New Eden base has created a disturbance so violent that it's visible from space. Tearing through the clouds of dust, a whirlwind opens up like an eye – the eye of Mars. As if the planet, after so many months of being permanently watched, was now staring back at Earth and its inhabitants.

Cut.

Static shot of grains of sand, blurred, in very close-up.

Caption: SUBJECTIVE VIEW FEMALE PIONEER NO. 6 – ELIZABETH

Slowly the angle of vision rises up from the ground against which it had been pressed.

A red sand dune appears, and then another, and yet another: the whole valley is revealed, all its dust miraculously swept away. The huge explosion of the base temporarily pushed back the storm front several miles around, carving out a circular opening in the cloudy vault, and the rays of the setting sun are pouring through. The howling of the wind has been temporarily forgotten – a peaceful silence reigns.

The English girl's voice comes on the radio relay: *'Tao . . . ? Léonor . . . ? Can anyone hear me?'*

One by one, the other pioneers appear from the neighbouring dunes. They're all there – including Tao and Kelly, their wheelchairs half submerged in the sand. Before the depressurisation command reached the base, they were able to put enough distance between themselves and it to avoid being caught in the maelstrom. The powerful decompression blast sent their suits – infinitely heavier than the dust – flying dozens of metres, but it wasn't able to crush them.

A voice comes through the speakers, loud and clear: *'This way!'*

There, in the middle of the dusk-inflamed valley, in front of the gleaming pyramid of the transit capsule, stands Léonor. She's holding up her red chiffon dress, which floats gently in the reduced gravity, like an unfurling flag.

120. Shot

Month 18 / sol 484 / 18:21 Mars time
[603rd sol since landing]
Transit capsule lift-off – accomplished

'*To summarise, then: yes, Serena is guilty of all the crimes she's being accused of,*' I conclude, staring straight into the on-board camera of the transit capsule where we all took our places half an hour ago.

It only took me a few words, after we had lifted off, to contradict everything I'd claimed in the Garden, point by point.

It was a super-bold bluff.

It was a huge gamble.

It was a risky move that put the whole future of the world under threat, for a few minutes.

But it was also the best bet for getting the lives Alexei had entrusted to me out of harm's way.

Down there, under the dome, when Samantha asked the question, I felt the wind change – I had visions of Serena depressurising the base before we'd made it to the capsule.

And to avoid that, I adjusted my sails.

I danced with the wind.

719

I took Serena on at her own game – and caught her in her own trap.

And when the depressurisation finally happened, as I'd dreaded, we were far enough from New Eden to survive the explosion.

'*The Noah Report exists, Serena and her team knew about it, and here's the proof!*'

It was thanks to the cellphone I discovered the truth two years ago, and now I hold it out to the camera. I scroll through the pages of the report so that everybody on Earth can familiarise themselves with it.

'*I've just been told the Wild Bees have taken control of Villa McBee,*' says Samantha from the small monitor that connects us to the Earth, as we rise with no collisions or turbulence up the microwave beams to the self-energised satellite. '*According to what I've heard, Ms McBee escaped at the last minute in a helicopter.*'

The way the young assistant is speaking, I imagine she's still intimidated by the woman who for so many years has been her role model – she's still calling her 'Ms McBee'. It will take some time for her, and for the millions of viewers, to completely digest the astonishing truth.

But not everybody has quite such oratorical delicacy.

'Death to the McBitch!' yells Kelly into the mic of her helmet, in a voice as resonant as when she used to be in perfect health – it's like she's been holding that shout in for two whole years.

For once, Fangfang doesn't feel any need to comment on the obscenities coming from our red-faced Canadian friend, who's now stretched out beside her, upright in one of the thermoform seats. On the contrary, she just laughs and laughs. Tao and Liz are holding hands, their trusting eyes meeting behind their visors. Samson and Safia, too, look sure they'll stay united whatever risks and encounters the future has in store for them. Even Louve and Warden are leaning obediently against one another, their black eyes devouring the stars with wonder through the windscreen of the capsule.

Their joy, all of theirs, does me good, even if I know the struggle is far from over. We will continue to fight, side by side with Andrew, and Harmony, and all the people on Earth who love freedom. Serena has lost a battle, but not the war. She is still officially president, with her networks, her militias, her secret allies – knowing her as I do, I suspect she has no shortage of those. I'd bet my life she had something to do with Kris's attack of craziness. For now though, my friend is sleeping like an angel, carefully strapped into her seat, her hand on her belly. We'll have to be careful when she wakes up. I'll take on the task of telling her about Alexei's death; and she'll be the first person I tell about Marcus's final journey and the incredible revenge he got against destiny too.

Marcus . . .

I look far away, through the little porthole to my right.

Beyond the reinforced glass, the hole created in the atmosphere by the depressurisation of the base has almost disappeared. The planet that welcomed us has closed up on itself and on its mysteries. The strange noises in the storm; the mysterious disappearance of the guinea pigs, and then Kenji; Kelly's inexplicable illness . . . There are still no answers to these questions. For two years, we've lived in a world that has revealed nothing to us, despite all our tablets and our sensors, our technological paraphernalia and our colonising pride. Even if – just to dazzle Serena – I pretended my chiffon dress was a flag, I know that it's not really a banner of conquest – it's just a private memento, which I will cherish until my final breath. Despite all the declarations of independence offered to us by our enemy, I know we've never really been Martians – we were just Earth people in a bubble – even Kenji himself, Earth's ambassador to those mirages with which the human imagination populates space.

But not Marcus – he didn't come to Mars to be a coloniser or an ambassador. He always knew that his real home was someplace among the stars.

And he made it to his destination.

He made it back home.

'*Léo?*'

I look away from the porthole and my eyes meet Mozart's, as he sits beside me.

'*I'm – I'm so sorry about the syringe . . .*' he stammers. '*I . . . I was just so scared of losing you . . .*'

'Forget about it. And we've still got five months ahead of us to prepare ourselves for our arrival back on Earth, to sort things out so that the Aranha can never hurt you. I promise, we'll manage.'

I put my glove on his, then turn my attention back to the giant umbrella of the satellite that's getting bigger and bigger every moment outside the windscreen; to the *Cupido* drifting slowly in orbit, to the distant figure of Phobos moving ahead of them both; and finally to the Sun, shining all the way out there, beside the place of my birth.

Yes, I'll fight to save Mozart. As for everything else . . . Whatever our futures hold, his and mine, we'll have to be patient.

Of all the sails we humans use for navigating our lives, those of the heart are the hardest to adjust – maybe it's even impossible. I've been pulled by opposing winds for too long. I've known the dizziness of a hurricane and the gentleness of a light trade wind. Now I need to give myself time to find my new course.

Liz plugs her tablet into the audio feed.

The notes of the 'New World' symphony fill my headphones.

I keep my eyes wide open: looking straight ahead, towards my world.

Towards Earth.

Acknowledgements

The time has come to thank all those who made this odyssey happen: my family, who provide me with joy and inspiration every day; my publishers, both in France and in the United Kingdom, who were always there at my side during the journey; my translator Daniel, who brought this story to English-speaking readers in the best possible way.

A book is like a ship.

A whole crew helped to adjust the sails of this one, so it could reach its destination: in your hands.

Explore the world of Phobos on Victor Dixen's site:
www.victordixen.com

Victor Dixen

Victor Dixen is the author of three series for teenagers: THE STRANGE CASE OF JACK SPARK, ANIMALE and PHOBOS, and twice the winner of the Grand Prix de l'Imaginaire, the most prestigious science fiction and fantasy award in France. His father is Danish and his mother is French, and as a child he travelled throughout Europe with them. Today, he shares his time between Paris and New York City with his family and his two inquisitive cats.

Want to read
NEW BOOKS
before anyone else?

Like getting
FREE BOOKS?

Enjoy sharing your
OPINIONS?

Discover

READERS FIRST

Read. Love. Share.

Get your first free book just by signing up at
readersfirst.co.uk

For Terms and Conditions see readersfirst.co.uk/pages/terms-of-service

HOT KEY BOOKS

Thank you for choosing a Hot Key book.

If you want to know more about our authors and what we publish, you can find us online.

You can start at our website

www.hotkeybooks.com

And you can also find us on:

We hope to see you soon!